Marilyn's Child

Lynne Pemberton was born in Newcastle-upon-Tyne. She had a highly successful career as a model before becoming a founding director of Pemberton Hotels, a Barbados-based group which encompasses some of the most luxurious hotels in the world. Her novels include the bestselling *Platinum Coast*, *Eclipse*, *Sleeping with Ghosts* and *Dancing with Shadows*.

Acclaim for Lynne Pemberton:

'A rags-to-riches story with plenty of sun, sea, sand and sex thrown in . . . Escapist bliss'　　　　　*Tatler*

'An ideal light, pacy summer read.'　　*Mail on Sunday*

'A tale of glamorous lives and ruthless ambition – impeccable.'　　*Manchester Evening News*

Romantic suspense, mystery and intrigue in a tropical setting – a terrific read.'　　　　　*Annabel*

'The material that great bestsellers are made of, a heady blend of success story, intrigue and a smattering of sex'　　　　　*Sheffield Star*

'Perfect holiday reading'　　　　　*Sunday Express*

'A bittersweet love story to keep you on tenterhooks'　　　　　*Woman's Realm*

Platinum Coast
Eclipse
Sleeping with Ghosts
Dancing with Shadows

LYNNE PEMBERTON

MARILYN'S CHILD

HarperCollins*Publishers*

This novel is entirely a work of fiction. The names, characters and incidents portrayed in it are the work of the author's imagination. Any resemblance to actual persons, living or dead, events or localities is entirely coincidental.

HarperCollins*Publishers*
77–85 Fulham Palace Road,
Hammersmith, London w6 8jb

www.**fire**and**water**.com

This paperback edition 2000

1 3 5 7 9 8 6 4 2

First published in Great Britain by
HarperCollins*Publishers* 2000

isbn 0 00 651328 x

Set in Aldus by
Rowland Phototypesetting Ltd,
Bury St Edmunds, Suffolk

Printed in Great Britain by
Omnia Books Limited, Glasgow

For Robin and Bobby
I love you both, very much

Part One

THE FATHER

When I was fifteen I knew how it felt to want some-one. I mean really want them in every sense of the word. It happened very quickly, in a flash of absolute clarity, and it made the most perfect sense. There are moments, I'm sure, in everyone's life, when absolute certainty stifles reasonable doubt. So it was with me. Of course he, the object of my adolescent longing, wasn't of like mind – well, not then, not in the begin-ning. His moment of truth would come later, much later.

The past is a place I visit often – too often. It's an unhealthy pastime, the retreat of the old and the dying who have nowhere else to go. I'm young, so why do I keep returning? Wallowing in it, embracing it? I even have to admit enjoying the pain. What use recrimi-nation? What use regret? Had his thoughts been of me when he chose to leave? Had he wondered what would become of me without him? I've tried to patch it up, my broken heart that is, but I'm still searching for the right dressing, so I continue to bleed. In my head I can hear his voice, it never goes away; the deep resonant music of memory plays over and over again in the dark corners of my mind. 'Our childhood bag-gage is merely pawned, to be retrieved or returned to us later in life, in one guise or another . . . There is no escape, Kate, nothing is ever what it seems.'

I close my eyes, my thoughts racing, my heart pumping hard. I'm travelling back, and the sensation is akin to a fast ride on an express train. The landscape of my life flashes past so quick I have no time to take any of it in. I can feel his presence, he's close, very close, closer than he's been for a long time. He looks exactly the way he'd looked the first time I set eyes on him, at precisely ten past four on a wet afternoon in March 1978.

Chapter One

In the quiet of St Winifred's church I listen to his move-ments; from under half-closed lids I watch him mount the pulpit steps. He hasn't seen me. I'm kneeling, hands folded in prayer, head bent, all manner of things going on in my head except worship. It's dark in the church; he's wearing a black soutane, his back towards me, clothed in shadow. Suddenly he lifts his head: a wedge of light from the window above the nave touches his crown, which is the colour of a roasted chestnut. Now he's facing the empty church and, as if practising a sermon, he begins to mime. Desperate to stay hidden, I wriggle my body down into a crouching position and in the silence listen for his footsteps. When after a few moments I hear him descend from the pulpit, I raise my head a fraction to see him start down the aisle. As he gets closer I can see Father Declan Steele has full curling lips, darker in the centre, and heavy lids above navy blue eyes. Irish eyes, framed with spidery lashes, below ruler-straight eyebrows, thick and coal black. My best friend Bridget Costello had been right when she'd said he looked like Robert Redford in *The Great Gatsby*, except the curate is better looking.

I want to sneeze; Sod's Law, when I want to be as quiet as a mouse. I pinch my nose with thumb and finger, inwardly cursing the weather. For the love of God, I wish the rain would stop! It's been lashing down for three days, the hard slanting type that stings bare flesh. In a mad rush as usual and thinking of other things I'd run out without my mackintosh. I hate my mac. It's long, reaching

3

almost to my feet, and made of a scratchy material in a dirty grey colour. But it's the only coat I own, part of a set of clothes given to me by the Sisters of Mercy.

So now I'm wet, soaked to the skin. But then we're always wet in Ireland, wet or cold, or both. The cold is the worst; it seeps into my bones because there isn't much flesh on them. Before November is out I'm wishing my life away. I'd cheerfully miss Christmas; it's not a happy time for me anyway. Christmas is for families. I've seen them on my way back to the orphanage from church, quick furtive glimpses through sitting-room windows dressed with fake snow and bright tinsel: florid-faced mams, ale-swigging dads, grandmas and kids with glowing cheeks all gathered around gaudy Christmas trees, a wholesome family picture, opening presents and feasting their faces full of chocolates from a selection box. Later they would eat turkey and ham and Christmas pudding with lashings of brandy butter.

Last year it snowed on Christmas Eve and the trudge to church, hand in hand with Bridget under a sky as blue as my eyes, had been like walking through another village, a magical place transformed to silver brilliance. Bridget and I, at the back of the snake of girls, as far from Mothers Paul and Thomas as possible, had played a game of placing our feet in the footprints made by the girls in front. On the surrounding hills a huddle of sheep formed a grey blob against the gleaming white. The unmarked snow lay in thick wedges on the rooftops of the village; the church spire was sullen in contrast. The trees surrounding the church were woven with white, and the snow cleared from the churchyard drifted into our faces and pricked our eyes.

At the Good Sisters of Mercy Orphanage we have a tree dressed by the parish Christmas fund, and a make-believe present. I say make-believe because it's an only-for-show present. On Christmas morning the parish priest visits to inspect the orphanage. The gifts under the tree are all

4

wrapped in shiny Christmas paper. After he's left they are all taken away. None of the girls knows where they go and no one dares to ask. One year we got to open the presents on the insistence of Father O'Neill. I got a pair of trainer shoes that were too tight: they nipped my toes. Foolishly I complained, and got a clip round the head for my trouble. The same year we got to eat the for-show-only meal. It was pork, rich and fatty, and it made me feel a bit sick. You could have played football with the pudding, and the custard was runny, like Maureen O'Leary's snot. All in all, I was rather pleased when the following year there was no inspection and we had the usual porridge and a rasher with fried bread.

I'd like to miss it all and jump straight into spring. Why do we have to have winter? Other countries don't. Some people wake up to sunshine every day. I suppose that would get a bit boring, but every other day would be nice. No more huddling under blankets no thicker than toilet tissue, bony legs close to my chest, hands as stiff as a corpse and as blue as Mother Superior's lips (she's got a bad heart). What joy never again to hear the nocturnal chorus of chattering teeth, hacking coughs, rasping wheezes and the constant sniffing from noses that become, from December to March, like running taps.

Thinking of winter causes the face of Theresa Doyle to surface. Countless times in the past couple of months I'd longed to throttle her or wished her phlegm would choke her. The sound of her coughing had made me feel physically sick. In that dark middle-of-the-night time when minutes turn to hours I would have given anything to stop the deathly rattle emanating from her infected tubes. After Theresa died of whooping cough, I'd confessed my sinful thoughts to Father O'Neill, who had given me double the usual ten Hail Marys and Our Fathers to say every day for a week. I'd been desperate to tell the priest that being in a state of grace and chanting Hail Marys in my head every day would make no bloody difference to poor old Theresa or, for that matter, to me wishing her dead. Well, not dead but quiet so I could get some sleep.

I'd also wanted to ask him why God let bad people live and good people die. Like Theresa, a few months off her sixteenth birthday, or the kind-hearted Colleen Corrigan who'd worked in the bread shop. Why was Colleen, a good mam, taken by cancer at thirty-two, leaving a husband and four lovely kids? These sorts of questions are forever nagging at me, yet they stay where they are in my head, unuttered and unanswered. My confusion has nothing to do with Theresa's death. No, my doubts had started much younger, as far back as I can remember.

In my mind I challenge the priest: So tell me, Father, why is it the pair of them, Holy Father and merciful son, let so many terrible things happen? I visualize the face of Father O'Neill looming above me; inwardly I quake at his imagined reaction. He scares me, this big man of God – not as much as Mother Thomas, but close. His hair is the exact colour of ripe tangerines. Even when he speaks normally, one to one, his voice rises at the end of every sentence like when he's in the pulpit. But it's his eyes that are really terrifying: deep set with coal-black pupils, the kind Mother Peter says can see right into your soul. I know I'm not the only one afraid of the bogeyman priest; even Mother Thomas, who I thought was unshakeable, quakes in his presence.

So, Father – I continue my imaginary conversation with the priest – why is it that this absentee father and way-ward son have caused more than enough trouble, for me at least, yet I'm expected to love, cherish, adore, and obey them? To believe that if I worship the pair of them all the days of my life everything will be OK? You see, Father, it's not that easy, at least not here in Friday Wells, not where I live in the Good Sisters of Mercy Orphanage. For a start they aren't all good, the sisters that is, and there's not a lot of mercy. I've never had a natural appetite for the rich food of the Lord, Father, I suppose it's because I was force fed. Do you know, Father, Jesus was the first word I ever heard and learnt?

I have these imaginary conversations often, and not only with the parish priest. I have some really heated arguments with the nuns, particularly Mother Thomas. How I wish I didn't have the sick feeling in my belly when she comes near me, and could muster the courage to tell her out loud what I really think. The mere thought of her reaction makes me shudder.

Hugging myself tight I feel my nose twitch and a moment later let out a loud sneeze. The young curate, level now with the pew where I'm kneeling, looks surprised, and his surprise turns to shock as I leap to my feet and, like a rabbit springing from a magician's hat, jump into the aisle and block his way. I can see Father Steele is startled, but to his credit he recovers quickly and appraises me with lazy interest.

He's taller than I'd first thought and broader, big-boned with a high forehead and a deep dimple in his chin. I'm beaming – I can feel it stretching my face to aching point. After a couple of minutes it begins to hurt and I'm forced to relax my mouth. To be sure, this film-star curate would make even the likes of Lady Susan Anderton lost for words. And, according to Bridget, since Susan had left Friday Wells for London she'd been going out with pop stars.

Mother Thomas had said the new curate had far too much charisma for a priest. I'd looked up charisma in the dictionary, and, after being in Father's Steele's presence for a few minutes, I was inclined to agree with her. With characteristic boldness I say, 'Do you think you've got charisma, Father?'

I watch the slight rise of his eyebrows. 'Do you know the meaning of the word, child?'

7

'I do that, Father.' I quote: ' "Ability to inspire followers with devotion, divinely conferred talent or power." '

In a bid to hide his surprise, the curate digresses. 'Did anyone ever tell you that it's wrong to be talking this way about your elders?'

I nod vigorously, my head bobbing up and down. 'All the time. Mother Paul is forever telling me that my chatter will get me into no end of trouble.' Placing my hands on my hips, I wag my finger, imitating the nun's voice: ' "You'll wear that tongue of yours out." To be sure, it's got me fair worn out. I wish the cat would bite it clean off.'

My eyes are smiling, and so is his mouth – I suspect against his better judgement, but I don't care. I'm pleased as Punch to have made him smile, it makes me feel warm all over. 'Kate O'Sullivan, at your service, Father.'

'Kate is a grand name, my mother's name.' He repeats: 'A grand name.'

'It was Mother Peter who called me Kate O'Sullivan, the first name to come into her head the night I was taken in by the Good Sisters of Mercy Orphanage. I've no mam and dad, see. Well, none that anyone knew of at the time – just a name, that's all.' I lower my eyes. 'My name wasn't chosen out of love or thought, or in memory of some dead ancestor.' I hang my head. 'I've no idea where I came from.'

I know he's beginning to thaw, to feel sorry for me, I can see it in his eyes. I have this effect on men, so Bridget is always telling me. But until now I'd never thought much about it, never cared about manipulating the opposite sex. From the age of ten Bridget had taught me how to flutter my eyelashes, to lower my head and peep sideways from under half-closed lids. She said all the film stars did it and they got the men they wanted. One night, when I was about eleven, encouraged by Bridget, I'd dressed up. We'd waited until lights out and all the girls were asleep. We had to be very quiet so as not to wake the nuns or Elizabeth Rourke, an older girl, the dormitory enforcer, who would go running to Mother Thomas to report us. With socks stuffed down my nightdress and my mouth pouting, I'd walked on tip-toe, wiggling my hips. Bridget had shown me how to throw my shoulders forward and jiggle my breasts, copying the showgirls she'd once seen at a travelling fair. A year later I ceased to need socks; my tiny plum-plums, as Bridget called my breasts, grew into melons.

It happened very quickly, creating so much attention that I set about denying their existence. The rest of my body was reed-thin, which made my breasts look even bigger. At bath-time Mother Thomas could not look at my body. She'd spin me around so my back faced her and scrub so hard that my skin smarted. The day before my thirteenth birthday she'd found lice in my head. Gleefully she'd shouted, 'Dirty head, dirty head!' Filled with shame and self-loathing I'd sobbed as she shaved and scrubbed my naked skull with a foul-smelling soap.

Afterwards I'd said to Bridget, 'I wish I'd been born a boy, life would be so much easier. Don't you wish you'd been born a boy?'

With a shrug she'd come back with, 'To be sure, Kate O'Sullivan, I've no wish to be a boy, but I wish I'd been born with a face like yours.'

Now, looking at the new curate, all thoughts of being a boy are banished. With a suddenness that scares me, I want to be a woman. I wish with all my heart I was wearing anything but the shabby pinafore and white blouse of the orphanage. I imagine myself in a figure-hugging long black dress, cut low at the front and back, like I'd seen film stars wear in old black-and-white films. I'd never seen anyone in a dress like that here in Friday Wells; I doubt the curate has either. What would he think, how would he react if I was all togged up like a film star? Would he, I wonder, be tempted?

Temptation: the evil word careers around my head. Men of the cloth, I tell myself, are not tempted by the sins of the flesh. Priests are not normal men, who, according to Bridget, are all the same, wanting one thing: the hole between a girl's legs.

Whenever she talks about her secret place she giggles in an odd way, as if nervous, pointing to her crotch and saying in a conspiratorial whisper, 'But you mustn't let them inside until you know they intend to marry you. Or, God forbid, you end up having a baby with no husband.'

I notice an edginess about the curate. He's shuffling from one foot to another, seeming eager to get away. I don't want him to go and search my brain for something to hold his attention. 'Where are you from, Father?'

'Dublin, if you mean where was I born.'

'I'm going to Dublin, as soon as I'm sixteen, in less than three months' time. I've got a scholarship to art college. I can't wait until I can leave the orphanage, for my sins.'

He interrupts: 'Hush, girl, don't talk so. You're lucky to be alive. You've the good sisters to thank for taking you in, looking after you, putting food in your belly. You should be thanking them and the good Lord every day of your life.'

I chew on my next words: do I swallow or spit them out? I decide to risk the priest's wrath. There was something about the young curate that loosened my tongue – not that it needed much unravelling. And unlike Father O'Neill this man was young – I reckoned about twenty-eight or -nine – and soft-spoken, with what I called the mushy look in his eyes, a bit like Dr Conway when he'd treated me for my burst appendix. 'Bad case of peritonitis,' he'd said. 'You're lucky to be alive, Kate.' With the same sympathetic expression as I now see in the young curate.

'I'll not be thanking them for much at all, Father, because I don't feel thankful. That's the truth. The good book tells us not to lie, or to sin. So how is it that the good sisters do both? When I'm famous, and I will be, they'll all read about me in the newspapers. Then they'll be sorry.'

Father Steele shakes his head. 'Strong words for one so young.'

'Not so young, Father, sixteen soon. Old enough to leave this Godforsaken place. When I go I'll not be looking back.'

'Wherever you go, child, try to go unencumbered.' His eyes leave my face for a moment; when they return I can see they've changed. There's something in them that had not been there before. I'm not sure what, but feel rather than see that he's sad.

'Our childhood baggage is merely pawned, to be retrieved or returned to us later in life, in one guise or another, so mark my words it will only weigh you down.'

My expression mirrors my confusion, and he seems to understand.

'Remember, Kate, wherever you go, you've always got God.' He pauses. 'Now I must be on my way.'

The curate begins to walk down the centre aisle towards the door. I fall into step beside him, aware that he's not pleased with this intrusion. 'I have my doubts about God as well, Father,' I say, walking briskly to keep up with his long strides. 'I've had them for as long as I can remember. I feel like his name has been on my lips ever since I could talk. Did loving Jesus save the sweet Colleen Corrigan, as good a person who ever drew breath? Will a thousand Hail Marys stop Paul Flatley beating his long-suffering wife? Or will saying the Lord's Prayer stop the badness spilling out of Mother Thomas's mouth every minute of every day? If I worship God for all the days of my life, will it make any difference? Will it bring back my friend Theresa Doyle? Will it help me to –'

We are at the door when he stops walking. 'Hush, child, stop it at once. Don't speak so.' Father Steele seems genuinely concerned, an angry red spot appearing on each of his cheeks. 'Have you confessed your doubts?'

'No, Father. I don't think Father O'Neill will listen to me.'

The curate looks stern. 'I'm sure he will, that's what he's there for.'

'For the love of Jesus, there have been lots of times I've wanted to ask Father O'Neill why he, the Almighty I mean, lets terrible things happen to innocent people. You see, Father, it's very confused I am. I don't know what to believe any more.'

I pause for breath: a quick glance to monitor his reaction confirms that it's all going better than I'd hoped. I've got his attention, the next step is to grab his interest, enough to make him think me a special case. Poor little orphan girl, mixed up, disillusioned, in need of religious direction. I'm pleased to see a look of self-righteousness come over his face. Piety I can deal with, I've seen it enough times on the faces of the nuns.

'You, Kate O'Sullivan, should find plenty to be penitent about.' When I'd first heard the word I'd asked what it meant. 'To repent your sins,' Mother Paul had said with the same look on her face as Father Steele is wearing now.

Throwing back my head I fix him with what I know is a probing stare. 'So, Father, tell me: is it a sin to say what I think? Does it make me a good Catholic to be filled with guilt for doing the very things that come as naturally to me as sleeping and waking, eating and drinking? I laugh a lot, too loud for the sisters' liking; I play practical jokes, but only to make others laugh. I'm rebellious, or so they tell me, strong-willed is another favourite term of theirs. I admit I tell lies but only sometimes, white ones usually – don't we all? A couple of times I've pretended to be ill to miss Sunday Mass, but I've confessed. Are they such evil sins? I don't feel bad or wicked inside. If there is a God, then surely he should be my judge?'

I suspect I've gone too far this time. I've never talked like this before to anyone, except Bridget, who warned me not to tell a soul of my doubts, unless of course I wanted a good hiding. Yet here I am spewing it all out to a priest, and a priest I'd just met. Bridget, I know, accepts things the way they are; sometimes I wish I were more like her, because, I suspect, life would be simpler. I've got a queer feeling deep in my belly like I want to go to the toilet. I squeeze my buttocks tight and say, with that look on my face, the one Mother Paul always wants to wipe off: 'I've had religion rammed down my throat since I was old enough to say Our Father, and I do, I really do have a most desperate desire to believe.'

For what seems like a long time the curate fixes me with a steady gaze, then he takes a step closer to me. I can smell his breath: a sugary smell; I suspect he's been eating a toffee or a chocolate bar. His expression has changed again; the 'I know best, my child' look has gone, and in its place I see genuine interest. Gotcha! I think as he begins to speak. 'You and I should have a quiet talk, Kate O'Sullivan. Maybe I can give you some of the answers you're seeking. Restore your faith. Come and see me soon. Early evening is a good time. But now I really must be off, I've got some house visits and I'm late. God be with you.'

If he could have heard my heart singing he'd have been deafened by the racket. 'And you, Father,' I manage to mutter, stepping to one side to allow him to pass.

The back of his hand touches mine; I want to hold it, if only for a brief moment. Rooted to the spot, my eyes glued to the back of his head, I watch him open the door. I look at my hands: they're shaking, and now my heart instead of singing is beating very fast, hammering hard, like when big Frankie Donegal chases me.

I'm in a kind of trance. It's the only way I know of describing this feeling. The only other time I've felt remotely like this – and really there's no comparison – was three weeks ago, when I'd had the strongest urge for Gabriel Ryan to kiss me. Gabriel is sixteen and the most handsome boy in Friday Wells – in the whole county, according to Mary Shanley. Mind you, I'd not taken much notice of her since she'd never set foot outside the parish. All the girls want him and he wants me. His father is a bank manager, and the Ryans live in a posh house with a long black drive and a white car parked in front of the house. Like me, Gabriel is in the local secondary school, and everyone says (including him) that he's going up to Trinity College in Dublin to study law when he's eighteen.

Two weeks ago, behind the science lab, he kissed me. At first I tried to stop him, afraid one of the teachers would see us. He was strong though, too strong for me, and his body pinned mine against the wall. The whole thing was very uncomfortable: the corner of a brick digging into my right shoulder blade; his hardness pushing against my thigh; his mouth forcing mine open. Then he stuck his tongue down the back of my throat. I gagged, pushed him away, and ran back to the main yard. I couldn't wait to tell Bridget and Mary about Gabriel. I told them his kiss had made me feel faint and I'd let him feel the top of my leg under my skirt, but only for a split second.

A few years before, Bridget and I had made a pact; we'd tell each other about the sex thing if and when it happened. As if I wouldn't have told Bridget – she's my best friend. I tell her everything. She was fifteen when she let Dermot McGuire touch her left breast.

Eagerly she'd demonstrated. 'Round and round his hand circled, then he squeezed my nipple.'

'Did it hurt?' I'd asked.

'A little,' Bridget had admitted before continuing with enthusiasm: 'Then he put his hand on my leg, it was hot – his hand, I mean – and shaking. I could feel it through

14

my tights. I opened my legs a little, let him feel me on top of my panties. Then I shut my legs tight, clamping his hand inside my thighs.'

I'd giggled at this and, curious, I'd asked, 'Did you want to go all the way?'

Bridget's face had turned bright red. She'd crossed herself and said, 'Temptation is a terrible sin. No more, I swear, until I'm married.'

Unlike Bridget I hadn't been tempted with Gabriel; well, not after the sour-tasting kiss. Anyway, I didn't intend to get married and have babies, not for a long time – if at all.

All sorted, or so I thought, that was, until Father Declan Steele, this film-star curate who looks to me more like God than any other living creature I've ever seen, had come to Friday Wells. Instinctively I know, with all the certainty that my hair is the colour of silver sand, my eyes are grey-blue, and I have a tiny birthmark on my left hip, don't ask me how, I just do, this man has been sent to this parish for me, Kate O'Sullivan. A rare gift of fate.

'You've got to be telling all, Kate O'Sullivan. What's he like?'

I'm enjoying myself, holding court amidst four girls hungry for every detail of the new film-star curate. We are in the dormitory; I'm standing, and the other girls are sitting facing each other on the edge of two cast-iron beds. The north-facing room is cold and dark, the walls a sour yellow, dull even on the brightest day. The orphanage was built of granite and grey stone in 1896 – so the plaque above the entrance says – as an industrial school. Enclosed by high granite walls and black wrought-iron gates, I often feel I'm living in a prison. The floors of planked wood are highly polished by the inmates, and God forbid that a speck of dust should be found by one of the nuns. There is a Sacred Heart of Jesus on the wall opposite my bed, a constant reminder of how Our Lord suffered on the cross for me, and on the opposite wall Mary Mother of Christ set in a 3-D gilt frame. Mary is clothed in a long, flowing midnight-blue dress and has the usual smile on her face, which looks to me like she's a bit daft in the head. I'd mentioned this once and got thumped so hard it's a wonder I'm still all right in my head. Under Our Mother is a candle that burns constantly night and day. There's not much furniture, and what there is was not designed for comfort. Two chairs stand either side of the dormitory, like soldiers on guard, there is a basic wooden table next to the door holding a bible, two prayer books, and the catechism.

The nuns live in separate quarters, two to a room. They have sunlight and white glossy walls. When I go to the nuns' domain, as we call it, I'm always dazzled by the brightness. Bridget says it's because their long sash windows face south. Rosemary Connelly once suggested that the sun only shone on the righteous, which had made me mad and I'd listed some of the things the nuns did that were far from righteous, in the name of the Father the Son and the Holy Ghost.

'What about suffer the little children?' I'd said.

She'd backed down with, 'Bejasus, Kate O'Sullivan, I was only joking. Keep yer hair on.'

I'd gone on to question why the nuns had masses of beautiful flowers in brass vases and bowls of fresh fruit everywhere, when we were lucky if we even saw a peach from a distance. At the back of the building there's a walled garden, with a lawn so green my eyes hurt to look at it, narrow paths that wind through fruit trees and great clumps of flowering bushes of every colour, and several wooden benches placed in shady spots where the nuns often sit in contemplation. We, the girls, aren't allowed in the garden and I've only seen it from the top of the wall of the school house attached to the side of the building. This is where we were taught until the age of sixteen, or fourteen if, like me and Bridget, we passed primary certificate and went on to the local secondary school. The house is spotless; it smells of disinfectant like a hospital, and damp. I learnt very young that Catholics are obsessed with washing – well, nuns most certainly are. How often had I heard the words: 'Cleanliness is next to Godliness, dirty people are pagan, clean ones divine.'

Four eager faces are looking into mine, eight wide eyes fixed on me. 'He puts Robert Redford in the shade. His eyes are the deepest blue, like the sea. And not the Irish Sea, more like the Indian Ocean. His hair is so smooth it shines like polished glass, and when he smiled, sweet Jesus . . .' I pretend to swoon. 'I swear he made me feel faint just to be looking at him.'

'Did he say much?' It was Mary Flanagan. Then in the next breath: 'How old is he?'

'I'd say he's in his late twenties, and yes we talked for more than an hour. He asked me millions of questions about myself. To be sure, he hung on my every word.'

'How long?' Bernadette Kennedy looks dubious.

'Well, almost an hour,' I say quickly. 'He even told me where he was born.'

'Where?' Bridget pipes up.

'Dublin. He misses city life a lot, so he says. It's going to be mighty quiet here in Friday Wells, I say. Very boring after Dublin. Nothing much goes on here apart from John Connor throwing up his wages every Friday night outside the pub, Paul Flatley giving his missus a black eye once a month, or me causing havoc in the orphanage. Jimmy Conlon sometimes has an epileptic fit, and John Joyce coughed up his insides last year.'

'Mother of God, Kate O'Sullivan, did you really say all of that?' That was Rosemary Connelly, her black eyes narrowed. 'I don't believe you. Tell the truth, or let the

17

good Lord strike you down dead this very minute.'

I point my forefinger in Rosemary's direction. 'Rosemary, will you stop it with the good Lord Almighty stuff? You know as well as I do I don't believe God will be my judge. I think I can be my own best judge. To be sure, don't you think I get enough of that from the sisters without you preaching? I'm telling the truth when I say that Father Declan Steele is a god amongst men, and I for one would like to kiss him full on the lips. I'm in love, I tell you. In love with Father Steele.'

Bridget screams, 'Mary, Mother of Christ, he's a priest!'

I'm enjoying myself. 'He's a man, the most handsome man I've ever seen in my whole life.'

'And who, pray, is the most handsome man you've ever seen in your life, Kate O'Sullivan?'

I swivel my head in search of the voice, and spot the stooped figure of Mother Thomas, her black habit shining like sealskin in the overhead light. Her eyes are button bright and piercing behind the rimless spectacles, and her cheeks are puffed out and red, bright red, like she's been daubed with scarlet ink, or has applied too much rouge. Since she doesn't wear make-up I assumed she's been running. She always gets red-faced when she exerts herself.

I'm shaking inside but, determined not to cower or show fear, I look her straight in the eye. What can she do to me that she hasn't already done, I ask myself. And the knowledge that I am leaving soon, in a matter of weeks, gives me added strength. 'The new curate, Mother Thomas, Father Declan Steele.'

'That's enough.' The nun raises her voice. 'It's himself, a Catholic priest.'

I shrug. 'That doesn't stop him being handsome. Surely God made him so?'

I can see the tip of the cane she keeps hidden inside

the wide detachable sleeves of her habit. With a look that would, less than six months ago, have filled me with terror, Mother Thomas takes three long strides, her rosary beads making a clanking sound as she comes to a halt a few inches from where I'm standing.

We face each other, adversaries as always, only now I'm not afraid. For the first time since Mother Thomas had come to the orphanage in the summer of 1967 when I was five she didn't scare me. The five-foot-three eleven-stone battleship of a woman has in the past year shrunk, and now seems to shrink even more before my very eyes. Ha! Perhaps there is a God. The thought makes me smile. She knows I'm no longer afraid, the knowledge makes her more aggressive, yet strangely less terrifying. When we'd first met I was small for my age, and Mother Thomas had seemed huge. Now it was I who towered above the diminutive nun; it felt good.

Within weeks of her arrival she'd singled me out for her own particular brand of discipline. 'Evil rebellious child, it's a hard lesson you need to be taught, someone has got to do it if we are to save your soul.'

Often I was to wonder, Why me? What had I done to make her hate me so much? We were all afraid of her, and most of the girls still are; I suspect even Mother Virgilus, the Mother Superior, is. The bead-eyed monster nun from hell I call her – behind her back, of course, and always in hushed whispers.

I'll never forget an incident that happened about four months after her arrival. The memory, I'm convinced, is one that will remain with me until I'm very old, maybe until I die. I hate liver. Is that so bad? I know it's good for me, or so everyone says, but I can't stand the taste and gag at the smell. One evening, with a loud disgusted grunt, I'd refused to eat a plate of liver and onions. Mother Thomas had rapped my knuckles hard with my knife and fork before forcing my head into the plate of rapidly congealing food. Yet still I'd refused to eat, even under threat of house arrest (all free time spent in the bedroom for at least a week). Four hours later the liver and I met again; still I refused to eat. Two days later, weak with hunger, my hands raw from the repeated beatings, I began to eat. With each bite I cursed Mother Thomas, and almost choked on the last morsel.

A few minutes later, the entire meal mixed with a glob of phlegm had flown out of my mouth to land on the hem of Mother Thomas's habit. I don't think she ever forgave me for that, and even now, after all this time, I can't bring myself to think about the look on her face as she'd carefully spooned my vomit from her habit on to my plate. She did it slowly and methodically, and as I watched the realization of what she intended to do had dawned, and I remember wishing with all my heart that I'd eaten the liver when it had first been served.

Now I can feel her breath, hot and moist; it smells rank like bad meat. I want to spit in her face, and think of the pleasure it would give me. I watch her tongue dart out to lick her thin and curly lips, the top one puckered like ragged scar tissue. It's a face better suited to a witch than an angel of the Lord. She's from the north; Belfast, I think Bridget said. 'That's why she's cruel, been taught by the English.' Her accent, unlike mine, sounds almost English, her voice high-pitched and squeaky like a child.

'A Catholic priest is not an object of desire. I won't have you talking about the good father in that way. Blasphemous it is, you know so, Kate O'Sullivan. If you dare utter one more word about Father Declan Steele, I'll see to it that you –'

I interrupt. 'You'll see to what, Sister Thomas? See me burn in hell? See me get my comeuppance?' I can see her anger rising and feel a familiar panic. I've got what I call jelly belly and I take a deep breath.

'What did you call me?'

'Sister Thom—'

I glimpse the cane, like a rigid snake sliding down her sleeve. Now the jelly belly has gone to my legs and I've got to summon up every ounce of strength to say, 'I called you Sister.'

'It's Mother to you, Mother, Mother, Mother! Say it, you evil girl. Say it, or I'll see to it that you –' The banshee shrieks have a familiar ring and I know she's lost it, her mind that is, and as of now anything can happen. With all my strength I fight my fear. At the very worst she's going to cane me, and I can survive that.

In a calm voice I say, 'I suppose you're going to do what you always do, give me a good beating, and not just a thump round the head, a really good hiding. How can anyone be taught a lesson unless they're black and blue and bleeding like our Lord on the cross with nails in his hands, suffering so that we might suffer? When I was a little girl I really believed grown-ups when they told me I had to suffer for my sins. I don't believe that any more, and I'm not afraid.'

I can't believe I've just spoken to Mother Thomas like that and I'm not surprised when I feel her hand swipe the side of my face. It stings. I want to lash back but daren't.

'Hell is where you belong, Kate O'Sullivan. You're a lying, evil child. Like I always said, the devil's own, that's what you are and that's where you'll end your days. With him, the devil in hell and damnation.' With her cane she points at the other girls, screaming, 'Get out of here, all of you, I need to teach this evil pup a lesson.'

The girls scatter. Before she leaves I catch a glimpse of Bridget. Her face reveals what I know she feels: concern and hatred. Now I have the nausea deep in my stomach, and it takes all my will power to keep from crying out. I take a long step back, away from the nun. My head hits the wall and for a moment the urge to throttle her overwhelms me. What joy to stanch the stream of abuse spilling out of her ugly mouth. Or, better still, I long to stick a knife in her fat belly, twisting it round again and again while she begs for mercy. For a few seconds I revel in the pleasure killing her would give me, then in a voice that doesn't sound remotely like my own I hiss, 'Don't touch me. I'm warning you, don't come near me.'

With her right hand she grabs me by the throat, cutting off my air supply. I try to resist but she's too strong and a moment later I hit the bed face-down. With vice-like strength she pins me to the bed. I can feel her nails digging into my spine. Suddenly my head feels hot, my temples and forehead are burning, and I have this terrible image of the first time she did this to me, when I was six. As she drags my dress up and pulls my knickers down, I'm talking into the horse-hair mattress, repeating mantra-like: 'I hate you, Mother Thomas, with all my heart, I hate you, hate you, hate you.'

The anticipation, those few suspended moments before cane meets flesh, is always the worst. I squeeze my eyes shut, thinking of how soon I'll be leaving this place, of my own bedroom with sun streaming through big windows, and a pink rosebud bedspread. The monster nun from hell takes a deep breath before bringing the cane down. My entire body freezes in spasm and I bite my tongue. It hurts like hell and I want to scream but don't. I won't give her that satisfaction. In fact, it's a long time since I've cried. I can hear her panting, and know she's lifting the cane for the next blow. 'You'll burn in hell, Kate O'Sullivan, that's where you're going. The devil's own, that's what you are.'

Suddenly there's a strange noise inside my head, like a light switch clicking on then off, and before she can hit me again I roll over and scramble to the other side of the bed.

My knickers are hanging around my ankles, my backside feels like it's been torched, but the shaking has stopped and I no longer feel physically sick. We face each other on opposing sides of the bed. My eyes are harnessed to hers, and I detect to my glee a little uncertainty in those glassy beads. 'Mother Thomas has eyes just like a raven,' Bridget always says, and until now I'd agreed, but today they, like her, have diminished to those of a common sparrow. In the same strange detached voice I say, 'You'll never hit me again because if you do I've got orders from the devil to kill you. And if it's hell I'm going to, you won't be far behind.' She's staring directly into my eyes; hers don't waver or blink, but she says nothing as I go on: 'When I'm rich and famous, and I will be, you'll be sorry, very sorry – that is, if you're still alive.'

I know, as soon as I enter and kneel, that it isn't Father O'Neill in the confessional box. Whiskey breath and sweaty feet do not smell of freshly squeezed lemons mixed with a trace of lavender. The smell is different from any I've ever encountered. I inhale, exhale, then say, 'Bless me, Father, for I have sinned. It's two weeks since my last confession.'

I know it's him. Holding my breath, I wait for confirmation.

'Tell me about it, my child.' Father Steele's melodic voice washes over me. I close my eyes and imagine bathing in spring water on a warm summer day. It isn't something I do regularly, but I had, a couple of times last summer, been allowed to go on a picnic with a girlfriend from school. We'd gone in her father's car to Kinsale, where we'd eaten tons of egg sandwiches and drunk gallons of lemonade. Then afterwards we'd swum in the river. It had felt like Father Steele's voice: warm and soothing.

I sigh. 'I've had a terrible row with Mother Thomas. I said some awful things to her. She beat me, not for the first time, and I've been punished by Mother Virgilus.'

I look down: my hands are red and sore, the skin peeling. Work-worn hands, like those I'd seen a thousand times in the village, attached to pink arms scrubbing front steps or polishing brass door-knockers. Ashamed, I try to cover them up. The sight of them makes me angry, and sad that I should have such hands at fifteen. My hands were intended to paint, not scrub floors and polish brass, or be submerged elbow-deep in boggy water in the laundry where I'd been since my tussle with Mother Thomas.

'Sure, I said things I shouldn't have, but she made me say them. She made me very angry, Father.'

'Are you sorry, my child?'

I know the simple way to get off the hook is to say, Yes, Father, I'm very sorry; I won't do it again. But today, with only a panel of wood and a foot-square grille separating me from the man of my dreams, I've no desire to get off lightly. And instead of feeling penitent, I'm busily inventing more sins to confess. The rate they're popping into my head I reckon I could be in the confessional box all day.

'Mother Thomas is mean and cruel, and if God were all he claims to be, he wouldn't let her live. I told her to go to hell, and that I wished her dead. In truth, Father, to be sure, I meant every word.'

'May the Lord bless and forgive you, my child.'

Exasperated, I raise my voice. 'I don't want forgiveness, Father. I want Mother Thomas to suffer for what she's done to me.'

I hear him sigh. 'Do you have anything else to confess?'

Before I can reply, a shuffling noise outside distracts me. I look towards the sound. I can see a pair of feet outside the confessional box. One black-booted foot is tapping impatiently. Another sinner waiting to be cleansed. Probably one of the men from the village, one of the many who get drunk every Friday night. I've watched them spew up their earnings in the alley behind the pub; heard the shouts – hasn't everyone? – and the screams from their women. The lucky ones, the wives that is, get off with a black eye. Most of the people I know sin regularly, confess at the same rate, are absolved and go on to do it all over again. Religion – what a waste of time; stupid, to be sure. The more I think about it the less it makes sense. Suddenly I'm seized with a strong urge to get out of the confessional box, and out of church. My knees hurt and I feel very tired. With a deep sigh I say, 'No, Father, I've nothing more to confess.'

'For absolution, say ten Hail Marys and five Our Fathers. God be with you, my child. In the name of the Father, the Son and the Holy Ghost.'

I rise and step out of the confession box muttering under my breath, 'I hate Mother Thomas and I hope she goes to hell.'

For the first time in years I'm looking forward to Sunday Mass. Since confession on Wednesday I've been counting the days, hours and minutes for my next sighting of the curate. Bridget and I chatter while dressing in our Sunday best. Our church uniform consists of black stockings, dark blue skirt, white blouse and navy blue sweater. As I force my feet into my black brogues I long for a dainty pair of peep-toe sandals in red or white with a heel, like Lizzy Molloy wore to church last week.

Leaning forward to lace up my shoes, I say, 'I wish I had a beautiful new dress to wear, like the one Aileen Shaunessy wore to church last week. Didn't you think she looked just grand?'

Looking me up and down she replies, 'Sure, Aileen's dress was grand, but she hasn't got your figure to carry it off. You'd look beautiful in a paper bag, Kate O'Sullivan. You've got the body of a bloody angel, a sight for sore eyes.' She lowers her voice to a whisper. 'Can you imagine Mother Thomas's face if you swanned into church dressed up like a bloody film star? She'd probably have a heart attack.'

I grin. 'I wish.'

'And to be sure, one glimpse of your titties would be enough to make the new curate forget his vows.'

Still grinning, I say, 'That'll do, Bridget, and it's very beautiful you're looking this fine morning too.'

She beamed. 'You really think so?'

I squeeze her hand. 'I do that. You look grand.' I'm telling the truth, not the whole truth but partly. The midnight-blue serge skirt trims Bridget's stocky body, taking inches off her generous hips, and the colour complements her dark auburn hair. But beautiful she is not, nor ever will be, lest it be in the eye of the beholder. Given a beholder that is short-sighted, or just plain blind with love. I hope Bridget will find the latter. She is, after all, my best friend, better than a sister, and I love her very much.

Hand in hand we leave the dormitory and pass Rosemary Connelly on the stairs. She whispers, 'Mother Thomas is on the warpath. She found a dirty sanitary towel on the floor of the downstairs lavvy.' Mary looks directly at me.

'Not guilty,' I mutter.

As we continue downstairs Bridget digs me in the ribs. 'Don't even think about it.'

I know she's referring to my first period. Mother Thomas had examined my knickers and after finding one spot of blood had made me wear them on my head for the remainder of that day. I have to fight hard to stop dredging up these unwanted memories, yet even in the doing I know it won't make them go away – well, not forever. What was it Father Steele had said about our childhood baggage? I think instead about the future, it has always helped me to cope with the past and the present. Soon I'll be sixteen. I've longed to be sixteen since

I was ten. The magic age, time to leave the orphanage, to be in charge of my own life. Yet now it's almost upon me I feel more than a little scared. You're going to be famous, I remind myself, you can look after yourself. But could I? Would I? The doubts jump around my head.

I'm very tall for my age, five foot eight, and still growing, as Lizzy Molloy was fond of saying, in all the right places. 'It's a model for them fancy glossy magazines you should be, Kate O'Sullivan. A top model you'd make, to be sure.' I can think of nothing worse than being a model: being told what to do; how to stand; what to wear. I was going to paint. The only time I felt truly happy was when I was painting. It made me feel different, whole and important, like I had something special to say. As we reach the foot of the stairs, I turn to Bridget. Tears well up in the back of my eyes and I'm not sure why.

'I'm going to be sixteen soon. I've longed for the day, but as it gets closer I'm feeling a bit strange. I've never known anything but this place.'

The glassy sheen of concern in Bridget's eyes makes my insides loosen, and I want to hug her when she says, 'You, Kate O'Sullivan, are going to be a famous artist. You're a brilliant painter. I only wish I was good at something.' She squeezes my hand. 'But I know how you feel.' Her bright smile fades. 'For as long as I can remember, I've dreamt about leaving here. When I was very small I used to dream that my mam and da hadn't died. They'd gone away to work, to make lots of money, and had put me into the orphanage until they had made enough to come back for me. The dream always ended with them leading me up a long path, their arms loaded with presents. At the end of the path there's a lovely cottage covered in ivy. Mam and da tell me it's our home; we're all going to live there. I always hated waking up from that dream, and every night I used to go to sleep trying to dream it again. Yet now when I think about leaving here I get the shits. I've no place to go, I don't have any family, only you, Kate, you're like a sister to me and you'll be leaving four months before me. I'm going to miss you so much.'

I can't stand to see her sad, or afraid; I've seen both too often. The trouble is it makes me feel the same, so with more enthusiasm than I actually feel I say, 'Why don't you come to Dublin, Bridget? You can get a job and we can share a flat.'

Even in the saying I knew Bridget wouldn't be coming to Dublin. She wasn't going anywhere. Bridget was small town, and, after all, there had to be the Bridgets of the world. She would, I knew, let one of the local lads get inside her secret box, as she referred to it. Then she'd get married and let him pump his hot sperm into her every Friday night after the pub, because that's what all the men round here did. She'd have babies, lots of them, be a good mother, try to be a good wife, and pretend to be a good Catholic. Doing without, and dying inside.

That wasn't for me. I wasn't like Bridget or Mary or most of the other girls I knew. I had my life all mapped out; I'd been planning it since I was ten. First I was going to go to Dublin, then London, perhaps even America. People would come from all over the world to buy my paintings, and I'd be rich; very rich. I'd be interviewed in newspapers, asked to appear on TV, on talk shows and the like. Of course I'd come back to the village to see Bridget and her fat babies. Then I'd cruise up to the orphanage in my chauffeur-driven car, dressed in beautiful clothes and smelling of expensive perfume. Mother Thomas would open the door. At first she wouldn't recognize me, but when I spoke shocked recognition would register on her wizened face. With my head held high and wearing my best smile I'd say, 'I told you so.'

Chapter Two

It's warm in church; steam rises from damp, closely packed bodies. Judging by the size of the congregation, I reckon most of the parish has turned out to get a glimpse of the new curate. My eyes follow the lead altar boy, Eugene Crowley, as he emerges from the sacristy. I used to like Eugene, but that was before he chased me around the school yard and tried to pull my knickers down. I have to admit he looks grand in his scarlet soutane and starched white surplice. I skip Father O'Neill and concentrate on the figure of Father Steele bringing up the rear of the small procession towards the altar.

A quick glance to left and right confirms the eyes of the entire congregation are focused in the same direction. If Gatsby had been in town he couldn't have asked for a better reception.

Father Declan Steele, to give him his full title, looks wonderful: tall and handsome, God-like – or how I imagine God should look. My left knee begins to tremble; it does this nervous jig from time to time, it's a damned nuisance and makes me feel stupid. I place the flat of my hand hard on my thigh just above the knee to stop the shaking. This sets the right one off and now both legs are jiggling like I'm having some kind of fit, a bit like Jimmy Conlon, an epileptic, who sits three seats in front of me in class. Only Jimmy froths at the mouth.

Bridget puts her head close to my ear, hissing, 'He's a film star all right, should be in Hollywood.'

I nod, whispering in her ear, 'It's handsome he is, the most handsome man I've ever clapped eyes on.'

Church, for the most part, bores me. Sometimes I listen to Mass, but rarely; I enjoy singing hymns, particularly for the harvest festival, and usually ask God selfish things during prayers.

I'm jammed between Emily Donaghue, the local publican's new missus, on one side (her hair stinks of stale Woodbines, and there's a sickly mixture of cheap scent and sweat wafting out from under her arms every time she moves) and Bridget on the other.

I repeat the prayers and responses parrot-like while studying the face of Father Steele. I focus on his deep mouth. I have, according to my class teacher, a fertile imagination. I smile to myself. If Mrs Rourke could see what's fermenting in the young fresh earth of my mind at this moment, she would drag me off to confession by the ear. The new curate features heavily in sinful thoughts of him being normal – by that I mean not a priest – and of how it would feel to kiss him. Under my breath I repeat, Forgive me, Father, forgive me, Father, for I sin in my thoughts. Then with quick furtive glances I look from side to side, certain that what was going on on the inside must surely show on the outside.

Once Mother Thomas had said she could see into my soul and, to be sure, the devil was there. Foolishly I'd believed her and for months I'd had nightmares of being devoured alive by evil spirits.

My imaginings of Declan Steele the man make me moist between my legs. It's not the first time I've been wet down there. I remember when I was thirteen and Elizabeth Bradley came to live in the orphanage. Elizabeth was from Cork, fifteen, and four months pregnant. She was big-boned and big-breasted and smoked Silk Cut cigarettes. One night I'd woken with a start to the tip of a cigarette glowing eerily in the dark, with Elizabeth

Bradley attached to it. Before I could stop her, she'd slipped under my covers and, lying on her back, had handed me the cigarette. My first drag had burnt the back of my throat and made me cough, the second not so much, and by the third I was enjoying the buzz in my head. It was then Elizabeth had put her hand up inside my nightdress. She'd asked me to open my legs. Confused, I'd asked what for, and she'd whispered that she was going to do something nice, something boys did to girls if they let them. She was a lot bigger than me and packed a mean punch, so without questioning I did as she asked. When I'd opened my legs I remember thinking that it was all right to let Elizabeth inside my secret place; after all, how could it be a sin if she had one herself – a secret hole, that is – and anyway she wasn't a boy. The tip of her forefinger had probed a little before beginning to rotate. Round and round her finger went, until I could feel the wetness on my thighs and I was embarrassed that it would wet the sheets. After a few minutes she'd guided my hand under her nightdress and had shown me how to do the same to her. She had thick hair on her legs and stomach and I was amazed at the big bush of hair between her legs. I had difficulty finding what she called her excitement button, but when I did, her back had arched and she'd spread her legs very wide. I did it to her for a lot longer and, unlike me, she made a lot of noise, moaning sounds, and kept urging me to go faster.

I wriggle my bottom on the hard pew wondering where Elizabeth Bradley is now. She'd left not long after her baby was born. Someone, I think it was Mother Peter, had said she'd returned to Cork.

I watch Eugene move the missal, then ring the bells for communion. Taking communion is the only bit of Mass I enjoy. There's definitely something kind of divine and sacred about receiving the host and contemplating the visitor inside my body. In fact, it's the only time I feel even remotely Catholic. I stand in line on the left of the altar rail and shuffle forward to take communion. It's Father Steele who places the host on my lips, and it's I who deliberately holds his eyes for longer than necessary. I'm convinced I can see a spark of interest in his midnight-blue gaze, but I'll dismiss it later as wishful thinking.

In single file we troop down the aisle out of church. The pace is slow, as the congregation stops in turn to be introduced to the new curate. Bridget is far ahead and I'm stuck behind Tom Donaghue, the publican, who has the lumbering gait of a big ugly bullock. Too much beer in his belly, Mrs Molloy says. Where his hairline stops and before his shirt collar starts there's a wedge of red neck covered in angry boils.

A thick slice of sunlight pours on to Tom's crown and as I follow him out of church I peer over his shoulder to the top of Father O'Neill's fiery head. It's moving up and down rapidly in time to his booming voice. The curate, I guess, will be standing next to Father O'Neill; they usually do. And if he's anything like the others before him, he will be smiling, the smile fixed as if it had been painted on his face. But then this curate isn't like his predecessor Father Peter Murphy, who always seemed, to me at least, to be play-acting. 'Got a secret agenda, that one,' I'd overheard Mrs McGuire who ran the post office say to one of her customers. She was right. Father Peter was caught with his trousers down, literally, around his ankles, his dick in the mouth of Robbie Donovan, a lad from the next parish, and him a choir boy an' all. I'd enjoyed the scandal enormously, we all had. It had broken the monotony for a couple of weeks. The men from the Pig and Whistle had raged: 'Jesus, Mary and Joseph, a man of God and him a slip of a lad! To be sure, the dirty curate should be horse-whipped. If I was the lad's father sure I'd do the job meself, priest or no bloody priest.'

Mrs McGuire had spoken of her outrage to the local newspaper, and Bridget and I had been thumped around the ears by Mother Thomas for calling Father Peter 'a dirty old poof'.

Father O'Neill had arranged for the curate to leave the parish quietly, under cover of darkness, else, so Mrs McGuire claimed, the mob from the Pig and Whistle would have lynched him. I didn't think the men frequenting the pub on Friday nights had the strength to do much lynching, it would interfere with the drinking, but I'd kept my thoughts to myself.

My brain is aching for something to say to the curate, something interesting to grab his attention. I could pretend to faint, have him catch me, and swoon in his arms. On the other hand, I might get Father O'Neill, who sometimes has rank breath and terrible dandruff. When I reach the entrance to the church I see Father Steele surrounded by a tight bunch of people. There's a young couple I've never seen before, the man thick-set with a bull-like neck, his wife a tall, painfully thin woman who looks like she's not long for this world. She's holding the hand of a small boy with big doe eyes and the same thin face as her. Bridget is next to them, standing awkwardly, goggle-eyed and slack-lipped, staring into the face of the curate like he's the new Messiah.

On Bridget's right is oul' Mary O'Shea, a widow who owns the village store where Bridget has just started to work on a Saturday – a trial period, according to Mary O'Shea, who might or might not offer her a full-time job depending on how she works out between now and October when Bridget turns sixteen. Oul' Mary's clutching her rosary beads as if her life depends on it, and edging closer to the curate, beaming for all she's worth.

It's the first time I've ever seen her smile. As I get closer I can hear her crowing about her trip to Lourdes last year.

Stepping in front of Mary O'Shea, I say in a deliberately loud voice, 'Well, Father, it's grand to see you again and on such a beautiful morning. What did I tell you last night, Bridget?' Before Bridget can reply, I continue: 'I said the sun would shine on the morning of Father Steele's first Mass in Friday Wells. True, it rained earlier, but just look at the sky now, won't you: not a cloud in sight. The sun shines on the righteous, that's what I say.'

'Is that so, Kate?' There's no mistaking a hint of mockery in Father Steele's voice, and suddenly it's unsure of myself I'm feeling.

Mary O'Shea trills from somewhere behind my back, 'Kate O'Sullivan, would you be so good as to step to one side. I was telling the good Father here about my trip to Lourdes last year. He was mighty interested, weren't you, Father?' I feel the tip of Mary's finger prod violently between my shoulder blades. It hurts, and I want to poke her back to let her know just how much. 'Before we were so rudely interrupted, that is. Honest to God, Kate O'Sullivan, you've got no manners. I don't know what the good sisters teach you up there; nothing, to be sure, nothing at all. Bridget here is just the same. No respect for an old woman.'

Bridget glares. With a shrug, I reluctantly take a small step to one side. Mary eases her stout body forward and with some skill manages to edge me back a few feet. Undefeated, I stand on tiptoe, looking over Mary's head in the curate's direction. He glances up, I catch his eye and we exchange a knowing look. I can tell he's feigning interest in Mary O'Shea's prattle. His eyes smile; he knows I know. I enjoy the shared moment, and bask for another in the warmth of his smile. I watch him lean forward towards the young couple and exchange a few words I can't catch before dropping to his knees to stroke the head of the small boy, who I assume is their son.

Bridget is also looking at Father Steele, her mouth open as if about to speak. She's not sure what to say. I know, because she's twisting her hair with her finger and thumb into a tight knot. She always does that when she's nervous.

'Father Steele, last July I organized the raffle at the church fête and we raised twenty-six pounds. I was wondering if I could do it again this summer.'

For the first time in my life I want to hit Bridget. We'd already decided that I'd do the raffle this year – she'd promised. That was, until she'd seen Father Steele, who was now smiling warmly in her direction. Not the same class of warmth as when he'd smiled at me, but then once again it could be wishful thinking on my part.

'Twenty-six pounds, that's grand,' I hear him say. 'I'll speak to Father O'Neill. I don't know what he's got planned for the fête this year. What was it you raffled to raise such a grand amount?'

Peeved but smiling in spite of it, I say, 'Two of my paintings, Father. An oil I did of the previous curate, and a watercolour of the village, and a –'

Bridget cut in: 'A day-trip to Dublin, a truly beautiful dried-flower arrangement, done by Mary Collins who trained in all classes of floristry in London and Dublin, and a meal for two people at the Pig and Whistle.'

Not so nervous now, are we, Bridget? I think as I watch her drop the knot of twisted hair and beam like a bloody lighthouse beacon.

'You must have been busy,' he's saying, still looking at Bridget. I'm seething and, though I'd never do it, I've the strongest urge to slap my friend hard. 'I'm sorry, I don't know your name.'

For one awful moment Bridget looks like she's going to do a cute little bob of a curtsey, as if she's being introduced to the Pope or something. Just in time she stops herself and says in a really silly little-girl voice, the one she affects when she wants something, 'Bridget Costello, Father.'

'It was yourself, Bridget, who organized all the prizes?'

Before she has chance to say another word I pipe up with: 'No, Father, I did.'

Bridget scowls, but says nothing; it's the truth.

He looks first at Bridget, who has a sheepish expression on her bland face, then his gaze rests on me. 'Well, I think if there's to be a raffle this year both of you should organize it. How's that?'

I want to refuse; I feel like stamping my feet and shouting, I don't want to do it with Bridget because for all I love her like a sister there's no denying she's downright lazy, bone idle, and will let me do all the running around while she takes the credit, or most of it – at least the amount I let her get away with. I want to organize the raffle myself, like last time, only this year I'm determined not to let Bridget take the glory. But since I'm not wanting to make a bad impression I hold back on saying what I really feel, and say instead, 'OK, Father, we do it together. On one condition: you let me paint your portrait for the raffle. Is that a fair deal?'

His blush surprises and delights me, and for the life of me I'm not sure why.

I repeat my question, 'A deal, Father?'

'I can't be sparing the time for the likes of portrait-painting, Kate, much as I'd like to, and I don't do deals.'

'Time for what?' Father O'Neill's foghorn voice drowns out every other sound. He towers above the small gathering, making Father Steele, who must be well over six foot, look small.

'Father O'Neill is built like a brick shithouse,' Lizzy Molloy had said once. I'd thought it a good description but had never dared repeat it to anyone.

'Kate here has suggested she paint my portrait to raffle at the church fête, but like I was telling her I don't –'

Father O'Neill interrupts, 'To be sure, that's a grand idea, Father, a grand idea.' He slaps a bear-like paw on Father Steele's right shoulder and the curate winces. Father O'Neill says, 'Never asked to do my portrait – this face too ugly for you, Kate O'Sullivan?'

I don't know what to say; he scares me, this huge priest. In truth, he puts the fear of God – or is it the devil? – into me at the best of times. Now my face is getting hot and I'm dying to pee. I'm about to make some silly excuse when he begins to laugh. 'Can't say as I blame you, my child, for wanting to paint the young curate here; he's a far prettier sight than an old man like myself.'

The same hairy paw moves and hits Father Steele full in the back. The curate coughs and Father O'Neill snorts like a pig, snot shooting up his right nostril. 'Must say, she's a good artist. Did a grand painting of the church last year. It's hanging up in Tom Devlin's front room, pride of place over the mantelpiece. Never thought he would take down our Sacred Heart but to be sure he did, put Our Lord on the bedroom wall – or so he says. Haven't been up there lately to find out.'

The curate looks uncomfortable. I'm not sure if it's Father O'Neill's hand, back now on his shoulder, weighing him down, or the thought of sitting for his portrait. I have my answer in his next words.

'I'm sorry, Kate, but I've not got the time to sit for a portrait, as much as I'd like –'

Father O'Neill's bellow stops him in mid-sentence. 'For God's sake, man, you can make time. It's a good cause and, to be sure, it's a grand idea: we'll have all the women in the parish bidding for it.' Father O'Neill laughs, the sound coming from somewhere deep in his belly and rumbling around the churchyard, attracting several glances in our direction. Bridget looks sullen. I'm grinning, secretly pleased with myself and at the prospect of long hours spent alone with Father Steele. But when I look at the curate he's wearing an odd expression, one I can't quite fathom. He definitely doesn't look pleased.

From where I'm sitting on the lavatory I can, if I strain my neck really hard, see through a narrow gap at the top of the door the branches of an apple tree in the orchard on the nuns' side of the wall. It's in full bloom this morning, after an earlier shower. It looks like a huge pink and white umbrella: the kind I'd seen in books, carried by ladies who called them parasols. Apples are not my favourite fruit, I much prefer plums and apricots. I don't get either very often, and the thought of a big ripe juicy plum makes my mouth water. I love it when on the first bite the juice squirts out and runs down my chin, so I can lick my lips and taste it for ages afterwards. Last summer I pinched a couple from outside O'Shea's shop. I ate one on my way home from school and saved one for Bridget, who hadn't been particularly grateful since that very day she'd been scrumping apples and had a store under her bed. To be sure, I'd eaten my fair share of Bridget's hoard, but only because I'd got the empty groaning in my belly. And when I get that I'll eat just about anything that I can lay my hands on. As usual I'd eaten fast, too fast, and had farted all night long.

I'm always hungry. Mother Peter is fond of saying, 'It's hollow legs you've got, Kate O'Sullivan.' Once I happened to say that it wasn't my legs but my belly that was hollow, due to the measly portions of food we got in the orphanage. Growing girls could not grow much on half a bowl of porridge, one slice of bread with no butter, watery cocoa, mashed potatoes, and the occasional rasher and raw egg a special treat. No sooner were the words out of my mouth than Mother Paul had boxed me around the ears so hard her next words had been accompanied by the ringing of bells. 'Ungrateful child! You should be thankful for the food Our good Lord puts in your belly, thankful for having a roof over your head. Spare a thought for Our Lord who suffered on the cross for you, and think yourself lucky to be alive, instead of complaining and gassing nonsense all the time.' As if to emphasize what she'd said about the suffering and all, she'd given me another thump, only this time in my belly. It had hurt so much I'd felt the tears leap to my eyes, and it had been really difficult not to cry in front of her. But I didn't; wouldn't give her or any of them the satisfaction I'm sure they'd feel if they reduced me to a blubbering idiot, like some of the other girls.

The only time I really enjoy apples is when I get invited to Lizzy Molloy's house and her mother makes apple pie. My mouth waters anew at the thought of the sweet apple taste, mixed with melt-in-your-mouth pastry and lashings of thick clotted cream. Lizzy is my second best friend after Bridget. I sit next to her in school. I'm much brighter than Lizzy, and I let her copy all of my homework. Bridget said that was the only reason she invited me to her house.

Once, when I fell out with Bridget – I can't even remember what about – I told Lizzy she was my best friend, and would be for ever and ever. Of course it was a lie; Lizzy could never replace Bridget. Lizzy was from another world, she had a mam and da, a sister and two brothers, one in America – an accountant in Baltimore, thank you very much. The Molloy house, though not big, was spotless, and it always smelt of cooking, the sort of smells that make the mouth water. I never wanted to admit it, even to myself, but Lizzy's main attraction was her mother's cooking. I had food at Lizzy's like I'd never tasted before. Thick gravy made from meat juices with chunks of onion in it, poured over floury potato mixed with real butter and not margarine; the same butter spread thick on doorstep slices of home-made bread and scones, washed down with gallons of cherry lemonade, the fizzy, quench-yer-thirst-from-the-pop-van kind. Yes, being

Lizzy's friend had its advantages. And you could eat off the Molloy floors, so Bridget said, although why you'd want to when you could eat off a lovely polished mahogany table with a white lace tablecloth was beyond me.

Every room in the Molloy house was crammed full of wooden ornaments Mr Molloy made in his spare time, and beautiful patchwork cushions and blankets Mrs Molloy made in her spare time. I often wondered when they had any time left over for five kids. One son had died when he was three; Michael, the lad in America, had married very well and was, according to Mrs Molloy, doing very nicely, thank you very much. Mrs Molloy had an odd habit of tagging 'thank you very much' on the end of all her sentences. And there were a lot – sentences, I mean. She never shut up. I'd asked Lizzy about it once, and had been told to mind my own bloody business.

My knickers are hanging around my knees, the right leg lower than the left owing to the loose elastic. I wipe my backside with a square of newspaper and pull my knickers up to my waist, thinking of the underwear Lizzy has ordered from her friend Sally Heffernan's mother's catalogue: a bra and pants set in black lace, the see-through type with little red satin bows on the waist of the panties and the bra straps. Lizzy is very thin with a flat chest and one of those stomachs that go in – concave, I think, is the word – and I'm not sure the bra and pants will look the same on her as they do on the model in the picture, but I don't say so. The underwear is being sent to Sally's house, 'cause if Mr Molloy got wind of it there would be hell to pay, and the only thing she'd feel next to her backside would be his belt buckle. Lizzy wants to wear them for her third date with Frank Sheridan.

'Honest to God, Lizzy, his eyes will pop clean out of his head if he sees you looking like that,' Sally had said, her eyes popping.

Lizzy had winked. 'Who says he's going to see me?'

At that point I'd piped up with, 'To be sure, if Frank's not going to see you in the sexy lace you might as well just wear your old blue school knickers with the holes in the arse.'

Sally had said, giggling, 'Kate's right. What's the point of spending all that money on underwear if nobody is going to see it?'

At this Lizzy had pulled a long face, the one that makes her look daft. 'Wearing sexy underwear makes me feel different. You know, grown up and sexy. Who knows, I might let Frankie have a quick peek. Let him see what he can have if he waits awhile.'

Giving Lizzy an affectionate pat on the arm, Sally said, 'If he puts a ring on yer finger and marches you down the centre aisle is more like it, Lizzy Molloy.'

Lizzy had stuck out her tongue but hadn't argued. She knew Sally was right, so did I, only Lizzy didn't want to admit it. She would tease and titillate Frank until she got a ring on her finger, then she'd let him into the secret place between her legs, and in her head she'd live happily ever after in a thatched creeper-clad house in the country, the one she went to in her dreams.

The one she'd have, more likely, would be a two-up two-down middle-of-terrace house with a new bathroom and a shiny kitchen on hire purchase – if she was lucky and Frank kept up the payments and didn't throw his wages down his throat like his father and grandfather before him. Both are dead now. The drink killed them, according to Mother Paul. 'The demon drink,' she'd said, 'puts the devil in good men.'

'To be sure, it'll be for me to decide when I wear the underwear, and who sees it. It's costing me four weeks' wages and I don't have to tell either of you how hard I work on Saturdays for that old miser Sheehan.'

I can't resist saying, 'Not half as hard as Bridget for the oul' bitch Mary O'Shea. Jesus, Bridget slaves in that

41

shop from seven in the morning 'til gone seven at night, sometimes eight by the time she's cashed up. Honest to God, she's as mean a woman as ever lived. Wouldn't give you the drippings off her nose, and that's no lie. The oul' bugger scrimps on everything: her clothes are darned to death, she's cobbled her shoes so many times she's two inches taller, and still she cuts up newspaper for the lavvie when the shelves are stacked full of toilet roll. Gives Bridget strict instructions when she makes her a sandwich to cut the bread wafer-thin.' I form a tiny space with my thumb and forefinger. 'She's got an old press in the back shop (full of rubbish, so she says), and keeps the key on a chain around her neck like a bloody gaoler. Bridget reckons it's stuffed with money, says that she's forever moaning about bank charges, and how when her pa was alive and running the store he never believed in banks, said all bank managers were daylight robbers – worse than the feckin' English.

'Apparently he'd fought for a free Ireland.' I imitate Mary O'Shea's thin voice: ' "If it wasn't for good men like me da, you, Bridget Costello and Kate O'Sullivan, would be working for some Englishman. A Protestant heathen, not God-fearing and generous like me. Yer should be grateful, thankin' the Lord and me every day of yer life to be living in a free country, after eight hundred years of the English." '

'Well,' I said, 'I'll not be thanking the likes of Mary O'Shea, or the good Lord for living in this wet hole of a place, nor will I be blaming the English for all of Ireland's problems.'

Sally, a finger to her lips, had said, 'Hush, Kate, you'll get me in no end of trouble talking like that.' She lowered her voice. 'Me da's an IRA man, believes in the cause, hates the English. You know how it is . . .'

Distracted by a noise in the yard outside the toilet I forget about Sally's dad and Lizzy's underwear. It's

Mother Peter talking to Paddy Fitzpatrick, the man who owns the farm shop a couple of miles from the orphanage. With the flat of my ear pressed against the door I strain to hear what they are saying.

'It's very sorry I am, Paddy, to hear of your troubles, but like I was telling you last week my hands are tied, there's naught I can do.'

'What about the three girls due to leave?'

'Bridget Costello, Mary Shanley and Kate O'Sullivan come of age this year. Kate's the first, sixteen in a few weeks' time. She's an artist, got a grand future ahead of her, paints like her hands were touched by something sent from heaven. And Mary, sure, she's a lovely child, going to enter a religious order. Bridget Costello, well, I'm not too sure about that one, forever talking about going across the water to that pagan country England. Sure that would be the death of her.'

A metallic sound drowns out all other noise, and I realize Paddy is closing the van doors. Then he's speaking again.

'Aye, she's a grand lass, Kate, a sight for sore eyes. I remember coming up here when she first came to the orphanage. If me memory serves me well we had a fearful thunderstorm that night. Mother Superior, God rest her soul, had asked for a delivery of potatoes and cabbage. I was near out of cabbage, so brought some beets instead. She was grateful, said she liked beets. I says they were good for her, and the kids, no rumbling bellies if you fill 'em up with beetroot soup and potato pancakes. That same night as I'm pulling out of the gates who should I see but Father Sean Devlin – almost knocked him down. You remember Father Devlin, don't you, Mother Peter?'

There was no reply. I assume she must've nodded, because I heard Paddy's voice again: 'He was in a fearful hurry, sweating like a pig, his cheeks bright red and all puffed out, like. He was carrying something in his arms,

43

a little bundle. At first I wasn't sure what it was, then it moved, and I could see it was a baby wrapped up real tight in a blanket. In fact it was the blanket that attracted my attention. I'd never seen anything like it: bright red and yellow zig-zags – Mexican, I think. I wound the window down and doffed me cap, as you do, but the priest just looked at me like he didn't know me from Adam, and him usually so chatty and friendly like, and me a God-fearing man who hasn't missed church since me communion. So I asks him if everything is all right, like, since he seems sort of agitated. Not stopping, he mumbles something about a baby having come a long way, and getting her into the warm. I don't drive off straight away; I watch the priest in the rear-view mirror, running up to the front of the house, and I wonder why he's so worked up, and why he's carrying a baby. Aye, I remember the day well. How could I forget? The same day me missus went into labour. Eight hours later our Molly was born. Now she's gone and got herself pregnant, Jesus, Mary and Joseph, and her not yet sixteen. If I wasn't such a God-fearing man meself, and for the love of God I love me daughter – our Moll has always been the apple of me eye – I'd send her far away up north to have the baby. The father, Sean, is naught but a lad himself. He's gone missing, can't lay salt to his tail, last seen boarding a boat headed for England. If I could lay me hands on the young bugger right now, I'd tan his hide so hard he wouldn't be able to walk for a month at the very least. But soon as he was able, I'd make him walk up the aisle with our Molly.'

'Now, now, Mr Fitzpatrick, calm yourself. Sean O'Halloran was an altar boy, I seem to recall. The son of Tom O'Halloran . . . A good man, Tom. The lad's no more than a slip of a thing, no bigger than an ounce of copper. In saying that, I'm not condoning what young Sean has done, not fer a minute. Sure, the young pup needs a good hiding

44

and to be made to do the right thing by Molly . . .' She sighed. 'But if it's God's will, so be it.'

'It's all well and good you saying that, Mother, but I've got ten mouths to feed at home. I can't afford another one. I thought you might be able to help out for a while. At least the baby would be near so as our Molly could see it from time to time. Just a few months would do, maybe stretch it to a year until our Moll gets on her feet, gets a job and a place of her own, like, then she can have the baby back. The orphanage is always needing more veggies: I'll see to it that you get them at the right price.'

'Mother Virgilus says your prices are too high now, Mr Fitz.'

'My prices, like I keep telling her, haven't altered in nigh on five years, and if she was to go and buy the same stuff down at the supermarket she'd be paying twice what I charge. So if you could have a word with her, I'd be mighty grateful.'

A jackdaw crowed, drowning out the nun's reply.

Then I heard Paddy's voice again. 'A good woman, so yer are, Mother Peter. I knew you'd try and help. You scratch my back, I'll scratch yours, so to speak.' Paddy chuckled. The nun said nothing, so Paddy went on, 'Good day to you, Mother Peter.'

'God be with you, Mr Fitz,' she says.

I hear the gravel crunch under his feet, the clunk of the van door, then the engine starting up. Without making a sound, I wait until the van rumbles past the lavatory then count out five minutes in my head before slowly opening the door to step outside.

The yard is empty. A quick peek in the scullery window reveals nothing. As I walk from the yard around the east wing to the front of the house Mr Fitzpatrick's words are running around my head: 'a baby having come a long way.' I'd always been led to believe that I'd been left on the steps of the village church, less than three miles away.

Well, surely that couldn't, even in the wildest imagination, be described as a long way. It sets off bells in my head, the ones that ring whenever I think about who my parents were, and if, as in my recurring dream, they are still alive. I suppose I'm like the rest of the girls, the same as orphans everywhere: we all want to know where we've come from, who we are. Mrs Molloy, after seeing a film on TV, had told Lizzy I was like a young film star. Lizzy had said it was one of the star's first films and she thought it was called *Bus Stop*. After that I'd become obsessed with films, to the extent of letting Eugene Crowley, warts and all, kiss me in the playground in exchange for a movie magazine. I'd spent hours poring over the glossy pictures, imagining my mother was a film star. That, I convince myself, would account for my platinum hair and beige skin tone. Who in all of Ireland looked like me?

I cling to the thought, the idea, the dream. It explains why I feel different. If I'd been born in America to a film star who couldn't keep me for some reason it would make perfect sense. When we were about eight or nine, Bridget had stolen a telephone book from a box in the village, and we'd spent days picking out the O'Sullivans and Costellos, making a list of the numbers, imagining that one of them might be related and intending to ring them all when we had the money. But of course we never did.

I've reached the front door now. A makeshift dressing of cardboard and tape seals a wound in one of its panes of glass. As I push the door it makes an eerie creak, the sort they always have in horror movies. And I think, not for the first time – more like the hundred and first – that the house should have been demolished years ago. It's damp: in summer the humid smelly type of damp, and in winter the bitter seeping-into-your-bones kind. There's a wet patch above my bed that's got bigger every year; now it covers half the wall and is furry to the touch. I know twelve girls shouldn't be sleeping in a room that

46

by rights should be condemned unfit for human habitation. After Theresa had died of the whooping cough I'd mentioned the damp to Mother Superior, who'd promised to look into it. True to her word, she'd looked at it, but that was six weeks ago and nothing's been said or done since.

The house is deserted. It's Saturday morning and most of the girls are working: the younger kids have household duties at weekends, on a rota system that includes cleaning rooms, washing floors, changing beds, gardening, swilling out the lavatories, and the dreaded laundry. The older ones are out working, like Bridget at Mary O'Shea's, and Mary Shanley on Fitzpatrick's Farm. Back-breaking labour: I know, I'd done it for two months last year before I got peritonitis – 'For my sins,' according to Mother Thomas; 'Our Lord works in mysterious ways.' Just as well I hadn't been out picking crops on my own, else I might have been a goner. As it was I had to be carried off the potato field where I'd passed out in the most terrible pain, rolled up in a tight ball, face-down in the damp earth.

I'd spent three weeks in St Francis of Assisi Hospital; in truth, the best three weeks of my life so far. For the first time I'd had constant attention without having to fight for it. The nurses had chatted and the young doctors had taken pains to explain what they were doing and why – especially Dr Conway, who'd only to look at me with the gooey-eyed expression, the one I knew he kept specially for me, and I'd go bright red and feel a bit faint. Lizzy Molloy had come with her mother, who had brought me a box of Cadbury's Milk Tray. I'd tried – not very hard, I have to admit – to make them last, but had ended up scoffing the lot in one long glorious chocolate afternoon. Once, Mother Peter came with a bunch of flowers. She said they were from all the nuns, but I knew she was lying; she'd bought them herself.

How anyone can say they are bored in hospital is beyond me. I wasn't bored for a moment, there's always so much happening. After I'd devoured my own supply of books and any others I could lay my hands on, I'd sketched all the patients on my ward, including a girl called Sinead Webster. She was ten, and had very white skin, even whiter than Bridget's; she looked like an alabaster doll I'd seen once in an antique shop in Cork. She could sit on her brown hair, and had hundreds of tiny freckles on her thin face. Her mother had been delighted with the portrait, and offered to pay me. I'd refused but had been over the moon when she'd bought me a Yardley soap and talcum set smelling of lavender. Sinead died two days before I was discharged. When I'd watched them take her body away I'd tried to cry, because I thought I should, but I couldn't. I was too busy thinking about presenting a caricature I'd done of Dr Trevor Conway, who had bright red hair and small owl-shaped glasses. It turned out he was less than pleased with it, said it made him look fierce, but the ward sister had chuckled and said, 'It's a very good likeness, Dr Conway, to be sure.'

As I mount the stairs that lead to the first-floor landing and the dormitory, I repeat in my head a promise I made to myself a long time ago. The first thing I'm going to have when I get to Dublin is my own room, and it will have a pink-and-white floral bedspread with matching curtains, and a kidney-shaped dressing table with a glass top and a frill around the base. Once I'm settled and selling lots of paintings, I'm going to hire a private detective to find my parents. I'm certain they are alive and, at this very moment, are no doubt searching for me.

I gather together my canvas, pencils, paints and treasured purse with the sheepdog on the front. Bridget had been given it, and she'd given it to me for my fifteenth birthday. It didn't matter that it was second-hand, or third- as it turned out, it was as good as new. I put all my things into my bag. The bag is large and square, the type I've seen hanging on the shoulders of young women from the village when, all dolled up, they go out to the pub on Saturday nights. It's green vinyl with two long handles and a zip. I wouldn't have bought it myself, but beggars can't be choosers. A few months before, I'd found it on a wall outside the library. After a quick look over my shoulder to check no one was watching I'd poked my head inside. There was an empty crisp packet, a dirty hairbrush, and a hard ball of chewed gum – nothing of any value. So I'd nicked it. Well, not exactly; I'd claimed it and not told anyone except Bridget, who'd urged me to confess. I'd promised her I would, then had deliberately forgotten. Honest to God, what was one old beat-up bag in the great scheme of things?

As I zip the bag I silently thank God that I've lost my Saturday job: sacked two weeks ago from Murphy's pork butcher's shop. I've missed the money, but I haven't missed, not for a single minute, cutting up pork belly and offal from half past six in the morning (with hands so cold I could barely move my fingers by the time I'd finished) until gone eight at night: nigh on fifteen hours with no more than twenty minutes' break, if I was lucky. Nor do I miss the feel of Billy Murphy's fat belly pushed into my backside every time he squeezed past me in the tight space between the cutting block where I worked and the hanging racks he went to twenty or maybe thirty times a day. I'd had enough even before he accidentally on purpose put his hand on my breast, hissing between beery breaths, 'Sure, Kate O'Sullivan, yer a nice piece of plump young meat for a hungry butcher boy like meself.'

After that I'd been deliberately late twice, refused to swill out the yard, dropped two pounds of sausage and bacon on the floor, and sold it to Kathleen Murtagh, who'd brought the dirty food back to the shop, ranting and raving about reporting the Murphys for selling soiled food. Mrs Murphy had railed at me like a banshee, threatening to thump me black and blue. I'd warned her if she did I might tell the whole village about her husband's sinful actions, which had made her scream all the more, calling me a lying whore with the devil in me, fire and brimstone were too good for the likes of me. Her threats of hell and damnation were still ringing in my ears when I was way down the bottom of the lane. I'd told Mother Superior that the Murphys wanted a girl to work full time; she'd believed me, I think, but I wasn't sure. I was never sure of Mother Superior; she said one thing and did another, and always with her own brand of a holier-than-thou smile. I didn't trust any of the nuns, except Mother Peter. She was a good woman, of that I was certain. The rest, especially Mother Thomas, were good on the outside and downright evil inside. I'd told Bridget the truth and had gone that very day to confession. Father O'Neill had listened intently to my long-drawn-out story of Mad Murphy (as he was known in the village), of how he'd come after me, made advances, and me a good Catholic girl, a virgin, saving herself for her husband, how I'd been 'just plain terrified, Father – to be sure, what's an innocent girl to do?'

The priest in his infinite wisdom had doubted Mad Murphy had had any sinful thoughts. 'Billy Murphy is a good Catholic, a good family man. A bit over-friendly, perhaps, but nothing more. But you, my child, have lied to the Murphys, and the good sisters, so now you must pray for God's forgiveness, and say ten Hail Marys and ten Our Fathers.'

I notice my cardigan has two buttons missing but I've no time to change and I start back downstairs, Mad Murphy forgotten, my head stuffed full of Father Declan Steele. Today I'm to start his portrait. He'd given me the money, from church funds he said, to buy the canvas and paints. I'm to meet him at the sacristy at eleven. He could spare an hour, he'd said, no more.

'An hour is plenty,' I'd replied enthusiastically. 'More than enough for the first sitting.'

I'm looking forward to painting Father Steele. He's special. The portrait will be special, I can feel it in my bones.

Chapter Three

A cold wind hits me full in the face as I step outside the orphanage. My hands, thrust deep in the familiar holes of my coat pocket lining, are warmed by my body heat. It's quarter past ten. I know, because I've just checked the time by the hall clock. It's never wrong. Not a minute fast, or slow. Mother Superior makes sure of that. She's obsessed with punctuality, and neatness.

The journey to the village takes, if dawdling, about thirty-five minutes, if route marching behind the nuns it takes twenty. I walk briskly, and am pressing my face on the glass window of O'Shea's shop at eighteen minutes to eleven, according to the clock on the wall above Mary O'Shea's head. At the back of the display I can see a row of dusty bottles and jars full of jam and chutney, that I know for a fact Mrs O'Hara makes and, according to Bridget, pees and spits in depending on how much ale she's had the previous night. In front of the display of jars there's an assortment of cans – baked beans, processed peas and carrots mainly – neatly stacked on top of three discoloured boxes, half-full of biscuits and crisp packets. I would love to buy six bottles of red lemonade, my favourite, and six half-moon cream cakes, and every chocolate bar in the shop. I imagine myself standing in front of Mary O'Shea with lots of money, slowly ordering all her stock while her eyes pop out of her head. With a couple of minutes to spare I duck inside to see Bridget.

'Top of the morning to you, Mrs O'Shea,' I say to the

back of Mary O'Shea's bent head. 'It's a fine morning, it is that. What's the crack?'

Mary O'Shea is standing on the second rung of a stepladder, stacking beans on to an empty shelf. She turns and scowls. 'It's yerself, Kate O'Sullivan. I've no crack, too bloody busy for prattle, and if it's Bridget you've come to see, she's busy.'

'It's important I speak to her.'

She continues stacking can on top of can. 'If it's life-and-death important, you can be telling me.'

'I'll take a Mars Bar, thanking you, Mrs O'Shea.'

With a deep sigh Mary O'Shea places the can she's holding carefully on the shelf and steps down from the ladder.

'It's a Mars Bar yer wanting, but I know what yer needing.'

I slap twenty pence on the counter. 'And what, may I ask, is that, Mrs O'Shea?'

'Insolent, to be sure, that's what you are, Kate O'Sullivan. Honest to God, if you were mine I'd give you a good hiding.'

'Well, since I'm not, give me a Mars Bar instead. And tell me, Mrs O'Shea, cause it's curious I am, to know why it is you think I'm insolent?'

If looks could kill I'd be dead on the spot. I stare her out, counting the long black hairs on her chin. I get to six before she says, 'In my day, children were seen and not heard.'

What is it with this 'seen and not heard' or 'because I say so' or 'I'm older so I know better'? Why do grown-ups think kids are stupid, I ask myself, a question I'd considered many times in the past, particularly when I'd heard so much rubbish pouring out of adult mouths.

'To be sure, I don't know who you think you are, with all yer feckin airs and graces. Yer a bloody gobshite, Kate

O'Sullivan, and I'm thinking that one of these days you'll be falling flat on your face.'

I've a sharp retort ready on the tip of my tongue when Bridget appears on the other side of the counter, red-faced and sweating. She sweats a lot, does Bridget, God love her. I have to admit sometimes, in summer and before her period, it's really bad. In the past I'd offered her my hard-earned, saved-up-for Lily of the Valley talcum powder. I'd only seen her use it once, when she'd gone out with Sean Connolly for the first time, and then she'd made me mad by using far too much between her legs. Most of it had ended up on the bedroom floor. I'd kept it hidden after that.

Mrs O'Shea hands me a Mars Bar and my change. With a loud grunt she mounts the bottom step of the ladder and continues stacking cans. I can see her ears prick up when she hears Bridget say to me, 'What time are you meeting the curate?'

Opening the wrapper with my teeth, I say out of the side of my mouth, 'Ten minutes.'

Bridget's mouth drops open, and she looks a bit simple. I've told her before about her slack jaw but she never listens. 'Wish it was me. Trouble is, I wouldn't, couldn't, for the love of God, say or do a thing fer just gawking at him.'

'That's what you do most Saturdays in here, Bridget Costello. I get tired of looking at your sour ugly puss, and you smelling like a bloody midden. Don't they have hot water up at the orphanage? If I was younger and had the energy I'd take a stick to you. Now stop your crack, git out back and bring me those beans.'

Bridget pulls a face behind the old woman's back. Mary turns just in time to catch the last of it, and looks ready to kill. I can't help laughing, which infuriates the old bitch even more. Bridget smirks.

'You –' she points at Bridget – 'git! That is, if you want

to keep yer job. Jesus, Mary and Joseph, why can't an oul' woman have some peace in her old age? Worked all me life, fer what? To be pestered by young hooligans like you two.' She steps down from the ladder with a wheeze.

'Out of me shop and out of me sight, Kate O'Sullivan. Go on off with you, else you're going to be late for the curate, and for the love of God that won't do.'

As I step out of the shop on to the main street I spot Maggie Murphy coming out of the post office. Quick as a wink I bend my head, but not quick enough. She sees me and makes a big thing of sticking her nose in the air and turning her face in the opposite direction. I want to laugh and shout to her and anyone else who happens to be listening that her husband is a dirty old bugger who plays with his own sausage in the back yard lavvie, and doesn't bother to wash his hands before going back to the front shop to serve sausages that are full of rancid pork fat and blood from the tins of cow's liver to colour them. If folk knew what Mad Murphy put in his sausages they'd never eat another one as long as they lived. In fact, I'm surprised anyone lives very long after eating them.

As I lift the latch on the churchyard gate I still have the lovely taste of chocolate in my mouth. I lick my lips and stuff the Mars Bar wrapper into the back pocket of my skirt. It makes a scrunching sound as I walk briskly up the path towards the sacristy at the rear of the church. After one rap, the door creaks open and he's there before me, in all his bloody glory, smelling for all the world like lemon sherbet. I wish I could pluck up the courage to ask him about that smell. I promise myself I will one day.

Silently I urge him to speak first. It's not often I'm tongue-tied – actually, never – so this is a whole new experience for me, this odd feeling of uncertainty, and the shyness that's giving me a sharp pain in my chest. I've been afraid before, many times. I've had the fear of God put into me by Mother Thomas and her partner in religious teaching, Mother Paul. Paul is to Thomas what I suppose Himmler was to Hitler. Often I've said to Bridget that the pair of them would have been kicked out of the Gestapo for cruelty. But this feeling is different, the butterflies in my stomach are similar, but I don't have the horrible sinking sensation or the jelly guts I get anticipating what she, or they, may do to me.

With a short nod the curate says, 'Come in, Kate.'

I step past him into the small vestibule that leads to the sacristy. It's dark, but then all churches are dark. That's another thing I don't understand: if church is supposed to be a place of joyous worship, why did God make his houses so bloody gloomy? The only good reason I can see for going to church is to shelter from the rain, dry off, and hope it has stopped by the time Mass is over.

I follow Father Steele into the sacristy. When he stops in the centre of the room I stop a couple of feet behind.

He says, 'Wait here a couple of minutes.'

I nod, and watch him leave by a door on the opposite side of the room. A few minutes later he returns. He's changed from the chasuble soutane, taken off the amice and alb, and is now dressed simply in a plain black soutane. He's carrying a small leather bag and a set of keys. Without a word, I follow him out the same way we came in. He locks both doors behind us, and we fall into step side by side down the narrow path that rings the cemetery.

'It's a grand morning, Kate.'

'It is that, Father.'

We both sink into silence once more. I sense he's feeling a bit like me, unsure and uncomfortable. I wonder why I'm feeling this way; to be sure, I didn't feel so stupid and tongue-tied the first time I met him in church. I suppose it's because I'm starting his portrait, something I've been looking forward to for three weeks. I want to relax, but the more I try the less it seems to work. My heart is beating faster than normal, banging against my chest, a bit like when I've been running, only we're walking at a leisurely pace. Strange, this feeling, very strange. We continue to walk in silence until eventually I take a deep breath and dare to ask, 'Where are we going, Father?'

Looking straight ahead, the curate says, 'To my house. I thought it would be peaceful there. Mrs Flanaghan, the cleaner, doesn't come in Saturdays, else it wouldn't be quiet at all . . . no, not at all.'

I smile, I know Biddy Flanaghan. 'You're right there, Father. She can talk the hind legs off a donkey.'

He nods. 'Two donkeys, or maybe four.'

The talk of Biddy breaks the ice and I feel a bit better.

As we walk up to the front door of Coppice Cottage, the curate's house, I'm thinking what a sad little place it is. This God-like priest should be living in a dazzling white mansion with long windows and sweeping lawns, something similar to Cashel Manor, the grand Georgian house on the edge of the village. It was built by Lord Anderton's English ancestors; the po-faced Lady Anderton and her snooty daughter still live there when they aren't floating around fancy parties in London. According to Angela O'Brian, a girl who used to sit next to me in class, the house has twenty bedrooms (she knew because her mother had cleaned them) and six bathrooms. Mrs O'Brian even had to dust the flowers in every room; not wild flowers – nothing so common – but specially imported flowers from far-flung places, like Casablanca and the Caribbean.

I follow Father Steele into the hall – well, you can't really call it a hall, more like a passage, grey-walled and narrow with stairs leading straight up to the first floor. He leads the way through a stout wooden door; it's low and he has to duck. The door opens on to a small square room, which looks a bit like my headmaster's study at school: lots of books and papers stacked unevenly on groaning bookshelves. A single floor-to-ceiling window overlooks a ragged bandage of untidy lawn broken by a small pond and a couple of fruit trees.

The curate stands facing me in front of the fireplace. The black grate behind his feet is shining, like a shilling up a darkie's bum, as Lizzy Molloy would say, and so are the brass dishes on the mantel; the desk you can see your face in and the window is gleaming like in the Windolene advert. Biddy has been busy. Above the mantelpiece the Sacred Heart of Jesus drips great globs of scarlet blood, and on the opposite wall the Virgin Mary in a long flowing dress is wearing her ever-present benign smile.

'So, what's it to be, Kate: do you want me sitting or standing? Sure, it's awkward I'm feeling either way.'

'It'll be no good, Father, the portrait that is, if you don't relax. You would do better if you sat or stood somewhere you feel most comfortable.'

With his eyes he indicates a chair in the corner of the room. It's dark brown leather, with a mass of wrinkles like the hide of a buffalo. Assorted newspapers and religious periodicals are stacked on the seat.

Eyes fixed on the chair, he says, 'To be honest, I'm not comfortable having my portrait painted, by you or anyone else. Father O'Neill assures me you paint like a young Rembrandt, but I don't believe him. What training have you had? I haven't even seen any evidence of your work. Last year you did a watercolour of the church – that's not exactly portraiture, is it?'

I take a deep breath, then say, 'I've done no less than thirty portraits since I was thirteen. I admit the early stuff of Bridget and Lizzy Molloy isn't headed for the Louvre, but last year Mother Peter and Mother Superior were both over the moon with theirs, and Mr Lilley, my art teacher, says I've got exceptional talent. He's convinced I'll get a scholarship to Trinity.'

Still gazing at the chair, he says, 'That chair belonged

to my father. Honest to God, a fairer, more hard-working man never walked this country.'

Tentatively I ask, 'Is he still alive?'

'No. Cancer got him in the end. He was only forty-five, no age for a man to die. I was thirteen – you know, that funny age when a boy stops needing his mother so much, and becomes badly in need of a father. I was very angry. I don't recall ever being so angry before or since. My father always wanted me to be a doctor. "Make something of yourself, Declan," he'd say, "you've got the brain for it." It wasn't what I wanted to do, but for his sake I went to Trinity, to medical school, and passed out with flying colours. When I was a junior doctor, a young child in my care died. He was eight years old. I remember sitting by the boy's bed – Liam was his name – willing him back to life. It was then I turned to God. I was twenty-six. I'll be thirty in September and there hasn't been a day since when I haven't thought about the priesthood.'

Shaking his head he mumbles, 'Sorry for rambling on, don't know what got into me.' Looking directly at me, and pressing a finger to his temple, he repeats, 'Sorry for rambling, nothing to do with you. Now, where was it you wanted me to sit?'

Unsure of what to say, I quietly begin to take my sketch pad and pencils out of my bag. I use my pencil to point. 'The chair it is then, Father.'

Father Steele gives me an odd smile before crossing the room to sit in his da's chair. He takes the pile of journals and dumps them on the floor, then sits down, arranging his gown neatly about his feet. He rakes his fingers through his hair and looks into the middle distance. 'Is this all right?'

I stand back. The light isn't good, and his pose is all wrong. He looks like he's straining to do a stiff shit and is having trouble. I imagine saying this to him, but ask myself how can I even think about saying such a thing to a priest. Then again, why not? Everyone does it, even the Queen of England, and I'm bloody sure it smells to high heaven.

'The light is not the best, Father. Would it be too much trouble to ask you to pull your chair towards the window?'

With a curt nod he stands up and, making no attempt to hide his impatience, drags the chair in front of the window. Panting, he straightens to his full height. With a deep sigh he says, 'Here OK?'

Quickly I reply, 'That's grand.' It's not perfect, but I can see he's getting edgy and at this rate the hour will be up before I've put pencil to paper.

Settled in the seat, he goes through the same ritual of raking and patting his hair, and arranging the folds in his robe.

'Lift your chin a little, Father, please.'

He obliges with an unwilling shrug.

'And turn to face the window.'

Silently he does so, blinking as a beam of sunlight pierces his eyes. They are the most unusual colour I've ever come across: dark blue with grey flecks, framed with curling eyelashes and straight eyebrows, thick and coal black. As I study his face I can't help wondering if he's got furry legs and chest. I'm not sure I like hairy chests. The only hairy chest I've seen up close, close enough to touch, belonged to Liam Flatley, the father of a friend from school who'd taken me to the swimming baths last summer. Mr Flatley's chest and back were covered in red hair, matted and horrible like an orange bearskin.

The skin on the curate's face is smooth, a dark cream colour with random freckles sprinkled over the bridge of his nose and temples. His mouth, in my opinion, is his best feature. I could, quite simply, look at it all day long. The bottom lip is deep, the top less so, yet fuller than most. It's a sensitive mouth; Bridget, I'm sure, would call it sexy. I thought it just plain beautiful.

I pull a high-backed wooden chair from the corner of the room and stand it a few feet from the curate. Sitting down, I place the canvas on my lap and begin to sketch. The pencil takes on a life of its own; I've entered another world, the one I inhabit when I draw or paint, the place where I feel at my best. Since I was old enough to hold a pencil, I've drawn. Even Mother Thomas, faced with a painting of the orphanage executed when I was twelve, had been forced to admit I had talent. A natural talent that Mother Superior, Mother Peter and Mr Lilley had nurtured.

The silence that follows is broken only by the sound of pencil skimming paper, the rustle of Father Steele's soutane when he moves slightly, and our breathing, mine soft and shallow, his deep, with the occasional sigh. After about twenty minutes I stop drawing and say, 'Can you move your head a little to the right?' I want to add, 'And sit still,' but daren't. Instead I say, 'Please.'

He does as I ask, gazing out of the window across the garden to where his cat Angelus is stalking a field mouse.

Now the light on his face is perfect. It's half in shade, gold and burnished copper lights spark from his crown. Now I have him, and draw his high brow and rounded skull perfectly.

After almost half an hour he starts to fidget, his left foot beginning to tap out a little rhythm. 'How much longer do I have to sit like this? To be honest, I'm getting a stiff neck.'

'Not much longer, Father. Please, I'm nearly there.'

With a deep sigh he directs his eyes out of the window again. But he's changed his pose.

'Sorry, Father, but you're not right – lift your head a little.'

He does so.

'A little higher.' He's getting impatient, his left foot is

tapping faster, and he's got that expression on his face again.

I drop my pad and pencil and cross the few feet that separate us. I say, 'Excuse me, Father,' in a very gentle voice, then lean forward and with my fingertips I lift his chin and place it in the right position. I smile. 'Just a few more minutes, then we're finished.'

'If anyone had told me sitting still could be so difficult I would never have believed them.'

I move back to the chair. 'It's not the sitting still so much as the concentrating on sitting still.'

He nods. 'You're right, Kate. Sitting still for hours reading is no problem, but you ask me to do it for twenty minutes and it feels like for ever. I've got a crick in my neck as if I'd been working at my desk on a row of figures all day.'

It's my turn to be impatient, but I quickly remember I'm with a priest and say in a pleading voice, 'Please, Father, can you find it in your heart to sit still, very still, for a few more minutes?'

Without another word he holds the pose for a further six or seven minutes before I stop sketching. 'All done for today.'

The curate lets out a long sigh of obvious relief and stands up. He stretches his torso and I can see his chest muscles rippling against the cloth of his robe. Walking over to me, Father Steele directs his eye towards the canvas in my arms. 'Can I see it?'

'Not until it's finished.'

'Why?'

'Because it's bad luck.'

'Stuff and nonsense, Kate. Who said it was bad luck?'

I'm cradling the canvas like a baby to my breast. 'No one in particular, just a feeling I have, Father. It's the same as when people say they are going to do something, then for some reason or another they don't. It makes them look foolish, specially after they've told the whole world and her grandmother about it. Me, I never say I'm going to do something unless I'm certain I will. I don't let anyone see any of my work until it's finished.'

The curate gives me the odd look again, the one I don't understand. 'You are an unusual girl, Kate.'

I blush, feeling hot and foolish. I've been called a lot of things in my life but never unusual. 'I am?'

He takes a step closer to me. 'You're an extraordinary young woman, Kate O'Sullivan, don't let anyone ever tell you different.'

Now my cheeks are on fire, and I imagine what a fright I must look, as red as a lobster fresh out of the pot. Again I'm struggling for words, and all I can think of is hiding my embarrassment and getting out of the curate's sitting room quickly.

I fumble with the zip of my bag, and when I look up Father Steele is waiting at the door. He's holding it open. I slide past him, grateful for the darkness of the hall. I head for the door, his footsteps echoing behind me. As he opens the door his hand glances the side of my head; I jump as if bitten. Jesus, Mary and Joseph, what is the matter with you, I ask myself. Pull yourself together, Kate O'Sullivan.

A blast of fresh air hits me full in the face. I breathe deeply before turning to face Father Steele. 'Thank you for being so patient and all, Father. It's not easy to be sitting for such a long time, and so still.'

'I hope it's going to be worth it, after all the bullying I've had from Father O'Neill.' He smiles.

Sure, his smile could warm the cockles of the coldest heart, and I think how happy I'd be, just standing on the spot being warmed by it all day long. 'I know it will be a most perfect likeness, the most beautiful painting I've ever done. When I'm long gone, Father, you'll be still

63

around, hanging in the Louvre.' I grin. 'To be sure, that's confidence for you.'

I pause, hesitant, toying with my next words, playing and replaying them in my head.

'Would you believe me, Father, if I was to say you are the most handsome person I've ever had the pleasure of drawing in my entire life?' I'm blushing, I can't believe I've just said that to a priest. I wait for his rebuke, my heart banging hard against my chest. I study his face, searching for a response, and, like wind on water, his expression changes from a sort of awkwardness that seems to me boyish to a look of deep tenderness, the like of which I'd rarely seen. One particular time sticks firmly in my memory. Lizzy Molloy had fallen and broken her wrist and I'd watched her father cradle Lizzy in his arms. With an intense pain in my chest I'd listened to his soothing words, and had felt my own tears pricking the back of my eyes when he'd ever so gently kissed away those of his daughter. The curate's expression is very similar. All my life I've longed for a father, and it makes me wonder if he feels parental towards me. I feel weird again, only this time it's different. I've got a terrible hunger, yet I'm not hungry.

My hands are shaking. I grip the strap of my bag tight, tighter as they shake more, and still I watch his face.

It's my turn to smile when he says, 'I'm not sure about the handsome part, Kate, but I'm beginning to believe you when you say the portrait will be good.'

I'm beetroot-red and tongue-tied again, and I just about manage to mumble, 'Till next week then, Father?'

He nods. 'Same time, same place.'

The door is closing, half his face visible. 'God be with you, Kate.'

In my head I say, At times like this, Father, I really believe he is. Out loud: 'And you, Father . . . and you.'

Chapter Four

My insides are melting, my head's hot and I've got a relentless throbbing above my left eye. I feel like I did last year when I'd eaten a rancid rasher and had been sent home from school early after vomiting over the back of the girl who sat in front of me in class. Only now I'm not sick, not in the stomach anyway. In the head, maybe.

My palms clogged with sweat, I glance in his direction; his expression is unreadable yet I suspect he's nervous.

During the past six weeks I've sensed (perception was the word Mr Molloy used for what I called my inner sense) that there are two Father Steeles. There is the pious, God-fearing, I-want-to-be-a-saint Father Steele. This face, I must say, he wears most of the time and with practised ease. I say 'practised' because I've glimpsed the other Father Steele, the person who, when Biddy Flanaghan broke a vase, had flown into an unnecessary rage, suppressing it as quickly as it had risen when Biddy dissolved into floods of tears. I'd defended Biddy, saying that accidents happen and it wasn't the end of the world to lose a gaudy vase. He'd glared at me, and I'd spent the remainder of the portrait-sitting smarting from the anger I'd encountered in his eyes.

Then there was the time I'd arrived early for our second sitting. The front door had been ajar and I'd crept into the hall softly calling his name. It was then I'd heard his voice. At first I'd thought he was talking to someone in the room, then after a couple of minutes I realized he was speaking on the telephone. Silently I'd waited in the hall, not deliberately eavesdropping but unable to avoid hearing Father Steele's side of the conversation drifting through the half-open door.

He was talking to a woman called Siân. Twice his voice rose in anger: once when he asked her to listen to his side of the story, and secondly after a few minutes of silence when clearly she wasn't prepared to listen he'd sighed deeply, saying she was a foolish woman who deserved everything she had coming to her. I sucked in my breath, not daring to let it out, when I heard him say, 'How could you even suggest such a thing, after all we've been through? You're a bitch, Siân Morissy, and I never want to hear or see you ever again, do you understand?' I heard the slam of the receiver hitting the cradle before I crept out of the house the way I'd come, retracing my route to the gate and back again to the front door. It was an ashen-faced curate who opened the door and I couldn't help thinking that there was a lot more to Father Steele than met the eye.

This did not put me off him; on the contrary, I found it endearing. It meant he was a man, a real flesh, blood and guts person, not a sanctimonious holier-than-thou super-being. He had faults and weaknesses just like the rest of us. It made him more acceptable and, to me, more accessible.

I never mentioned the telephone conversation to anyone, not even Bridget, but I did think about it a lot, often wondering what the woman called Siân was like. I built up an image of a tall, beautiful creature who had been, or was still, Father Steele's lover. The thought made me feel odd, sort of possessive, sick-in-the-pit-of-my-stomach odd. A bit like the way I'd felt when, a few months before, Bridget had become overly friendly with a new girl called Magda who had been sent to the orphanage to have her baby.

Now the portrait is finally finished. My right hand, holding the edge of the canvas cover, is trembling.

'Come on, Kate, what are you waiting for?'

'I'm afraid.'

He takes a step closer to me and the concealed portrait. 'Of what?'

'Of you not liking it,' I say, giving the cloth a sharp tug to reveal what is in my opinion the finest piece of work I've painted in my life so far.

It's my creation and I've seen it every day, sometimes for fours hours at a stretch, yet today Father Steele's portrait looks like it has never looked before, and in that split second I understand what I've done. I've captured the soul of the man. It is more real than the real thing standing in dazed wonderment in front of his own image.

Neither of us speaks and I'm aware of an unearthly hush. After a few minutes I hear him let out a long breath, like when the doctor asks you to breathe in and out. The anticipation and the urge to pee are killing me. I cross my legs and squeeze my vagina tight. Lizzy had taught me how to do it when I'd almost wet myself waiting until the end of class to go to the toilet.

'It's not often I'm stuck for words, Kate, but right now, I'm ashamed to admit I don't know what to say.'

'Just tell me if you like it, yes or no,' I demand sharply, my need to know far greater than any fear of risking his wrath for speaking disrespectfully.

He moves towards the painting; when his nose is almost touching the tip of the painted version he says, 'The likeness is quite incredible.'

I'm losing patience. 'Do you like it?'

'Yes,' he says, turning to face me. 'Very much.'

I swallow the thick swelling in my throat and feel an overwhelming surge of satisfaction.

'Good. That's all I wanted to know.' I drag my eyes from the still image to the real thing. His gaze is glassy and, unlike his portrait, his generous mouth is taut. My arm, as if being motivated by some outside force, moves from my side towards his face. I long to touch him, to seal this special moment with physical contact. I know it's wrong, but I can't help wanting his mouth to relax and his lips to touch mine. I imagine his breath warming my face, of tasting it while it fills my mouth. I start as he grips my wrist, stopping my advancing arm in mid-air. We stay like that for a few quiet moments before the spell is broken and he replaces my arm by my side.

'Father O'Neill is right. You have great talent, Kate. Don't waste it.'

'I don't intend to, Father. I'm going places.' I press the flat of my hand to my stomach. 'I feel it in here, deep inside. Do you ever have those feelings, Father, like you know what's going to happen for sure but can't explain how or why you're so certain?'

'It's called perception, Kate, or instinct. And, yes, I do feel instinctive sometimes.'

'Does it always come true?'

'Nearly always, and I'd say if you feel very instinctive about something or someone, don't let go.'

I'm secretly pleased he's told me about the instinct thing because it confirms everything I've ever felt about Father Steele. I want to tell him how certain I am and have been since the day I first met him that one day he'll be mine. But I hold back. There's a time and a place for everything, so Lizzy's ma always says, and she's right. My instinct kicks in again. It'll keep – I'll keep – until the right moment arises, and I know deep in my heart it will.

The portrait of Father Steele never appeared in the church fête. A few people asked why and I told them the truth. The curate had loved it so much he'd wanted to keep it himself.

I recall my heart sinking as Father O'Neill approached

me before Sunday Mass a week after Father Steele had seen his portrait. He'd come straight to the point, his voice barely containing his frustration.

'Father Steele wants to keep his portrait. He's made a good deal of fuss over not wanting to part with it, even offered to pay for it. I can't say I'm not disappointed – I was looking forward to raising a good bit of money for the painting at the fête. Remember, last year your work caused quite a stir and the local press picked it up – all good publicity for the church. Friday Wells, as you probably know, is not a wealthy parish. I've had all this out with Father Steele but he's adamant to the point of being downright stubborn.'

I'd no idea why Father O'Neill was confiding in me like this, and I found it difficult to contain my shock.

'But, being a fair man, I'd feel downright churlish if I refuse. Now, if you, the artist, were to say it had to be the raffle prize for the church fête, well, that might present a totally different story.' The priest scratched his head, leaving a hole in his sparse hair where his finger had been. 'If I'm honest, I can understand why he wants to keep it. Grand likeness and perfectly executed. Sure, one of your ancestors must have been an artist.'

I felt a tug in my chest for all the times I'd wondered the same thing. Would I ever know who I was? Or was I destined spend the rest of my life scarred with question marks? I knew Bridget felt the same as I did, but had, with her enviable complacency, accepted her lot. On numerous occasions she'd tried to convince me that digging for my past would create a hole so deep I might never be able to fill it.

Father O'Neill lowered his head. Two identical hairs poke out of each nostril and as he speaks they move simultaneously. 'You painted the portrait for the church, Kate; what do you think about the curate keeping it for himself?'

It was the first time in my life an adult had asked for my outright opinion, on any subject, and to come from the lips of a priest, a ferocious terrifying man of God, was the last thing I would have expected. I racked my brain for something non-committal. 'If Father Steele wants the painting that much, I'm sure he's got good reason. We know you are a generous man, Father, and I think it would be a very kind of you to give it to the curate.'

For a long moment he was silent, then, puffing out his chest and looking for all the world like a huge carrot-topped pouter pigeon, Father O'Neill said, 'I've decided the curate must have his portrait.' Then he slapped me on the back between my shoulder blades, winding me and making me splutter. 'It's a grand portrait, incredible likeness. You've got a rare talent, Kate. That's for sure.'

Catching my breath, I said, 'Thank you, Father. Soon I'll have more time to concentrate on my painting. I'll be sixteen next week, time to leave the orphanage.'

'How time flies. I remember you when I first came to the parish. You were no bigger than –' he holds his hand out level with my waist – 'this, and with a head of golden hair the like of which I'd never seen before, except in films. Sure, you were and are a beautiful child. I recall saying to Mother Peter, "She's like an angel, that one."' He chuckled. 'Mother Peter nodded, all knowing like, and said, "Not an Irish angel, to be sure."'

I put on my best innocent smile. 'It would make me very happy for the curate to keep his portrait. If I had time, I'd paint another for the fête, Father.'

'Perhaps you could find the time, young Kate, to dash off a quick drawing of the church, or the village?'

The fête was next Saturday, less than a week away. I had no time but could make time. 'If you were to speak to the good sisters about my chores, Father, then I might be able to dash off more than a drawing of the church – a watercolour, perhaps?'

The priest's eyes twinkled mischievously and to my surprise he grinned, suddenly boyish, and said in a conspiratorial whisper, 'Consider it done.'

Father O'Neill is true to his word and the following few days after school I arm myself with a pad and pencils and scurry to the churchyard. Perched on a stool, I sketch the Norman church. St Winifred's in Friday Wells is no grand edifice, yet to avoid criticism by the entire village I feel compelled to give the building some elegance and dignity.

I draw the stone columns rising either side of the arched entrance taller. I labour over clouds, like fake Santa Claus beards stuck to the towering spire, and I marvel at the way the cut-glass windows above the nave catch the light in a kaleidoscope of purple and green. For hours I mix and re-mix colour to get the exact shade. I paint until my hand and wrist ache and the light fades from sallow dusk to inky black. Most nights I miss supper; thank God for Bridget, who one night saved me half a slice of dry bread and a chunk of cheese, and another managed to nick a hard-boiled egg.

Late Friday afternoon, the day before the fête, the painting is complete. It isn't a patch on Father Steele's portrait, but I'm positive Father O'Neill will be pleased, and I'm certain it will fetch what the priest calls a pretty penny. Perhaps, I speculate, more than the portrait. After all, a portrait of a priest is not everyone's cup of tea. Sure, most of the folk around Friday Wells would much rather hang a painting of the parish church than the parish curate looking for all the world like a film star in the role of a priest. Small-minded people, I conclude, and hypocrites: they say one thing and mean another. Fear, that's what it's all about. They are afraid of what other people might say or think. Why should it matter what others think? I ask myself. Recently I'd had this conversation with Mr

Molloy, who had, I sensed with the perception thing, a different kind of attitude. He was always reading: books with unusual titles, books on philosophy, he called it. He'd encouraged me to read, lent me books, saying I had a bright enquiring mind. I loved reading, and enjoyed the discussion Mr Molloy insisted on after I'd finished a book. The 'post mortem', he called it. 'Reading', he said, 'gives you an insight into the human condition, and with that knowledge comes greater understanding.'

Even without books I do understand some things. I know for certain some people need to believe in something, anything, and the church fulfils that role. If you believe in God and everything he stands for, then you don't have to face yourself and who you really are.

'It's very good, Kate.'

The voice is behind me and without turning I say, 'Not in the same street as your portrait, Father.'

'Perhaps for some being in a different street is better.'

I nod, then screw my neck around to face him. 'You're right. I was thinking about just that a few minutes ago. I believe the folk around here will be more comfortable with a painting of the parish church hanging over the mantelpiece than a portrait of a film-star curate.'

He inclines his head, but not before I've seen his cheeks turn crimson. I stand and begin packing my things into the cheap PVC bag, thinking, not for the first time, how much I'd love a proper art portfolio in soft brown leather with two long carrying handles and shiny buckles, exactly like the one Gabriel Ryan's parents had bought him for his fifteenth birthday.

'Can I walk you to the end of the lane, Kate? There's something I wish to say to you.'

It's my turn to blush. I mumble, 'Of course.'

It's unusually warm for June, and dry. There has been no rain for ten days, a phenomenon in Ireland. Yesterday I heard a girl at school say the weather was as hot as

Spain, she knew because she'd been there twice to stay with her grandparents. Spain seems a million miles from Friday Wells even on a humid evening like this one. I wonder if the sky in Spain is the same as the one above our heads. Shades of indigo streaked with gold stretch beyond dour rooftops, above tall yellow grass clumped below charred hills smudged against the horizon. A plane unzips the sky and I try to imagine how it must feel to be flying through the air on the huge mechanical bird.

'Have you been in an aeroplane, Father?'

'Yes, several times.'

Still gazing at the retreating aircraft, I ask, 'Where to?'

'Italy, South America and England.'

'For holidays?'

'No, working. I lived in a monastery in Italy, in the most beautiful part of the world – a place called Umbria, and in Spain I worked in a small parish in Andalusia.'

'Do you speak Italian?'

'Yes, fluently, and Spanish. At one time I wanted to live in Italy.'

'What stopped you?'

His upper lip tightens. 'My mother died. I came back to Ireland and stayed.'

'I'm sorry.' Then: 'We have something in common – we're both orphans.'

'Yes, Kate, but I know who I am and where I came from. It makes us very different.'

We fall silent, a comfortable silence, the type friends share. It warms me. Side by side we walk down Potter Lane. Before we reach the end, Father Steele stops walking. As he turns to face me I stop and look directly into his eyes.

'I want to explain about the portrait.'

With a perplexed look I ask, 'Why didn't you ask me if you could keep it?'

73

His hands open as if holding a book. 'I can offer no excuse except to say I was embarrassed. When I saw the painting for the first time, I was surprised ... No, more than that, I was shocked to the core.' He pauses. I open my mouth to speak but close it when he continues: 'What I saw in your interpretation of me wasn't what I wanted to see. During the sittings I tried very hard to adopt a reverend air, an expression of goodness and serenity. But you cut through all of that, stripped the priest bare and found the man. That's why I want the portrait. It's not about ego or vanity, it's about my calling, my dedication and my commitment. I desperately want to do the right thing, to be a good priest. You see, Kate, every time I look at the portrait it will awaken memories of the man I was, and still am sometimes, and the priest I want to become. Does that make any sense, Kate? I know you're still a child but ...'

My voice rises. 'I'm not a child!' Then it drops: 'I'm sixteen next week. I'm a woman, and, yes, it makes sense. What I think you mean is we all have different faces, and some people are not always what they seem.'

My thoughts stray to Mother Thomas, who could, when she chose, be the kindest and most considerate person in the world. That was the face she wore to hide the evil, her dark side.

His deep mouth parts and he sighs. 'You are without doubt a beautiful young woman with enormous potential, but, forgive me for saying this, Kate, you're still an innocent. The orphanage, I'm sure, has taught you how to use your wits and every resource to survive, and you have a strong will and driving force that's going, I have no doubt, to take you far. Yet you are still a lamb with no knowledge of the world outside this sleepy village. I can help you, Kate.'

My eyes widen quizzically. 'I don't understand.'

'Biddy Flanaghan is leaving to have a baby. Why don't

you take her place in the cottage? It's not hard work – only me to look after and I'm not too messy, I promise. I can afford to pay you eight pounds a week, all found. Not a fortune, I know, but it'll help out when you get to Dublin. I know you can't wait to leave Friday Wells, but look on it as a stop gap for a few months before you go to art college.'

He senses my hesitation and rushes on. 'If you'd like to learn, I'll teach you Italian and Spanish and some knowledge of the world outside this parish, if in return you promise to give me painting lessons. Ever since living in Italy I've longed to paint. Will you think about it, Kate?'

I nod. 'When do you need me to let you know?'

'As soon as possible.'

He was right, I did need the money. I had a student grant but the extra money would come in handy for canvas and paints. It was only for a short while and it would give me an opportunity to get to know Father Steele better. I weigh all of this against my desperate craving to get out of Friday Wells.

I make a snap decision. 'I'll do it, Father, until the end of September. College starts the twelfth of October – that gives me a couple of weeks to settle on campus.'

He's smiling and I know I've made him happy. I find myself smiling too. I had a lot to smile about. I was leaving the orphanage, going to art college, and Father Steele obviously liked me – he was even willing to give up his free time to teach me the ways of the world. He cared. God for once had listened to my pleas. Sometimes God was good.

I'd expected to feel different. Yet I feel the same as I did yesterday and the day before. I'd dreamt of this day for such a long time, how could it cheat me this way? Being sixteen meant freedom, so why didn't I feel free? And why this heavy feeling in the pit of my belly, like I've swallowed a lump of lead? My hand under the covers slides across my groin; it aches just above my pubic bone. It's June 2, too early for my period. Perhaps I've got a temperature. With my other hand I touch my forehead: it's cool. I've felt like this a couple of times before, once after eating too much pudding at Lizzy's house, and the time I try not to think about too much, when a couple of years ago Mother Paul punched me in the stomach. That had hurt a lot and I'd cried a lot, but not in front of her. At the sound of coughing, I swivel my eyes right. Christine Donovan has the worst cough I've heard since Theresa Doyle died. Her nose scabs and she makes it worse by picking at the scabs until they bleed. Bridget reckons she's got bronchitis, but Mother Thomas won't have it. 'Nothing that a bit of Vick and cough medicine won't sort out.' The nun's been saying that for the last six weeks; it's not sorting it out, in fact it's worse. Some nights her tubes rattle so much I think I'm on a railway siding. I can't watch as she hacks then spits into a metal dish on the floor, but I can hear and I feel sick.

I'm sorry for her, we all are, but I wish she slept somewhere else. In that instant I remember I'll be sleeping somewhere else very soon. Tonight. With both arms I pull myself into a sitting position, my legs sprawled wide. My mouth is dry, as are my lips. I run my tongue over the top lip and bite a piece of loose skin from the bottom. It's early, very early, about six a.m. I yawn, glancing up and right to the window above my bed. Idly I watch a bird land on the windowsill; it pecks at the glass for a few seconds before hopping along the sill. I think it's a thrush but I'm not certain. I turn over, the bed creaks and the bird, startled by the sound, takes flight. I close my eyes tight and think of where I'll be tonight, and the ache in my belly starts to ease.

I'm going to be with him, in his house, just the two of us. The thought fills me with joy and a just a tiny frisson of fear. Afraid of being alone with the curate? I ponder the question then dismiss it as silly and childish. The curate is a good man, I tell myself, his outburst over the broken vase an isolated incident.

I believe, rightly or wrongly, that Father Steele and I have formed a friendship, a bond. After the initial portrait sitting when the cat had given me back my tongue we'd talked a lot. He'd talked about his family, mostly his da, who he'd had a very close relationship with. I recall the pride in his voice when he'd talked of his father working all his life in the shipyards, till at forty he got to be foreman, the proudest day of his life. 'God-fearing and honest, salt of the earth, my Dad,' he'd said. 'Allowed himself one Woodbine and a pint of Guinness a night. Said he'd seen too many good Irishmen go bad with the drink.

'"Aye, there's a great big wide world out there, Declan," he'd say. "Way past Dublin and Ireland even. It's out there for the taking, lad."'

The priest was interested in me, I knew by the amount of questions he asked. No one had ever shown so much interest in me and I'd found myself responding to him in a way I'd never done before. He made me feel special and grown up. I think for my part I made him laugh a lot, and once he said I was like a breath of fresh air.

Since meeting Father Steele I'd thought about God a lot. Perhaps getting the job with the curate was the work of the Lord. Could He, who had for so long overlooked me, have had a hand in this twist of fate, I ask myself. Perhaps I wasn't all bad, as the nuns would have me believe. I'm not, I have never been, convinced I was truly bad – deep inside that is. Mischievous, yes; cheeky, or lippy as Mother Thomas said; and I'll give them wilful sometimes, but evil, never. Is locking Mother Paul in the lavvy and hiding the key evil? Or creeping downstairs with Bridget on a Thursday night after the weekly grocery delivery to ease the ache in our howling bellies? It had been my idea to shave thin slices off the cheese and corned beef then re-wrap it, and then water down the milk. We'd got away with it for five weeks until Bridget dropped a milk bottle. It had shattered into hundreds of tiny pieces on the stone floor and Mother Paul had caught us red-handed, desperately trying to clean up. I don't want to think about what happened later – not today, not on my birthday.

Sliding my legs from under the cover, I let them dangle from the side of the bed. My toenails are dirty and the soles of my feet hard with a thick scaly layer of dead skin. This makes me think about a hot bath, with bubbles and deep water right up to my chin. My feet are long and slender, I take a size eight. Bridget, who is a tiny four and a half, always says they are too big for my body. I'm five feet eight and most of that height in my legs, so I've always thought my feet match my legs.

I'm the tallest girl in my class, and by far the tallest in the orphanage. I don't look like any of the other girls from the village. I suppose it's because I don't look Irish. I recall Father O'Neill's words when repeating what Mother Peter had said: 'Not an Irish angel.' I make a silent promise to ask her about that. For a start (as a rule) the Irish have different skin to me, very different: pink and freckled, and they rarely tan. At the first sight of the sun my skin turns a golden brown. Nor are they (again as a rule) tall and willowy, with hair the colour of a tropical beach and eyes that can be grey or blue depending on the light.

In the past I'd often wondered if the way I look had made some of the local villagers treat me with what I felt was a sort of suspicion. They often whispered behind their hands as I passed; some of the women looked at me with blatant disapproval; and lately I'd seen the odd look in the eyes of some of the men. Bridget said it was the eye of lust. They wanted to poke inside my knickers. From a very young age I'd decided that the only man to enter my secret place would have to love me, a lot, and be prepared to show me just how much he cared. If he didn't come along then I wouldn't settle for second best. I'd be celibate. I'd learnt the word last week when reading a magazine piece on feminism. I'd have my work and surround myself with friends and like-minded people. Then I wouldn't need the sex thing at all.

Idly I wonder how people will react when they find out I'm to be living and working for the curate. Ha, the news will get the tongues wagging.

I brighten at the thought of that and of Mary O'Shea's anger. Rumour had it she'd wanted her own daughter Marjorie to get the job. Marjorie who has carthorse legs, black hair on her upper lip and on her stomach (according to Lizzy Molloy) and a distinctly fishy body smell. How anyone would even consider putting mangy Marj in the same space as the divine curate is beyond me. She'd best stay with her monster mother; at least then there wouldn't be two houses spoilt.

Dropping my feet to the floor I stand up very straight, stretch, then pad quietly towards the window. I was right about the time, the milk van is pulling out of the gate. Terry O'Leary always delivers no later than six-fifteen every morning, except Sunday, when it's seven a.m. But I was wrong about the sun: a whitish mist hangs above a ragged strip of wall in front of my window. Tiny lavender flowers blossom from a deep crack, prompting a memory of when two lads from the village, one of them Noel Duggan whom Bridget had a crush on, but whom we found out later was secretly in love with me, had tried to sneak into our dormitory. They'd been caught and Bridget and I had been punished. For a couple of minutes I watch a sharp shower pound out a beat on the corrugated roof of the laundry, then I turn away from the window. With a jolt of anticipation I think about the day ahead and of how everything is going to be different. A fresh start, the first day of my new life.

Dressed and downstairs in the breakfast hall before anyone else, I'm greeted by Mother Peter. In her right hand she's carrying a package. 'Top of the morning to you, Kate O'Sullivan.'

I'm smiling. This woman, I believe, is a good woman. She behaves the way I think God-fearing people should behave, and most surely are supposed to behave. Polite and considerate, she shows kindness even when being firm. Also, she has an inner calm. She's someone you feel you can talk to, and trust.

'So, Kate, you're leaving us today. I must say you've grown into a fine young woman.'

'Thank you, Mother Peter. Thanks for all your kindness. I . . .'

'Hush, child, no need for thanks. I do God's work, it's what I was put on this earth to do, it's why I'm here.' She sighs and, stepping closer to me till her face is almost touching mine, fixes her eyes on me. She has one blue eye, and one green flecked with brown.

The paper on the parcel rustles as she places it in my hand. 'This is for you. Take good care of it, Kate, and don't ever forget that you're a very special person.'

I glance down at the package lying in my hands. It's wrapped in brown paper; my name is written on it in bold black letters, and underneath are the words *Happy Birthday, and many happy returns. God be with you all the days of your life.* I'm not sure what to say – I've only ever had three presents in my entire life. Two were from Bridget: my sheep-dog purse and a jug she'd made in pottery class. It was misshapen, painted a dirty clay pink and had a lumpy handle and two crudely painted rosebuds on the side. None the less I'd treasured it. The third was a set of watercolour paints Mrs Molloy had bought for Lizzy to give to me when I was fourteen. The lid of the rectangular tin was painted with a typical Irish country scene: green hills, rushing blue rivers with bright blue sky, birds on the wing and couple hand in hand walking towards a rose-clad cottage. I knew that kind of Ireland existed, but I'd never been there. The paints inside were made up of tiny squares, every colour under the rainbow. I used each square right down to the last scrap. That was, without doubt, the best present I've ever had. I didn't tell Bridget; I lied, saying her jug was the best and most cherished. Anyway, I still have the jug. The paint tin is now being used for keeping my clean brushes.

I stroke the package, then with my free hand grab Mother Peter's. It's damp and warm, much warmer than mine. Gently she squeezes my fingers. 'You're going far, Kate O'Sullivan. Don't ask me how I know, because in truth I couldn't say.' Tapping the gift with her forefinger she says, 'I love poetry, the resonance, the depth . . . I suppose it puts me in touch with the romance in my soul.' This admission makes her blush. 'Some of the finest and most profound poems ever written are in this book. I hope it brings you as much pleasure as it has me.'

I'm kind of embarrassed to look at her because she'll see my eyes filling up and I'll feel daft. One teardrop falls on to the parcel, making a watermark on the brown paper. With her free hand she lifts my chin and when our eyes are level I manage to utter, 'I really don't know what to say . . .'

' "Thank you, Mother Peter," would be appropriate, you ungrateful little pup. Leaving today doesn't mean leaving your manners behind.'

The voice belongs to a dark shadow to the right of Mother Peter's shoulder. I don't want to look at this woman; the mere sight of her is enough to tarnish this most special moment. Silently I pray for her to go away and find some other victim. And, once again, God forgive me, I wish her a painful death – and soon. Now would be appropriate, on the morning of my sixteenth birthday, Mother Thomas suddenly struck down by a terrible attack of some unknown disease that no amount of drugs can help, rendering her helpless and in terrible agony. That would be the best birthday present of all.

Without turning, Mother Peter calmly says, 'Kate has thanked me several times. There really is no need for further thanks. Nor, I might add, is there any need for your interruption, Mother Thomas.'

I can't see because I'm not looking in her direction, but I sense Mother Thomas bristle, and with a sigh of relief I hear the swish of her habit then the dull thud of her footsteps as she leaves the room.

'Now, Kate, breakfast. And remember what I've told you. Listen to God: he'll be your guide, he'll never fail you if you are prepared to let him into your heart.'

I long to say that God hasn't done much for me so far, and I doubt things will change. I intend to rely on my own instincts to guide me, listen to the feelings I have all the time, the ones that tell me what I should do and when. But I know she won't understand. She has her God; I have to seek mine.

All I can find in my heart to say is, 'I'll try, and thank you again for everything you've ever done for me, every kindness you've shown.'

With a serene smile, one the Virgin Mary would have been proud of, she places a hand on the crown of my head. 'God be with you, Kate, always.'

I'm sick of the God stuff and happy when she lifts her hand and I'm free to go. Several girls are now sitting down on the long pews eating breakfast from a tray. I spot the back of Bridget's head and slide into an empty place next to her, so close our thighs touch. She's eating a bowl of porridge. My stomach yawns with hunger but I can't face the porridge. It would be OK if it was made with milk and had sugar, or stuff of dreams like jam or honey, poured over the top. 'This food is not fit for humans,' I hiss. 'In fact, Lizzy Molloy's dog gets better grub.'

In between spoonfuls of porridge Bridget mumbles, 'Do you think Lizzy will adopt me as her new best friend now you're working for the curate?'

'She might, but I'm not sure you'd be happy doing most of Lizzy's homework for her.'

Bridget winks. 'For a slice of Mrs Molloy's apple pie, I'd do just about anything. Even show my knickers to her gormless brother Jack.'

Next to Bridget's left hand I spy a long thin package crudely wrapped in what I suspect is school exercise paper. I'm right; Bridget has painted exercise paper bright red and tied it with blue velvet hair ribbon. The ends are frayed; she probably nicked it from the girl she sits next to in class. Under the gift is a large white envelope. After her final spoonful of porridge, Bridget pushes both items towards me. 'This is for you, Kate, I hope you like it. I could think of a million things I'd like to buy you, if I had the money that is, but since I don't I thought you might like to keep this and every time –'

'For the love of God!' I interrupt. 'Will you shut up, else you'll be telling me what it is and spoiling the surprise.'

Bridget blushes, two red blotches spotting her cheeks. I'm dying to open Mother Peter's present but decide to concentrate on Bridget's first. Placing Mother Peter's gift on the pew next to my leg I start to tear at the red exercise paper. It opens easily and I can't contain my surprise when I spy a paintbrush. It's not any old common-or-garden paintbrush; this one is very special. It has a long bone handle with a ring of mother of pearl and a ring of silver at the base, and the brush is made of pure horse hair.

'Bridget! it's beautiful! Where on earth did you get it?' I stroke the handle of the brush, which is cool to the touch and perfectly smooth, a sensuous object, inanimate yet somehow alive. 'I've never seen anything like it.'

Bridget, her head down as if looking for something in her empty bowl, whispers, 'I'm pleased you like it.'

'Like it? I love it. It's the most beautiful thing I've ever seen. But you didn't answer – where did you get it?'

Lifting her head, Bridget points to her nose. 'None of your business, Kate O'Sullivan, to know how or where. I had to get you something special for your sixteenth birthday . . . Will you promise me something, Kate?'

Still fondling the handle of the brush, I say, 'Anything.'

'Every time you paint with that brush, will you spare a thought for me.'

'Oh, Bridget!' I'm fighting tears again. 'I'll always think of you wherever I go, whether I'm painting or not.'

'I've never had a friend like you. I don't know how I would have got through the time here without you. I don't want you to go, and that's the truth.'

'I'll not be far away. The curate's place is no more than a couple of miles.'

'I know you're going to go far away, Kate. Everyone says so.' Mimicking Mary O'Shea, Bridget adds, '"To be sure, there'll be no holding that one back."' She pauses, chewing on her next words. 'You're different to me and the rest; you've got something special. Sure, you're tall, and very pretty, and blonde, but it's more than that. It's what they call the charisma thing, you know like film stars have. You've got it.'

I can feel my cheeks burning as Bridget urges me to open the envelope. It contains a card. On the front is an image of a girl with flowing blonde hair; she's dressed in an ankle-length white dress with a midnight-blue sash cinched at her waist. It's a classical card edged in gold leaf. Inside, there's a mushy verse. I begin to read but Bridget insists I read it aloud. I hesitate and look up as Sally and Mary Neesom sit down opposite, identical twins so alike it's scary. I know they can't help being ugly but one would have been more than enough.

On the opposing leaf, Bridget had written in her childish neat hand: *Happy Birthday to my best friend Kate. I love you and am going to miss you (LOADS).*

I kiss Bridget on the cheek and at the same time whisper in her ear: 'Ditto, and thank you very much. I'll cherish this –' I touch the brush – 'for the rest of my life.'

'So how does it feel to be getting out of this place?' Sally Neesom asks, nudging her twin in the ribs. 'Looking forward to working for our heavenly Father?'

'I can't start to tell you what it feels like to be leaving this Godforsaken place, and as for working for Father Steele – I'm very excited!'

Simultaneously the twins stick out their tongues. 'You, Kate O'Sullivan, get all the bloody luck. It's not fair.'

'Sure it's fair. And anyway, like I've always said, you make your own luck in life. We –' as I utter the word I glance around the dining hall – 'we lot were in the back of the queue when they gave out the luck, so all the more reason for us to make our own. We've no mams and da's looking out for us, nobody to run back to if it all goes wrong. It means we've got to be extra strong to get where we want to be.'

'And where's that, Kate – in Father Steele's bed?'

It was Sally, the louder of the twins. Her sister giggles. I feel irritated, and pleased a second later when Bridget snarls, 'Remember it's a priest you're talking about. Just don't let anyone hear you blaspheming.'

They both shrug and speak together: 'Sure, it's only a joke.'

'And what is it you'll be doing for the curate?' Sally again.

The word char stuck in my throat. 'Answering the telephone, paying bills, keeping the books, making appointments ... You know, like a PA. He's even asked me to teach him to paint.'

The twins look suitably impressed.

'It's only temporary, for a few months before I leave Friday Wells.'

'Where will you go, Kate?' a wide-eyed Mary Neesom asks.

'I intend to go right to the top. Nowhere else will do.'

Chapter Five

After breakfast I'm summoned to Mother Superior's study. I know why, but the knowing does nothing to dispel the dread. All girls have to say a formal farewell. To summon up the courage to refuse, to make a stand to leave right there and then, head held high, feet as light as air, was tempting. Don't think I hadn't considered it, yet I knew for certain my action would deem me unfit to work for the curate. On my solitary march to the nuns' domain I talk to myself every step of the way. There is nothing any of them could say or do to hurt me. It's a formality, something to endure for a few minutes before I get a life.

My rap on the door is followed by a brisk, 'Come.'

On stepping into the room I'm momentarily taken aback. All the sisters are there except Mother Thomas: eight in total, lined up like tin soldiers on either side of Mother Superior, who sits menacingly still, her long back stiff as a board behind her highly polished mahogany desk.

'Good morning, Kate,' Mother Superior says, her lips barely moving, like a ventriloquist.

'Good morning, Mother Virgilus.'

Unsmiling she beckons me to approach her desk. Once there she hands me a brown parcel tied with string saying, 'It contains regulation garments given to all girls leaving the Sisters of Mercy Orphanage. There's a good set of clothes: a dark blue woollen skirt, a white cotton blouse, a six-button blue cardigan, and a grey mackintosh. You will find ten pounds in an envelope, and your birth certificate.'

I take the package from her right hand as she picks up a large brown manila envelope with her left. 'This arrived for you yesterday. I've no idea what it contains.' She thrusts the envelope into my hand. A quick glance tells me it's from a firm called Shaunessy & O'Leary in Dublin.

'And this –' Mother Superior taps the cover of a bound book – 'is a gift from the Sisters of Mercy. A specially embossed and bound bible. I hope it will be a reminder of your time here and the goodness and mercy bestowed upon you by this charitable organization.'

She hands me the bible; I make no effort to take it.

'I hope you will cherish this fine gift, Kate.'

I manage a nod.

'Do you not have a tongue, girl? I asked you a question. I expect a civil answer.'

'Do you want me to tell the truth, Mother Virgilus?'

'Of course. What else have we taught you here but to tell the truth in the name of the Father, the Son and the Holy Ghost?'

Under my breath I mutter, You asked for it. Aloud, I say, 'I don't want the bible or, for that matter, anything that might remind me of my time here.'

I see her face begin to turn red, in anger I suspect, but I don't care. She asked for the truth. 'Apart from Mother Peter's kindness, I want to forget this place ever existed.' I glance in Mother Peter's direction; she averts her eyes. 'Have you any idea, Mother Vigilus, how it feels to be an orphan child, totally alone and at the mercy of monsters like Mother Thomas and Mother Paul?'

'How dare you, Kate O'Sullivan, you ungrateful pup? How dare you accuse me of –' Mother Paul moves forward as if to strike me. I stand my ground, triumph lighting up my eyes.

Rising like a black spectre from behind her desk, Mother

Superior refuses to meet my gaze. 'I think it's time you left.'

'Don't worry, I don't have to be asked twice.'

I start towards the door and, as I open it, I hear Mother Peter say, 'God bless you, Kate O'Sullivan, all the days of your life.'

Scarcely able to contain my glee, I bounce back to the dormitory on freshly sprung feet. The orphanage is quiet as most of the girls are at school. I mount the stairs thinking that in less than twenty minutes I'll be going down the same flight for the last time.

Once in the dormitory I sit on the edge of my bed. The mattress feels hard, the horse-hair spread coarse to the touch. Images are beginning to filter into my consciousness. I blot them out with thoughts of tomorrow. A new bed with a bright candlewick counterpane, I hope, and a wooden headboard; a dressing table and a chair with a floral-covered cushion and matching curtains.

Next to each bed is a locker, mine empty now, and above that a shelf where each item of clothing I've ever owned has been folded and neatly stacked in exactly the same way every day of my life. Daily inspections kept us neat – God help anyone who had a fold out of place. I wonder if I'll ever get out of the habit of folding my clothes and stacking them in neat piles.

The parcel of clothes rests on my lap. I fumble with the string; it gives way easily and I slide the clothes out of the package. I rummage for the envelope and, tearing it open, I find a ten-pound note and a neatly folded document. With shaking hands I unfold my birth certificate. My heartbeat quickens as my eyes scan the page. Kate O'Sullivan, born June 5 in the parish of Friday Wells, County Cork, parents deceased. I stare at my birth certificate for a long time before folding it neatly and placing it back in the envelope with the ten pounds. I put the envelope in my bag, and leave the clothes on the bed. I want nothing from the sisters, I want nothing to remind me of this place.

Suddenly I remember the brown envelope. Excited, I tear it open. I've never had a letter posted to me before. Sure, I've had letters from Lizzy and Bridget, and once I got a love letter from Gabriel Ryan, but they were all hand-delivered. Inside is a letter from a law firm in Dublin and pinned to the top of the letter is a cheque. For several minutes I stare at the cheque thinking that there must have been some mistake. The cheque is made out in the name of Miss Kate O'Sullivan to the sum of five thousand pounds. I can't believe what my eyes tell me, and holding the cheque in one hand I begin to read the letter.

Dear Miss O'Sullivan,

You are the sole beneficiary of a trust fund founded in your name in June 1962. We have been instructed to act on behalf of the trustees who will remain (at specific behest) anonymous.

Please find enclosed cheque for £5,000, monies representing first payment on your reaching sixteen. Further sums will mature at eighteen, twenty-one and twenty-five respectively. I suggest you contact me at your earliest convenience to confirm receipt of cheque, and to discuss forwarding address for future correspondence.

I look forward to meeting you.

Yours sincerely,

Mr James Shaunessy

My chest is as tight as a drum and an adrenaline rush makes me feel faint. I reread the letter, than stare at the cheque again. Now surely I had proof, definite proof that my parents hadn't forgotten me. They'd provided for me – sure, money doesn't make up for what I've lost and suffered but it gives me something real to cling to instead of fanciful dreams. Anonymous, the letter said. The only reason to remain unknown that I can think of is that my parents, or at least one of them, was someone very important and wealthy. Five thousand pounds! A fortune; people bought houses for less.

Without warning I begin to cry, tears plopping on to the letter. I'm not sure why I'm crying, I should be happy. I am happy, I tell myself, so why the tears? Every time I'd cried in the past I'd been hurting, badly. I understood that sort of crying. Once I'd seen Mr Molloy cry when he'd cradled his grandson for the first time. I'd asked him why he was crying and he'd said, 'Tears of joy, Kate; tears of joy.'

I sniff, fold the precious letter very carefully, and then I replace the cheque and the letter in the envelope. Hugging it against my chest I sit very still, thinking of my new-found freedom. I'm rich, rich beyond my wildest dreams. If I wanted, I could get on a train to Dublin today. With five thousand pounds I could order a sleek black limousine to take me all the way there. I could even fly to London and buy a fine easel and brushes, fancy clothes and all the books I've ever wanted to read.

In fact, I could have or do whatever I wanted. But what of Father Steele? I couldn't let him down – or could I? I'll tell him about my good fortune, and offer to work until he finds a replacement for Biddy. I can't say fairer than that. He'll be happy for me, I'm sure, and he'll understand when I explain I've no need to work for a meagre eight pounds a week when I've got five thousand pounds. Now I've got a huge nest egg: enough, if I'm careful, to see me through until I get the second payment at eighteen. I wonder if it will be the same amount . . . It might be more! I can't get my head around more than five thousand pounds – that's beyond my wildest dreams. I'll write to James Shaunessy as soon as possible and arrange to meet him when I get to Dublin. I'll use all my persuasive skills to find out who sent the money. I'll make him understand how important it is for me to know. All sorted – or so I think.

Grabbing the vinyl hold-all Bridget had lent me, I open the side pocket and put the envelope inside. With a flourish I zip the bag and, throwing it over my shoulder, I stride to the window. The broken pane of glass has recently been fixed after months of tape and cardboard; the greyish tinge of fresh putty is in stark contrast to the dark green frame. When I look out of the window I see the black-clad figure of Mother Thomas striding briskly across the yard, the folds of her habit fanning out behind her, long rosary beads bouncing off her protruding stomach. I shrink back before she has a chance to see me. I haven't seen her since our brief encounter earlier with Mother Peter.

'So you're leaving us. Not a better person, I'm afraid.' I jump at the sound of her voice. 'You, Kate O'Sullivan, I consider one of my most spectacular failures.'

The shock of seeing her in the dormitory causes my throat to tighten and my heart to hammer hard. I face her head on, a black tank filling the open door. With my eyes I defy her and imagine I see her shrink from my malevolent glare. But this woman is no shrinking violet, this is the monster nun from hell, the last person I want to see before I leave, a final reminder of the loveless, cold and cruel upbringing I've had in this sham of a holy place.

According to Lizzy, all nuns are bitter and twisted because they never have sex. In my head I hear Lizzy whispering, 'Mother Thomas has never had a man. No one would fancy the ugly old bitch even if she wasn't a nun. Me brother Jack says women who never get poked shrivel up and die. It eats away at their insides like a cancer.'

I'm not sure Lizzy's brother is right, but I don't care any more. I'm armed with the knowledge that my parents cared about me; they must have loved me to want to provide for me so generously. This part of my life is over, history. I'm free, and nothing Mother Thomas says or does can ever hurt me again.

I'm wrong. Without warning and as quick as a flash she lunges at me, and before I have a chance to defend myself I'm pinned against the wall, her hand over my mouth, her eyes gleaming with something I haven't encountered before. Lust.

'I bet you're not a virgin, Kate O'Sullivan, you dirty little whore. I bet you let all the boys poke their dirty fingers in you. Stick their things inside, do they? In your mouth?' Roughly she drags my skirt up, bunching it around my waist, exposing my bare legs and white pants. I wriggle under her strong grip, stretching my mouth under her hand in a silent scream. I feel a great surge of anger as her fingers yank my pubic hair and I bite down as hard as I can into the back of her hand. She lets out an agonized yelp, like a wounded dog. Encouraged, I jump, using my full weight, on to her left foot. Before she has time to recover, I grab her rosary beads and, knotting them at her throat, I pull tight. Tightening my grip I watch with undisguised glee the colour drain from her face. She's trying to speak but I've cut off her windpipe. It's exhilarating, this adrenaline-pumping power. I can smell her fear, see the terror in her eyes; she thinks she's going to die. I want to laugh, and wish she could see herself, a sad and pathetic little creature with nothing to live for except abusing innocent kids. With a loud pant I relax my grip. 'If you ever come near me again, I'll kill you – that's a promise.' I'm not sure she can hear me, so I repeat, 'I'll kill you – do you understand?'

There is a quietness, a deathly hush, and I feel a quick beat of fear. Mother Thomas is rubbing her neck and making strange noises in the back of her throat. Her fingers are like the small chipolata sausages I used to sell in Murphy's, and again I feel the urge to laugh. What an odd thought to enter my head after I'd come so close to strangling the bitch. Quickly I gather my things together. Not glancing in Mother Thomas's direction, I scurry towards the door, her voice hoarse, snapping at my heels. 'Don't think you'll get away with this, you little whorepup. I'm going to have you, Kate O'Sullivan. One of these days I'll have you, make you pay so much you'll beg me to forgive you. Then and only then will you see and understand the power of Our Lord.'

'Kate O'Sullivan, are you there?' It's the voice of Dan Collins, the driver. He's standing in the middle of the hall, big wet footprints charting his route from the door.

'Just coming,' I bellow from the top of the stairs. Then, taking them two at a time, I bound down to join him.

'Top of the morning to you, Miss Kate.' Dan touches the peak of his cap.

I smile radiantly, it's a reflection of the way I feel. My step is as light as air and instead of feeling shaken by my encounter with Mother Thomas I feel empowered.

'And to you, Dan.'

Taking my bags, Dan leads the way outside to his car parked a few feet from the front door. I dodge a muddied puddle to jump into the back seat.

I'd met Dan once before when he'd driven some big brass from Dublin to the orphanage. Bridget and I had watched from the roof of the outside lavvie as the huge black car swept through the entrance gates. We'd seen Mother Superior and Mother Thomas, all beaming smiles and contrived enthusiasm, greet two men and one woman. Later, I'd hung around the yard talking to Dan. He'd told me that the car was a Daimler like the Queen of England used for big state occasions, and that he had two others: a white Rolls Royce that he hired out for weddings, and a Ford Cortina for his straight taxi service.

It was the Cortina today, and I couldn't help but feel a little cheated. I'd hoped for a ride in the same car as the Queen of England used. Every few minutes, I catch Dan spying me in the rear-view mirror. As I'd climbed into the back of the car I'd spotted him lingering much too long on my legs, and I'd noticed he'd not closed the back door until I'd arranged my skirt around my knees. What is it with men and that funny look in their eyes? I don't like it, not for one minute. It makes me feel funny – and not jokey funny, more uncomfortable funny, dirty, as if I'm what Mother Thomas called me. A whore, the sort of woman men poked for a few bob down the side of the pub on Friday and Saturday nights. I don't want any of that.

The car pulls slowly away from the front of the building. As it bumps down the gravel drive and through the open gates, I resist the urge to glance over my shoulder. What pull could this prison have that I want a last look? As if I haven't seen enough grey walls and ugliness to last me a lifetime. Would I ever escape? Or would the last sixteen years imprison me for the rest of my life? I bite my lip and look stoically ahead, determined that I will never look back, not now, not ever.

'You're looking grand this morning, Miss Kate. Very grand, to be sure, and sixteen now. All grown up and off to work. Earning your own money. So, how much they paying you down there to look after the curate?'

Stony-faced I stare out of the window. 'I don't think that's any of your business, Dan.'

'Maybe not. Just making conversation, like, needn't get so hoity toity. Just being pleasant.'

I say nothing and the silence hangs in the air, broken by the swish of the windscreen wipers sweeping great plumes of water aside. It is at least five minutes before Dan speaks again. 'Must say, I liked the painting of the church you did for the fête. Good enough to hang in them posh galleries in Dublin, I reckon.'

'Thank you, Dan.'

'I hear tell you want to be an artist. That true?'

I nod and wish he would shut up and drive, but I might as well ask a dog not to bark.

'I used to do a bit of sketching myself few years ago. I loved to go down to the sea, at Cork or Kinsale, and sketch the boats. Something about the sea and sailing excites me no end. I once went all the way to the Dingle. My God, I saw some sights up there, sights like you've never seen in your life. The scenery fair took my breath away, it did that.' He paused, changed gear, then continued: 'You ever been up to the Dingle, Miss Kate?'

'Never. I've been as far as Cork once, on a school trip.'

'Well, I could arrange it, if you'd like a trip up there. I've got a friend who has a pub looking out over Dingle Bay. Lovely little place, got a few rooms. I'd drive you up there, you could paint and I could watch. Might learn a thing or two about art. Have your own room, no messing about like that. I've been a widower now for nigh on six years, and I don't go in for any of that nonsense. God-fearing man – ask anyone around these parts. I admit I'm on the lookout for another wife but there's no one on the cards at the moment. Had one girlfriend – Sally, lovely girl – but she decides she wants to be a nurse and ups and offs to Dublin to train in one of them big teaching hospitals. Yep, I'm not a bad catch, if I say so myself. Got me own house all paid for, and a good business. Going to buy another Daimler soon, lot of demand for wakes. When the right girl comes along I'd be prepared to wait for our wedding night, you know what I mean, none of that hanky panky. There's not many round these parts who can say that, not many in all of Ireland, I'll be bound.'

'Right now I can't make any plans, and even if I could I wouldn't want to go to the Dingle or anywhere else with you, or any man old enough to be my father unless he was that very same man.'

Dan stiffens his back and hunches forward to see through the downpour. The car slows down to pass a bus parked at the bus stop. Cursing the bus driver, Dan stalls the car, only starting the engine again with a stream of abuse.

The remainder of the journey to Coppice Cottage is conducted in blissful silence. I use the time to plan how to tell Father Steele I won't be staying for the four months we'd agreed. A month, I decide, will give him ample time to find a replacement. That gives me plenty of time to find a place to live in Dublin, and to fly to a foreign land. Spain, perhaps, or France – something I've dreamt of doing since I was a little girl. I'd take Bridget if she were free, but as she isn't, I'll offer to take Lizzy. The Molloys had been like family to me. In fact, I'd offer to take them all. I can afford it. I know several girls who would jump at the chance to work for the curate. Susan Reilly springs to mind. She lives in the same street as Lizzy, and works part-time in the fish and chip shop in the village. She's one of those people who always has a smile even when there's little to smile about. 'She's got a big heart,' Lizzy always says. 'Not very bright, but a big heart.' I've seen Susan Reilly chuckle when the young lads tease her, and on Friday nights after the pub her good humour deals with a stream of drunken abuse. A couple of times she'd given me a bag of chips when I'd no money, whispering that I could pay next week. Yes, Susan Reilly deserves a bit of luck.

As Dan slows down outside the curate's cottage I can see deep rivulets of water streaming down the shingle roof to gather in a pool at the edge of the neat square of lawn. Dan stops level with the picket fence. Without a word, he jumps out of the driver's seat, and with agile grace opens the passenger door for me.

Extending his hand, he says, 'I'm not old enough to be yer da, Kate. I'll be twenty-nine next birthday, in August. A Leo by birth, but honest to God I don't roar.'

Stepping out on to the pavement I manage a small smile.

'I meant what I said earlier, Miss Kate. I'm not the pushy sort. I can wait, not like some I could mention.'

If Dan could have read my mind he would have happily crawled into a hole, curled up and died on the spot. Dan Collins was the very last man on God's earth I would let poke between my legs. For a start, he looks like a pig. It isn't just the pink flesh and poker-straight milk-white eyelashes I detest; it's his nose and what he does with it. Dan sniffs a lot, and when he does his nose wrinkles up at the end exactly like a snout. And many years ago I'd promised myself I would never have sex with a redhead. Dan has a mop of the stuff, the colour of ginger biscuits. I'd made a silent promise after seeing Patricia Guthrie naked in the showers. The risk of a clip around the ears from a sixth-form girl hadn't deterred me from staring at her bulging red pubic bush, white see-through skin, and nipples so pale they could hardly be called pink. From that day forward I'd imagined all redheads to have the same long straggly pubic hair, and the boy's willies to be the same colour as Pat's nipples.

In spite of my thoughts I smile sweetly. 'I was only kidding about your age, Dan. Sure, you don't look old enough to be me da.' I pause. 'Since I don't have a da, I'm not even sure how old he'd be.'

'Older than me, that's for sure.' My hand is shaking, and he notices. 'You OK?'

'Bit nervous. It's my first day out of the orphanage.'

From under half-closed lids I can see Dan responding. He's telling me with his kind expression that he understands. 'Bloody hard on a young girl like yourself. I've heard lots of stories 'bout them nuns up there. Sisters of no bloody Mercy, so they say. You must have had a rough time, need someone to look after you proper like, no more worries.'

'You're right about the nuns, Dan. And, yes, I do and will need someone to look after me eventually, but not right now. Right now I've got to do the looking after: I've got to take care of the curate.'

'A lovely girl like you shouldn't be skivvying. You could be one of them top models in magazines and the like.'

I ache to tell him I'm rich and don't have to do for anyone any more, but I keep my mouth shut. After reading the solicitor's letter for the second time I'd decided to tell as few people as possible. It's the best way, I tell myself, else the tongues will be wagging non-stop in the village – and beyond, I've no doubt.

'Kate, there you are!' Dan and I turn to see Father Steele trotting down the path towards us. He speaks directly to me. 'I was expecting you earlier. Mother Paul said you'd be here before Mass. So I raced back from church expecting to find you on the doorstep soaked to the skin.' Dressed in a traditional black soutane, he looks exactly as he had on the first day I'd seen him in church, except for his hair, which is wet and plastered to the sides of his head like a skull cap.

'Good morning to you, Father.' Dan touches the tip of his hat. 'Well, I'd best be off. No charge for the ride, the orphanage settles my account.' Then to me, 'Remember what I said earlier, Miss Kate. If you need a friend, you know where I am. Take care and God be with you.'

I nod and mumble, 'Thanks,' as Father Steele says, 'God be with you, Dan.'

In silence we both watch Dan climb into the car, do a U-turn and drive off with a curt wave. Still looking at the back of Dan's car, the curate says, 'He's a good man, Dan Collins. You could do a lot worse for a friend.'

'Sure, it's pointless making friends in Friday Wells,

99

because I've only to leave them very soon. I've got Bridget, a friend for life. I don't need any more.'

Father Steele tries to take my bag. 'Here, let me take that.'

Clutching the handle so tight it bites into my palm, I shake my head and with a hint of sadness say, 'I can manage. I haven't got much. All my worldly goods aren't very heavy.'

'Possessions mean very little, Kate. It's what's in here –' he places his hand on his heart – 'that make us rich or poor.'

I know what he means but I'm not sure I agree, so keeping my mouth shut I follow him through the gate and up the path, stopping while he opens the front door. Pushing it open with the toe of his shoe he stands to one side, allowing me to pass.

'Welcome to my humble abode, Miss O'Sullivan. It's good to have you on board.'

'It's good to be here, Father, very good.'

'This is where you'll sleep.'

The bedroom on the first floor of the cottage faces south and west. It overlooks part of the back garden and a thickly wooded coppice. Many years ago, I'd hidden under a beech tree a few feet from the cottage wall and read a Famous Five adventure from cover to cover instead of going to church.

Panelled to dado-height in some sort of dark polished wood, the room looks more like a study than a bedroom. A large rug, threadbare in places, covers the majority of the boarded floor. There is a lot of yellow on the walls, quite faded, and a damp patch at the left side of the windowsill. A single bed with a crude wooden headboard pushed hard up against the wall is covered in an egg-yolk yellow candlewick bedspread which doesn't quite reach the floor. Our ever-present Lord is, as usual, on the cross, dripping blood above the bed. A small chest of drawers doubles as a bedside cabinet. Neatly arranged on top are a water jug, a lamp with a green shade, and a box of tissues. Next to the window stands a simple wooden chair with a cane seat alongside a crude wardrobe painted bottle green. Yellow curtains with tiny blue flowers are the only relief in the otherwise Spartan room. A functional room, not much better than the orphanage, and definitely not the bedroom of my dreams.

I try not to look disappointed but realize it must show when Father Steele asks, 'Don't you like it?'

Stepping into the centre of the room, my voice shrill with enforced enthusiasm, I say, 'It's lovely.'

He's not convinced and, pointing to the window, says reassuringly, 'It faces south, so you'll get the sun in the morning.'

'Really, Father, it's very nice. After sleeping in a dormitory with eight other girls for most of my life, this room is like the Ritz.'

This seems to satisfy him. 'You can leave your things here, then if you follow me I'll show you around the rest of the house.'

Dutifully I follow him downstairs to a narrow hall. At the end he turns right, heading towards a closed door ahead. It leads to the kitchen, and Father Steele has to duck to enter. I'm surprised when he steps to one side and, passing him, I find myself in a very large room. I reckon it's about thirty-five by twenty-six feet with four tall windows almost filling an entire wall. One, I notice, is a sliding door leading to the garden. In one corner there's a very large oven, bright red and polished to a high gloss, the word Aga written in chrome, shining like a newly minted coin. Next to the oven a range of fitted cupboards forms an L-shape.

'This room was once three: a scullery, outhouse and small kitchen. The curate before me was a bit of a handyman. In his spare time he did the conversion.' With a flourish, Father Steele opens one of the cupboard doors, running the palm of his hand across the wooden surface. 'All solid oak. Hand-crafted the entire kitchen himself. Not bad, eh?'

I know little or nothing about joinery. I'd only been in three kitchens in my life: the one in the orphanage, a huge scullery with a long range of equipment, a bit like the canteen at school; Murphy's butchers, where I'd worked; and Mrs Molloy's, a room that resembles an overgrown cupboard, so much so it never ceases to amaze me how she produces such wonderful food.

'He did a great job,' was all I could find to say. I wanted to add that kitchens weren't my thing. Bedrooms, yes; I'd always dreamt of how it would be to have my own bedroom. In my imaginings it had tall narrow windows – sash, I think they are called – opening on to a paved terrace crammed full of flowering plants in big terracotta pots like I'd seen in pictures of Italy. The bathroom would lead off the bedroom, with a bath big enough for at least four. And all the walls would be white, with glass shelves packed with every conceivable type of oil and scent and soap. I'd have a dressing table with a printed cloth that fell in folds to the carpeted floor. Every morning, after I'd been served breakfast in my king-sized bed, I'd float through to the next room, which would be my studio. Here the light would be perfect, and I'd paint all day, sometimes late into the night. Of course, I'd have a maid who would bring me drinks and food as and when I needed, and I'd never have to go to the kitchen. My hands would be smooth and flawless, protected from detergent and hot water. After this morning my dream seemed more a reality, and the thought made me feel light-headed again, a bit like when I'd been given drugs in hospital.

'Kate, did you hear what I said?'

'Sorry, Father, I was miles away.'

With a mildly irritated click of his tongue Father Steele points to a pantry. 'For the third time, this is where all the dry food is kept. Coffee, tea, sugar, etc. Obviously milk, eggs, butter are kept in the fridge and all cleaning materials under the sink. I've made a list of your duties and my daily requirements. I like a simple meal in the evening, nothing too heavy. Fish on Fridays, of course, and chicken or lamb the remainder of the week. I don't eat beef.'

'You didn't mention cooking. I've never done any. In truth, Father, I wouldn't know where to start.'

'Don't look so worried, Kate. It's very simple.' He taps the cover of a cookbook sitting on the top of a scrubbed pine table. 'It's all in here, just follow the recipes letter for letter and you can't go wrong.'

The image on the cover of the cookbook is of a young woman in front of what looks like a pie of sorts, all golden and perfect. A smug smile splits her round face; it says, Do it my way and it will be perfect every time.

That afternoon Susie O'Connor and I get together for the first time, and by the end of the day I'm certain ours is not going to be a match made in heaven. I hate cooking. At school I hated domestic science and would much rather have done woodwork like the boys. Once, Pat Devlin and I had asked to swap places: he wanted to be a chef and it made perfect sense, but not to our class teachers – they said we'd disrupt the classes and that everyone would want to do the same. As far as I'm concerned, cooking is a waste of time. Time that could be spent doing much more enjoyable things.

'You may well smile, Susie –' I'm talking to the image on the cover of the book – 'I just wish you'd told me to remove the giblets from the belly of the chicken before I roasted it. And why, since I followed your instructions to the letter, is the gravy so lumpy?'

In despair I stir the gravy yet again, and decide the

only way to get rid of the lumps is to use a sieve. I rummage through every drawer and cupboard cursing the gravy and Susie until eventually I find one.

As the steaming hot gravy strains, my ears prick up at the sound of the front door opening. Like a thief caught red-handed I drop the pan and sieve with a clatter, spinning around to face the door with my back to the sink. A moment later the door opens and Father Steele is filling the space.

'Are you OK, Kate? You look very pale.'

'I'm grand, Father, grand.' I point at Susie's smiling image. 'We are getting acquainted. It's a new relationship and might take a little time, but I'm sure we'll get there in the end.'

Taking a step into the room, Father Steele smacks his lips. 'It certainly smells good. Did you get a chicken as I suggested?'

I nod.

'And apple pie?'

I'm afraid to tell him about the apple pie, then decide I might as well.

'Sure, it's not the most perfect pie, golden crust and all. But it was hot, you see, and I forgot to use the oven gloves, and . . .' I pause and begin to chew the side of my bottom lip. I can hear the drumming of rain on the window behind Father Steele. 'Sure, this rain hasn't let up all day. My bet is it'll be flooding in Mallow.'

'Don't change the subject, Kate. What happened to the apple pie?'

Spreading my arms wide in a gesture of hopelessness I mumble, 'There was a loud clap of thunder like nothing I've ever heard before. It gave me such a shock. I swear, Father, I thought the British Army had come down from the North and were letting off grenades or something.'

The curate frowns. 'I won't ask you again, Kate.'

'I dropped it, Father. I tried to retrieve it, but it kind

of got all mashed up and didn't look so good. More like stew than pie.'

'And the gravy?'

'That . . . Oh yes, the gravy.' I grimace at the mention of the gravy hidden behind my back, no doubt swimming in a few inches of dirty dishwater. Without a word I point over my shoulder to the sink. Father Steele crosses the room and, standing next to me, follows my finger with his eyes.

'It'll be better next time.' In my head I vow it will be perfect, even if I have to sneak Mrs Molloy into the cottage to give me secret cookery lessons.

The corners of his mouth tighten. He looks angry, so I'm surprised when a moment later he begins to laugh.

I thrill to the sound. He isn't angry, he couldn't be if he's laughing, people don't laugh when they're angry. They snarl and shout, and hurt. A sense of relief pushes aside some of my apprehension.

'I'm really sorry, Father, I desperately wanted the first meal I made for you to be perfect. Instead it's a disaster.'

Abruptly he stops chuckling. 'No disaster. There's cheese in the fridge and some ham left over from yesterday, and we have fresh bread and tomatoes. A veritable feast. What more could a man ask for? Now, I'm going to take a bath, and when I come down I want you to join me for supper.' He turns on his heel, then, glancing over his shoulder, says, 'Do you think you can get the cheese and ham out of the fridge without mishap?'

I grin. 'I can try.'

'Good. I'll see you same place in half an hour –' he glances at his wristwatch – 'seven thirty-five on the dot.'

I nod and watch him walk across the room. Through the open door I concentrate on his back as he strides down the hall. At the foot of the stairs he stoops to pick up a letter from the doormat. The black cloth of his soutane is stretched across his broad shoulders and when he stands up to his full height the cloth flaps like the wings of a huge black bird at his feet. I feel warm inside, and tingling. He'd laughed at my mistakes and forgiven me. He wanted me to eat with him. It's my chance to tell him about the money and the trust fund.

With a tug, I pull the chain attached to the plug and watch the dark brown gravy water wind down the drain, thinking at the same time that the only way to have intelligent conversations, be it with Father Steele or anyone else for that matter, was to fill my head with knowledge. If I read every night for a few hours I could get through a couple of books a week and many more newspapers.

In my heart I know I want to impress the curate. I haven't analysed the reasons, I just know it makes me feel good. In my head I hear Bridget: Admit it, Kate, you're in love with Father Steele.

Don't be ridiculous, he's a priest, says my own voice of reason. I simply enjoy being with him – is that so bad? The nagging voice fades as aloud I say, 'When I make him smile it makes me happy. Is that so wrong?' As I cross the room towards the fridge I consider my feelings for the priest. Since I'd met him I'd had a huge crush on him – who wouldn't? That isn't love, is it? I accept we cannot have the normal man-and-woman-type love. But what about a brother–sister type, or even the father–daughter sort?

Is that what you really want, Kate? The nagging voice again. A blast of cool air hits the side of my face as I open the door of the fridge. In a hushed whisper, I say, 'I want to be loved, that's all. It's not a lot to ask.'

The mattress is hard, but thankfully thicker than the mattress in the orphanage, and the pillowcase smells of lavender. Shame it's not made of soft down, the stuff of dreams. If anyone as recently as last week had told me I'd miss the familiarity of the orphanage dormitory I'd have laughed in his or her face, yet tonight, disturbed by sounds of a different kind, I might be inclined to agree. I feel a bit like a kitten pushed out of the litter, and I miss Bridget. In my entire life I can think of few occasions when I hadn't seen her first thing in the morning and last thing at night. The creak of the second from top stair and the squeal of Father Steele's cat Angelus are determined to keep me awake, and try as I may sleep eludes me. I scold myself for not telling Father Steele about my trust fund and giving him notice. I'd fully intended to during supper, but the opportunity hadn't arisen, and I'd been loathe to spoil our first night together especially since he'd been so understanding about the food. I promise myself I'll do it before the end of the week, and offer to stay until the end of July, which in fact is more than a month.

I slide out of bed and pad as quiet as a mouse to the dresser. In the top drawer where I'd put it earlier lies the manila envelope containing my future. Gripping it tight I cross the room and, barely daring to breathe, turn the door handle and say a silent thank you as it opens with ease. With my back touching the wall, I feel my way across the dark landing to the top of the stairs. Taking a deep breath, I begin to descend, careful to miss the one that I notice creaks. At the bottom I turn right and head towards the sitting room. Once there I switch on the light and cross the room to Father Steele's desk where earlier I'd noticed a writing pad, pens and envelopes.

Sitting down I open the pad and choose a pen from a selection standing in a ceramic tumbler. A fountain pen with a fat nib.

I write the date and the curate's address in the left-hand corner, exactly as I'd been taught, and in my neatest hand confirm receipt of the solicitor's letter, my thanks and my intention to meet him in Dublin at my earliest convenience. I instruct all correspondence to be sent to the above address and sign it with a formal, *I remain, yours faithfully, Kate O'Sullivan.* The letter complete, I search for blotting paper and on finding none I blow on the damp ink.

'I'm out of blotting paper, I'm afraid.'

Spinning round I'm faced with Father Steele filling the door in ankle-length dressing gown and a grim expression. 'What are you doing, Kate?'

Covering the letter with my hand, I say, 'I'm writing to someone.'

'That much is obvious, but why sneak about the house in the middle of the night like a thief? I couldn't sleep and I heard noises. I thought you were an intruder.'

'I'm sorry, Father. I couldn't sleep either and it seemed like a good idea.'

'Is the letter so important it couldn't have waited until tomorrow morning? At least then you could have asked my permission to use my stationery.'

'It's only one page and a bit of ink.'

He sighs. 'It's the principle, and you haven't answered my question. Why is the letter so important you have to write it in such secrecy?'

Scooping up both letters, I rise and cross the space that separates us. I hand him the letter from the solicitor. 'Mother Superior gave it to me this morning. Sure, I was going to tell you, Father, and to give you notice.'

There is silence as he reads and when he finishes I can see his body language has changed: it's no longer stiff and guarded.

Handing me the letter he says, 'Most families have secrets. Some are not worth keeping. Clearly yours was and is.'

'I can't start to tell you how happy this has made me. Believe me, Father, it's not just the money, it's about a whole stack of other things. You know, emotional stuff. I feel . . . less abandoned. It helps a lot to know my parents

– whoever, wherever they are – cared enough to do this for me. It takes away some of the pain and the guilt. For most of my life I've believed deep in here –' I touch my breast bone – 'that I wasn't born in Ireland, that I was sent here for a reason. A secret love child perhaps, or the daughter of someone who was under threat. I know it sounds romantic, fanciful even, the stuff young girls read about in novels. But this –' I hold out the letter – 'proves it.'

'I hate to pour cold water on your theory, Kate, but you have to accept the facts and stop living in a fantasy world. Has it occurred to you that there could be a very simple explanation for all of this? Your mother when she had you may have been very young, probably unmarried, and unable to look after you. She left you with the church thinking you would be cared for. Presumably she went on to make something of her life, and to eradicate some of her guilt she set up a trust fund for you.'

I can feel my frustration rise and I want to lash out at Father Steele. 'Even if that were true, it still proves she loved me.'

A slow smile parts his lips. 'Of course it does, Kate, and I'm sure if she were to see you today she'd be very proud.'

For the second time today I start to cry. 'Do you really think so, Father?'

'I know so.'

Chapter Six

'So how is it living with Robert Redford Steele?' Bridget pinches my leg and before I can reply whispers in my ear, 'How far away is your bedroom from his?'

'Bridget, what sort of question is that?' I pinch her back.

We are both seated at the back of St Winifred's. Bert O'Flanagan is reading the lesson, a perfect time for Bridget and I to catch up.

'I miss you, Kate. It's not the same without you.'

'I miss you too, when I get a moment to myself.'

'So tell me, what do you have to do?'

'Well, I'm up at the crack of dawn. The curate likes his breakfast at half six, always the same. He has porridge smothered in honey, a glass of milk and an orange. Makes me have an orange too, says it's full of vitamin C, keeps the flu away. Then he's gone for most of the morning. I zip around the house: dust, polish, vacuum, laundry, all the usual stuff.' I fake a yawn. 'Dead boring. Then I walk to the village to buy the food for the day. When I get back I make his lunch and prepare the stuff for the evening meal.'

'I didn't know you could cook. You were hopeless at school – remember your vegetable soup?'

My expression is smug. 'Our domestic science teacher didn't have Susie O'Connor. I've been friendly with her for a week. Another couple of weeks and I'll be one of them cordon blues.'

'Who's she and what's a cordon blue?'

'A famous cook who's written several books. On my first day Father Steele gave me this book and said if I followed her instructions to the letter I couldn't go far wrong.'

'What sort of things have you cooked so far?'

'I've done roast chicken with a rich onion gravy to die for.'

'As good as Mrs Molloy's?'

'Nearly.'

Bridget digs me in the ribs. 'I know where to come for Sunday lunch when I leave the orphanage.' Then she leans close to me, her lips almost touching my ear. 'So what do you do at night?'

'He reads. He's got millions of books, with hard backs; most of the writers I've never even heard of. Sometimes he listens to music. He's teaching me Italian and I'm giving him art lessons.'

'Will you girls hush up?' It's Mrs Flatley, who's sitting directly behind. 'I'm trying to listen to the lesson.'

Ignoring this, Bridget asks, 'Have you seen him without his soutane?'

Before I can answer, Mrs Flatley pokes the handle of her umbrella hard in the middle of Bridget's back. 'If you don't shut up, Bridget Costello, I'll tell Mother Thomas how you behave in church.'

In defiance Bridget sticks out her tongue, but doesn't dare say another word. That sort of threat could silence Joe Dunne, the toughest boy in the village.

I follow Bridget down the aisle to take the wine and host. As I walk I thank God I don't have to go back to the orphanage.

Hand in hand, Bridget and I leave church. In the far distance I spot Mother Thomas standing on the steps of the sacristy. She's talking to Father Steele, who is either coming or going, I'm not sure which. I shrink back into the darkness of the vestibule, pulling Bridget with me.

What's she saying to him, I wonder. What evil is she filling his head with?

'Did you see her?' I hiss.

'Who?'

'The witch Thomas. She's talking to the curate, probably telling him I'm the devil's own, and to watch out for me.'

'I wouldn't worry about that old bugger, word's out that she's not got much longer. A few days ago Sally saw her coughing up blood all over her hanky, and it spotted on the front of her habit. Cancer, that's what she's got, I reckon.'

I can hear the venom in my voice and barely recognize it as my own when I say, 'I hope it's the long painful type of cancer – you know the kind that eats away at your flesh so you become a bag of bones, and all your hair falls out, and your body gets covered in open sores and –'

'Stop it, Kate, for the love of God! Not in church.'

'Oh, Bridget, don't you think he knows?' I jerk my head towards the altar. 'He knows all about her evil, and this is his way of punishing her.' I nod solemnly. 'We all get our just desserts, it's only a matter of time.'

Bridget shuddered. 'You're scaring me.'

'What goes around comes around, that's what I say.'

'Speaking of going, that's what I've got to do right now. I'm on floor-cleaning duty today and if I'm not on my knees by the time she comes around at eleven-thirty I'll get not a bite to eat.'

An image of myself doing the same job and Mother Thomas kicking the bucket out from under me, then forcing me to clean the entire floor for a second and third time enters my head. It lingers only briefly; I'd made a promise to myself the day I'd left, if the bad thoughts came – and I knew they would visit me sometimes – I'd banish them quickly and thoroughly. Instinctively, I know that to dwell on the past, my kind of past, would stop me having a future.

It's a hot day and threatening to get hotter. A whitish haze blots out the sun as Bridget and I walk to the end of Potter's Lane where we have to part. We hug, clinched in a tight knot, clinging to one another as if we were parting for ever. I kiss her on the forehead like I've seen parents do to their children. I'm not sure why I did it, I've never kissed her like that before. When our arms drop, Bridget is the first to speak.

'I miss you, Kate.'

'I miss you too.' I try to sound optimistic. 'Sure, it won't be long before you leave, and we can spend time together.'

Warming to this, Bridget manages a tight smile. 'Will you send for me when you get to Dublin, like you promised? You won't forget me, will you?'

'How could I forget you? We're family.'

'You're all I've got, Kate.'

Suddenly I feel suffocated, as if I'm drowning, and I want to push Bridget away. I'd planned to tell her about my trust fund but without any clear reason I hold back. Why not have a secret, I ask myself. I've never had one before. Anyway, I decide I don't want to part with it just yet.

'Look after the curate good, and keep praying that Mother Thomas doesn't recover.'

A wide grin splits my face. 'That I will, and you look after yourself good, Bridget. You know where I am if you need me. I'll always be there for you. If all else fails, we've got each other. Remember what we used to say when we were kids?' I sing: '"Never mind the weather as long as we're together." Go on now, else you'll be late, and I don't want you to get into trouble.'

Bridget glances over her shoulder up the lane that leads

to the orphanage. 'Sometimes I just want to run away, far away, and never look back.'

'To where? With no money and no further education, you'd end up on the streets. Jobs are not ten a penny in Ireland. How many times have we talked about this? It's the only way. Don't give up, Bridget, so close to getting out.'

She's anxious, I can tell, and restless – not her usual self.

'Now you really will have to go, or you'll be in big trouble.'

'I'm in trouble now.' Bridget hangs her head. 'Mother Thomas has shifted her affection from you to me.'

'What do you mean?'

'I mean . . .'

'Look at me, Bridget!'

She refuses to lift her head. 'I mean, she's tried to . . . you know . . . do that.'

I lift Bridget's face, yet still she won't look me in the eyes. 'Tell me, has she tried to touch you down there in your private parts?'

Still not looking at me, Bridget slowly nods.

'I'm going to report the evil bitch. She tried it once with me on the day I was leaving and I nearly killed her.'

'I'm scared, Kate, very scared. I'm afraid that I might do something bad, something I'll regret, and me so near to getting out, being free.'

I'm seething, a great rage is turning my innards to steel. The anger is like nothing I've ever felt before and instead of feeling afraid I feel powerful, strong and fearless, as if I could do or say anything I want. And right at this moment I want to march up to the orphanage, storm into Mother Superior's office and confront her there and then. But I know it won't do any good, she'd have me thrown out. No, what I need is proof, hard evidence; it's the only way to punish the bitch.

In the back of my brain a small seed of a plan is beginning to form and with a stroke of luck it might just work.

Gripping both Bridget's hands in mine, I hold them very tight.

'Stay away from her, sit tight and wait to hear from me. I've got a plan.'

'What is it, Kate?'

'I can't tell you right now, but as soon as I've worked out all the details I'll let you know.'

This seems to cheer Bridget and she manages a tremulous smile. 'I miss you, I really do. I can't tell you how much.'

Looking down at Bridget's knotted fingers I notice her nails are bitten down to the quick. 'I know,' I sigh. 'I know.'

Gently I push her in the direction of the orphanage. Her hands slip from mine, she blinks rapidly as if fighting back tears, then turns and begins to run down the lane. I watch her back, expecting her to turn. I'm not disappointed. Halfway down she does, and, arm half-raised, she waves. In spite of the warmth I feel a shiver run up my back and a vision of Bridget a few days after I'd met her, when she was four, appears with startling clarity before my eyes. She had a round face with dimpled cheeks and she'd been crying: her eyes were raw and swollen, the lashes stuck together with what looked like glue. I didn't know at the time she was suffering from chronic conjunctivitis.

I stand very still, my eyes fixed on her back, until she turns the corner and is out of sight. On the slow trudge back to the village I'm seething with anger. My stomach feels empty, but not the hungry-type empty, more like I've had my guts ripped out. Stopping twice, I lean against a wall and take long deep breaths. By the time I've reached Caroline Street I'm determined: regardless of my own safety, I'm going to get Mother Thomas. Raising my eyes,

I shout, 'And you, what bloody use are you, letting innocent kids suffer? Why the hell don't you do something
about it?'

'You all right, miss?' It was a kid on a bike.

I lunge towards him, blocking his path. 'No, I'm not,
I've just got out of the loony bin.' I slacken my mouth
on one side, and, narrowing my eyes to slits, I shout, 'I'm
after a lad just like you.'

The kid looks scared. 'Out of me way, else I'll –'

'Else you'll what?'

He swerves off to my right, his skinny legs peddling
furiously. When he's put a safe distance between us he
yells over his shoulder, 'I'll tell the coppers on you.'

I yell back, 'Go to hell!' Then a second later say three
Hail Marys.

I feel a bit better, and my step lifts as I think about the
day ahead.

Unused to leisure time, Sunday stretches endlessly in
front of me. In Doyle's newsagents I buy two newspapers
and a Mars Bar, then board a bus to Mallow, five miles
south. Aimlessly I wander into MacHugh Park. It's quiet,
except for a few kids kicking a football, and a couple
walking their spaniel. I circle the small boating lake before
finding an empty park bench. I'd prepared a packed lunch;
it isn't lunchtime but I'm ravenous and tear into the
cheese sandwiches like I haven't eaten for days. Idly I
feed the crusts to a couple of fat ducks who seem totally
uninterested. The park is getting busier by the minute.
An assortment of folk walk dogs and children in prams
and gaily painted buggies. Every time I'm faced with a
happy domestic scene I try hard not to feel sorry for
myself. It's difficult sometimes, but the older I get the
easier it becomes. I suppose it's because I know I'm not
the only one with problems. Sometimes having mams and
dads is worse than having none at all. Karen Leesom who
was in my class for a couple of years used to come to school

some days looking like she'd done a couple of rounds with Muhammad Ali. It turned out her father had been having sex with her since she was ten. The authorities took her into care and the last I heard she was living with foster parents.

When it starts to spit with rain I meander down the High Street. I gaze in shop windows, before boarding the bus for the journey back. On the top deck of the bus I eat my apple and Mars Bar, taking alternate bites then saving an inch slab of Mars till the end to savour the sweetness on my tongue. By the time the bus stops at the end of Elswick Lane, the stop before mine, most of my 'Get Thomas' plan is formulated. Later that night, in bed, the final piece drops into place. I can't wait for next Sunday to tell Bridget, and to put the first part into action.

But I don't have to wait until next Sunday. The following Wednesday Mother Thomas is dead. She was alive when Mother Paul found her, at eight-thirty in the morning at the foot of the main staircase in the orphanage. Twenty minutes later she died of a fractured skull, in the ambulance en route to hospital. Foul play was suspected. She hadn't fallen, she'd been pushed.

Father Steele breaks the news in a flat monotone. 'Mother Thomas is dead.'

I feel a ripple of elation. 'When? How?'

'She was found at the foot of the stairs in the orphanage with a fractured skull.'

I can feel the colour slowly draining from my lips. This always happens when I'm shocked.

'They think she may have been pushed.'

I lower my eyes, afraid he may see the glint of satisfaction, joy even. I long to tell him how evil she was, and how I'm glad she's dead, but I mumble a lie instead. 'I'm sorry.'

'Are you really sorry? Is that the truth?'

My head still bent, I nod vigorously.

'Look at me, Kate.'

I do as he says, certain he'll see the truth in my eyes.

Studying me with intent he says, 'You're not sorry, are you, Kate?'

Taking a deep breath, silently I shake my head.

His sucks his mouth in at the sides. I'd seen the expression before and know he's angry. 'I think you should go to confession, Kate, as soon as possible.'

Before I can reply, Father Steele leaves the kitchen without closing the door. I'm only vaguely aware of the front door opening and closing before I cover my face with my hands and feel my body crank with an angry sob.

I dress carefully for confession: simple white blouse, black pleated skirt covered by a long dark grey raincoat. It's dark when I step out of the cottage, and as I pick my way along the unlit narrow lane towards the church I regret not bringing a torch.

Father Steele is in the confessional. I'd hoped he would be; I want him to know the truth, it's important.

When ten minutes later I step out of the confessional I'm very angry. Not as angry as I'd been when I first heard about Mother Thomas molesting Bridget, but close. I'd expected to feel better after confession, but strangely enough I feel worse. I'd told Father Steele everything – things I hadn't told another living soul except Bridget. Patiently I'd listened to him harping on about forgiveness until I could stand no more and, gripped with the terrible anger again, I'd said, 'Why should I forgive someone so evil?'

I'd wanted, expected, a reasonable answer, not: 'God will be the judge. You must find it in your heart to forgive.'

'But what if God, busy as he is, happened to overlook the wicked nun and she got off scot-free, got a place in heaven instead of where she belongs, in the bowels of hell? What then, Father?'

He'd replied with controlled patience, 'Mother Thomas will not find a place in heaven if she has sinned.' It isn't good enough and I leave church in turmoil. Later, much later, in my bed while the village sleeps I lie awake haunted by demons. I try, with every scrap of willpower I can muster, to get Mother Thomas out of my head, but however much I think about good things, the future, my plans, I keep returning to everything she did to me, things I'd buried deep, so deep I'd forgotten them. It's as if Mother Thomas is reaching out from the grave for one final torment. Her voice mocks: 'You'll never be free of me, Kate O'Sullivan.' The sound echoes around the small room. Hunkered in a ball, I rock to and fro, muttering, 'I need to tell you, Father, I'm glad she's dead. I'm just disappointed it was so quick and painless. I'd hoped for a long, lingering, terrible end for Mother Thomas. I don't think she's with you, I hope not, I think she'll be down below with the other bloke, where her soul will rot in hell. I want to ask your forgiveness, Father, for feeling this way, but you have to understand I can't help it, after all she did to me.' It's then I hear a sound outside and with a pinch of terror I watch the bedroom door slowly open. Father Steele steps inside, closing the door quietly behind him. He's wearing a long dressing gown. I can see a few golden hairs poking out of the top, one resting on the dark blue braid of the collar. His skin is pale, but not pink like most Irish skin. He leans against the door, making no attempt to enter the room.

'You mustn't blame yourself for hating Mother Thomas, nor must you feel any guilt for what she did to you. What you must do, and I know it will be very difficult, is find it in your heart to forgive her. Do you think you can do that, Kate?'

Silently I shake my head.

'I urge you to try. If you can, it will prove to be your salvation. Believe me, you will feel much better.'

I don't believe him. 'How will forgiveness make me feel better?'

'Because quite simply it absolves you of any blame you might attach to yourself. Do you want a life of self-disgust? Of pain and suffering? Never being truly free, holding these terrible things inside, suspended in case they should be needed? You'll never be able to move on. Do you understand, Kate?'

I manage to whisper, 'Sort of.'

'Will you, for the love of God, try to forgive her?'

For a long moment I think about what he's said. 'I'll try.'

'Is that a promise, Kate?'

'Yes, Father, you have my word.'

'The little devil's run off. I reckon it was her, that Bridget Costello, who pushed the good sister to her death. That's the thanks the good sisters get for all they do for those bloody orphans. I'd horsewhip the young pup if I caught her.' Helen Mooney is chatting and wrapping bread at the same time. 'Two soda breads and a flat cake – that'll be fifty-two pence, Eleanor.'

Eleanor Brady pulls a pound note out of a small leather purse and slaps it on the counter. 'Young pups today, wayward, not enough bloody discipline, not like in our day – we got a bloody good hiding.'

Passing Mrs Brady her change, Helen Mooney notices me for the first time. I'm glaring and biting my tongue so hard it stings. 'Did you know the Costello girl has run off?' Then, 'Seems mighty suspicious to me.'

In silence I continue to glare at Helen Mooney. She's got a vicious tongue at the best of times, it matches her temper.

Glaring back, she says, 'Answer me, girl: did you know that Bridget has run away?'

My voice shaking with anger, I shout, 'No, but I

wouldn't blame her if she did push that monster Thomas down the stairs. The evil witch deserved it. Good sisters, my backside! Sisters of evil, more like. And let me tell you, Helen Mooney, Mother Thomas was the worst of the lot. She's the one who should have been horsewhipped.'

Eleanor Brady looks aghast. 'Hush, girl, don't speak ill of the dead, the good woman's not yet cold in her grave.'

I'm so angry I think I might do for one or both of the women. How dare Eleanor Brady tell me to shut up when I've seen her taking men into her house all hours of the day and night? She was, so they said, a tart; she opened her legs for money. What right had she to be moralizing and going on about discipline?

Digging me in the ribs, Eleanor growls, 'Get off with you to confession before the good Lord strikes you down, you cheeky young pup.'

I round on Eleanor Brady, pushing my face so close to hers that I can see what I think are veins on her upper lip, then realize it's where her lipstick has seeped into the cracks. 'I've been to confession. I'm in a state of grace. But I'll never forgive that woman for what she did to me and the others, including Bridget.' I move even closer. I can feel her breath; it's warm and smells very rank, like rotting meat. 'Mother Thomas was a monster, and I'm glad she's dead.'

With that I stamp out of the shop, leaving the furore behind me. But I know it will follow. Within less than an hour the entire village will have heard of my outburst, and by tomorrow, after the fracas has made its way around the pub, Bridget and I will be labelled as evil killers. On my march up Doyle Street I'm planning how to explain my outburst to Father Steele. I decide to tell him the truth. In my experience it rarely works, but it's worth a try. The sight of my empty basket reminds me I need to buy bread, and I trudge half a mile to Flanagan's bread shop to buy crusty brown rolls and soda bread, Father

Steele's favourite, especially when spread with lashings of butter and thick home-made strawberry jam.

During the walk back to the cottage I'm consumed with thoughts of Bridget: where is she? Is she OK? Why hadn't she come to me for help? I visualize her alone, terrified and helpless. The thoughts make me feel the same way, and I long to be with her wherever she is. I'm still thinking about Bridget when I reach the cottage and see a black car parked outside. In it are two men.

My hand is on the gate latch as the passenger door opens and a man steps out. 'Are you Kate O'Sullivan?'

I nod.

The man then leans forward to speak to the driver of the car before slamming the door and approaching me.

'I'm Detective Inspector Frank Keane.' He flashes his ID in my face before continuing: 'I'd like to ask you a few questions, if I may?'

'Is it about Mother Thomas?'

'Yes.'

'I suppose you'd better come inside.'

I open the gate and the inspector follows me up the path. We don't speak again until we are in the kitchen.

Dropping my basket on the floor, politely I ask, 'Would you like a cup of tea?'

'Never say no to a brew.'

I busy myself filling the kettle and putting tea in the pot while the inspector glances casually around the room. From the corner of my eye I scrutinize him. He's got what I call an open face, wide-spaced eyes of a soft-focus brown, and a full mouth, the sort of face advertisers like to use. He's dressed incongruously in the type of clothes I always associate with English landowners: baggy corduroy trousers of nondescript brown, lace-up brogues, a V-neck sweater over a striped shirt and what looks like an old school tie.

'How long have you worked for the curate?'

Pouring hot water into the pot, I reply, 'I started work here on June the fifth, the day I left the orphanage.'

'Enjoying it?'

I stir the tea. 'Anything's better than the orphanage.' I place a mug of steaming tea on the table in front of the inspector. He sits down, and I sit opposite holding my mug in both hands.

Pulling a notepad and a pencil out of the breast pocket of his shirt he places both on the table. He takes a quick nip of tea then lifts the pencil and begins to chew on the end.

'So, you and Bridget Costello are best friends?'

I nod enthusiastically. 'We've known each other all our lives, like sisters, only better because we don't fight.'

'You knew the deceased?'

'Only too well.'

'Tell me about Mother Thomas.'

'She is – sorry, *was* the most evil person I've ever met.'

'A nun? Evil? Unusual, I'd say?'

I widen my eyes and, looking directly into his, repeat a couple of lines I'd read in a newspaper the previous day. 'Why is it that nuns and priests can do no wrong in this country? They preach to everyone about goodness and love, when lurking under their oh-so-pristine habits is a teeming mass of hypocrisy.'

The inspector raises his eyebrows, obviously surprised and, I detect, impressed by my little speech. 'You haven't explained why Mother Thomas was so evil.'

Now I can't look at him. How do you start to explain abuse? For the abused, talking about it makes the memories surface, and with them the pain and the guilt comes flooding back. The telling never seems to come out right; it sounds exaggerated, unbelievable. It had been difficult enough to talk in the dark of the confessional.

Concentrating on my mug of tea, I fixate on my thumb

and forefinger gripping the handle of the cup. 'It's not easy to explain. Like I said, she was evil.'

There is a long uncomfortable silence, followed by the inspector's sensitive query, 'Would you like to talk to a policewoman?'

Shaking my head I say, 'No.' I can feel my heart hammering, and my palms are moist. 'Mother Thomas beat me, a lot, and said things, terrible things, things I can't repeat.' I'm getting very hot and feel light-headed.

'Did she beat Bridget?'

'Yes, she beat most of us. She hated me because I stood up to her. Once she made me eat days-old liver. It made me sick. I threw up all over her habit, then she made me . . .' I can't go on, my throat closes around a sob.

Neither of us speaks. In the silence I listen to the inspector's breathing and the buzzing of a fly on the windowsill.

'What did she make you do, Kate?'

'She made me eat my own vomit.' There, I'd said it. For the first time since it happened I'd told someone. Odd that it should be a complete stranger; even odder I felt no shame, only the most terrible anger.

'She hurt Bridget, too. She touched her down there –' I pointed to his groin.

'Did Bridget tell you this or did you see it?'

'Bridget told me. She tried it with me once but I was too strong for her, I wouldn't let her get away with it, but Bridget . . .' The top of my head is burning as if it's on fire. 'I'm glad she's dead. I just wish she'd had a long and painful death. It was too easy.'

I drop my head in my hands and am barely aware of the inspector's hand stroking the crown of my head or the arrival of Father Steele. Only when I hear his voice do I lift my head.

'What is going on, Inspector?'

I answer for the policeman. 'It's Bridget, Father. The police want to know about Bridget and Mother Thomas.'

The tone of the inspector's voice has an unmistakable ring of reverence as he rises to his feet to address Father Steele. 'A routine line of questioning, Father. In the early hours of yesterday morning Bridget Costello turned herself in at Friday Wells district court. Today she's being moved to the women's unit in Limerick Prison, where she will be remanded in custody pending a hearing and, I assume, a subsequent trial. She's being held in custody in Cork for questioning.'

The shock of his words causes my throat to tighten so much it's an effort to speak, but I manage to splutter, 'Is Bridget OK?'

The inspector nods. 'Yes. Tired, a little shaken, but apart from that fine. She's made a full confession.'

With a quick glance in my direction, Father Steele asks, 'Have you finished your questioning, Inspector?'

'For now. But I may have to speak to Kate again.'

I'm only vaguely aware of Father Steele leading the inspector to the front door and their hushed voices. I'm in the same position when the priest returns.

'Do you want some tea, Father?'

'No, but perhaps I should make you a fresh cup.'

I look suitably aghast. A priest making tea for me, unheard of – unthinkable. 'No, Father, no, I wouldn't dream of such a thing.'

It was then he touched me deliberately for the first time. It felt like the electric shock I'd once had when trying to change a plug in Lizzy Molloy's front room. Mesmerized, I watch his hand stroking mine and pray he won't stop.

'I want to ask you something, something that might be painful but you must tell me the truth.'

With my eyes downcast I wait in silence for his question.

'Look at me, Kate.'

I raise my eyes to look directly into his.

'Did Mother Thomas ever sexually abuse you?'

I gaze at him, transfixed by the black of his pupils.

'She tried but I was too strong for her. I scared her a bit – not as much as I would have liked, but enough.'

'Did she abuse Bridget?'

My mouth feels dry and there is a metallic taste in it. 'I think so.'

Abruptly the stroking stops. I'm disappointed; I was enjoying his touch.

'You know what this means, Kate?'

'What does it mean, Father?'

With a long sigh Father Steele places two fingers on the side of his right temple and rubs in small circular movements. 'It means there will be an investigation. The orphanage and the entire village will be involved.'

'Good, it's right and proper that everyone should know about Mother Thomas, and if Bridget did push her down the stairs, everyone will know she deserved it. I've lost count of the times I've dreamt of killing her myself. The joy that one moment of power would have given me would have been worth all the pain.'

'No, Kate, never.' Father Steele looks angry. 'Power corrupts. Never forget that, and never give in to it.'

'She was corrupt, Father.' My voice is very small, child-like. 'She used her power to hurt me, and Bridget, and others, innocent kids. It started for me when I was five. Why was she like that, Father? Can you explain?'

The priest begins to pace up and down the kitchen, back and forth, talking at the same time. 'Perhaps at some point in her life something very traumatic happened to Mother Thomas. It's possible she herself was abused as a child and suppressed it.' He touches his chest. 'If anger is locked away deep inside and never let out, people become very twisted, paranoid, sick in here –' he points to his head – 'and they take it out on others. It's the only way they can live with the pain, by transferring it.'

'But to kids put in their care!' I spit out the words. 'They pretend to be holier than thou, act like saints while being evil. I can't understand them.'

Suddenly he touches me again, this time in a more intimate way, on the side of my cheek. His palm is warm, it warms me to the soles of my feet. I would be very happy for him to leave his hand there for ever.

'It's difficult for you to understand, Kate, and maybe it will take a long time – perhaps the rest of your life – but you must forgive.'

'Why should I forgive her when all I can think about is how pleased I am she's dead?'

'If you can find it in your heart to forgive her then you'll be able to move on yourself. Don't carry any guilt. It's an impossible burden, and one I wouldn't wish for anyone, let alone you.'

I can feel the tears welling up and am powerless to stop them trickling down my cheeks. With his fingertips he wipes each individual tear away, murmuring softly, 'My poor, poor Kate.'

I want him to hold me; this most fundamental human need overwhelms me, obliterating shyness and fear of impropriety. 'Father, will you hold me, if only for a moment?'

I see shock register on his face and his mouth forming the negative, but too late: I'm next to him, my head resting on his chest, my arms around his back, my body pressed close to his.

'No, Kate, please. I'm a priest. Have you forgotten I'm a priest?'

My need is stronger than his rejection and I ignore his pleas. 'Please, Father, hold me, just for a moment.'

A sigh escapes him as slowly he lifts his arms, one at a time, to rest on my shoulders, his hands hanging limply down my back. He smells of incense and candle-wax and cigars; he doesn't smoke so it must have been someone near him earlier. I shudder as his right arm leaves my shoulder and drops to the small of my back, then I experience a surge of shock as he grips my waist with both hands, pulling me towards him, like I've seen lovers do on film. I can feel his heart through the fabric of his soutane; it's beating hard and fast like a drum. I'm rigid, afraid to move a muscle, terrified to break the spell. At the sound of the doorbell we both jump apart like startled cats, and without a word Father Steele leaves the kitchen. I strain my ears to hear who is at the door.

I'm at the kitchen sink when a few moments later he returns. 'That was Father O'Neill. He wants to talk to you. I told him you were upset and to come back in an hour.'

'Thanks. And thank you for talking to me, listening to me.' I long to add *holding me*, but think better of it.

With an embarrassed shrug, he says, 'I'm a priest. It's what I do.'

I sense he's uncomfortable. 'What will happen to Bridget?'

Again a shrug. 'I'm not sure, Kate. If she's found guilty, she's a minor so she won't go to prison. But however much she was provoked, if she has committed a grave crime she will be punished.'

His words sting. It's unfair – why should Bridget be punished when it was Mother Thomas who was at fault? There's no bloody God, I've decided, because if there were he wouldn't let all these terrible things happen. 'Will she have to go to court?'

'Probably.'

'Will she have someone on her side to defend her in court?'

'Yes, she'll have the right to legal aid.'

'What does that mean?'

'It's legal representation for people who cannot afford

to pay for barristers. But don't worry, Bridget will have good defence.'

'I'll be a witness and I'll tell the court about Mother Thomas, about how she hurt Bridget. My Bridget, the softest sweetest girl in the world, who wouldn't harm a fly. They won't punish her because she doesn't deserve it. I won't let them.'

I can see Father Steele is becoming exasperated. He's got that patronizing look on his face. Why is it, I ask myself, that I have this effect on most people? My school-teacher, Miss Dwyer, said it was because I'm strong-willed, prepared to confront issues, and most people don't like that in a person.

'I think you should clear up in here, Kate, then freshen yourself up before Father O'Neill returns.'

'Do I have to talk to him?'

'I think you know the answer to that.'

In silence I begin to stack the dirty cups in the sink. I'm conscious of his presence – he hasn't left the room. Without turning round, I say in a clear and distinct voice, 'I love Bridget and I'll do anything to help her. She doesn't deserve to be punished and if I can stop that happening, I will. Mother Thomas will turn in her grave when she hears what I've got to say.'

The visiting room in Limerick women's prison reminds me of the laundry in the orphanage, depressingly damp. The ceiling is high, and painted a sludgy colour. The walls are cow-pat brown and peeling in places, and except for a tattered poster of a young hooligan under arrest, head-lined *Crime Doesn't Pay*, they are bare. Bridget is stand-ing very still and upright, next to a small table in the centre of the room. She's white, very white; even her lips are drained of colour, and she's lost a lot of weight. At least a stone.

My first words – 'How are you?' – seem unnecessary when it's clear she's not good.

'Fine.'

I take two long strides to stand next to her. 'You're not fine, are you?' I can see her tears drowning her coffee-brown eyes. Her bottom lip begins to quiver, and she hangs her head muttering, 'No.'

A moment later she's in my arms. I hold her very tight, so tight I can feel the quickening beat of her heart, and her body-heat through her cotton shirt. I let her cry, muttering all the soothing things I can think of: 'It's going to be all right, I won't let anything bad happen to you. You're going to be fine. I promise. It's going to be OK.'

When at last she stops crying, I gently lift her chin and with my fingertips wipe her tear-stained cheeks. She sniffs, I rummage in my pocket for a tissue and hand it to her. She blows her nose, then screws the tissue into a tight ball in her fist. 'Do you remember Mrs Doyle reporting me to the headmaster for using my sleeve to wipe my nose?'

I'm grinning. 'Yes, and you telling him if you had a hanky you'd be happy to use it.' Out of the corner of my eye I can see the policewoman leaning against the wall.

Bridget tries to smile yet doesn't quite manage it. 'She left me no choice, it was her or me.'

I lean close to her ear and whisper, 'You don't need to explain, Bridget. I've lost count of the times I wanted to kill her.' Then I take both her hands in mine, my eyes communicating my absolute understanding, and I see some of the pain leave hers.

'I'm scared, Kate.'

'Don't be. Believe me, it's going to be all right, I'll make sure of that. I've come into some money.'

With a question in her eyes Bridget starts to speak. 'How . . .'

I interrupt: 'It's not the time or the place to explain.

Enough to say I can pay your legal fees, and see justice done. The evil bitch abused you, didn't she?'

Bridget is on the verge of tears again. 'Will they believe me, when I tell them she deserved to be pushed downstairs after what she did to me?' A sob catches in her throat, an animal sound. 'She put her cane . . .' she pauses, then sobs, 'inside . . .' She lets her head drop to her chest. A moment later she lifts it, and to my surprise her eyes are dry and shining with a brilliance I'd never encountered in her before. 'God forgive me, but I'm glad she's dead.'

My eyes not leaving hers, I say, 'So am I.'

Chapter Seven

I'm not a natural liar. It's not in my character. But growing up surrounded by the Sisters of no Mercy I learnt to lie, barefaced lies, shocking in their complete denial of the truth. It made life easier. I told the other kind as well, white lies, innocent stuff: if someone had a new dress you didn't like you said, if asked, that you thought it was very nice. Or if you were late for school, or played truant, you pretended to have a headache, or like Bridget once, a touch of cancer – that one got her into a whole heap of trouble both at school and at the orphanage.

I think a lot of people lie to appear better in the eyes of friends, loved ones, superiors, or to get what they want. The truth doesn't always achieve that. I suppose they do it to make them feel better, bigger or more powerful, stronger, faster, brighter, wittier, more interesting or desirable; generally to provide fuel for their self-esteem. Not so for me: I did it to survive. And when I told the truth about Mother Thomas it was not only for Bridget but for myself and for what is called integrity.

It was important that everyone in Friday Wells knew about our pain and suffering.

The directions Katherine Mowlem had given me were very confusing. Probably they'd have been less confusing for people who travelled a lot, but I'd been too embarrassed to admit that I'd only been out of Friday Wells twice in my life. Eventually I arrived at the legal offices of Katherine Mowlem, after getting lost twice and beating myself up for not catching a taxi. But I'd listened to the man sitting next to me on the train who said – and he seemed to know – that South Mall was a ten-minute walk at most from the station. I'm twenty minutes late and flustered because of it. I'd so wanted to impress with my efficiency and punctuality. I wouldn't be here if it hadn't been for Mrs Molloy telling me all manner of horror stories about legal-aid people. They only act for poor folk, so Mrs Molloy had said, 'Don't work nigh on as hard as the rich folk's lawyers. Seen it happen a million times, rich folk getting off scot-free 'cause they had a good barrister.' I'd asked Mrs Molloy for examples and she'd reeled off a dozen film characters. When I'd pointed this out she'd returned with, 'It happens in real life just the same. Got to have a good lawyer. They can twist the jury right around their little fingers.'

It had been a hard decision to part with my money on legal fees, but I knew it would be harder to live with myself if I didn't do all I could for Bridget. It had been easy to find a barrister. One call to Mr Shaunessy the solicitor in Dublin and Katherine Mowlem had called the next day. She'd sounded very nice on the telephone and I'd felt very grown up talking to her while seated at the curate's desk. She'd asked me a few questions, then said she would have to meet Bridget before deciding if she would take her case. I'd told her I had five thousand pounds, it was all I had in the world, and I'd asked her if it would be enough. She'd made no comment about the money and said she'd get back to me in due course.

Due course took eight days, eight days spent in torment until an envelope addressed to me landed on the mat. It was a brown manila one, the same as Mr Shaunessy's, and it contained a letter from Katherine Mowlem. She'd met Bridget, and now wanted to meet me. Could I come to her office.

The building is stone and tall and built in 1792, so it

says on the stone pediment above the entrance door. A receptionist takes my name and asks me in a very prim voice to take a seat in the waiting room. A few minutes later a young girl with wild hair held down with two clips and the face of a beautiful imp greets me: 'I'm Miss Mowlem's assistant, Kylie. You must be Miss O'Sullivan.' She's smiling, warm and inviting. I return an equally warm smile and follow her out of the waiting room to the fourth floor where Kylie informs me Katherine is waiting.

The room Kylie shows me into is disappointing; I'd imagined something grander. My limited experience of lawyers has been confined to a couple of films seen at Lizzy's, and in them the lawyers had vast offices with wall-to-wall carpet, panoramic windows and impossibly big desks.

Rising from behind her normal-sized desk, Katherine Mowlem walks around the other side to greet me. As she moves I can see she is tall and pear-shaped, with a tiny waist, button breasts and a wide backside. Her hair is copper with gold streaks and rests on her shoulders like a slick of paint. She could never be described as beautiful, or even pretty. Her nose is too big and her chin too weak, but there's no doubt she's striking. Yes, striking, that's how I'd describe her. I was pleased with the adjective: it fitted her perfectly.

Today she's dressed in a black trouser suit with wide shoulders and a cinched waist. She's sophisticated and I feel very small-town girl in Lizzy's ill-fitting cotton dress and jacket that her Aunty Meg had made for the church fête.

'Pleased to meet you, Miss O'Sullivan.'

I take her outstretched hand saying, 'And you, and please call me Kate.'

'Kate it is. Have a seat. Coffee, tea, biscuits?'

'I'd like tea, please – and biscuits.'

Miss Mowlem nods in Kylie's direction and she leaves the room at once. Miss Mowlem returns to her chair and begins to flick through a file of papers on her desk. 'As I said in my letter, I met Bridget in Limerick and we had a long talk. I find the case very interesting. It's not the first time the Catholic Church has been on trial for misconduct. A case like this is not for everyone. I believe James Shaunessy recommended me because I'm a liberal.'

'I've no idea why he recommended you, Miss Mowlem, except that he thought you were the right person for the job.'

Katherine lights a cigarette and, blowing out smoke, says, 'Does it bother you?' I shake my head and look up as Kylie returns with the tea and, joy of joys, a plateful of custard creams.

I dig into the biscuits while Kylie pours the tea and Miss Mowlem inhales deeply and exhales noisily.

'Now, Kate, tell me about Mother Thomas. Why did you not report her to the Mother Superior?'

'The nuns stuck together. She wouldn't have believed me. Like it was them and us. Except for Mother Peter – a good woman with a big heart.'

'So why didn't you confide in her?'

It's a good question and I think about it long and hard before answering, 'Because I was afraid.'

'Afraid of what might happen to you, or afraid of what Mother Thomas would do in retaliation?'

Without hesitation I say, 'Afraid of Mother Thomas. We all were.' My eyes wander over the barrister's head to a row of books stacked haphazardly on a bookcase. Irish Case Law for the last twenty years.

'Does it take a long time to study law?'

'Four years to go to the bar.'

'What's the bar?'

'To be a barrister – to go into court and defend or prosecute.'

'Do you have to go to university?'

'Yes. Is it something you're interested in, Kate?'

'Oh no, not at all. I'm going to become a famous painter, and in my lifetime. You see, I don't want fame when I'm dead. What's the point of that?'

She's smiling. She has nice teeth, very white and square. 'I'm sure most, if not all of the great artists who found fame after their deaths would have preferred it when they were alive.'

'Well, they should have done more about it then. If at first you don't succeed . . . , that's my motto.'

She rifles through the papers on her desk again. Her white hands are the same colour as the porcelain figurines Mrs Molloy had sitting in a cabinet in her front room. Her high cheekbones are very prominent, making her deep-set eyes appear sunken. I'd like to paint her in a long scarlet dress made of a luxurious fabric, velvet or a shimmering satin. I consider asking her to sit for me, then think how ridiculous that would sound to this posh lawyer woman: a sixteen-year-old orphan, who at the moment works as a housekeeper for the local curate in a village at the arse end of the world.

'As we speak, the book of evidence is being prepared by the prosecution, and if I'm to defend Bridget I've got a lot of work to do. I've got a sworn statement from Mary Shanley, who alleges she was beaten and witnessed repeated abuse to several girls over a period of eight years. None of the other girls are talking.' She lights another cigarette and exhales before going on: 'In the police statement you allege that you were systematically beaten by Mother Thomas from the age of five. That's a long time not to tell anyone – eleven years and not a word?'

Her tone and expression suggest doubt; it makes me think she doesn't believe me. 'Bridget and the other girls knew. They won't talk because they're afraid, terrified of what will happen when this is all over. You won't be around to protect them then. And believe me, the nuns won't let them forget. Like I said before, you don't talk about these things. You bury them away deep inside, it helps you to deal with it.'

I watch her grind her cigarette out in a glass ashtray, my eyes returning to her face as she says, 'Three girls out of forty-two are singled out for beatings? Why do you think you, Bridget, and Mary Shanley were chosen? Were you disruptive? Did you push the nuns too far? You have been described as headstrong, insolent, difficult and wilful. Are these descriptions of your character accurate?'

My anger is on the boil. All the signs are there: the hot thrusts in my belly like fists punching the air. 'What are you trying to say, Miss Mowlem? Do you think I'm lying? Do you really believe I'd invent such terrible things? Sure, I've got a strong will, I wouldn't be sitting here today without it – but I'm not bad or evil, as the nuns would have you believe. They hate me because they can't, to quote Mother Thomas, knock the stuffing out of me. She tried – oh, how she tried! How would you like to eat your own vomit? I was five when she forced me to do that. Or sit on the chamber pot at night, your backside freezing and sore, and if you couldn't do it, a number two that is, you stayed there until you did, sometimes all night. When Bridget was twelve she got terrible piles and had to be treated in hospital.' My chest tightens and I swallow hard, afraid I might begin to cry.

I see Miss Mowlem blanch. Good, is all I can think. If she's moved, she'll move others. But does she, I wonder, have the power of words and the delivery to convince an entire village? I have my doubts.

The date of the trial was set for December 5. I postponed my entry to art college; it was the least I could do. Bridget needed me. The days leading up to the hearing I spent in deliberate seclusion. The village was buzzing with gossip, and speculation. Lizzy was a regular visitor to the cottage, stopping for a cup of tea and to bring me up to date with the latest news. Apparently, several people were convinced that I was the devil incarnate. Since we were children I'd possessed Bridget, commanding her to kill Mother Thomas. Instructed by me, Bridget had made several other failed attempts. Maeve Gowan, a pretty twelve-year-old from the orphanage, had confessed that Mother Thomas had tied her to her bed with rope and sexually abused her, several times, with her fingers.

Dan Collins, bless his heart, is a witness for the defence, and Mr Molloy intends to testify that he's often seen me distressed and crying, after one of Mother Thomas's repeated beatings.

Bridget's defence, according to Father Steele, is weak. It angered me when he spoke of it, and angered me more when he talked of Edmund Muldoon, the prosecutor. 'A champion among men,' he kept saying. 'You've only to take one look at him to know he's a winner.' Once, when he'd been singing Muldoon's praises, I'd been unable to resist saying, 'Do you want evil to triumph, Father?'

For a long moment the priest had been silent, then in a very controlled voice he'd said, 'How dare you ask me such a question?' before leaving me in the centre of the kitchen with my cheeks on fire.

I bought, encouraged by Mrs Molloy and Lizzy, a new dress and jacket for the trial. It was midnight blue, with a calf-length skirt and short cropped-at-the-waist jacket. When I tried it on in the shop I thought it looked lovely; now, standing in front of my dressing-table mirror in thin dawn light, I feel over-dressed, as if I'm going to a wedding – not that I've been to one, a wedding that is, but I'm sure this is the sort of thing I'd wear.

The trial is being held in Cork Circuit Court. Mr Molloy is picking me up at 6.30 a.m. for the 6.45 train. He's on time and I'm opening the door as he's walking up the path.

He's grinning. 'Morning, Kate. You look grand. Fancy the races instead of court?'

I smile. 'I wish.'

We start towards the station, he links arms with me, pulling me close to his side like he does with Lizzy. I like it a lot.

'Our Lizzy's in a huff, desperately wanted to come today, but I told her she has to go to school. Important time, doing her exams. I want her to get a place in university. She's a bright lass, our Lizzy, would make a damn good doctor. It's what she wants, but she's not prepared to work.'

I don't have the heart to tell him Lizzy hasn't got the brain or the commitment to get through medical school. Only last week she admitted to me she was struggling without my help.

As we approach the station the train is pulling in. Mr Molloy has splashed out on first-class tickets. When my eyes widen at the sight of them, he says, 'Just for today – thought we'd travel in a bit of style. It's going to be a long day.'

As he helps me into the carriage I smile. 'I hope it's over very soon. I want to move on.'

The hearing lasted eighteen days. Eighteen days of being sandwiched between Dan Collins and Mr Molloy. Dan Collins, I'm certain, enjoyed the proximity to my left thigh as much as I detested it.

During the entire hearing I ignored the whispering behind hands, the averted eyes, the hisses and the blatant stares.

'Rise above it,' Mr Molloy had said after the first day. 'Take no notice. Small-minded folk, they're pathetic.'

He was right, and on the second day, armed with

sketch-pad and pencils, I concentrated on drawing the judge, the jury, Katherine Mowlem, and Edmund Muldoon – and I have to agree with Father Steele: he's an imposing giant of a man.

Katherine Mowlem, I'm sorry to say, was no match for the great Muldoon. She tried, and damned hard. I admired her spirit. Mother Peter almost broke down under her cross-examination. The Neesom twins, who had witnessed many beatings, both left the stand in floods of tears, and Mother Superior was made to look like a dithering, incompetent old biddy who should have been pensioned off long ago.

But it was Edward Muldoon who shone, lighting the dull courtroom with his dazzling brilliance. He was tall and handsome with warm brown eyes and a killer smile, but it was his voice that did it, and his articulation; every sentence so beautifully constructed it was like poetry. The jury loved him, worshipped him, and by day six he had them eating out of his hand. We didn't stand a chance.

Katherine, I admit, has a saccharine tongue, but clearly not sweet enough for the jury's taste. Like me, she thought the truth would come blazing through the courtroom like some white knight on a charging stallion of justice. But by the end of the first week I knew that it wasn't going to happen.

Bridget was found guilty of manslaughter and, being a minor, was sent to reform school in Sandyford, Dublin. Mother Paul and Mother Superior were both dismissed and two other nuns applied for posts elsewhere. The Sisters of Mercy orphanage was subjected to intensive investigation and there was talk that it might be closed down.

I'd spent most of my money on legal fees and was left at the end of the trial with £120. I was interviewed for the *Irish Times* and the local rag, the *Wells Post*. The reporter was young, about eighteen, and funny; he made me laugh a lot and asked me for a date. I refused him, yet he still said a lot of nice things about me in print.

The court hearing had been my first brush with the law, and my first lesson in the real world outside Friday Wells. Truth does not always triumph over lies, and people, however much you trust them, sometimes let you down.

The week after the trial I give Father Steele notice. Now there is no reason for me to stay. Before, during and since the trial I've been aware of fingers pointing in my direction, the constant whispering behind hands, downcast or sideways glances, eyes afraid to meet mine. Hiding behind their own backs. You're paranoid, Father Steele had said when I'd mentioned the hostility I felt. Patiently he'd explained the meaning of paranoid and I'd thought about it for a long time before coming to the conclusion he was wrong. The village had cast me in the role of villain, and nothing I did or said would change its small-minded mentality. People don't change, Mr Molloy said, and if they do it's by slow degrees, in darkness and silence.

'I want to leave Friday Wells as soon as possible, Father. Will you accept a week's notice?'

With a gentle smile he asks, 'Is it that bad?'

'It's got nothing to do with you, Father, it's the village, the gossip. I just want to get away, and I've made an appointment to see the solicitor in Dublin – you know, the one who sent me the cheque. I've got very little money left after paying the legal fees, and I was kind of hoping he could forward me some from the payment I'm supposed to get when I'm eighteen. I have to get on with my life. When I was a kid, about ten, Bridget and I made a pact. We'd find our parents and whoever succeeded first would have to give the other twenty pounds. Kids' stuff, I know, but I still feel the same way. I'm determined to find out who my parents were ... are. The trust fund is the first real clue I've had.'

'No need to explain. I understand, but understanding doesn't make me feel less sad. I can't pretend I won't miss you.'

'I'll miss you, Father, a lot. I'll miss our long talks and my lessons. But we can write and you can visit me when you come to Dublin. Teach me some more Italian. At the moment I'd still struggle to get past the post office and pizzeria in Florence.'

His eyes are twinkling. 'I shouldn't worry, Kate. I'm sure you'd have every hot-blooded Italian male falling over themselves to help you.'

I blush, wishing as I did every time it happened that I had some control over it. 'In the short time I've been here you've taught me a lot, Father. I've got a much bigger vocabulary, I know a little – ' I indicate a space with my thumb and forefinger – 'about politics, and have a greater understanding of how the world out there works.'

'It's been a two-way lesson, Kate. Don't think for a moment I didn't get anything in return.'

Again I feel the colour enter my cheeks. 'What did I teach you, Father? Apart from how to construct a sketch.'

'Sure, I'm no Michelangelo.'

I grin. 'That's for sure.'

'You're a free spirit, Kate. You open your arms and let life in. You have the ability to soar. You've brought a different sort of music into my life. All my life I've been the opposite to you. At your age I'd never have had the courage to stand up to Mother Thomas like you did. To say what you believe in and not be afraid. Inside I rage at a church that is riddled with hypocrisy and shackled to an antiquated doctrine and too stubborn to move forward, but, unlike you, I suppress instead of confronting issues. I've always hated emotional conflict.'

'I'm often afraid, Father. I don't give into it, but it's there all the same. My belly turns to water and my legs go weak, and sometimes I feel full of uncontrollable rage.

That's scary because I don't know what I might do. Mother Thomas used to terrify me but I knew if I showed my fear she would have won . . .' I pause as a vision of Bridget's distraught face emerges. 'But she did win in the end, didn't she? Mother Thomas, I mean.'

'No, Kate, you won. What happened last week in court was not a battle lost, don't ever think of it that way. I had to remain neutral, I had no choice. But you stood up for what you believed. You had a voice; people were forced to listen and form their own opinions. I watched the people in court when you were giving evidence, I studied the faces of the jury, and do you know what I saw, Kate?'

I shake my head.

'I saw concern and admiration.'

'So why didn't they believe us?'

'They did, of that I'm sure. But a nun is dead, pushed by Bridget – under severe provocation, we all know that now, but pushed to her death nevertheless. If Bridget had not been punished it would open the floodgates for every child in care to retaliate in a similar way. The orphanage, as you know, is being thoroughly investigated; the abuse you suffered will never happen again.' He pauses. 'You did win, Kate.'

'Thank you, Father. That means a lot to me.'

'Now let's change the subject. I think we've been melancholy for far too long. How about some Italian?'

I groan.

He claps his hands. 'I meant music, not a lesson.' Father Steele bounds to the record player and a moment later the room is filled with the strains of *Così fan tutte*. With his eyes closed, he mimes and sways from side to side. 'Don't you think this is the most beautiful song in the world, Kate? Music like this makes me glad to be alive. *Bellissimo*.'

I'd never listened to opera before working for the curate; the only music I'd ever heard were tunes on the Molloys' radio, and a few pop songs Lizzy played in her bedroom. Of those I liked Elton John best.

I close my eyes but don't sway and a moment later am startled when I feel the curate's arm round my waist and his voice in my ear saying, 'Will you dance?'

'I can't, Father. I mean, I've never done it before, I don't know how.'

Pulling me closer, he murmurs, 'Just follow me.'

Like a wooden doll I allow myself to be led around the small room. I feel very silly and want to laugh, but daren't; by the look on Father Steele's face he's taking it very seriously.

'Relax, Kate, let all your muscles go floppy. You're too tense.'

'I'll try,' I mutter, closing my eyes and concentrating on relaxing my legs first and working up through my body.

'That's better,' he says after a few moments. 'Much better.'

As the music reaches a climax he spins me around and catches me with both hands either side of my waist. I giggle. He holds me at arm's length and says, 'Will you stay for Christmas?'

I hesitate.

'Less than three weeks. At least you won't be alone in some dingy bedsit. I can't bear the thought of that, Kate.'

'I've never liked Christmas, Father. Sure, I've never had one, not a real Christmas with turkey and pudding and all the trimmings.'

'We're friends, aren't we, Kate?'

I nod.

'Good friends are like family. Just like you and Bridget. We can be brother and sister, how's that? It's not too much for a brother to ask his sister to stay for Christmas, is it?'

Fourteen days isn't long, and being totally alone, like Father Steele said, is a grim prospect.

'OK, Father, I'll stay until New Year. That way we can bring in the New Year together and I can make a new start on the first of January.'

Encircling my waist, he pulls me towards him and plants a kiss on my brow. 'Family, Kate. Brother and sister – it feels good. I always wanted a sister.'

I'm not sure about Father Steele being my brother, but to please him I add, 'And I've always wanted a relative, any relative.'

'Well you've got a brother now, but don't tell anyone. It's to be our secret.'

Father Steele has the same tired look on his face that he's been wearing as constantly as his soutane for the week. Something is nagging at him and clearly won't let go.

Every night after supper he sits in front of the fire not speaking, not even reading, just lost in thought. Lately I haven't sat with him, he hasn't asked, and once when I'd mentioned Italian lessons he'd fobbed me off with a lame excuse. I fill my spare time painting Christmas presents for all my friends and, with some misgivings, work on a very special piece for Father Steele.

Often in the quiet of the night when the priest is downstairs in the living room, I undress and stand naked in front of the small dressing-table mirror. I watch my hands explore my body and fantasize about Father Steele. I know he's cast himself in the big brother role, but he isn't a blood relative and I can't stop myself dreaming about him. Sometimes late at night I imagine him coming to my bed; he tells me he loves me and I call him Declan and I let him touch and enter my secret and innermost parts. Often I chastise myself for these evil thoughts and mumble, 'Jesus, Mary and Joseph, I've done it again.' Then I repeat

Hail Marys in my head until I fall asleep. But no amount of Hail Marys and Our Fathers can make me stop.

Christmas Midnight Mass is the one time I really do enjoy church. There is something about the nativity, the carols and the community spirit I only enjoy at Christmas time.

Father Steele has asked me to wait for him after Mass so we can walk back to the cottage together. It's cold and, according to Father Steele, getting colder. I hope he's right, a white Christmas would make me very happy. I've been waiting nigh on fifteen minutes and I'm frozen stiff. Stamping my feet, I inwardly promise myself a pair of fur-lined boots when I get to Dublin. I've lost the sensation in my fingertips and am cursing Father Steele as he emerges from the sacristy with a bright smile.

'Happy Christmas, Kate.'

'And to you, Father.'

Side by side we walk along the path leading to Coppice Cottage. Great plumes of white breath billow out in front of our faces.

'I think it might be a white Christmas, Father.'

'No, it's too cold for snow. The forecast is for frost tonight and a crisp sunny day tomorrow.'

'Good, that's the sort of weather I like.'

'Me too.'

When we reach the front door he takes off one woollen glove. I notice it has a small hole in the thumb and I make a silent note to darn it. He opens the door with a pant, his body a dark silhouette against the light from the hall. I follow him inside and, taking off my hat, gloves, scarf and coat, I hang them in the hall cupboard.

Cupping my hands, I blow into them, saying between breaths, 'A cup of tea, Father?'

'No, Kate, I think something a little stronger tonight. It's Christmas Eve, after all. How about a sherry?'

I point to my chest. 'Me?'

'Is there someone else here?' He grins at my obvious confusion. 'Aye, a dram of Irish whiskey for me and a tot of sherry for you. Keep out the cold – what do you say?'

'What does sherry taste like? I'm not sure I'll like it.'

I follow him into the living room and watch him take a bottle out of the cupboard next to the fireplace. Holding it aloft he says, 'This one is sweet, I think you'll like it.'

Pouring the sherry into a small glass he hands it to me. I wait while he pours himself a whiskey, and giggle when he clinks my glass. This is like in the films, I'm dying to say, but feel silly and say instead, 'Cheers, Father, and a very merry Christmas.'

His cheeks are rosy like polished red apples. He looks better than he's looked for weeks. 'You look grand this evening, Father, just grand.'

I study his face and, encouraged by his benign expression, I say, 'May I ask you something personal, Father?'

Peering over the rim of his glass he says, 'You can, but I may not answer it.'

'Have you been worried about something lately?'

I notice his cheeks burn redder; he takes a quick nip of whiskey. 'Why do you ask?'

'Just a feeling. You know, I get these feelings all the time.'

He's studying me with intent, and suddenly, without reason, I feel uncomfortable. I'm sure I've upset him and feel powerless to do anything about it. There are lots of things I want to say but can't. Not to a priest.

'I've got a Christmas present for you, Father. Can I give it to you now?'

His reply stings. 'No, Kate, go to bed. We'll exchange gifts in the morning.'

Yet something makes me stay. I try again. 'Please, Father, let me give it to you now. Tomorrow you'll be busy at church and there'll be so little time. It would make me very happy to . . .'

I see his body relax a little, perhaps it's the effect of the whiskey. I don't really care as long as he isn't angry with me. I'm overjoyed when in the next breath he gives in. 'You win.'

I gulp down the remainder of the sherry and place the glass carefully on the hall table before racing upstairs to the bedroom. The painting is where I'd left it earlier, on the bed wrapped in red paper with a gold bow in the centre. The gift was lucky to have the bow; I'd struggled to part with twenty pence for a bit of gold paper, but had argued with myself that Father Steele was worth it and had given in to extravagance. It just meant that all the others would have to make do with no ribbon at all.

As I re-enter the sitting room carrying the painting in front of my face, Father Steele is on his knees, putting more coal on the fire. The clock above the mantelpiece reads twenty minutes past one. I make a mental note of the time; the date is unforgettable: December 25, 1978. I'm beaming as I hand him the present with a flourish. 'Happy Christmas, Father.'

He's smiling, his cheeks dimpled, and I'm overjoyed. I've made him smile. It's the warm one I like to kid myself he keeps specially for me.

Turning the package upside down, he shakes it. 'Now what on earth could this be?'

I shift awkwardly from one foot to the other. 'I'm sure by the shape you can guess what it is.'

He begins to peel back the paper, letting out a loud gasp when he looks at the portrait.

With narrowed eyes I scrutinize his face. For weeks I've been struggling with my reasons for giving Father Steele this gift. Countless times I've questioned myself. Do I want to shock him? If so, why? Or did it go much deeper, did I want him to look at the painting and want me? Twice I'd felt the urge to destroy it, yet an inner force had stopped me. I can't decide from his expression whether he's pleased or not. 'I hope you like it. I wasn't sure about painting a nude, but then I thought all the masters have done it. And it is a thing of great beauty.' I blush, realizing what I've said. 'Not my body, I mean, the female form, and God made us this way, so why should we be ashamed of our bodies . . . the naked form is . . . What I mean is, we . . .' I'm struggling for the right words and decide to give up when I notice the change in Father Steele.

In all the time I've known him I've never seen him this pale, even when he'd had a bad bout of flu a few months back. His lack of colour unnerves me, and I feel a great surge of relief when he says, 'It's beautiful, Kate. Quite beautiful.'

'Oh, Father, I'm so pleased you like it. It took hours to paint. I did it at night, after I'd finished work, long after you'd gone to sleep. I didn't have the money to hire a model so I decided to use my own reflection.'

I cast back to the first night I'd started the painting. I'd questioned my vanity and the pleasure I'd derived from the discovery of my own body. Until that point I'd barely looked closely at myself, and never full-length, except once when trying on Lizzy's underwear in front of Mrs Molloy's wardrobe mirror. Was I beautiful like people said? Did having a generous mouth, the bottom lip fuller than the top, and a slim nose make me more attractive than Bridget with her wide nose and thin mouth? Are wide-spaced eyes that turn up at the corners with sleepy lids better or worse than any of the other kind? 'You've got the light in your eyes,' Lizzy Molloy always said. 'And what light is that?' I'd asked, intrigued. 'The kind film stars have. My dad says you've got it. When you come into a room it lights up, like you kind of glow.'

In the painting I'd rounded my boyish hips, taken an inch or so off my waist and lessened the size of my breasts. Artistic licence, but necessary after hours of my reflection telling me I was still a girl and so wanting to be a woman for Declan Steele.

His voice brings me back to the present. 'I think you should keep this, Kate. Give it to someone who will really appreciate it. A man who is in love with you, someone who will cherish it forever.'

The acute disappointment must have shown on my face. 'You don't like it, do you?'

Still staring at the portrait – I'm sure to avoid looking at me – he says: 'It's the most beautiful present I've ever been given, but I can't keep it. I can't hang it – what would the parishioners think? I'm a devout man, a Catholic priest. I've taken a vow, Kate, you understand. Can you imagine Father O'Neill's face if he saw this? It would probably give him a heart attack. Did it never occur to you, at any point while you were painting, what sort of effect it would provoke?'

I'm loathe to admit that I had thought about it a lot. 'It's art, Father. If people want to read something else into it, let them have their petty dirty thoughts. I wanted to paint something special for you, something for you to keep, to remember me. Even if you hide it under your bed, I want you to have it. It's a gift to you. You never know – in a few years' time it might be worth a lot of money.'

'Thank you, Kate, thank you very much.' Still he can't look at me. He places the painting at his feet, facing the wall. I know then I've embarrassed him, pure and simple, and he doesn't know how to deal with it. I watch him pour himself another whiskey. He doesn't offer me a sherry. I'd have refused anyway – I hadn't enjoyed the last one and had only drunk it to please him.

He drinks half of the whiskey before handing me a

small package. It's very neatly wrapped in plain blue paper tied with a red ribbon. Excited, I tear at the wrapping and let out a little whoop as I see a jewellery box. An old one, but a jewellery box no less. As I open the lid I have this horrible sinking feeling that it's a joke, and he's put something else in an old box. Inside, nestling on blue velvet is a chain and cross. Carefully I lift it out of the box and, holding it up to the light, realize it's gold. I'm lost for words and can only stare at the chain as he speaks.

'It was my mother's. She gave it to me before she died. She made me promise to give it to a woman worthy of wearing it. She said it had brought her good fortune. She'd had the love of a good man, and the joy of three wonderful sons. Since I'll never have a girlfriend or marry, I want you to have it, Kate. You've got a big heart, and a good soul, and I know my mother would have liked you. In the last six months since you've worked here you've brought a special kind of joy into my life. Your laughter, your enthusiasm, your feisty attitude, your inner strength, that intangible thing, a song in your soul.' He finishes his whiskey. 'May I put it on for you?'

My cheeks are on fire. 'Yes, please. I've never had anything like this before in my entire life. I don't know what to say . . . except thank you.'

Walking across the room he stops behind me. 'You don't have to say anything, just wear it. I hope it brings you luck.'

Handing him the chain, I'm aware of his breath, hot on the back of my neck, then his warm hands fumbling with the clasp. 'There, all done.' he says, patting my shoulder.

I touch the cross with the palm of my hand. 'I'll never take this off. They'll bury me with it on.'

'I hope that's a very long time off.'

My hands drop to my sides. I see his face change, his eyes narrow and his mouth become taut as he reaches across to touch the cross. He lets it fall between his fingers for a few minutes, then very slowly his hand trails across my neck. He's shaking. I begin to shake too as he moves his face close to mine. I feel paralysed, like I'm set in stone. Now his fingertip is tracing a line across my lips; suddenly I feel his lips brush mine. They are very warm and I detect a faint hint of whiskey. I open my lips a little, I'm not sure what else to do, and a moment later his mouth is on mine. Not gentle, but hard and demanding, forcing my mouth open wider, his breath hot and coming in short, sharp gasps. Then suddenly he steps back as if bitten, his hand covering his mouth, and without another word leaves the room. I stand in the same position watching the clock tick, hoping for his return. After sixteen minutes I kill the fire, put out the lights and go to bed.

The next day when I come down to the kitchen at seven-thirty Father Steele has gone. We'd planned to spend the evening together but after last night I'm not sure how he will feel. I'm invited to spend the day with the Molloy family, but decide to go to Mass first to catch a glimpse of Father Steele. I'm disappointed when Father O'Neill takes Mass and there's no sign of the curate.

Mrs Molloy has cooked the biggest, fattest turkey I've ever clapped eyes on. 'We'll be still eating that big bugger come New Year,' her husband comments with an affectionate glance in her direction. There's stuffing made from fresh chestnuts, the like of which I've never tasted before, and roast potatoes, buttered cabbage and crunchy carrots. The pudding is sublime, the melt-in-your-mouth kind, and I'm over the moon with the Cadbury's selection box, and Elizabeth Arden perfume. I'm not sure about the smell, but Lizzy's brother assures me it's lovely and keeps coming close, too close, to sniff my neck.

Lizzy has bought me a pair of frilly knickers she'd chosen from her mother's catalogue, and I give each of them a painting. Mrs Molloy loves her still life of a bowl of fruit. Mr Molloy, I can tell, isn't sure about his, a lone figure of a man crossing the brow of a hill. Lizzy goes into noisy raptures over the pretty ballerina in a tutu, Degas style, and her brother screams with glee at his Rubenesque nude, running upstairs that instant to hang it in his bedroom next to our Lord on the cross. We watch *Casablanca* in black and white on TV; I cry buckets and so, strangely enough, does Mr Molloy.

We all go to evening Mass together. Mr Molloy and Lizzy walk me back to the cottage. The house is in darkness.

'You'll be fine now, Kate?'

'Fine, just fine, Mr Molloy, and thanks very much for a lovely Christmas.'

I'm grateful for the darkness, else they would see the tears in my eyes. 'It's the best Christmas I've ever had. I'll never forget it.'

With this Mr Molloy takes me in his arms; the rough fabric of his coat scratches my face. I could have stayed like that for ever. I wet the front of his shirt but he doesn't seem to notice. He kisses my forehead like I've seen him kiss Lizzy, and I feel like I've just been given a million pounds.

'Happy Christmas, Kate, you deserve it. And I think I speak for the entire Molloy family when I say we wish you all the best in Dublin.'

Lizzy kisses me on the cheek and squeezes my hand for a couple of minutes, before linking her father's arm and pulling him close to her in a possessive kind of way, as if to say he's *my* da.

I watch them walk down the path until they are gobbled up by the blackness. I'm still standing in the same position a few minutes later when Father Steele comes up the path.

'Good evening, Kate.'

'Father.' I nod and push the key into the lock. Before

153

I have chance to open the door, he growls, 'I've had a very long day and I'm whacked. I'm going to have an early night.'

I turn the key in the lock, push the door open and flick a switch to light the hall. Unbuttoning my coat, I'm only vaguely aware of him shrugging out of his.

'Did you have a good time with the Molloys?'

'Yes, thanks. I'm very fond of them all. They're like family.'

His shoulders are hunched. 'Good. I'm pleased.'

My coat is open, the cross he'd given me glinting on the black of my sweater. I touch it, something I'll do instinctively for many years to come.

Stepping past me, Father Steele walks towards the living room. 'Goodnight, Kate. Happy Christmas.'

'Goodnight,' I manage to mumble before climbing the stairs to my bedroom. What had happened to our family Christmas? I had ham and pork and a huge pudding Mrs Molloy had made, steeped in sherry since September. Sure, I felt stuffed but I would have gladly joined Father Steele. Lying on top of the bed still wrapped in my coat, I relay the events of the last twenty-four hours, every minute detail analysed and dissected. Was it something I'd said? Something I'd done? I decide it is the nude that has upset him. I should never have given him the painting, it was stupid of me. I'd shocked him and, I suspected, thrown him into a sort of turmoil. He'd kissed me, and what was it I'd seen in his eyes just before the kiss? An emotion that had been there – fleetingly, I admit – but there all the same. Fear. I know what it looks like – I'm very familiar with that particular emotion. Father Steele was afraid of me. Afraid of what? I can't harm him . . . or can I? Then it suddenly dawns. He's afraid I make him feel like a man instead of a priest. I feel a frisson of triumph and long to go downstairs and confront him with it. Who is this man hiding behind big brother's back? Did he show himself last night? Tell me the truth, Father, I need to know. But for once my courage fails me. I could brave the wrath of Mother Thomas yet when faced with Father Steele's conflict I'm a coward.

At dawn after a fitful sleep I get up and, on tiptoe, careful not to make a sound, I creep to the door of Father Steele's room. Peering through a small crack I see he's sleeping like a baby. My eyes roam the room. His clothes are folded neatly on a chair next to the bed, and on the other side near the window I spot my nude portrait. I gasp and, shrinking back, flatten myself against the wall. The portrait has been deliberately destroyed, defaced with black marking pen, so much so it is almost impossible to recognize any of the original.

A rage, akin to the one I'd felt when Mother Thomas had attacked Bridget, overwhelms me. Taking a deep breath, I try hard to contain it but know I've lost when I storm into Father Steele's bedroom shouting, 'How could you do that?' My throat tightens. I'm struggling to speak as I point to the painting. 'How could you, Father? I thought you cared for me.' Choking on a sob, I stagger from his room back into my own. Tearing off my pyjamas, I dress hurriedly in jeans and a sweater. When ten minutes later he appears at the open door I'm throwing my few things into a bag. He's fully clothed in his soutane and collar.

'What are you doing, Kate?'

He's facing my back; I make no attempt to turn. 'What does it look like?' I say tartly. 'I'm leaving.'

'I thought we agreed you'd stay until New Year.'

Grateful now he can't see my tear-stained face, I reply, 'That was before you betrayed me, Father.'

'Will you allow me to explain?'

Scalding tears burn my cheeks and like a small child I wipe them with the back of my hand and compose myself before facing him. 'No, Father, I don't want to hear any more of your sugary words. Anyway, I think I know why you destroyed the painting.'

With raised eyebrows and a composure I find slightly menacing, his voice cold, he says, 'You tell me, Kate.'

I breathe deeply, 'Because it makes you feel like a man. You know, the one you want to deny.'

'And what exactly do you mean by that?'

Gripping my bag very tight, I take two steps towards the door.

'How did you expect me to react to a nude painting of yourself? You are a very beautiful young woman. Answer me, Kate, what did you expect?'

When I am almost upon him I breathe deeply again, formulating my words in my head very carefully, the way he'd taught me. 'Exactly what I got. I now know you want me.'

On hearing his sharp intake of breath I feel a beat of triumph. I was right. 'All this brother–sister stuff is a cover. You don't want to be my brother, Declan Steele, you want to be my lover.'

Shaking his head, he moves to one side saying icily, 'I think you should go.'

Straight-backed and with my head held high, I walk past him and begin to descend the stairs. Halfway down I stop at the sound of my name. Looking up I see him at the top. 'God be with you, Kate.'

'God can go fuck himself,' I mumble. Not sure whether he's heard me or not, I open the front door and leave without saying goodbye.

Part Two

THE SURROGATE FATHER

If I'd been like the other girls in the orphanage, if I hadn't dreamt of a brighter future, things would have been different. But I'm not like the others. I'm not like anyone I know. Everyone should have a dream, a story, because the undreaming live empty lives. It's funny how little we know of ourselves; at sixteen almost nothing. I felt certain I'd survive but had no idea how lonely it would be at first.

Oddly enough, I missed the orphanage. Not the bad bits but the camaraderie, the being surrounded by people, the never feeling alone. Most of my life I'd longed for privacy, but in the darkness and the silence of my bedsit this pungent desolation seemed like a prison sentence. There are definitive moments in everyone's life, most people don't recognize them and they slip by unnoticed. Others, like me, know instinctively. Life, he said, is about timing, getting it right and not wasting a moment. I was seventeen when I met him; a child, a damaged child inside the body of a mature woman, desperate to learn and to love.

I was never in love with Brendan Fitzgerald, not in the true sense of the word, but I will be eternally grateful to him. Brendan made a difference.

Chapter Eight

Mr James Shaunessy isn't the least bit how I'd expected. That's the trouble when you allow your imagination to run free, the end result is either disappointing or totally surprising. In Mr Shaunessy's case it was the latter. To start with, he's younger than I'd assumed from his telephone voice. I'd come to Dublin with a preconceived image of all solicitors as sour-faced old men, hunched over stacks of dusty papers in grey offices like Mr Donovan the senior partner in Donovan & Doyle of New Street, Friday Wells. I've never seen Doyle and don't think he exists, but Mr Donovan looked less like Mr Shaunessy than the man in the moon. Mr Shaunessy's office in Fitzwilliam Square is the grandest place I've ever been to in my life. James Shaunessy stands, I reckon, just under six feet, with the kind of body I've only ever seen in magazines and on film: athletic and lithe, a body more suited to an Olympic training ground than the austerity of the early Victorian office I'd entered twenty minutes earlier. His nut-brown face looks natural but could be sun-tanned, and a thick wedge of hair flops over one eye when he speaks. I concentrate on the other eye. It's black, coal black like his hair.

Mr Shaunessy is wearing a dark suit with chalk stripes, a striped shirt in various shades of blue, and a tie the colour of egg yolk. Thinking of egg yolk reminds me of the first time I'd had a whole egg and not just the top (that's all we ever got in the orphanage – the top of the egg; I never did find out what happened to the rest). It was at Lizzy's house after Mass on Sunday morning.

She'd showed me how to dip the fingers of toast she called soldiers into the runny yolk. I'd sucked on the toast, savouring the melted buttery taste, and later that day had made Bridget's mouth water when I'd described this particular treat.

'I'm very sorry, Miss O'Sullivan, I can't tell you any more than I told you when we spoke last – remember, when you called to explain why you couldn't get up to Dublin to see me ... something about a friend of yours in trouble. I hope she's fine now.'

I nod. 'She's grand.'

'Like I was saying, it's impossible to disclose who the trustees of your estate are because, quite frankly, I don't know. Our instructions are explicit; we were contacted by a firm of lawyers in New York.'

He shuffles a few files on his desk, pulling out a letter addressed to himself and handing it to me with a curt nod.

I read: *Morgan, Morgan & Spencer; 56th and Madison, NY, NY.*

'They may be able to help, but don't hold out much hope. If someone goes to an enormous amount of trouble to conceal something and is determined to remain anonymous, the chances of you finding them are slim.'

'I'd sort of hoped ... You know how it is, Mr Shaunessy. You spend your life wondering about your parents or relatives and cling to anything, any clue. Your letter gave me a shock and a glimmer of hope. Someone out there cares about me.'

A flicker of compassion colours his eyes for a moment, then is gone. 'I'm very sorry I can't help you more, but there's nothing I can do. As for the other matter we discussed on the telephone, I spoke with Mr Morgan yesterday. Unfortunately, under no circumstances can any monies be forwarded to you before the allotted times. As you can see in his letter, he lists the dates. You are to receive a further three payments on your eighteenth, twenty-first and twenty-fifth birthdays respectively. The sum doubles each time, so at eighteen you will have ten thousand pounds, and the final payment will be forty thousand, making a total of seventy-five thousand. It's possible you may be able to secure a loan against your inheritance.'

Puzzled, I say, 'I don't understand, Mr Shaunessy.'

'Simple. Banks lend money against collateral. You have a valid trust fund and will presumably be able to pay off your loan when you receive your next payment in eighteen months' time. I'd advise you to try and borrow five thousand pounds to help you get started. In fact' – he picks up the telephone and begins to dial – 'my own manager will, I'm sure, help.'

Patiently I wait while he speaks to a Mr Tim Corrigan, and smile when I hear the solicitor say, 'Good. I'll send her over.'

When he replaces the telephone his eyes are gleaming like black ice. 'Tim Corrigan is prepared to offer you a loan of five thousand punts over the next eighteen months at the base rate of 11.85 per cent.'

Again I look confused. 'When you get your next payment' – his eyes move to my file – 'in June 1980, you will have to pay the bank five thousand, plus the interest.'

'Money is expensive,' I mutter.

He's smiling. 'You catch on quick. Tim wants me to stand guarantor.'

'What does that mean, Mr Shaunessy?'

'It means I guarantee the money is paid back with incurred interest or I'm liable.'

'Oh, I . . . it's very kind of you. I mean, you don't have to do that. What if I were to squander all the money and run off?'

Knotting his fingers, he cracks the knuckles. The sound makes me squirm. 'No great risk, even if you were to do what you've just suggested. The monies are administered by our firm.'

'I'm not going anywhere.'

'Mr Corrigan will see you,' he pauses to glance at the ormolu wall clock, the only decorative object in the otherwise clinically white office, 'in an hour and a half at three-thirty. His office is located in the Bank of Ireland on College Green. You can't get lost. Sure, everybody knows where it is.'

'I really don't know what to say, Mr Shaunessy. You've saved my life. I don't know how to thank you.'

He rises and, holding out his hand, says, 'Don't thank me, Miss O'Sullivan. I think you should save your thanks for whoever has bequeathed seventy-five thousand pounds to you.'

'If I ever get the chance.'

'In my limited experience, anonymous benefactors invariably come to light at some point or other. A death in the family, the clearing out of property, the opening of locked cupboards, the finding of skeletons, names written in dust . . .'

I grip his hand very tightly. 'I hope I find my mother's name written in the dust. That would make me very happy.'

Mr Tim Corrigan is gushing. I put it down to the fact that he thinks I'm worth a few bob. I can't think of any other reason for his saccharine charm. I listen intently to the banking terms and leave his small office with a pronounced spring in my step. I'm to call back in two days' time for my stationery, he'd said, cheque book and the like. Clutched in my right hand I've Rose Nolan's address, who, according to her nephew Tim Corrigan, lets rooms to students. 'Aunt Rose's place is grand, not far from here and will, I've no doubt, suit you down to the ground. Basic but spotless, and she's a fair cook, Aunt

Rose – had many a meal there myself when I was a young student.'

I've been in Dublin for less than forty-eight hours and already things are looking up. I've got enough money to get by, at least until I can find some work, and if Aunt Rose is everything she's cracked up to be I'll be looked after just fine. Life is grand, sure it is.

I'm wearing my Sisters of Mercy mackintosh and under that the same jeans I'd left Friday Wells in and a red sweater with a furry cat motif in the centre that Mrs Molloy had knitted for me on her new knitting machine. Some of the shops have started their sales and I'm tempted to buy a new coat. Plunging my hand into my coat pocket I pull out my dog purse, the one Bridget had given me. I count out the money in my hand. After paying for a week's board and lodgings, my train fare, a pack of cheese sandwiches yesterday, and a bacon sandwich this morning, I've fifty-eight pounds left.

I've no idea the price of a coat in fancy Dublin stores and I wander aimlessly up and down Grafton Street staring in brightly lit shop windows twinkling with Christmas decorations already gathering dust. A coat in one shop catches my eye. It's camel with big buttons and wide lapels. It's calf-length and when I try it on it swings around my legs like a movie star's coat. 'I'll have it,' I say to the young shop assistant who starts to help me out of the coat. 'No – I want to wear it.'

With her head on one side, she gives me an short odd look. 'Sure, but you'll have to take it off for me to take the price label out of the sleeve.'

Reluctantly I shrug out of the coat and wait while she cuts the label and spends a ridiculously long time messing about with a stock list, ringing the transaction up on the till, and folding my hated mac very neatly before putting it into a big bag with the name of the shop – Scruples – on the side. Once outside I walk down the street towards the bus stop, my body as warm as toast, an icy wind biting into my cheeks. I join the back of the short queue waiting for the number 54. We don't have long to wait. Within a few minutes the double-decker lumbers to a standstill. I shuffle forward, dropping the shopping bag into a nearby garbage bin. A woman behind me asks, 'Old clothes?'

I say, 'Yes, in one sense.' As I mount the bus I turn and add, 'Clothes from an old life.'

Aunt Rose lives in the middle of an Edwardian terrace. The houses share a sameness in their shabby attempt at respectability. Mr Molloy used to call it the net curtain culture, explaining to me that most people are like sheep, needing to be part of a flock; if Mrs O'Brian has net curtains so will Mrs Callahan and so on and so forth. Thankfully, he'd gone on to say, some black sheep strayed. 'Like you, Mr Molloy,' I'd piped up. 'You haven't got net curtains.'

As I walk up the path leading to number 79 I spot a cat sprawled across the windowsill, so still it doesn't look real. As the door opens the cat stirs and with a flick of its tail leaps from the window and out of sight.

Aunt Rose is everything her nephew had said: warm, friendly, tall and talkative. I guessed her to be in her mid fifties; she was, I learnt later, sixty-two, but had the exquisite and extraordinary bone structure that time cannot destroy. I conclude after ten minutes in Rose Nolan's company that talkative had been an understatement. She barely drew breath; she had verbal diarrhoea, some would say, and was totally incapable of listening. Yet for some reason it suited this ebullient woman.

'The room is ready for you, Miss O'Sullivan. Tim called earlier, said you were a good girl and I was to look after you. An orphan, he said. Sisters of Mercy. I've heard bad stories about some of them nuns.' She crosses herself. 'Sure they should be ashamed, give the Catholic Church a bad name. It's hard enough being bloody Irish without the likes of them evil sisters making it worse. You look tired.'

I'm about to say, I'm not, but she races on.

'Follow me, miss, up the wooden hill, like my old daddy always said. Sure, I've got you a lovely room overlooking the park at the back. Nice view – not so good at this time of year, no leaves, but in the spring fair takes your breath away. Can only let you have it for three months, I'm afraid, because it's let out for two years after that, but perhaps I'll be able to find you something else when the time comes. How long you going to be with us?' I open my mouth to reply but not quick enough. 'What did they feed you in that orphanage? Not much, by the looks of you, a right bag of bones. But beautiful, I must say, Tim was right when he said you was a fair-looking gel.'

We trudge up two flights of stairs, Rose puffing and talking, me listening – well, half-listening would be more honest – and studying the house. I'd read somewhere that houses take on the personality of their owners. This one certainly had. It was exactly like Rose: tall and slim with a faded elegance, shabbily attired, eccentric in the extreme, entrancing, and as warm and welcoming a place as I'd ever set foot in. It was a house with a past, I was to learn, a past coloured with love and romance.

'This is your room,' Rose says, opening the door and stepping to one side to let me pass. I look around me in wonder. The huge bed is brass, tarnished but none the less grand, and covered with a lace spread that trails on the wooden floor like a long wedding train. On top of the bed are piles of cushions in fabrics I've never seen before. Following my gaze she points to a huge cushion, 'Indian and Far Eastern, given to me by a lover: a merchant sea-man who' – she hurriedly crosses herself – 'died in this very bed.'

I shudder and wish for all the world she hadn't told me that. Pushing thoughts of the dead merchant seaman firmly out of my thoughts, I cross the room, the floor creaking underfoot. Rose was right about the view. The window is deep and opens out from the middle. I look out across frosted grass; the sun for a moment breaks free of the clouds and Rose's cat appears, a black lance in a sunny patch between two trees. 'What did I tell you? Pretty, isn't it? But just you wait for spring and summer, then you'll come and hug old Rose, telling me, as if I don't know, how your room has the best view in the whole of Dublin.'

'I just want to say, it beats the room I had last week.' It is, I realize with a start, the first time I've heard my own voice since entering the house. Rose looks startled too and, as if to combat that, begins to gabble again. 'I hope you'll be happy here at Magenta House.'

'Why Magenta?' I ask.

An enigmatic smile flickers across her thin lips. 'My man always called me Magenta, said it suited me much better than Rose. What do you think?'

Tilting my head to one side I grin. 'I disagree. I think Rose suits you fine.'

She shrugs. 'Makes me think of old ladies and English gardens, but it's my God-given name and I'm stuck with it.'

Placing my bag next to an antique chest of drawers, I sit on the edge of the bed. Rose, as if reluctant to leave, lingers next to the door. 'How long have you been in Dublin?' she asks.

'Four days. I arrived here on Boxing Day. I stayed in a crummy boarding house near the station, cost me nigh on eighty pounds with Irish breakfast. I wandered aimlessly around the city, kind of sight-seeing, and read a couple of old books the dragon landlady lent me. She even made me pay a deposit, in case I took off with them. Mean oul' bugger. I needed to see Mr Shaunessy urgently, but he wasn't back from his Christmas holiday until this morning. He was very helpful. Now I have to make an appointment with the admissions office at Trinity, and I'll be all set.'

'You going up to Trinity then?'

'Yes, but I'm not sure when. I was supposed to start an art foundation course last October, but I had family troubles and couldn't leave Friday Wells. Mr Lilley, my art teacher, submitted my portfolio early this year. He was positive I would be offered a scholarship. I was supposed to come to Dublin for an interview, but Mother Thomas put a stop to that.'

With arched brows she asks, 'Who is Mother Thomas?'

'Was,' I say, 'she's dead.' Then, 'I'd rather not talk about her, Rose, if you don't mind.'

Rose shrugs. 'Suit yourself. Now, if there's nothing else you're needing to know, I'll be off.' With her hand on the door-handle she turns to add, 'The bathroom and toilet are at the end of the hall. At seven prompt I put on an evening meal – nothing grand, but it's wholesome. Guaranteed to put hairs on your chest. Can't say as I'd want hair there.' She winks. 'Unless they happen to be attached to a man.' She's chuckling as she opens the door, and I can still hear the faint echo of her laughter as her footsteps recede.

When all is silent I lie fully clothed on top of the bed. I've slept very little since leaving Friday Wells and I'm very tired. I listen to the faint sounds of the city below my window: the screech of car tyres, a dog barking, and a mechanical noise I can't recognize. I glance at the bedside clock; it's twenty-five past six. My thoughts are jumbled. I mutter a prayer for Bridget and myself before I close my eyes and fall into a deep sleep. It is ten minutes to five the following morning when I awake with a jolt. Disorientated, I feel a throb of panic, I don't know where I am. Wide awake now, I dart out of bed and run to the window.

The light from the streetlamp below my window glows

in the pre-dawn darkness. Still fully clothed, I cross the room to the door and flick a switch on the wall. I blink in the sudden brightness, and look around the room, re-acquainting myself with my surroundings. It feels, as it had last night, warm and comforting, a nest, a home. I undress, fold my clothes neatly on the chair, and unpack my fleece dressing-gown, wash-bag and the suit I'd bought for the court. I straighten the bed and lie the suit carefully on top. I slip on my dressing gown and, clutching my washbag, creep barefoot along the corridor to the bathroom. I discover, after several failed attempts to get into locked rooms, that the bathroom is at the other end. When I eventually get there I'm not surprised to find it as eccentric and flamboyant as the rest of the house.

The large room is dominated by an equally large slipper bath, one end of which is raised, the other surrounded by a semicircular brass panel with a huge shower head attached. Two deep pedestal basins of white porcelain stand side by side in front of a set of long sash windows, covered in vertical blinds, painted cherry red. One wall is lined with shelves stacked high with towels in an assortment of colours. I kneel at the bathside examining the taps, slightly intimidated by the mechanism of what is clearly an antique. The taps turn easily and the water, after the first trickle, gushes out generously. I scan the room for bath salts; finding none, I jump into the steaming water armed with a bar of soap.

When an hour and a half later I come downstairs, I hear Rose's voice drifting out of what I assume is the kitchen. A moment later she appears in the hall. She's wearing an emerald green velvet smock dress, a green and black silk scarf tied haphazardly at her neck. Her sooty lashes flutter below emerald green lids.

'Top of the morning. You sleep OK? Do you always get up so early? I'm an early riser, always have been, get more done between six and eight than for most of the day. In springtime I love to get up at dawn, walk the dog – sure, the world seems like a different place at that time of the day. You want something to eat? Look like you could do with some feeding up.'

I nod. 'I'm famished.'

She points to a room on my right. 'Sit yourself down in there. I'll see what Maudy can rustle up.'

I wander into the room she'd indicated and sit down at the head of a rectangular oak dining table, bare except for a bowl of dusty silk flowers. A few minutes later the smell of bacon cooking wafts into the room. Surely it has to be one of the best smells in the world, ranking alongside onions and Mrs Molloy's roast pork. My mouth is wet and my stomach feels so empty I doubt I'll ever be able to fill it. I'm thinking of the rashers when Rose appears with a plateful of food: two fried eggs, mushrooms, tomatoes, one big fat sausage, four back rashers and a mountain of toasted sour dough. This feast could rival any I'd seen Mrs Molloy serve up to her husband on a Sunday morning after Mass.

Placing the plate in front of me, she says, 'Special treat. Don't go thinking you get this every morning. Ordinarily, you fend for yourself. Maudy makes a big pot of tea, and I expect everyone to buy their own cereal and bread, if you're wanting toast. Like I was telling a young student only yesterday, this isn't a bloody hotel.'

Between mouthfuls of food I manage to mutter, 'Thanks a lot, Rose, it's the best.'

'Tuck in, it's good to see folk enjoying their food, especially skinny ones like you. Got to get some meat on them bones,' she says touching my arm in what I sense is a maternal way. 'A mug of tea.'

With my mouth full I nod. A couple of minutes later she returns with two steaming mugs. She sets one down in front of my plate, and cupping hers in both hands she sits down opposite.

'Is it today you're going to Trinity?'

I swallow and say, 'Yes, I've got an appointment at ten.'

Looking down into her mug she says wistfully, 'I wonder if Daniel Joyce is still there. He's an art tutor. I was in love with him once. I swear he was the most handsome man in all Ireland. I wasn't the only one – me and a hundred others. All slavering over Danny boy, but he was only ever interested in one, that Shannon woman, black Irish, hair like ink . . .' She pauses and takes a sip of tea. 'He said he was in love with me. I suppose for a wee while he was, or thought he was. We all like to kid ourselves we're in love when we're making love.'

Using half a slice of toast I wipe the plate clean. 'Why is that?' I ask before stuffing the bread in my mouth.

'Self-esteem, I suppose. Makes you feel better about yourself, and anything that does that is worth doing.'

I chew, thinking about what she'd said. 'But it's not the same if it isn't real.'

Looking directly into my eyes, Rose asks, 'What's real?'

I consider this for a long moment, then say, 'Do you believe in real love?'

Rose directs her eyes back to the middle of her mug. 'I did once when I was very young.' A second later her tone changes and I realize I've touched a chord. 'He was young too – far too bloody young to die.'

'The good Lord takes the best first, or so they say.'

Rose swigs her tea, emptying her mug. 'Try telling that to mothers who lose children, families torn apart by war. Young lovers who suddenly have no future together. He's got a lot to bloody answer for – the Almighty, I mean. Sure, I was raised to be a good Catholic girl, but there have been many times in my life I've longed to turn my back on the church.'

'Why didn't you, Rose?'

She rises. 'Because I was afraid. Crazy, I know, but the honest truth. Scared shitless to leave the bloody flock.'

Shaking her head, she apologizes. 'Take no notice of my prattle. You'll get used to it – have to, if you live here.' She grins. 'You're a new victim.'

I sip my tea and watch her as she glides, and glide she does, as if on roller skates, around the table towards the door.

Before she reaches it I say, 'I just want to say I'd love to paint you, Rose. You've got a beautiful and animated face.'

She preens, putting on her best smile and nervously patting the sparse hair at her temples.

With growing affection I watch her turn on her heel and start back down the hall.

Later that morning when I return from Trinity, Rose is struggling up the path laden with supermarket bags.

'Here, let me help.'

She hands me one light bag while she opens the front door. I follow her into the hall. She drops the bags and immediately asks, 'How did you get on?'

I feel warmed by her interest. 'My place has been filled and they can't offer me a place until next October. The woman suggested I apply to Dun Laoghaire Art College, but I'm not sure that's what I want. I might go over the water, try a couple of London colleges.'

'England! You just got to Dublin. Apply to Dun Laoghaire, why don't you? No messing about.'

'Sure, I'm not messing, Rose,' I grumble. 'I'm disappointed, that's all. I'll get over it.' I walk to the foot of the stairs.

Rose's eyes fix on the portfolio I'm carrying.

'Let's see what you're made of, then.'

I'm in no mood to show her my work, but have a feeling she won't take no for an answer. I'm right.

'I've got a mutton stew in the oven, and pear crumble. Want some?'

I grin. 'In exchange for showing you my paintings?'

She winks. 'You catch on quick.'

I follow her into the dining room, placing my portfolio on the table. I unzip the case and slide out a few paintings. I study her face as she examines my work: her expression changes subtly, from slightly patronizing to open admiration.

When she's finished looking at every piece, she turns to me saying, 'Who taught you to paint like this?'

'No one. I taught myself.'

She lets out a long sigh. 'I don't know much about art, but from what I can see you've got serious talent. So, when do you want to start my portrait?'

'After the mutton stew and pear crumble.'

She chuckles. 'It's a deal.'

The food is wholesome, filling and delicious. Maudy could give Mrs Molloy a run for her money – and that was saying something!

After lunch I set up my easel and paints in what Rose refers to as the best room: a sacred place at the front of the house, overlooking the street. It is used rarely, on 'high days and holidays and for when the priest pops in for a cup of tea', according to Rose. It's dark because Rose keeps the thick velvet drapes permanently closed, 'To stop the wallpaper fading,' and unlike the rest of the house has none of Rose's ebullient personality. When she throws back the drapes a pool of wintry sun trickles between the rug and the tall glass-fronted chest containing an odd jumble of china and glass.

When I hear the door open I turn and cannot resist a gasp of admiration. Rose is dressed in an ankle-length wrap skirt made of the most exquisite silk, hand-embroidered in vibrant shades of red and purple. From her waist up she is covered in black velvet and lying across her chest is a gold baroque necklace set with amber stones. Her hair is hidden under a twenties-style silk turban in the same red and purple tones as the skirt. Statuesque in high heels and head-dress, her bright eyes twinkling in anticipation, she looks like a beautiful tired courtesan still enthusiastically aware of her sex appeal.

'You look wonderful!' I exclaim.

Teetering precariously on the heels, Rose does a little twirl. 'William, the love of my life, brought me this outfit back from the Far East.' She winks and I see a hint of mischief enter her youthful eyes. 'I remember trying it on for him, and – ' she giggles girlishly – 'not having it on for long.' She sighs, the brightness fades, and her eyes grow sad. 'He was only twenty-eight when he died. Too young, much too young . . .'

To distract her I say, 'Over there, Rose – ' I point in the direction of the window – 'draped across the chaise in a . . .'

'Provocative pose?' she suggests.

'However you feel most comfortable.'

She laughs, a moist gurgle. 'Then provocative it is.'

Finishing Rose Nolan's portrait and getting my first job as a life model coincided. I've been in Dublin for a month and three days, and I'm still waiting to hear about a place at Dun Laoghaire Art College. It doesn't normally take me more than a month to complete a portrait but Rose had cancelled more sittings than she'd attended, and I'd been equally busy working on my portfolio. It was Rose who suggested I find part-time work. We talked about life modelling, something a friend had done for many years until she'd developed breast cancer and subsequently died. The following day I placed a small ad on the bulletin board at Dun Laoghaire College, and another in the want ad section of the local newspaper. My first reply was from a man with a high-pitched falsetto voice who I thought might be a weirdo, the second was a woman who ran an agency for models of all types. I made an appointment to meet with her the following Monday. The third was from a Mrs Tremayne who informed me in an upper crust, plum-in-the-mouth – as Bridget would say – English accent, that she was Mr Brendan Fitzgerald's secretary.

'Mr Fitzgerald', she says, 'tutors private life classes three days a week.' Her pronunciation of 'classes' sounds like 'arses'. 'He's constantly looking for new models. He pays highly and I can assure you the conditions in his small classes and comfortable studio are excellent.'

I agree to send her a recent photograph and my CV. A week later, Mrs Tremayne calls again; she sounds agitated.

'Would it be too much to ask if you could sit for Mr Fitzgerald's class this evening? I know it's short notice, but the model he normally uses has called in sick.'

'What time do you need me?'

Sounding hopeful, she says, 'As soon as possible?'

'I'll do it. Give me the address.'

'Where are you, Miss O'Sullivan? Since you've been so obliging I'll send a car to pick you up.'

Delighted, I reel off Rose's address.

'The car will be with you in less than half an hour.'

'I'll be ready.'

Before putting down the telephone she says, 'Thank you very much, Miss O'Sullivan. I'm very grateful and I know Mr Fitzgerald will be too.'

I replace the receiver and bound upstairs, taking them two at a time. I wash in my bedroom sink, making sure all my private parts are scrupulously clean. Then I douse myself with Elizabeth Arden perfume and pull on jeans and a cotton sweater. As I return to the hall I hear the doorbell ring. It's the driver. He introduces himself as Joe McNamara. I follow him down the path to the street where a black Mercedes is parked. Not until I'm settled in the back seat do I start to feel nervous. I've never taken my clothes off before. Never exposed my nakedness. But I'm not shy – well, not in front of artists. It's different with them, there are no sexual overtures, no lust, no desire.

As the car pulls to a halt at the end of an elegant Georgian terrace I think of my nude portrait and the turmoil it had stirred in Father Steele. Thinking of the painting brings back a recollection of something Father Steele had said the day after he'd seen his portrait. 'If we have a rapport with something greater than us, it's our duty to produce something that touches the heart. You, Kate, have been given such a gift.' His words had touched my heart and it is with a step as light as a child that I alight from the car and walk up the path to meet Brendan Fitzgerald.

Chapter Nine

The melting light from the tall window throws my naked body into shadow, elongating my legs to giant proportions. My backside aches and I long to move, but I can't, not yet. I swivel my eyes right; the wall clock reads four minutes to five. At five I can move.

A dog barks in the far distance, a bus engine cranks into life, then the most glorious sound of all fills my head: the strident ringing of Mr Fitzgerald's alarm. It's music to my ears.

Before the bell ceases I'm clothed in a cotton kimono and smiling at the small knot of art students packing up their things and expressing their thanks. Slinging my bag over my shoulder I start to walk across the studio towards the bathroom. I'm almost at the door when I hear my name.

'Miss O'Sullivan!' Then again, louder: 'Miss O'Sullivan, wait!'

I turn to see Mr Fitzgerald, his finger crooked, beckoning me. I'm tired. All I want to do is lie in a hot bath, work on my own still life, then crawl into bed and sleep for at least ten hours.

Defy Brendan Fitzgerald at your peril, I'd been told by one of his students after my first life class three weeks previously. With deliberate ease I stroll back to where Mr Brendan Fitzgerald, a tall and imposing figure, is standing squarely in front of Rory Butler's study.

'Can you spare a moment, Miss O'Sullivan?'

Unable to suppress a hint of irritation I say, 'What is it?'

He looks at me for a long moment. 'Impatience will not get you very far in this life, Miss O'Sullivan. Believe me, I know.'

You think you know everything. The phrase jumps into my head. I'd dearly like to say so but he pays more for life classes than anyone else in Dublin, in all of Ireland, I shouldn't wonder.

'I'm very tired.'

'We all are. This exhibition is pushing everyone to the limit, which brings me to my next question. Can you work extra hours next week? I'm very excited about Rory's piece but feel it needs extra work.'

'How many extra hours?'

Brendan is studying the canvas, his knotted fist stuck under his chin. He towers at least a foot above the runt of the litter, Rory. I glance at the study. It's good, but there's something missing.

I joke, 'I just want to say, my tits are wrong – they don't droop.'

Indignant, Rory bites back, 'That's the way I see them.'

I shrug. 'OK, Rory, just a bit of fun. I wasn't serious.'

Rory frowns. 'Anyway, what do you know about painting?'

It's my turn to be indignant. 'A lot more than you, judging by this piece.'

Rory looks poised to slap me. Just in case, I step back before continuing with my assessment.

'You've painted the form well but you haven't captured the soul of the woman. It's a good study, but that's all it will ever be.'

'I care nothing for your opinion, Miss O'Sullivan. I really think you should stick to what you do best: taking your clothes off.'

Determined not to be rattled by the prissy Rory, I decide to kill him with kindness and, smiling sweetly, say, 'At least I do that well.'

'Children, children,' Brendan interrupts. 'All this squabbling will do no good, no good at all.'

Since our first meeting, Rory has been openly hostile, making it clear he dislikes me intensely. I'm not sure why but suspect Brendan Fizgerald's presence is the only reason he's silently glaring in my direction instead of raining abuse on my head.

Still looking at Rory's painting and stroking his goatee beard, Brendan says, 'You've got a point. There is something missing, but I can't put my finger on it.'

I drop my voice to a conspiratorial whisper. 'I don't think Rory likes women. It comes through in his work.'

Leaning close to me, Brendan mutters back, 'You could be right. But it's easy to criticize. I couldn't do better, could you?'

'I could do much better.'

He looks surprised. 'I didn't know you could paint.'

'You don't know everything, Mr Fitzgerald.'

A glint of mischief enters his pale green gaze. 'Promise you won't tell anyone?'

I grin and change the subject. 'Has anyone ever told you your eyes are the exact colour of a pistachio nut?'

'No, but it's a damn good description and, what's more, original. I like originality.'

There's a prickle of sweat on his brow. He lifts his hand to wipe it and I can see his fingers are long and tapered, with neat square nails. 'I've seen many promising artists come and go. Few know how to tackle the basis of life drawing: contact with the human soul. Do you think you can relate to that, Kate?'

'Why don't you be the judge of that, Mr Fitzgerald?'

Brendan studies my face with the same concentration he'd given the portrait. 'Why not indeed? Show me.' Then with a dramatic sweep he lifts and spreads his arms wide. 'Show me now.'

In a state of confusion I watch him set up a large canvas

on an easel next to an open box of pencils and oils. Speechless and no longer tired, I continue to stare in a stunned apprehension when he takes all of his clothes off except his boxer shorts.

The shock of seeing Mr Fitzgerald, the aesthete, the scholarly art tutor, baring all in the pristine perfection of his expensively lit studio makes me hysterical and I want to roar with laughter. It seems so out of character and totally incongruous. The rest of the class, huddled in a tight bunch, are mumbling under their breath, something about Mr Fitzgerald having gone mad. Brendan bellows in their direction, 'Class is over for today, be gone.'

Silently they troop out. Rory, the last to leave, slams the door hard behind him.

When we can no longer hear their footsteps Brendan jumps up on to the podium I'd vacated. 'So, Miss O'Sullivan, how do you want me?'

Still in shock I say, 'Are you sure about this?'

'As sure as I've ever been about anything.'

Recovering my composure, I make a suggestion: 'Standing in profile, perhaps.'

He poses, one hand on his hip, one on his jaw.

'No, definitely not right, too classic. I want modern new man. Open your legs slightly and put both hands on the wall as if you're being frisked, like in the American movies.'

He does as I ask.

'That's great. You've got marvellous legs, like a champion stallion.'

He laughs again. 'Another descriptive first.'

'Great pose. Only one thing wrong . . .'

Twisting his neck, he looks at me. 'What?'

'Do you really think I can paint a man in that position with his knickers on?'

He grunts something I can't catch but makes no attempt to take them off.

'They break the line of your back, sir. Really, it would be better if you took them off.'

He begins to pull his underpants down a fraction then stops and, twisting his neck, winks in my direction. 'Only if you say please.'

Inspired by Brendan Fitzgerald's ebullient enthusiasm I set to work with gusto. No longer tired, I sketch like someone possessed. The sketch takes three hours to complete and remains to this day the best I've ever done.

While I sketch, Brendan talks without restraint, as if I'm an old friend he hasn't seen for years. I've read that some people find it easier to talk in depth to a stranger than a close friend, and I put Mr Fitzgerald's intimate revelations down to that. During the course of the night I learn that he's single, in his forties, and had, at the age of twenty-five, on his father William's untimely death from a stroke, inherited a fortune in land, property and international investments. A descendant of Lord Edward Fitzgerald, an Anglo/Irish aristocrat who had lost his life in the Irish uprising of 1798, William had been twenty-six when he'd met Brendan's mother Frances Macguire. Ambitious, determined and impoverished, the beautiful Frances had wasted no time in seizing her opportunity. The chronically shy and unattractive William Fitzgerald hadn't stood a chance and had gone against the wishes of his friends and family like a willing lamb to the slaughter. All his life William had adored his wife, worshipping the ground she walked on, showering her with gifts and indulging her every whim. She, sadly, had never loved him and, once she'd given him two children, had pursued her own life.

When at last he stops talking of his parents he sighs deeply. 'Never marry for money, Kate.'

'It never entered my head. I want to make my own.'

'Good, that's the spirit. Now I must rest, my back is killing me.'

'One minute, please.'

He's fidgety, and I can see he won't stay still. 'OK. Let's take five.'

During the night we take several 'fives' that last for twenty. At each break, Mr Fitzgerald, naked and seemingly totally uninhibited, busies himself making thick treacly espresso coffee on his state-of-the-art Italian coffee machine. While I, whenever I am certain he isn't looking, cast furtive glances at his genitalia, wondering if all men had such low-slung, big balls. Mr Fitzgerald's are similar to those of my landlady's Boxer dog Duke. I'm fascinated by his penis, or cock as I've heard it called for most of my life. It's short and fat, and the foreskin doesn't fit properly. It isn't pretty. But then, what do I know of men? Nothing. Most of my life has been spent in the company of women. The male species are so alien, they might as well be from another planet. As far as I can see most of them do nothing more interesting than going out with their mates, swilling beer, and swapping dirty stories, and poking their wives and girlfriends on a Saturday night after the pub.

Since arriving in Dublin I've avoided men, which is no mean feat since they are always coming on to me. Most of the life-class students have asked me out at least once. I've declined their various proposals (ranging from a quick cup of coffee to all-night parties) politely. Usually I use the first excuse that comes into my head. The truth is I haven't yet met a man that can hold a candle to Father Declan Steele. So far no one has even come close. Every night, in the suspended moments before sleep, I clear my tumbled thoughts and begin to piece together, like a jigsaw puzzle, his face. I start with his eyes and end with his mouth. When complete, I hold the image in my mind's eye until I fall asleep. His voice is always there, repeating his last words to me: 'God be with you, Kate.' I try not to think of mine to him, and pray he didn't hear. Sometimes I touch myself, imagining it's Father Steele's fingers working me to a shuddering climax. Afterwards I feel guilty and a bit sad, and wish I hadn't done it. For penance I sometimes say a few Hail Marys and Our Fathers, and promise myself I'll never do it again.

At ten past noon the following day the painting is finished. Brendan, unable to contain his excitement, leaps like a two-year-old colt from the podium, landing next to me with a thud.

I've always found it difficult to judge my own work, but I know this is good. It's the best piece of work I've ever done, even better than the self-portrait I'd painted for Father Steele, the one he'd destroyed. I feel a sharp pain in my gut at the memory.

In silence we both study the painting. I'm dying to look at his expression but am afraid I might see something I don't want to see. Criticism, disappointment, or, even worse, sympathy.

When at last he speaks I turn to face him and see his eyes are watery.

'You did do better, Kate, much better.'

'You mean better than Rory?'

Without a word Brendan crosses the room. He disappears, reappearing a few moments later dressed in a long silk robe. In three strides he's standing next to me in front of the painting again.

'I can't say what I'm about to say naked. It's not fitting, somehow.'

I'm light-headed, my tongue feels woolly; I've got a dry throat and for the first time since we started the painting I feel tired. It's a familiar sensation, as if all of my insides have been sucked out.

Taking my hand Brendan leads me to a small sofa next to the window. As I sit, I'm aware of rain spattering the window pane and nothing else, except Brendan Fitzgerald's presence, his mouth drained of colour, sombre intent in his green eyes.

'There have not been many times in my life when I've been rendered speechless. In fact I can only think of three. One has just occurred.'

It's my turn to be speechless. I can't think of a thing to say and wait in anticipation for him to continue. In silence he strokes his beard. A perpetual habit, I'm soon to learn.

'You have talent, Kate. Exceptional talent.'

I start to say thank you, but with a wave of his hand he silences me. 'Let me finish. Lots of artists, writers, actors have talent, but a select few have a little more. No one knows why they are chosen for this extra special brand of greatness. I believe you are one of the few.'

My astonishment must have shown on my face.

'You had no idea?'

'No. I've painted for as long as I can remember, it's what I've always wanted to do. It comes as naturally to me as breathing.'

With a long sigh Brendan takes both my hands in his. Carefully, as if looking for something, he examines every finger.

'All my life I've strived for greatness. I can paint reasonably well; I play the piano, again moderately well. I've written a few poems, had a couple published, the reviews were good but never great. Have you ever heard the saying, "Some men are born great, some achieve greatness, others have greatness thrust upon them"?'

I shake my head.

'You, my beautiful child, were given a gift. I envy you. My God, how I envy you.'

I can feel my cheeks burning. 'Thank you, Mr Fitzgerald. I'm pleased you liked the painting.'

Dropping my hands, Brendan jumps up and quickly crosses the room to stand in front of the finished oil.

'My God if you can paint like this at sixteen and in one night, what, I ask, will you be doing when you are twenty-six?'

'Married and having babies, most probably.'

His voice rises with emotion. 'No, Kate, absolutely not! Your kind of talent will never be smothered. Nor will it cease. You will never stop painting, I can say that with absolute conviction.' He points to the painting. 'It's impossible to put a value on this sort of talent. By all means, have your lovers, husbands, babies even. But let none of them stand in the way of your painting. Do you realize you could become one of the most important painters of the twentieth century? And if it's got anything to do with me, you'll be recognized soon, very soon.'

'What do you mean, Mr Fitzgerald?'

'I want to become your patron.'

I'm confused. 'I don't understand.'

'Sponsor your career. You can live and work here in my home. Have the run of the place. I tutor four private classes a week, but that's a hobby, not a necessity. I'm fortunate to have been cushioned all my life by money. It gives me the freedom to choose. That's the best thing about money, Kate, don't ever forget that, and the only really good reason apart from collecting wonderful art to have the damn stuff. The rest is boring; investments brokers, lawyers, financial advisers. People who know the price of everything and the value of nothing.'

I haven't got a clue what he's talking about and continue to stare dumbstruck when he says, 'We'll mount an exhibition that will excite and shake the very foundations of the pretentious art world. Both sides of the Atlantic.'

'I've applied for a foundation at Dun Laoghaire.' I say lamely.

He laughs scornfully. 'You could teach that load of old buffers a thing or two about painting.' He taps the base of the canvas. 'I'm telling you, this is the stuff of budding genius. How can a college teach you to paint when you've got it in your soul? Your work comes from in here – ' he flattens a hand against his breast. 'I feel as light as a boy. What more is there to say? I will be your Svengali.'

I've no idea who Svengali is, or was, and feel foolish asking.

Running across the room, he falls at my feet and takes hold of my hand. I can see his own shaking like that of an old man. Placing one of my hands on his chest, he presses hard; I can feel his heart beating very fast.

'Feel that, Kate, that's the effect your work has on me. Think of your future. With my money, reputation and connections and your genius, there are no limits to where we can go together: London, Paris, New York . . . I predict that in less than five years every dealer will be fighting for your work.'

My head is swimming. I feel intoxicated, caught up in his frenzied enthusiasm.

'Will you do it, Kate?' he urges. 'Live and work here with me. I'll guide and care for you. As a mentor, teacher and friend. I promise I want nothing more. On that you have my word. You will have all your expenses found, and I'll give you a small work-in-progress advance on the sale of your first piece. You can talk it through with your parents, they can come here and meet me, see where you will be living. My housekeeper lives in, so there is always another woman around.'

It all sounds too good to be true. Since I was a child I've been aware of my talent. I can't get my head around genius but know instinctively I'm in the right place at the right time and have to seize the opportunity before it passes. Parents – he'd mentioned parents. I didn't want to lie to him, nor did I want to tell him the truth.

'It won't be necessary to speak to my parents, but I will have to let my landlady know. I've given her three months' rent in advance.'

'If she won't reimburse you, I will. Then no one is out of pocket. I think it's better if you live and work here. That way you can be flexible.'

'What about my modelling contracts with the agency? I signed a contract for a year, and I –'

He interrupts with a dismissive wave: 'Leave all of that to me.'

I feel hot on the outside, my skin is clammy, my underarms wet and there's a trickle of sweat in my cleavage. Yet inside I'm cool and very calm; my instinct tells me to trust this man.

'No obstacles, Kate. Opportunity is banging hard on your door. Will you let it in?'

With my best smile I say, 'When do we start, Mr Fitzgerald?'

'My father always said there's no time like the present.'

Before I can gather my thoughts Brendan is striding across the room towards the door. Opening it wide he leans against the frame and bellows downstairs, 'Mrs Keating, are you there?'

From the bowels of the house I hear a muffled response quickly followed by footsteps. A few moments later a squat body appears in the open frame, topped with a moon face. I assume it's Mrs Keating. She's panting. 'Them stairs are going to be the death of me.'

'Stop complaining, woman, it's good exercise.'

'I can think of better ways, like a long walk in Killarney National Park or –'

'Hush up,' Brendan interrupts. 'Kate here is going to be our new lodger.'

With a perceptible lift of her right eyebrow Mrs Keating makes a loud grunting sound.

Mr Fitzgerald grimaces but ignores her reaction. 'I want you to prepare the spare room on the third floor and make sure she has everything she needs.'

Dubiously she looks me up and down, making no

attempt to hide her hostility. I'm still wearing the kimono; it's gaping a little at the front, exposing half of my left breast. It's clear what she's thinking and I want to put her straight. Brendan does it for me.

'Kate is a painter, a painter of rare talent, the like of which I haven't seen in years. She's going to work towards her first exhibition, here under my tutelage. I want her to work free of all encumbrances. Her concentration has to be entirely, constantly focused on her art.'

This seems to satisfy Mrs Keating and she manages a terse smile in my direction. Then, turning her attention to Brendan, she says, 'I'll prepare the guest room. Will the young lady be needing lunch?'

'Why don't you ask her?'

'I'm famished. Would it be too much trouble to have a bite of something now?' I pause. 'Please?'

The brittle light in Mary Keating's eyes begins to fade. 'How about a good Irish breakfast, lass? You look like you could do with feeding up.'

I feel my mouth watering as Brendan adds, 'Mrs Keating makes a mean breakfast. In fact she makes a mean everything. Best cook in Dublin, according to my mother, who has in the last forty odd years been through her fair share of staff. Been trying to poach Mary here for as many years as she's worked for me.'

'Eighteen, coming up September,' Mary comments with pride.

'Doesn't time fly when you're having fun?' Brendan adds with a wink.

'Speak for yerself, Mr Fitz.' A long strand of dandelion hair escapes the knot at the nape of her neck to fall on to her brow. She blows at it, then with an impatient huff fastens it back. 'You want your usual fresh fruit and toast, I assume, Mr Fitz?'

'No, I want a gargantuan breakfast – the works. I, like Kate, am famished.'

187

'Two Irish breakfasts coming up. With tea or coffee?'
I raise my hand. 'Tea for me.'

'I'd best get cracking. Give me fifteen minutes.'

Brendan nods and Mrs Keating turns on her sensible heels and leaves the room on the trot. As soon as she's out of earshot, Brendan turns his attention to me. 'She's a good soul, a bit tetchy from time to time, but her cooking more than makes up for her temperament. Talks a lot if you let her, most of it rubbish. You know, banal stuff, the kind that goes in one ear and out the other.' He claps his hands three times. 'Now, I'll show you to your room and you can freshen up before we eat.'

In a kind of daze I follow him down the front stairs. I've never been in this part of the house before. Brendan's studio spans the entire fourth floor of his Georgian house. It's self-contained with a kitchen, bathroom and separate side entrance on to the street. I've often been curious to see the rest of the house. The first time I'd come to the studio I'd entered by the front door and had caught a quick peek through the long windows at the front. In the fading dusk I hadn't been able to see much.

Since childhood I've been fascinated by how other people live. Particularly the rich. Once when I was about ten, a girl I knew at school had in our lunch break taken me to Cashel Manor where her mother worked as a cleaner. I recall following Angela on tiptoe into the drawing room, gaping at the sheer extravagance of the place. It was the first time I'd seen wall-to-wall carpet. It was deep red with a gold-leaf design. I remember kneeling down and rubbing my palm across the velvety nap. I'd promised myself that one day I'd be rich, very rich, and have red wall-to-wall carpet in every room.

The guest bedroom is on the third floor, directly below the studio. It's a large room twenty feet by eighteen. Two tall identical windows face the back of the house overlooking a small walled garden; an opposing set front the street. All the windows are framed in long drapes, silk I think, in baby-flesh pink, with a tiny rosebud pattern. They are pinned open with thick rope tassels. My eyes widen when they rest on the bed. It's not exactly the bed of my dreams but it's close. The headboard is buttoned and padded in the same fabric as the curtains; the bedspread, which is the same colour as the rosebud print, has a pleated valance reaching to the carpeted floor. Three delicate antique cushions are propped at the head of the bed and there is an embroidered spread draped across the foot.

The walls are painted the same pale pink as the curtains and are covered in pictures and paintings. One, a portrait of a stern young man, catches my eye. I recognize the face.

'Yes, it's me,' Brendan says sadly.

'I thought so.'

'I'm loath to admit it's a self-portrait. Done, I might add, when I was very young.'

I'm secretly pleased he doesn't ask me to comment.

I glance to my left and my gaze rests on another portrait, of a young woman. She's very beautiful in a haughty don't-you-dare-come-near-me sort of way. Brendan stands next to me. 'My mother. She was forty-one when that was painted.'

'She's very beautiful.'

'The portrait doesn't do her justice. The artist has made her look harsh, untouchable, he hasn't captured her true beauty.'

'Who painted it?'

With a deep sigh he says, 'Me again. I tried, I was young – nineteen. God knows I tried, for months. I so wanted to please her, make her understand that painting was worth while, and that I was good at it. She wasn't impressed. Can't say I blame her. She said she had no room to hang it in her own home and insisted I hang it

189

here, making the lame excuse she could appreciate it when she came to stay. I know that wasn't the real reason. In truth, she just didn't want her fancy friends deriding it.'

I thought that Brendan's mother sounded as cold as she looked.

With a quick grunt of distaste, Brendan walks around the perimeter of the bed to a door in the far corner of the room. He opens it and indicates for me to follow. I expect a wardrobe and am overwhelmed when I find myself in a huge bath and dressing room. The room is the same shape as the bedroom, and almost as big. A huge walk-in shower occupies one corner, the bath another. All the fittings are gold. I gawk at the tap above the bath (it's shaped like a swan's neck) and wonder if the gold is real. Under my feet are tiny square tiles in an aquamarine colour, and piles of white fluffy towels stacked on deep glass shelves.

'My mother has spent most of her life bathing, creaming, exfoliating, dressing, undressing, crimping, preening, and generally pampering herself or being pampered by professionals. I decorated this room for her. No other woman has been near the place. Her bottles, potions and lotions are exactly as she left them.'

I'm a little confused. I'm sure earlier Brendan had spoken of his mother in the present tense. 'Is your mother dead?'

'No, she's alive – if you can call it life. Some days she may think she's dead, some days she thinks I'm dead and am reincarnated as my father – that's a good day. She has chronic dementia, but, like most old ladies, stubbornly refuses to be institutionalized. Can't say I blame her. All those places, however expensive, are like leper colonies run by well-meaning tyrants. She has round-the-clock nursing and, in her lucid moments, can still play a mean game of bridge.'

'I'm sorry.'

'Don't be. On my father's death my mother inherited a small fortune and is going out in great comfort, in the home she always adored and swore she would never leave until they carried her out. She has her dogs, snappy Spider and petulant Perkins, bad-tempered pugs both of them, and a house full of staff who pander to her every whim – and believe me they are many and frequent. My sister Madeleine lives at home in a very grand apartment, and spends most of her time fussing and fawning over Mother, positive she will inherit the lot when Mother eventually decides to make a nuisance of herself with the big man upstairs.'

He winks. 'Madeleine's in for a big surprise. If I know Mother, she'll leave all her money to some obscure charity no one has ever heard of, just to be perverse. I remember a few years ago, before she became ill, she said something to me I've never forgotten. She was here, we'd had a quiet supper and had both drunk too much wine. We'd climbed the stairs together and I'd done as I always do, kissed her on both cheeks before saying goodnight.

'But on this particular night she'd gripped both my arms, pulling me close to her face. "Your sister has done nothing all her life, except marry that no good son of a bitch Fergus. Fancy marrying a bloody Scot, and a penniless one to boot! I wouldn't have minded half as much if he'd been handsome, got her pregnant a few times, made me a grandmother, but no, couldn't even give me a child."

'Then Mother loosened her grip. She started to cackle and shout, "Revenge yourself on your children – spend all your money." She was still laughing as I mounted the stairs to bed.' The sides of his mouth curl. 'I think my mother lost something when she lost her parents. They were killed in a car crash when she was only eighteen. She once confided in me that all her life she'd felt as if she were on the outside, living behind a sheet of glass, an onlooker unable to join in.'

Quietly I say, 'I know that feeling. Sometimes it makes it difficult to relate to other people.'

Distracted for a moment, Brendan stares out of the window. 'I'm sorry, I shouldn't be bothering you with my family, or for that matter any of this stuff. It's none of your business. I don't know why I'm confiding in you.'

'Don't be sorry, Mr Fitzgerald. Sometimes it feels good to talk to a stranger.'

'I talk far too much. It's time I shut up and gave my tongue a holiday.' He points to his left. 'This is your boudoir. Clothes in there.'

I step into a vast dressing room, awed by the sheer scale.

Brendan is standing at the door. 'You like?'

'My clothes will fit very easily into one corner.'

'You haven't answered my question. Is it to your liking?'

'I've never seen anything to match it in my life. Not even at the pictures.'

'Where did you live, Kate, before you came to Dublin? Where is your family?'

A lie begins to formulate. I'm ashamed to tell him about my background – what will he think of me, this man of taste and wealth? He might change his mind about letting me stay, think I'm no good, not to be trusted; he might even ring the orphanage. Yet one lie begets another, a nagging little voice intrudes, where will it all end? He might have read something in the *Times* about the trial, or one of his friends might mention it. It would be much worse if he found out you'd lied to him. Tell him the truth. In a shaky voice, my head held deliberately high, I say, 'I've got none – parents, I mean. I was brought up by the Sisters of Mercy, in Friday Wells, County Cork. They took me in when I was a baby, a few months old. I was abandoned.' There it was, out in the open, and it didn't feel half as bad as I'd expected. 'What you never had, you never miss.'

It was a lie, of course. All my life I've craved a family, one to call my own. Surrogate families like the Molloys are kind, but how can they be the same? Better to have parents, even bad ones; at least you know who you are.

'And sometimes it would be better to have missed what you've had.' Simultaneously we both smile.

I'm still smiling when Brendan turns towards the sound of a voice in the bedroom. He walks to the door. As I follow I can hear Mary Keating: 'If you want to eat breakfast while it's hot, you'd best be coming now.'

At six-thirty p.m. on 12 February 1979 Brendan Fitzgerald's black Mercedes pulls up outside Magenta House. Rose is at the door before me. We face each other on the doorstep.

'Good luck, Kate.' She hugs me, whispering, 'You know where I am if you need me. And there will always be a warm Irish welcome on my mat anytime you want to drop in.'

I hold on to her tight. 'Thanks for everything, Rose.' I long to tell her I'll never forget the kindness she's shown me for the past six weeks, and that when I'm rich I'll pay off the mortgage on Magenta House and give her a big fat allowance, so she never has to work again.

I begin to walk down the path, my feet leaden. As I turn, using both her hands, she blows a theatrical kiss; it makes me chuckle and I do the same. The driver is out of the car and holding open the passenger door. Before I step into the car I hear Rose shout, 'Don't ever look back, Kate.'

It is exactly seven-thirty when Mrs Keating opens the door of 91 Elgin Crescent. I know because as I step inside I can see the time on the grandfather clock in the hall.

I make a mental note of the time and date of my move,

so as never to forget. Brendan leaves the house an hour after my arrival, apologizing most profusely for leaving me on my first night, but he has a pressing supper engagement with friends that he can't cancel. I'm secretly pleased to be left alone. Mrs Keating makes me a fish pie, followed by chocolate-chip pudding with lashings of cream. It sends me, much to her amusement, into loud dramatic raptures. After supper I run a deep bath, filling it to the brim with oils. Submerging myself up to my neck in bubbles, I stay there until the water turns cold. Then wrapped in a big fluffy towel I parody Marilyn Monroe's breathy voice, surprising myself how much I sound like her: 'I wanna be loved by you, just you, and nobody else but you . . .' I sing, whirling round and round the room until I'm so dizzy I have to stop. I long to slip into an ankle-length nightdress, the shimmering will-o'-the-wisp type, and pose in front of the full-length mirror like I'd seen film stars do in the movies.

Naked, I slide between white linen sheets. I notice the pillowcases are monogrammed with a tiny blue F in the right corner. I've never slept on linen before, it feels cool next to my warm skin. Lying on my back, I let my head sink into the soft down. Contemplating my good fortune, I decide that at long last the good Lord has seen the error of his ways and is through punishing me. In my head I make a solemn pledge: I will work my fingers to the bone, all hours that God sends, to repay Brendan Fitzgerald for the opportunity and his kindness. I'm determined he won't regret it. My eyes scan the ceiling. There's not a crack or blemish visible, but I'm aware of something missing. A moment later I realize what. No Lord on the Cross dripping blood, no crucifix, no religious icons of any description adorn the room. Come to think of it, I haven't seen any in the entire house. It's possible Brendan isn't a Catholic, he'd said his father was of English descent, so perhaps he's a Protestant, or worse still a heathen.

Leaning across the bed I switch off the bedside lamp, then, lying very still, my head lost in folds of duck down, I close my eyes and wait for the first piece of Father Steele to appear. But nothing happens. No image, no voice, no Declan. For the first time in I can't remember how long he hasn't come to my bed. I can't decide if this is a good thing or bad. I conclude it's good. It means I'm moving on, leaving my past behind. Perhaps he can't visit me in the house of a heathen. I smile. Well, so be it.

I'm slipping into sleep when he does eventually appear. He's dressed exactly the same as when I first laid eyes on him, but his hair is different, wet and scragged back from his face. I run my fingers through it, then pull him down on top of me. The coarseness of his soutane is tickling my naked belly and the blood is rushing to my head and groin. As I open my legs and slip my fingers inside, my thoughts are of him, and how pleased I am he hasn't left me.

The next morning I'm woken by an insistent knocking. I sit bolt upright, a feeling of disorientation gripping me. My brain in a fog, I stumble to the door, opening it to see an unsmiling Mrs Keating gripping a breakfast tray. She hands it to me.

'I think in future we'd best be setting the alarm. Mr Fitz is getting what you might call uneasy. He's not used to being kept waiting.'

'What time is it?'

'Gone ten. He's an early riser, so he's been pacing about the studio since eight-thirty. If I was you, I'd put a spurt on.'

'Why didn't he wake me?'

'I suggested that at nine, but him being a gentleman and all said you might need your sleep. Young people do, he says to me.'

'I'll get a move on. Could you – would you tell Mr Fitzgerald I'll be with him in five minutes?'

'I'll say ten, to be on the safe side, no point in aggravating him further,' she says before turning on her heel and marching down the hall.

Stuffing a slice of toast in my mouth I bound to the bathroom, pee (no time for a shower), finish the toast and dress in my painting dungarees and black T-shirt. A quick swill of my teeth, a gulp of orange juice, and I'm racing upstairs towards the studio in less than ten minutes.

I arrive panting. 'I'm so sorry I'm late, Mr Fitzgerald, I overslept. I've never slept in such a comfortable bed in my life – and so peaceful.'

He's standing close to the window, his long neck stretched as he gazes out. His head turns. 'I assume everyone wakes at dawn as I do. I've never needed a lot of sleep, even as a child. Hyperactive, my mother said. I think not. Inquisitive is better: I can't bear to think I'm missing something.' Then with his finger crooked he says, 'Come here, Kate.'

I cross the room to stand next to him. 'First and foremost, I think you should call me Brendan. Mr Fitzgerald makes me feel old. I am old, but I certainly don't admit to it.'

'How old are you, Mr Fitz . . . I mean, Brendan?'

'First rule of life: never ask anyone over twenty-one their age, especially women. It's a closely guarded secret, but if you promise never to reveal it to another living soul.'

'I promise.' I make the sign of the cross on my breast. 'Cross my heart and hope to die.'

'I was born on the tenth of November 1931. My God, it sounds worse when I say it like that; forty-seven is preferable.'

'That's not old.'

He laughs, his pointed ears sticking out of his hair pixie-like. 'You know how to charm an old man.'

He moves behind me and places his hands on my shoulders. Dropping his head close to my neck, he says, 'What do you think of that?'

I study the painting propped against the wall and, borrowing adjectives I'd heard Father Steele use, I say, 'Dramatic, powerful, intoxicating?'

'Do you know the artist?'

'El Greco?'

'Right. Does his hand clutch at your heart, Kate?' I can feel his nails biting into my collar bone.

'No, but he does take me to a place I'm sometimes afraid to go. He puts me in touch with my dark side.'

'Do you have a dark side, Kate?'

I move my head and he loosens his grip. 'Don't we all?'

Reflective for a moment, he strokes his goatee. 'Except, some would say, God. Yet he can be as ruthless as any mortal.'

I make no comment but have already decided I like Brendan Fitzgerald – a lot.

At the sound of the door opening we both turn simultaneously. It's Mrs Keating with coffee and digestive biscuits. She sets the tray down on top of a long drawing board. As she crosses the room her low heels click on the boarded floor. She stops in front of me and speaks to Mr Fitzgerald as if I wasn't there.

'Must get this one an alarm clock.'

'You can be her alarm, Mrs Keating.'

Her lips curl inwards and I long to tell her not to do that because it makes her otherwise pleasant face look very ugly. I wouldn't dare, but I sense that there will come a time when I won't be able to contain the urge to say something to this prickly woman that I might regret. For the first time since she entered the room I notice she's carrying some mail.

With a curt bob of her head she hands me two envelopes. 'Mrs Tremayne asked me to give you these. Apparently they were forwarded from a Mr Shaunessy's office.

She also asked if she could see you for five minutes, Mr Fitz. Said it was very important.'

Focused on the letters, I'm vaguely aware of Mr Fitzgerald's irritated grunt and nod absently when he says, 'Will you excuse me for a few minutes, Kate?'

I wait until they have left the room before sitting on the sofa near the window. The small blue envelope I instantly know is from Bridget. When I'd first arrived in Dublin I'd tried to visit her only to be told she'd been moved to Century House – a reform school in Limerick. I feel a beat of guilt for not having written and promise myself I'll write this evening. I don't recognize the writing on the large brown envelope.

On opening it I can scarcely contain my joy when I see Father Steele's signature at the bottom of the page.

My dearest Kate,

I do hope this letter finds you well – indeed, I hope it finds you. Mr Shaunessy was the only person I could think of who might have a forwarding address. On Boxing Day, after you left, I felt consumed with remorse. I'm very sorry I defaced your portrait. It provoked an emotional conflict in me, and this made me angry. To destroy a beautiful piece of art is a crime in itself, but to destroy something that had so clearly been executed and given in love is unforgivable. It saddens and alarms me that I could do such a thing and begs the question, am I ever to become a good priest? Not for all the world would I hurt you, my lovely Kate, nor would I have ever wished us to part on such bad terms.

Soon I'll be leaving to take up a missionary post in Argentina. My love of all things Latin may well persuade me to stay in South America.

So it's possible we'll never meet again. Yet I feel,

*deep in my heart, that we will. Meanwhile I want
you to know that you are in my thoughts.*

*Every day I ask Our Lord to keep you safe and to
guide you on your long journey, because I think we
both know that you are destined to travel far. Take
care, my dear Kate, and may God bless you all the
days of your life.*

Yours,

Father Declan Steele

*PS Mother Peter came to see you on New Year's
Eve. She asked if I could forward a package to you.
I've no idea what it contains. I hope it's good news.*

A dry sob catches in the back of my throat. Breathing
deeply I rummage in the bag. My fingers close around a
small package. Inside is a tiny bracelet. Tarnished black
and misshapen, as if had been lying under something
heavy. With it is a note tied with blue ribbon. I read:

*You arrived with it, I think it fitting you should
leave with it.*

I hold the bracelet up in the light from the window.
I'm still holding it aloft when Brendan returns. Hurriedly
I try to hide it, but I'm too late.

'Someone sent you a gift?'

'Sort of,' I say, closing my hand around the bracelet.

Sitting down next to me he asks, 'May I see?'

I don't want Mr Fitzgerald, almost a total stranger, to
delve into my past but feel churlish refusing. Slowly I
open my fingers. The bracelet lying in my palm like a
twisted black eel.

'What is it?'

'I think it's a christening bracelet. My christening
bracelet.'

Picking it out of my palm he says, 'Who sent it to you?'

'One of the sisters at the orphanage.'

'Why, I wonder, didn't she give it to you before you left?'

I shrug. 'Search me. I've no idea what goes on in their heads. They are not like normal people, to be sure. Many times I asked God and anyone else who would listen to explain the nuns' actions.'

'Did you get any answers?'

'Not from God.'

Brendan, still looking at the twisted metal, comments, 'That doesn't surprise me.' Then, 'Stay here, I'm going to get Mrs Keating to clean it. I think it's inscribed.'

Ten minutes later he returns with a triumphant, 'I was right.' Standing next to the window he says, 'Look here.'

The bracelet, clean and gleaming like a freshly minted sixpence, is inscribed *Anne – 28 February 1962* close to the clasp.

He's speaking: 'Definitely not Irish, and I doubt English. In my opinion it was made overseas. Canada or America would be my guess.' Brendan squints. 'Worth about fifty pounds.'

'I don't want to sell it. To me it's priceless.' I reach up and take the bracelet from his grip. Cradling it in the palm of my hand, I fight the urge to cry. 'I was born in March not June, and my Christian name is Anne.'

'How can you be certain the bracelet belongs to you?'

I offer no explanation. 'I'm absolutely certain,' I conclude with passionate conviction. 'And if it takes me the rest of my life, I'm determined to find out who I am.'

Scrutinizing me intently, Brendan says, 'Do you think you could manage to do a bit of painting in between?'

'Try and stop me.'

Chapter Ten

Five Years Later

'Excited, Kate?'

'Excited is an understatement, Brendan, ecstatic would be more appropriate.'

Looking me up and down in appreciation, as if admiring a beloved daughter, Brendan says, 'You look beautiful. I think the St Laurent was a very good choice.'

'You chose it.'

'If I'd left it to you, Kate, God only knows what sort of outfit you'd have turned up in.'

I scowl petulantly.

Firmly he says, 'Here in New York things like that matter.'

'I'm twenty-two, Brendan. I can get away with funky, and it only matters if it matters to me.'

'A black tuxedo with silk vest is elegant and sexy. My mother always dressed impeccably, and she swore no one could cut a pair of trousers like Yves.'

'In that case, why don't you wear the St Laurent?'

He winks. 'I'd love to, darling, but not in public.'

Crossing the room I lift the heavy drape to look out on the Manhattan skyline. 'It's awesome.'

Joining me, Brendan says, 'You're right. It is awesome. A city with a dual personality. On the one hand galvanizing and generous; on the other, ruthless and unforgiving. I was a similar age to you, a little older, perhaps, when I first came here. I'll never forget the adrenaline rush I experienced when I saw the skyline for the first time – I felt I'd arrived at the centre of the civilized world. I was in many ways an innocent, a sophisticated innocent. Of course I thought of myself as an urbane man about town, my head brimming with what I considered to be inspired ideas, most of which came to nothing.' He takes my hand in his. 'Unlike you, I wasn't staging my first major US exhibition.' He sighs. 'I wish.'

Squeezing his hand, I murmur, 'I couldn't have done it without you.' I blink, my mind racing back five years, then slowly recalling the commitment it took to be standing here tonight on the eve of my first major exhibition. 'You were the driving force, Brendan. Remember when I wanted to go out to discos, and you warned me that if I did I'd never get up to work the following day? Do you remember the night I went out with that Sean bloke, and got very drunk and told you to fuck off?' I smile, but he can't see my face.

Leaning over my shoulder, he plants a kiss on my neck. 'I remember everything. You naturally want to be part of your peer group. But you are not like them, not one of the pack; you are special, and I truly believe your sort of talent would have been spotted with or without me.'

'Don't underestimate your contribution. You've bullied, cajoled, praised, criticized and kicked ass. You've driven me both to distraction and my first exhibition. I'll never be able to repay you, Brendan.'

'Money is always acceptable.'

I'm smiling. 'If it were that easy . . .'

There's a knock on the door and a moment later a waiter enters the suite with a tray holding an ice bucket containing a bottle of champagne. 'Shall I open it, sir?'

With a dismissive wave Brendan says, 'I'll do it.' Then to me: 'Sorry, it's such a cliché, but I can think of nothing better than a glass of vintage Krug to wet the baby's head, so to speak.'

I giggle as the cork pops and flies through the air. He pours, and hands me a glass. 'A toast to Kate O'Sullivan

– talented, resourceful, and beautiful. The world, my dear Kate, is yours for the taking. Make sure you get a big slice.'

The Carlyle Hotel where we are staying is almost directly opposite the gallery venue on Madison and 72nd. It's an unusually warm night for mid October and I don't need a wrap or coat. As Brendan and I cross the street I can hear my pulse thump in my ears and feel my legs buckle. Brendan supports me. 'You all right?'

I inhale deeply. 'OK. A bit nervous.'

'It's going to be fine. In fact, it's going to be more than fine, it's going to be a resounding success.'

Brendan, as usual, is right. As I walk through a panel of smoked glass into the shimmering white glare of the gallery, the last five years of my life line the walls: mainly portraiture, but also some large abstract pieces Brendan had encouraged in the last two years. I can think of only one thing: I wish my parents could have been here to share this with me.

Susie Simons, my agent, is standing in front of a painting called 'Rose of Magenta', the portrait I'd done of Rose Nolan before I left her to live with Brendan. It has been likened to Lautrec. I'm not sure whether to be flattered or dismayed; he isn't my favourite artist. Deep in conversation with a hungry-faced young man who looks like a fellow artist, Susie does not notice Brendan and me immediately. When she does, she wastes no time in extracting herself to move in our direction.

'The dragon approaches. I'm going to make my escape,' Brendan mutters and with a light touch on my arm moves towards a waiter bearing a tray of champagne.

Susie, according to Brendan, is typical of a breed of ambitious, driven New York women who know exactly what they want and rarely fail to get it. 'Minus a set of balls, but apart from that little to differentiate Susie from her male counterpart,' he'd commented after his first meeting with her.

Not long after I'd signed with Susie, she'd married a man called Nicholas Simons, an influential dealer who had taken her several rungs up the fine art ladder. Two years on and Susie is the head of one of the most influential art agencies in the Western hemisphere.

'Darling Kate, you look divine. Let me guess – Dior?'

I shake my head, mildly irritated that it should matter what designer, if any, I'm wearing. I say, 'Try again.'

'St Laurent.'

'Right.'

'Perfect. But then you would look wonderful in a paper bag, with those long-enough-to-be-continued legs and film-star looks. Rebecca, my PR girl, said you had definite star quality. A joy to work with.' Taking my arm, she leads me across the room. 'There's someone here you have to meet.'

A quick glance over my shoulder confirms Brendan is fine, deep in conversation with a very handsome young man.

Susie moves her lips close to my ear. 'Robert Jansen is an extremely big dealer, very important, he buys a lot of stuff from me for private collectors . . . Robert, darling,' she gushes. 'My protégée, Kate O'Sullivan.'

'Hardly your protégée, Susie. We only met last year.'

'A figure of speech, darling,' she says, smiling insincerely before excusing herself to check on the canapés.

Robert Jansen is tall and lean with the raffish good looks that some women find very attractive. 'I'm delighted to meet you, Kate. I've heard a lot about you from Susie. She said you were very beautiful, and that your work was superlative.'

I can feel it coming, hot at the base of my neck, this curse; my blushing never fails to embarrass me. Dropping my chin I look up at him from under long lashes.

'On both counts she's right.'

I mutter a polite, 'Thank you', and, feeling the heat drain from my cheeks, lift my head to meet his eyes, dull-day grey, deep-set and empty.

'How long have you been painting, Kate? May I call you Kate?'

'I've been painting since I was old enough to hold a brush, and you can call me Kate.'

'You have –' he glances at an abstract I'd painted about six months ago – 'extraordinary talent, and so young.'

'I'm twenty-two and my painting has been prolific for the last five years.'

Glancing at his catalogue, he says, 'I see you had your first exhibition in London at the age of eighteen. Was it successful?'

'Reasonably, but in my opinion it was too soon. Brendan insisted I was ready but in my heart I knew I was still, as an artist, immature. Yet I went along – cursed with the disease of youth, I suppose: over-confidence.'

'Who is Brendan? Don't tell me I have a rival?'

'My tutor and best friend, and the man responsible for getting me this far.'

'Is he here?'

Turning my head, I point to the other side of the room where Brendan is now in conversation with Susie's husband Nicholas.

'Yes. Over there, talking to Nicholas Simons.'

From the corner of my eye I notice Susie plying her way through a knot of people in my direction. A moment later she's next to me saying, 'You mustn't monopolize her, Robert,' in a mummy-to-naughty-son tone.

'I can't think of anything more intoxicating,' he gushes.

Unimpressed by his silken tongue, I can't resist: 'Sure you weren't born in Ireland, Mr Jansen?'

He looks quizzical. 'Why do you ask?'

'It seems to me you've kissed the Blarney Stone.' I grin. 'Several times.'

Clearly confused, he changes the subject. 'How long do you plan to stay in town?'

'Until Saturday.'

He's smiling but it doesn't reach his eyes. 'That gives us three days to renew our acquaintance.'

I can feel Susie's long nails through the fine fabric of my jacket. When I don't reply he directs his attention to Susie. 'Call me tomorrow. I'm interested in several pieces, particularly the large nude.'

I sense he's trying to impress me, and wonder if he'd pay what I considered an astronomical amount of money ($150,000) for the large nude merely to achieve that.

Susie assures me differently. 'Robert loves your work. He's very impressed, thinks you're destined to become very important and highly collectable. He's got a marvellous eye and is rarely wrong. As well as being extremely eligible.' She nudges me in the ribs. 'Not many bachelors like Robert Jansen in this town.'

As we weave through the throng a man turns, hitting my shoulder with his elbow. Champagne spills from his glass on to my sleeve and the back of my hand. Looking genuinely dismayed he pulls a handkerchief from his pocket and begins to dab at my sleeve. 'I'm terribly sorry. I hope I haven't ruined your suit.'

'So you should be,' Susie growls. 'You ought to be more careful.'

Taking his handkerchief I wipe the back of my hand. 'Don't worry about it, it's nothing. A bit of bubbly never killed anyone.'

Obviously relieved, the man grins, showing big square teeth, a gap between the front two big enough to hold a cigarette. I find it attractive.

'Tom Gregson's the name. And you, I assume, are the artist, although I have to say I'd never have recognized you from your photograph.' He points to my image in the catalogue. 'This shows a beautiful woman, similar to a hell of a lot of other beautiful air-headed women: models, film stars, wannabe's. Fish fingers, I call them, not real women.'

Susie butts in. 'I think we can do without your opinion, Tom Gregson. Save it for your column.'

'The girl's got character – what can I say?' To me he adds, 'I'm not coming on to you, miss –' he glances at the catalogue again – 'O'Sullivan. I'm happily married.'

'When it suits you,' Susie snarls.

He glares at her, anger tightening his mouth. 'You've never got over the forgery piece, have you, Susie? Truth always hurts, I'm afraid.'

'I don't think this is the time or the place to discuss any of your downmarket investigative articles.'

Turning his attention to me, he asks, 'Would you say the *New York Times* is downmarket?' Then to a man next to him: 'Do you think the *New York Times* is downmarket?' Then, looking directly at Susie, he snarls, 'Can I quote you on that, Susie?'

It's obvious Tom Gregson and Susie have history. Their barely restrained animosity is building up to a fracas unless someone diffuses it. Susie takes the lead and, ignoring Tom Gregson, she forcibly steers me in the opposite direction.

Not to be deterred he follows and, patting me on the shoulder, says, 'I think your stuff is great. I'd love to buy a piece for my wife's birthday. Since I'm an impoverished journalist, I wonder if you've got a sketch standing around your studio that you'd let go cheap.'

Responding warmly, I say, 'Call me tomorrow at the Carlyle, suite 826. I'll see what I can do.'

Pulling me to one side Susie mutters, 'I can't believe he'd dare ask you in front of me, your agent, for a deal on a painting. It's fucking outrageous. He's scum and, worse, he's cheap.'

I have to retaliate. Susie has of late become very tedious in her possessive control of me and mine. 'He seems very nice – fun and mischievous. Why not ask me? It's not a crime to have a go. Nothing ventured . . .'

'I'm warning you, Kate, stay away from Tom Gregson. He wasn't invited; came with a colleague from *Vanity Fair*, I think. He's an arrogant son of a bitch. I've had dealings with him in the past. He exposed an international forgery ring and implicated me. Sure, I'd bought paintings from one of the dealers – in good faith. Christ, I'd no idea they were fakes! If I had I would have run a mile.'

'Did that come out in the investigation?'

Grudgingly she admits, 'Yes, but he's a fucking journalist and they always have to have an angle. I begged him not to print my name. Believe me, Kate, he's not to be trusted. Don't get involved.'

I'm about to say it's my choice whom I get involved with when someone catches Susie's eye.

'Shit, it's Spencer Cartwright Junior. Seriously old money. Come, Kate darling, you must meet him.' I allow myself to be led across the room and play the social game. With an aching smile, I struggle for small talk and concentrate on improving my networking skills as I long for the exhibition to be over.

Not before time the last guest air-kisses me goodbye at nine-thirty. In the contrasting quiet I stand very still in the centre of the gallery under the glare of the overhead halogen spotlights. I'd been invited to join Brendan and a gaggle of fast-talking effervescent people for dinner at Le Cirque. I'd declined, feigning a headache, and am alone now apart from the caretaker and Susie, who is upstairs in her office calling her driver. I move trance-like through the quiet of the gallery. I stop and stand very still in front of each of my paintings, every one a memory as surely as if I'd drawn them on my heart with indelible pen. I feel exhausted and anticlimactic, a deflated balloon after the party. But more than that I feel very alone.

I'm no closer to knowing who I am; the secret of my birth feels as distant and unattainable as when I lived in the orphanage. My trust fund had paid out as promised at eighteen, and last year at twenty-one, but all attempts at tracing the benefactor had proved fruitless. The day I arrived in New York I'd been to the lawyers who administer my trust fund. Morgan, Morgan & Spencer were unable to tell me any more than Mr Shaunessy. A conspiracy of silence, Brendan had commented, when I returned to the hotel.

Memories of childhood consume me. Characters from my past pop like phantom jacks out of my memory box to taunt me. I hear a mixture of voices, layered one on top of the other, and above the din I hear one clearly, the voice that never leaves me. *Our childhood baggage is merely pawned, to be retrieved or returned to us later in life, in one guise or another.*

He was right. There is no escape and nothing is ever what it seems.

Chapter Eleven

Before daylight I'm woken by an urgent rapping. I stagger to the door, hearing Brendan on the other side. 'Kate, it's me, let me in.'

I yell, 'Give me a minute,' before running to the bathroom to wrap myself in a towelling robe.

As soon as I open the door I know there's something wrong. His face is white, filled with anguish. His tall frame filling the doorway, he says, 'Will you marry me?'

If he'd asked me to accompany him on a trip to the moon I couldn't have been more surprised.

'You're drunk,' is all I can find to say.

'I've never been more sober or more serious in my entire life. Watch me walk a straight line.'

Marching past me he walks up and down the room while I shut the door and stroll into the room.

'What about Liam?'

'What about him?'

'I thought you and he were an item?'

'We were – we are, but to be honest with you, my love, I've had it with men.'

'Liam Hennessy cannot be classified as a man.'

'OK, I've had it with boys. I'm fifty-two. It's time I settled down. And I've decided I want to have a child. What do you say, Kate?'

I'm laughing; it's laughable, the most outrageous thing I've ever heard.

'You're gay, Brendan, or has that slipped your mind? Queer as they come. Bent as a nine bob note. Remember

210

once you said to me you'd rather eat a four-day-old-haddock than a woman?'

His turn to laugh. 'That's why I love you so damn much. You make me laugh. I've never laughed as much with anyone as I do with you.'

'Ditto. But I don't turn you on. If I took my clothes off and made a pass at you now, you'd probably throw up.'

The corners of his mouth curl in disdain. I've seen the expression before, rarely directed at me I might add; it's usually reserved for his sister or a discarded lover.

'Sex, my lovely Kate, is not everything. Lots of married couples do not copulate. There's no reason why we can't have a very good marriage, better even, without sex. Messy business, and complicated at the best of times. Think of the child we might have, with my brains and your beauty.'

'Wait a minute, Brendan: are you accusing me of being stupid?'

'Absolutely not. I was merely painting a pretty picture, and as far as sex is concerned, you'd be free to do as you please. I mean, take lovers if you choose, as long as you're discreet. The same would apply to me, of course.'

'But I can do that now, Brendan, if I choose.'

Regarding me with concentrated intent he says, 'Do you choose, Kate?'

I stammer, 'Sometimes, there have been a few occasions.'

Staring into the middle distance I reminisce. Tim Duval's reputation had preceded him: one of the most influential art dealers in the world, he had an international clientele and galleries in London, Geneva and New York. The first thing that struck me the day he came to look at my work was his eyes: intelligent dark brown pools, the left one flecked with green. I'd warmed to his voice, deep and gurgling as if he were permanently on the verge of laughter. The second time we'd met he'd offered to stage an exhibition of my work. Our third meeting was in London ten months later on the eve of my first exhibition, me as excited as a six-year-old at her first birthday party.

Indignantly I say, 'I had a love affair with Tim Duval.'

Knowingly Brendan nods. 'I thought as much. It was, I must say, pretty obvious at the time.'

'Was it? I was so naïve and gauche. I probably wandered about with it written all over my face.'

'I suppose, in retrospect, it was inevitable. Tim was handsome, intelligent, urbane, well read, well versed in all the things you at the time wanted to learn and understand. You, my sweet, were clothed in a thin coat of sophistication, the fabric so flimsy it gave scant protection to the fragile vulnerability underneath. Any man would have been captivated. Pity he was such a shit, and old enough to be your father.'

'Wrong, Brendan, on both counts. Tim was OK, he treated me well. I was only eighteen, he was thirty-five. The love affair, if you could call it that, was brief. It began in London after the exhibition – predictable, I know – with all the usual clichés: me heady on champagne and adulation, Tim getting off on having discovered the beautiful young artist everyone was raving about. We ended the night in my hotel room drinking more champagne and giggling a lot. To this day I'm sure Tim pretended to be drunk. I seem to remember thinking how sober he was when he undressed me. But I will say he took me in a gentle and gentlemanly way.' Initially penetration had hurt, then, once I'd relaxed, his slow rhythmic thrusting had felt mildly pleasant. On reflection I know I was driven by curiosity rather than desire. But unlike most women who recall their first experience with disappointment or distaste, I enjoyed it, in a detached sort of way. 'Since I've intellectualized the experience I've come to the conclusion it was the power I enjoyed more than the actual act. I didn't achieve orgasm with Tim, nor did I fake it. He never questioned me and seemed quite happy to satisfy himself quickly. But his boredom threshold was very low.'

Brendan grunts, 'No staying power. He's the type who quickly moves on to the next thing. For Tim there would always be a new venture to pursue. I wasn't surprised when it came along in the shape of a New York socialite, that super-rich bitch with more money than sense and her brains between her legs.'

I chuckle. 'The last I heard he'd married an Italian countess and was living in Rome.'

'Is that it then? Tim Duval the one and only lover?'

I thought of all the times I'd made love to Declan Steele in my head, remembering Friday Wells, the cottage, his footsteps on the stairs, his movements in his bedroom only a few feet from where I'd slept, dreaming of him. I blink hard, trying to erase the memory. Beware the murky waters of your past, Brendan had said not long after I'd met him, they may muddy the clarity of the present.

'Kate, are you listening? You look miles away.'

'I am.' Shaking my head, I glance around the suite. The two opposing sofas remind me of Brendan's drawing room where we always sit after supper putting the world and Ireland to rights, usually in that order. Flopping down on the sofa, Brendan makes himself comfortable before crossing his legs at the ankles, his expression inscrutable. I sit down opposite, completely still. My hands are resting in my lap and I'm asking myself the same question I've asked myself a million times before: Why am I still living with Brendan Fitzgerald?

'Do you remember when Bridget was released, and she came to the house for the first time? She was very nervous about meeting you, even though I'd assured her you were not, I quote, "the big intimidating toff" she imagined.'

Brendan nods. 'Yes, I remember how shy she was at first.' He grins. 'That didn't last long.'

'After that first meeting with you, Bridget said she understood why I loved you so much.'

I can see interest spark in his eyes.

'"He's your father." That's what she said. I recall being indignant and dismissing her theory as nonsense.'

'Do you still think it's nonsense?'

'No. I think you are my surrogate father, and that's a very good reason for not marrying you.'

'It could also be a very good reason to marry me.'

Suddenly he looks very old. His eyes seem to fill with a longing – for what, I'm not sure; his youth perhaps. The luxurious taste of freedom and choice.

'Why do you want to marry me? Why can't we stay as we are? I'm very happy. Without you I'd never have achieved the same degree of success and notoriety. People from my background rarely succeed without a support system. Chronically low self-esteem, feelings of inadequacy and self-loathing usually lead them into a life of crime or uselessness. But I got lucky. I got you, Brendan, and my art. I feel protected, secure; not only are you my business partner but you're my best friend. I can't imagine my life without you.'

After a long interval, Brendan says, 'You would have been successful with or without me. Your suffering as a child comes through in your art. Pain works. I'm not being flippant when I say angst channelled positively rarely fails to produce great art. Look at all the great writers and artists, tortured souls most of them. You got rid of some of your demons, but I suspect not all.' He pauses and strokes his beard. 'Daughters leave home, leave their fathers, make a life of their own, sooner rather than later. I think you want to believe I'm a surrogate father, it helps you to cope with the fact that you're not interested in men.'

Hotly I deny his accusation. 'That's not true. I was interested in one man.'

'May I enquire who?'

'It was a long time ago, so long it hardly matters any more.'

As I gaze downwards I can see my hands are trembling. For an instant I'm back in Friday Wells. The room is filled with his presence, his voice booming from the pulpit. My throat is swelling with love. An urge to confess forces the words out. 'A priest, Father Declan Steele.'

Brendan's eyebrows rise. I'd certainly surprised him. 'Where is he now?'

'I've no idea. He went abroad to join an order, on missionary work. South America, I think. I haven't heard from him for years.'

'But you haven't forgotten him?'

I turn to face the wall. 'No.'

Articulating slowly, he lets each word sink in before uttering the next. 'All my life I've wanted to be normal – you know, straight. I despise my sexuality yet cannot deny it. It's hard enough to live in peace with yourself when you don't conform to the sexual norm, but even harder when all your life you've been expected to produce an heir. A few weeks ago I was confronted with something that forced me to acknowledge my own mortality. For a while I was in despair. The uselessness of my life almost overwhelmed me. What had I done? What real achievements? What would I leave behind? I racked my brains but found nothing of any real value, nothing I could put my finger on and say with pride, "I did that." Then it came to me and it made absolute sense. I want a child, Kate, our child.'

I can think of many achievements but hear him out politely, trying to conjure up a vision of Brendan and me living in domestic bliss, of his baby growing in my womb.

Brendan gets up from the sofa and, crossing the room,

pours himself three fingers of whiskey. He knows better than to offer it to me. I loathe the taste and the smell.

'You drink too much.'

'You even nag like a wife.'

Holding his glass with both hands, he takes a sip before returning to his seat. 'You are a very beautiful woman, Kate, and I don't mean just skin-deep. You've got a big heart, much bigger than mine. I think you'd make a wonderful mother. Will you at least think about it?'

I rise and, crossing the space between us, sit down lightly on the sofa next to him. 'Can you remember the night I tried to seduce you?'

'How could I ever forget?'

The scene jumps into my head. 'I'm still embarrassed to talk about it to anyone but you. How stupid, how naïve, trying to seduce a homosexual.'

'Naïve, I accept, but not stupid. Actually I was tempted.'

'What a revelation! You've never admitted that before.'

'You were very beautiful – you still are, and so vulnerable. What I remember most was your skin. Flawless, with a luminous quality that even *you* find hard to capture on canvas, as if slicked with pale gold paint.'

The recollection of going to his bedroom about a year after I'd gone to live at Elgin Crescent is as vivid as if it had happened yesterday. For some time I'd entertained a certain image of myself as a femme fatale. Intent on looking like one, I'd tied my hair up in the kind of a messy knot that I'd seen models wearing in magazines. I'd shaved my pubic hair to a fine golden line, and doused myself in perfume, feeling very decadent when dabbing a little between my legs. I'd bought a sheer black négligé and matching panties. I'd waited until he'd been in bed for about half an hour before slipping noiselessly into his room. It was silent apart from his muted snoring.

From the foot of the bed I'd called his name. After the third time he'd woken and, sitting bolt upright, had immediately pressed the personal attack button. A second later I was on the bed kissing him full on the mouth, enjoying the warmth of his lips pressing against mine and the faint taste of Cuban cigar. I'd deliberately let the robe fall open and was busy peeling back the bedclothes when the alarm bells sounded. Throwing off the bedclothes, Brendan jumped up, shouting for me to go back to my bedroom. Shocked and confused, I'd slipped heavily to the floor.

I'll never forget his angry words. They were like knives jabbing at my heart. 'You're a child, Kate, trying to do a woman's job. Now get back to your own room and get some sleep. And I beg you, don't try to seduce me again.'

I'd fled from the room, my cheeks burning, choking on dry sobs. It wasn't until much later, months later, when Brendan admitted he was gay that I was able to understand and completely forgive him for his rejection.

'You were seventeen, a child, a damaged child; you simply needed to be loved. For the first time in your life someone had shown you consideration and unconditional affection, expecting nothing in return.'

I feign indignation. 'Nothing in return? My God, Brendan, you were relentless. It's a wonder I survived those first eighteen months of nonstop bullying.'

'It was necessary. Remember your first exhibition?'

I groan. 'I wasn't ready.'

'Agreed, it was too soon. Do you also remember weeping in my arms, and the next day refusing to read the reviews and threatening to give it all up?'

'You know the answer to that.'

He finished the remaining whiskey in his glass.

'Yes, I do, Kate. What I don't know the answer to is – will you marry me?'

I can feel the tension in the back of my neck. When I'm stressed it always precedes a headache. With my fingertips I press where it aches and massage in small circular movements.

'I want a real marriage, Brendan.'

'And what, pray, is that?'

'I want the perfect monogamous relationship with a man who loves me, desires me as I do him. You know – like, we'd do it as often and every way we could.'

'But you don't do it, Kate, you've said so yourself. Not in so many words, but you can't hide the truth from me.'

I blush. 'I would if I could find the right partner.'

With a sigh he places his glass on the table to his right. 'Do you really believe such marriages exist? They might for a few years but human nature is such that once passion diminishes – and that is inevitable when coexisting – infidelity kicks in. Men love the chase, my darling Kate, and need to spread their seed. It's a very remarkable woman who can keep a rampant, testosterone-pumping male in between her legs for more than a couple of years.'

'You're an old cynic, Brendan, and you can't talk. What do you know of the joys of women?'

With a long sigh Brendan says, 'I know enough about men, Kate. Face it, the species is not genetically programmed to fidelity. I've spent a lifetime studying the human race, and in my experience men rarely change after marriage. You can afford to criticize me for being a jaded old cynic. You have the magic, the potency of youth, the indescribable joy of feeling invincible.' Again he sighs. 'All that power in the hands of inexperience is terrifying.'

I stand up, stretching to my full height of five feet ten (I've only just stopped growing). I weigh the same as I did at eighteen, and have, so Brendan tells me, improved with age. He has not. Never classically handsome, Brendan when I'd met him had seemed to me a giant of a man. His once thick chestnut hair is now noticeably thinner and threaded with grey, as is his beard. The last few years have seen inches disappear from his backside and cheeks to reappear as chins on his stomach and groin.

I can't imagine making love to him, but then remind myself he doesn't expect me to submit more than a few times. I stroll to the window and sitting on the sill I rest my back against the pane.

A comfortable silence descends between us. I concentrate on positive thoughts of Brendan. His intellect and overwhelming generosity know no bounds. He's taught me so much about life, about myself. Through him I've learnt to confront my past, laugh at myself and to understand a great many things that otherwise might have passed me by. What or where would I be today without him? I know I could do worse.

'You could do worse, Kate.'

'It's uncanny the way we often simultaneously think and say the same things.'

'How about I make you an offer: if you get pregnant in the next six months, will you marry me?'

Avoiding his intense gaze, I look over his left shoulder to the mantelpiece, concentrating on the black hands of an ornate ormolu clock.

'I'll think about it.'

'Don't take too long, Kate, because I haven't much time.'

That makes me glance in his direction, alarmed. 'What do you mean?'

'I wasn't going to tell you, but you've forced it out of me by being so bloody-minded and stubborn. If you'd said yes straight away I could have spared you the truth.'

'Spared me what, for God's sake?'

'The cancer, of course. What else could have persuaded me to take a wife and attempt to have a child? It would have to be something pretty drastic, don't you think?'

Shaken, I take two steps towards him. 'What are you talking about?'

'Bones, dem bones dem bones dem bloody old bones.

Incurable, inoperable, the usual terminal shit. They reckon about eighteen months max.'

I stagger, grabbing the back of the sofa for support. I grip tight, my knuckles gleaming white. 'Oh Jesus, Mary and Joseph – Brendan, I'm so sorry.'

'Don't bring that family into this, and don't be sorry, just be kind and humour an old queen. Say you'll marry me and try to have a baby before it's too damn late. My sperm count is still reasonably high and, I might add, very healthy. I had that tested before asking you. So, Miss Kate, with a bit of luck and skilful manipulation I'm sure we'll manage to get it up once in a while.'

Sadness and sympathy sway me. 'I'll do it – on one condition . . .'

'Anything.'

'I want to get married in a Catholic church.'

'Why, Kate? I thought you'd done with religion.'

'I had – I have, but since I was a little girl I've had a romantic image of a white wedding and when I was sixteen I made a solemn promise to Mr Molloy that if I got married it would be in a Catholic church and he could give me away.'

'Then it has to be the Sacred Heart. From the age of eight until twelve I walked to school past that church, and always admired it. I once asked my mother why we couldn't go to the Sacred Heart on Sunday, and she snapped, "It's a Catholic church and we're Protestants. Remember, Brendan, what I've always told you about Catholics? Hypocrites, the lot of them. Drinking and fornicating, then confessing to put themselves in a state of grace. All over the world they do it, and get away with it. Hypocrites, I tell you, Brendan. Mark my words, boy, have nothing to do with Catholics." ' Brendan winks mischievously. 'Getting married in the Scared Heart will, if nothing else, make the old bat turn in her grave.'

* * *

The flowers arrive at ten, filling the suite with their hot-house fragrance. I've never received so many blooms, not all at the same time. I count a hundred white roses, and a hundred red, plus great sprays of white gypsophila. The card reads: *Enchanted by our brief encounter, Robert.*

I'm still holding the card when the telephone rings.

'Hi, Miss O'Sullivan?'

'Yes. Who's speaking?'

Expecting to hear the caller say Robert Jansen, I'm surprised to hear, 'Tom Gregson, the man who doused you with champagne.'

'Morning, Mr Gregson.'

'Don't sound so disappointed.'

'I'm not. I'm distracted.'

'Have I called at a bad time?'

'No, well, sort of, but it doesn't matter. What can I do for you?'

'Do you remember our conversation last night?'

'About the sketch for your wife? Her birthday, I think you said.'

'Right. Listen, I was a heel to put you on the spot like that, and I just want you to know I'm not broke – well, not completely – and would love to commission one of your less expensive paintings. I can't deal with Susie Simons; quite frankly, she won't speak to me. Relations between us were bad before last night, and now I assume she's got the big guns out for me. I suppose she gave you a glowing run-down on me?'

Carefully I say, 'You're not her favourite person.'

'It's mutual. I'm an investigative journalist and, if I say so myself, a good one. People like me make a lot of enemies. It's par for the course. But my mother adores me, and my wife Jenni. I want to make Jenni happy, and can't wait to see her face when I give her one of your paintings.'

Warming to Tom Gregson I rack my brains for a painting I could let him have reasonably cheaply. 'What sort of study do you want? I've got a work-in-progress land-scape, a Limerick dusk – watercolour. I have to be honest, it's not my best piece, but then my real forte lies in portraiture. When I get back to Ireland I'll send you a photograph and a price.'

'It's a deal. It'll remind me of the old country.'

'Are you of Irish descent?'

'Third generation American. My maternal great-grandparents were from Ireland.'

A red light on the telephone is blinking. 'I've got another call waiting. Can you leave your address at the desk?'

'No problem, and I meant what I said last night about your face having character. There's a lot more to you, Miss O'Sullivan, than meets the eye.'

Perceptive, Mr Gregson, I think to myself. 'It was good meeting you. Now I really have to go.'

'I'll look forward to hearing from you, and thanks. I really appreciate it.'

'I hope your wife will too.'

The other caller was Robert Jansen, who'd left a mes-sage. I return his call but hearing his honeyed tones I feel like throwing up. 'Good morning, Kate, I hope you slept well. Unfortunately, I didn't, couldn't.' When I don't ask him why he tells me. 'I spent the entire night tossing and turning, thinking about you.'

His insincerity is insulting and makes me wonder if this sort of shit actually works for some women. 'Thanks for the flowers. They're very beautiful.'

'A trifle.'

I'm tempted to say, Cut the crap, Robert, and get to the point, until I remember Susie's remarks about him being an important buyer.

'I'm throwing a small intimate soirée here in my apart-ment tomorrow night. Would you like to come?'

'I'd love to, Robert.' I pause. 'But could I bring my fiancé?'

The line is silent. Patiently I wait for him to speak.

'I didn't know you were engaged.'

'It was very sudden. In the early hours of this morning Brendan Fitzgerald asked me to marry him. I accepted. We're to be married early next year.'

Chapter Twelve

It's a hot day, unusually hot for September. A white haze hovers above the church spire, blotting out the blue of the sky and the sun.

We'd planned a spring wedding, but Brendan had become very ill two weeks before and had to be hospitalized. After a three-month intensive course of chemotherapy he'd made a miraculous recovery, and today looks fitter than he's looked for years.

The peel of bells lifts my step and fills me with a great surge of optimism. Have no regrets, I tell myself. I have only one. Bridget is not with me today. She was in America, in Chicago with her husband, Pat Flynn. I recall how angry and hurt I'd been when eighteen months ago I'd received a few scrawled lines from her telling me she and Pat had married in his home town in Connemara. We'd argued a few times about Pat Flynn, and I assumed that was why I wasn't invited to the wedding. It had taken me a long time to come to terms with her rejection after all we'd been through. With Brendan's help I'd found her work as a dental receptionist, and encouraged and supported her through night school to study English. I defy any sister or friend to have felt more pride than I did when she landed a job on the *Irish Times*. Six months later, on assignment, she'd met Pat Flynn, entrepreneur property developer with aspirations far beyond his intellect. I'd disliked him on sight. Having Bridget with me today would have made it complete. Last week, I'd mentioned this to Brendan, who'd said, 'Don't be sad, Kate.

Bridget has moved on. She doesn't need you right now, that's all. She's got a new life, but that doesn't mean she never thinks of you, nor does it mean she won't need you in the future. You two went through hell together. That kind of bond never dies.'

As I enter the church to the organ strains of the wedding march, I smooth the front of my dress, take a deep breath and gently squeeze the arm of Dan Molloy, who'd been overjoyed to be asked to give me away. Gliding slowly down the aisle I recall something Father Steele had said to me a few weeks after I'd started work at his cottage: 'Never have regrets. Mistakes are important; we learn from them and move on.'

Cheered by this I concentrate all my attention on Brendan, his head held high, his straight back neatly encased in grey lightweight wool. When I reach his side he turns to me with a smile but not with his usual confidence. He's tentative and just a little tremulous and I know he's nervous. He mouths the words, 'You look beautiful,' and instantly I'm pricked with affection for him and wish with all my heart it was passion.

The organ ceases, the congregation sit and the voice of the priest fills the quiet of the church.

At the sound of his voice I feel the blood slowly draining from my face. I can hear my pulse bang under the Alice band holding my veil and I'm positive everyone must be able to hear the thundering of my heart. Letting my head drop to my chest I cast my eyes down. I can't look into the face that has lived in my head since I was fifteen years old.

I blame him, the man upstairs. Clearly he's not finished with me yet. This I assume is my punishment for not visiting him for the last few years.

My legs are paralysed and I think I'm going to faint.

Yesterday Father Malone was rushed to hospital suffering with acute peritonitis. Brendan had mumbled something to me about a new priest who was taking over from

Father Malone when he retired at the end of the year.

In my head I ask God, How could you do this to me? Married by the only man I've ever loved to a man I'll never love in the true sense of the word?

To avoid looking at Father Steele I concentrate on the crown of an altar boy's head; his black hair is slicked flat with gel. As the priest begins the service I keep my eyes down. When it comes to the wedding vows I can feel Father Steele's eyes on me, burning into my flesh, and I can feel my cheeks colour.

'Do you, Brendan Francis Fitzgerald, take this woman, Kate O'Sullivan, to be your lawfully wedded wife?'

Brendan's big voice sounds small in the vastness of the church as he replies.

When Declan addresses me I keep my eyes fixed on Brendan. 'And do you, Kate O'Sullivan, take this man, Brendan Francis Fitzgerald, to be your lawfully wedded husband?' I'm convinced his voice falters on my name but I'm in such turmoil I probably imagined it.

Brendan's hand shakes as he lifts the ring from the bible, and mine in turn trembles uncontrollably when he places it on my finger.

When Father Steele pronounces us man and wife Brendan gestures with his eyes in the direction of the priest. As I turn to face Declan the blood rushes to my head and for a couple of seconds my heart stops beating.

The first thing I notice is how much he's aged. The smooth patina of youth has been replaced by a lined yet none the less handsome face. A lived-in face, Brendan would say, one that's seen a bit of life.

I calculate his age: he must be at least thirty-six or -seven. He's smiling the same lazy smile I remember so well. The air, laden with the scent of gardenia and incense, is heady. A wedge of sunlight drives through the dust-veiled window above the nave, igniting the crown of his head. In that instant the church empties and there are only Declan and I. I'm back in Friday Wells, in his cottage, my heart galloping as his arms entwine around my waist; the world outside is an empty canvas.

Gently tugging at my arm, Brendan leads me by the hand to the sacristy for the signing of the register. I'm drowning in memories so vivid that I'm almost consumed with the need to be alone with Father Steele.

Keeping a tight grip on Brendan's hand I go through the motions. I imagine I'm an actress on a set signing the register, smiling serenely, behaving as if nothing untoward has happened. I even manage to thank Declan for conducting the service. Brendan chats amicably to Father Steele and I learn he'll be taking over the parish in three months' time.

Brendan and I walk down the aisle hand in hand. With a smile and a nod I acknowledge Rose Nolan, peeping out from under her huge flowered straw hat, Lizzy Molloy and her mother, Brendan's sister Madeleine, and a few of Brendan's close friends. Inwardly I admire the gardenia garlands looped at the entrance to every pew. I'd thought this an extravagance but Brendan had insisted.

'I want you to have your favourite flowers everywhere, in profusion. No expense spared. It's not every day of the week a jaded old homosexual marries a beautiful, talented, sensitive, generous, remarkable young woman.'

When Brendan has his mind set, nothing and no one can change it. I call it stubborn, he thinks determined is a better adjective. He'd thrown himself into planning our wedding with such enthusiasm it was heartwarming to watch. Every detail had to be perfect, from the extravagant reception for fifty in the garden at Elgin Crescent to the honeymoon in Capri. I'd tried to help but he'd insisted it was his gift to me. Detached, I'd observed from the side-lines, an outsider withdrawing by slow degrees as the day had approached.

Inhaling deeply I fill my nostrils with the scent of

gardenia and, suddenly overwhelmed, I feel a sob rise into my throat. Fighting tears, I think of all those new brides who cry on their wedding day, but for most of them I imagine it is out of happiness.

Pretend to be happy, I tell myself, for Brendan's sake. He's a good man and he deserves to be appreciated.

As we step out of church I catch sight of Father Steele leaving by the side door of the sacristy. I harness an overwhelming urge to call his name, run to his side, fall into step next to him just like old times.

'Kate, this way!' a paparazzo photographer shouts. I smile and blink as a flash explodes. When I open my eyes Father Steele is out of sight.

'Look this way, Kate.' It's the official photographer. 'Look at your husband and smile.'

When I face Brendan he's beaming brightly; too brightly, it's not natural.

I lick my lips, fix a smile and hold the pose for the next fifteen minutes like a model at a photo shoot.

Strolling towards the waiting car, I throw my bouquet. It whistles through the air to land in the arms of Lizzy Molloy, who, with a whoop, clutches it possessively, tight to her breast like a new-born infant.

As the camera shutter clicks for the final time I think of how in years to come I'll look back on these images with deep regret. Not regret for marrying Brendan, just regret for not being brave enough to face the truth. I'm in love with another man.

'Bless me, Father, for I have sinned.'

I hear a sharp intake of breath, then his voice. It's chocolate-sweet to my ears. My heart soars; I was beginning to think he'd changed diocese. Twice a week for the last six, since I'd returned from my month-long honeymoon, a honeymoon spent counting the days and the hours until my return to Dublin and the hope of seeing

Father Declan Steele. I'd been coming to confession, and recently had ran out of hope as well as sins.

'Tell me about it, child.'

I long to flatten my palm against the grille, to feel his breath touch my skin.

'I've married a man, a good man, but I'm in love with another.'

I detect a slight tremor when he says, 'We can love many people in different ways. That's not a sin.'

'My thoughts are sinful, Father . . .' I wait but there is no response. Again I say, 'My thoughts are sinful, Father. I can't live with the way I think about this other man. It's not right or proper.'

The air is thickly layered with silence. There's not a movement nor a rustle; I can't even hear his breathing. At last he speaks, his words filling me with an indescribable sense of relief.

'You must tell me about it, Kate.'

'I've loved the other man since the first day I saw him, when I was fifteen years old. Most people would say I was a child, what did I know of love? The point is, they were right. I knew nothing of love, nothing at all. I'd never experienced it until that day. At first I thought it was affection I sought, fatherly, or even brotherly affection; someone to need me, care for me, just to be there. But soon I realized it went deeper, much deeper. I wanted this man with every part of my being. I tried to think of ways to please him, to gain his attention, to make him laugh, to bask in his pleasure. At night in bed I longed for his body lying naked next to mine, skin on skin, his touch, our bodies connecting, his breath in my mouth. I thought the longing would cease, I thought time would erase his memory, but no, still he haunts me, still he comes to me night after . . .'

'Stop it, Kate! Stop it!'

Pushing my face an inch from the grille that separates

us I hiss, saliva spraying, 'I can't stop it, Father, because it won't go away. Help me! For God's —'

I watch his mouth form the words: 'Step outside the confessional.'

I do as he bids. Standing a few feet apart we stare at each other, the church melting into dark shadow. I can read nothing in his eyes, yet know he must be able to see the naked longing in mine.

'I think we should take a walk.'

I nod in agreement, following him out of church. Silently we walk the perimeter of the church, not stopping until we reach a gate at the north end of the graveyard. Father Steele opens it and I follow, falling in beside him on a footpath leading to a block of flats. At the end of the path, instead of walking past the flats he turns right and heads towards the centre of town.

'Where are we going?'

'To my house.'

'Is it far? My car is parked near the church.'

'No, five minutes' walk.'

We fall silent again, not speaking until he places a key in the door of a small Georgian terraced house.

'How long have you lived here? It's only a mile from where I live.'

'Two years.'

'Two years,' I mutter, and think, Two years of living around the corner from the love of my life.

As I enter the narrow hall I smell furniture polish and onions. A voice drifts from the rectangle of an open door at the end of the hall, 'Is that you, Father?'

'It's myself, Mrs Denihan.'

'You're back early. Will you be wanting your supper now?'

'In a short while.'

A clatter of pans precedes, 'It's my yoga class tonight so I have to be away by seven.'

230

The door directly to his left is slightly ajar; with the toe of his shoe he pushes it open. 'Come in here, Kate.'

We enter a small L-shaped room panelled from floor to ceiling in light oak. A desk occupies one wall. I gasp as my eyes rest on the portrait I'd painted of Declan; it is hanging above an original stone fireplace on the opposing wall. One deep bay fronts the street where a streetlight gleams in the melting dusk.

Forcing his words through gritted teeth he utters, 'Take a seat.'

I sit stiffly on the edge of a small sofa, resting my hands neatly in my lap. Filled with nervous anticipation, I feel like I'm in a doctor's waiting room. Father Steele sits facing his desk. He flicks through a couple of letters, then with a deep sigh swings his chair round to face me. Still with polite stiffness he asks, 'How are you, Kate?'

During the walk to his house, I'd decided if I got close enough to talk to him on an intimate level I'd tell him exactly how I felt. I'd started in the confessional, now I had to finish. I will myself to tell him how it was – and still is – for me.

'Do you want to know the truth, Father?'

Instinctively I know he's lying when he comments, 'Of course.'

Everything about him reeks of sanctimonious insincerity. The contrived poise of his body language did not for a moment fool me, or his polite formality. He was, as usual, wearing armour.

'Or would you rather I went away, quietly, and left you alone, Father?'

'The truth?'

I nod.

'OK, Kate, you asked for it.' Sighing deeply he knots his fingers and his knuckles make a loud cracking sound. 'The priest in me wants to banish you from my life. You represent temptation and warmth, affection and joy. All the human emotions men and women enjoy together.'

I seize the moment. 'But what about the man in you?'

I see his body stiffen and a nerve begins to jump in his left temple. 'That's the dilemma. We are at odds, the man and the priest. It's an ongoing conflict, and you, Kate, are at the centre. When I was ordained I gave myself to God. I embraced celibacy with zeal. It was, at the time, no great sacrifice for what I believed I would receive in return. My life would be full, I'd live not like other men but on a higher spiritual plane. I'd been chosen, or so I thought. Back in Friday Wells I felt strongly attracted to you but the battle was easily won. You were an innocent, a sixteen-year-old child in my care. I swear I would never have taken advantage of you then.'

'Are you absolutely certain?'

Evading the question he says, 'It wasn't obvious, until you moved into the cottage, that you were infatuated with me. I made light of it, telling myself that lots of young girls fixated on older men. You, I believed, needed a surro-gate father figure, and I was more than happy to cast myself in that role. That was until you gave me the paint-ing of yourself, and I realized how much you wanted me to desire you. If you hadn't left at that point, I would have insisted you did. We were living in close proximity, and your physical presence had started to become a con-stant temptation. Have you any idea how enticing you are?' I'm blushing as he goes on without waiting for a reply. 'As you are aware, the day before your wedding, Father Malone was rushed to hospital and I was forced to take the service. It's highly irregular to conduct a wedding ceremony without having met the couple, but the circum-stances were extreme so I went ahead. I was shocked to see your name on the register. But not as shocked as when I saw you in church. You looked very beautiful. You were a beautiful child, Kate, but nothing compared to the woman. As I watched you glide down the aisle I felt my breath being sucked out of my body ... and do you know what I thought?'

Standing up, he moves a couple of feet, stopping in front of the fireplace. 'It should have been me you were marrying.' A trickle of sweat furrows his brow. As he wipes it, he sees his hand is trembling. 'God forgive me.'

'Why should he forgive you? You've done nothing wrong. You're responsible for your actions, but not your thoughts. I'm sure he understands. I doubt you're the first priest to be tempted.'

His eyes roll in exasperation. 'I don't think you fully understand, Kate. I'm an ordained priest, a servant of God. The very fact that I entertain lustful thoughts is wrong. It threatens everything I've strived to achieve, makes a mockery of my vow of abstinence.'

'I believe you need to understand and recognize this for what it is, Father. God, if you'll forgive the cliché, works in mysterious ways. He's thrown me in your path twice. To test you? Or to make you realize the church is not your natural habitat? How often have I heard you express your frustration and anger at the inner mechanisms of a Church you believe to be archaic and riddled with bigotry and fear? Has it ever occurred to you that you were destined for another life?'

He shouts, 'Never,' with such violence it alerts me to the fact that I've prodded a raw nerve. Swiftly I change the subject.

'What did missionary work teach you?'

'Nothing I didn't already know. Deprivation; death; men, women and children dying and maimed simply for lack of the things we take for granted. The pointlessness of it all was very hard to bear, the helplessness even harder. And what of you, Kate? I've read about your success. It doesn't surprise me. You had talent, and the extra ingredient that bakes the winning cake.'

'I just want to say, my childhood taught me several

things. The most important was that if you want something badly enough, there is only one person who can make it happen: yourself. I'm lucky I was given a gift, so in that respect for me it's been easier. I came to Dublin after leaving Friday Wells. I secured a loan of five thousand pounds, enough to get me started. I enrolled at art college, and worked nights and weekends as an artist's model, doing life classes. That's how I met Brendan Fitzgerald, a very wealthy man, with a lifelong love of the arts. He became my benefactor.' I notice a slight rise of Declan's eyebrows and jump to Brendan's defence. 'Our relationship was entirely professional. We lived together, in separate rooms, and eventually became business partners and devoted friends. I found my surrogate father in Brendan Fitzgerald. Our relationship was never sexual.'

'With a woman like you, I find that hard to believe.'

'Let me finish before I address that. Brendan Fitzgerald is a good man, one of the best. Since we met in 1979 he's been my life. My mentor, best friend, business partner, father and now husband. I adore him as he does me, but our marriage is one of convenience.'

'What do you mean, Kate?'

'Brendan is a homosexual. I agreed to marry him and have his child.'

'Why?'

A great sadness engulfs me. 'Brendan is dying. He wants to leave something behind. He's given me so much, how could I refuse? When I first left Friday Wells I thought I'd forget you, along with all the other memories that place held for me. I managed to bury most of the ghosts, and with the passage of time the images have got clouded. My work takes me all over the world. London several times a year, New York and latterly to the Far East. For some reason the Japanese and Hong Kong Chinese are going crazy for my paintings. A few years ago I had a brief love affair which lasted less than three months. I've been celibate since. Brendan jokes about me not liking men, he's even suggested I'm gay. Not true on both counts. I've been waiting, patiently waiting, for someone to make me feel the way I do right now. I ache in here –' I touch my heart – 'and in here . . .' my hand drops to my groin.

For a long moment he concentrates his gaze on my hand. I know he's tormented but I don't care. I've waited years, more than I care to count, for him and I can't wait any longer. When he lifts his head I can see undisguised lust gleaming from his eyes. A beat of triumph throbs in my chest.

'I want you to go, Kate.'

I take a step towards him. 'You know that's not true.'

Turning his back he places both hands on the mantelpiece and lets his head drop between his arms. The rounded haunch of his shoulder blades is clearly defined under the fine summer-weight soutane. They act like magnets to draw my hands to his upper body. It shudders under my touch. Encouraged, I move closer, resting against him, my head between his shoulder blades, my lips mouthing his name over and over again.

'We have to stop this, Kate. I'm an ordained priest. We have to stop.'

Ignoring his pleas, I encircle his waist and, standing on tiptoe, I brush the back of his neck with my lips. He shudders again, uttering, 'God forgive me, God forgive me.'

Quickly he turns and, caught off guard, I'm totally unprepared for my first encounter with Declan Steele the man. He looks different, almost unrecognizable, tautmouthed, wild-eyed and slightly deranged, and for a fleeting moment I regret having pushed him to this point of no return. His gaze is white hot. 'I want you, Kate, I've always wanted you. That's why I left Ireland. To get away from you. I thought if I put enough distance between us

I'd forget this madness, this ... lust.' He spits out the word in disgust. 'I gave myself to God, all my passion, my love is reserved for him. I thought I'd got rid of your image until I saw you in church.' Now he's shaking uncontrollably. 'Help me, Kate,' he pleads.

'What can I do?'

'Walk away, out of my life, and don't look back. Go to your husband, have his child. Do it now, if you care about me, do it, please, Kate. Just go.'

A little silence is broken by a rap on the door, then the housekeeper's voice from the hall: 'I have to leave soon, so do you want me to serve your supper now, Father?'

Striding across the room he throws open the door. 'Perfect timing, Mrs Denihan. Mrs Fitzgerald and I had just finished our business. I'll see Mrs Fitzgerald out and then I'll be right with you. Can't be keeping you from your yoga class, can we?'

He smiles at the housekeeper and holds it as he turns to me. 'Good to see you again, and I do hope you and Mr Fitzgerald will be very happy. Can you see yourself out?'

Chapter Thirteen

It was Brendan who wanted to come to the English coast. He said he liked the cry of the gulls (Irish gulls didn't sound the same), the smell of salt and seaweed, and fish and chips from newspaper. Happy memories of bucket-and-spade holidays spent near Brixham in South Devon. It was spring with the promise of summer warm in the air; a whitish mist blots out the sun when we step out of the taxi in front of the ivy-clad Grayshott Manor, a seventeenth-century vicarage once owned by friends of his mother. She'd spent many happy times there before he was born and when several years later it had come on the market she'd persuaded her husband, who detested all things English, to buy it. It was a house of crafty beauty; I understood immediately how it must have bewitched Brendan's mother. When Brendan was eighteen his mother sold it to a couple who had converted it to a country house hotel. Fortunately it had lost none of its romanticism to faux architecture and twee furnishings. Brendan had reserved a suite in the west wing, adjacent to where his mother had slept. His father had only come once, loathed it, and vowed never to set foot in the house again.

After checking in we stroll around the grounds, which are bordered on three sides by warm forests of elm and beech. Splashes of daisies in great clumps litter the lawn next to thick meadows of yellow grass that sweep down to rocky paths curving away to an unknown destination. We take a path downhill; the sea enters our nostrils and ears.

Brendan, more animated than he'd been in recent weeks, chortles, 'I was the boy wizard of Grayshott. Master of great schemes, inventor of the most outrageous adventures. A typical ten-year-old scamp. I drove my sister to distraction, after all I was the arch wizard and Madeleine had to obey or suffer. She was a sickly girl, with white skin and rat-tailed hair. I longed for a brother, or a sister like Charlotte who lived in Grayshott Lodge. She was a tomboy who called herself Charlie. Charlie was fearless, as strong as me and never bothered about getting dirty or scratched. She was two years older than me but seemed very happy to be my assistant in sorcery, and together we hatched spells and went off on mysterious escapades. I remember when I was about twelve, coming to Grayshott to find her gone. I was very angry. I kicked Madeleine and didn't speak to my mother for days because she hadn't told me Charlotte's family had moved abroad.'

As we begin to descend towards the sea Brendan suddenly stops. 'This is the exact spot where Madeleine broke her ankle. I was chasing her, she tripped and was lucky she didn't break her neck. I got into a lot of bother over that and Madeleine milked it for the rest of the summer.' There follows a short silence as we pick our way down a steep section, then Brendan speaks again: 'When is your period due?'

Unable to contain my despondency I whisper, 'I had it last week.'

No response and we carry on down the cliff path in silence, save for the vigorous smash of water meeting rock. Every month since we'd decided to marry we'd made love on two consecutive nights in the middle of the month. The first time, in New York, had made up for lack of passion by being a lot of fun. We'd both needed Dutch courage and had got drunk – well, I had, Brendan was a little inebriated but lucid, and he'd surprised me with his ardent skill. Afterwards I'd asked him if he'd made love

238

to many women. He'd chuckled and winked. 'You are the first.' Then added, 'Sex is mainly in the mind.'

'So what are you thinking when we make love?' I'd asked.

He'd grinned. 'That would be telling.'

Every month since September we'd counted the days leading up to my period. Before Christmas I was ten days late; during that time Brendan had driven me mad discussing names and nursery furniture. But since the onset of New Year his enthusiasm for lovemaking had noticeably waned. I blamed myself. It must be my fault, I couldn't have children. I had tests, everything normal, yet still I felt the guilt. Every month I prayed and choked back dry angry sobs when I saw the tell-tale spotting.

At the base of the cliff lies a wide sheltered cove. We land lightly on the sand. 'This is where I used to come crabbing with Charlie. I remember once putting a tiny crab down Madeleine's shorts.'

I giggle. 'No wonder she hated you.'

'Still does,' he comments, then, distracted, he gazes out to sea. A gull swoops low, his beak lancing the shallows, a fishing boat bobs in the distance and the sun peeks through a break in the haze. Brendan shades his eyes with his hand. 'I've an empathy with this place, my childhood sea. I'd spend hours in the rock pools, patiently waiting to see the sudden flash of a small fish, or the glint of a crab back in the barnacled boulders.' He points towards the horizon. 'We had a little boat, and on warm days my mother and I would row out. I used to fish with a net while she just lazed, trailing her hand in the water. It made a silver trail in the indigo sea. I was conceived here, so she says. Couldn't always believe everything she told me – she was prone to lies, when it suited her.'

'Like all of us,' I add.

'I'd hoped that you might conceive here, Kate.'

'I wish I could conceive. It makes me very sad that I

can't give you a child, a parting gift. After all you've given me.'

His hand drops away, his eyes full. He croaks, 'I don't want to die.'

Rushing to him, I wrap him in my arms, my heart swelling in my chest. I can feel his ribs through the thick wool of his sweater, and know he grows increasingly frail. 'Don't dwell on it, Brendan, it's a long time off, the doctors have all said how fit you are and . . .'

'I haven't got long, Kate. Believe me, I know. That's one of the reasons I wanted to revisit Grayshott.'

'Nonsense. Only the other day Dr Clancy told me a year at least.'

'Now that is nonsense. The man is either a liar or a fool. I'll be lucky to see my roses bloom, and I now know in my heart we won't have a child.'

'What makes you so sure, Brendan?'

Pulling me towards him he holds me very tight. 'It was selfish of me to expect you to bear my child and bring it up alone, I accept that now. Your first child should be with a man you truly love.'

A violent pang of pain, akin to a menstrual contraction, grips my stomach as I hear him say, 'I don't want to die in hospital, Kate and I want you to make sure that doesn't happen.'

'How can I prevent it if you get very sick?'

'Morphine – I've got a supply. I may not be able to do it myself though, you know my horror of syringes.'

Ignoring my shocked expression, he continued in the same frivolous manner as if he were talking about walking the dog.

'Apparently it's very easy to overdose and I have it on good authority morphine is a great way to go. You feel on top of the world: no rough edges, no pain. Much more civilized than all that wasting away and having to endure the constant stream of friends and sycophants expressing embarrassed sympathy as they linger awkwardly at your deathbed. Or, better still, rent me a beautiful young man to fuck me to death and bury me with a huge erection.'

Then he'd laughed uproariously. I'd tried to join in but my feigned laughter had stuck in my throat. 'I'm going to miss you, very much.'

'I'm going to miss you too, my lovely Kate. I'm going to miss the whole bloody lot.'

It was then he began to cry. It was the first, the only, and the last time I saw him cry.

Then holding me at arm's length, he says, 'Enough of this maudlin nonsense – I'll have none of it. There's life left in the old dog yet. How about a vicious game of chess?'

'If you promise not to cheat, Brendan.'

'I have no choice if I want to win. I taught you too well.'

We both smile and hand in hand start back to the house. On the climb up I lead the way, stopping several times for Brendan to catch up. 'I used to run up here as a lad,' he comments after one particularly arduous stretch. At the summit we link arms and like an old married couple stroll slowly towards the house.

It is during our month at Grayshott that I see Brendan rapidly deteriorate. His energy levels plummet at the same rate as his weight.

At night, long after he has gone to sleep, I sit close to the window in a wing-backed chair, my legs curled under me, listening to his shallow breathing, totally occupied with recollections of our life together. I've put Father Steele on hold. I haven't forgotten, nor have I given up on him, but to think of him at a time like this would be the ultimate betrayal.

Three days before we are due to return to Ireland I awake in the early morning to find Brendan sitting bolt upright in bed. His left hand is shaking uncontrollably, it's clear he's in pain.

'I want to go home.'

I stroke the back of his hand. 'We're going on Saturday.'

'I want to go now.'

Sensing his agitation, I move closer to him. 'Leave the arrangements to me. We'll go in the morning.'

And so we leave the magic beauty of Brendan's childhood summers to travel to London under a slate sky, landing in Dublin late that afternoon in a turbulent rain storm.

It rains for six days and six nights. When it stops, the sun, as if in celebration, shines relentlessly for two weeks.

Brendan is very sick. This morning on his insistence Mrs Keating and I had to help him stagger to the garden to see the first rose of summer. A sight that a year ago would have delighted him today barely produces a wan smile. He makes a lot of fuss about being helped back upstairs yet he could not make it without our support.

When he is safely back in bed I plump and prop two pillows behind his head. His face contorting in agony, he groans, 'The morphine isn't effective any more, Kate. I feel like I've been cut in a thousand places.'

'How can I help?'

Angrily he growls, 'You can help me to die. Get David Clancy here . . . tell him I want to go. The pain is unbearable. I've had enough. Tell him to give me something to end it.'

'Don't get angry, Brendan, it will make it worse.'

With what little strength he has left, he grips the back of my hand. 'It can't get any worse, Kate, believe me. Every night I pray to God to take me. This I suppose is his way of punishing me for my lack of faith and my homosexuality.' Suddenly he screams, 'Take me, you old bugger!' His eyeballs roll up in his head, and his fingers crawl down the bed like the spiny legs of a spider crab. Then his eyes roll back into their sockets and connect with mine.

In that instant I see the blood drain from his lips and I know he's about to die. 'I'm scared, Brendan.'

He knows too and smiles serenely. 'At long last he's heard me. I'm . . . going, Kate. Hold me.'

Scrambling on to the bed I lie very close and very still. I stroke his cheek, hear him murmuring, 'I love you, Kate.'

'Please don't leave me, Brendan. What will I do without you?'

He starts to shiver; he's cold and getting colder. In a pathetic attempt to keep him warm I wrap the quilt around his body. 'That will keep you warm.'

'Too late.'

I'm crying, the sobs racking my body. 'Don't die, Brendan, I know we all have to do it sooner or later, but can't you do it later? I'm not ready yet.'

His eyelids droop and I can see it's an effort to keep his eyes open. He's struggling to speak. 'Don't . . . grieve for me, Kate. I want you . . . to promise.'

Through my tears, I manage to utter, 'I promise.'

I watch his eyes close for the final time, his hand go limp and his head slump on to his shoulder.

For a long time I stay in the same position, talking continually about my next exhibition, our plans for the new studio, and his plans for a folly in the grounds of his country house. Every now and then I squeeze his hand and kiss his cold cheek, assuring him that he's going to get better very soon.

More than an hour later Mrs Keating knocks on the bedroom door. 'The doctor is here to see Mr Fitz.'

I yell, 'He's not here.'

In response Mrs Keating bursts into the room, stopping abruptly at the foot of the bed. Quickly taking in the scene she firmly prises me from the dead Brendan and with gentle perseverance leads me to my own room. I wait for her footsteps to retreat, then, pulling a paint-splashed cardigan over my cotton dress, I slip up the stairs to the studio and out of the house by the back stairs.

The stately spire of St Joseph's cuts a dash above a sullen row of terrace houses. It's ten past five; the church is empty. Brendan was christened, confirmed and, as a child and young man, worshipped here. Crossing myself, I stride towards the altar, then remember I'm in an Anglican church. 'They don't hold with all that guff,' Brendan had once said. Holding the altar rail I shout, 'You've got him now – I hope you're happy. They say you take the best first – why is that? For the life of me, I can't understand it.' In the silence I hear my own echo. 'What will I do without him?' Who was I going to confide in, ask advice of? Who would make me laugh? 'I'm not ready, I tell you I'm not...' I sob. 'Why didn't you give us a child? Was it too much to ask for? That would have made him very happy.'

I feel my legs weaken and I slide to the floor. Once there I lean against the rail and, pulling my legs into my chest, I let my head fall on my knees and I rock. I'm in the same position an hour later when a young vicar leans forward to touch my shoulder.

'Is there anything I can do to help?'

Struggling into a sitting position, I wipe my hand across my face. 'I've just lost my best friend.'

'I'm very sorry,' he says, helping me to my feet. I'm hunched, my arms dangling like limp string.

'It's killing me, his death I mean. I should have been prepared. I've known about it for a long time –he had cancer, you see. We knew ... we all knew...'

'We are never fully prepared. Was he a Christian?'

I nod.

'Try to think of him as not having died but having been reborn into a better life.'

'It doesn't help.'

'I promise you it will.'

244

With my eyes narrowed and my chin jutting forward I turn from his sanctimonious smile to wander out of the church. The sky is charcoal and heavy with rain. Like someone feral and half-possessed I stumble through the streets. Up and down Grafton Street, looking in lighted shop windows; in and out of the station, snarling at men trying to pick me up. At five past two I duck into a darkened doorway to dodge a slowly patrolling police car. It's possible Mrs Keating has sent out a search party.

At last I find myself outside Father Steele's house. It's no accident. It had been my first thought on leaving church. After ringing the bell three times I'm about to give up when the door opens, a crack at first, then wide. Father Steele fills the rectangle, a sleepy silhouette, the light from the hall picking out his tousled hair and pyjama'd legs.

Before he can send me away I say, 'Brendan died this afternoon.'

'I'm sorry, Kate.'

But I want to hear more from him than sorry. 'Is that all you can say?'

Peering out of bleary eyes he mumbles, 'Of course not. Come in.' He holds the door open and steps back to allow me to pass.

When I am in the dimness of the hall I murmur, 'If it's not too much to ask, would you do something for me?'

'What?'

'Will you hold me? Make it better, make the pain go away . . .'

His expression is tense, like that of a trapped man. 'You shouldn't have come here, Kate.'

Angry now, I scream, 'I've got no place to go, no one to turn to. You're a priest, for the love of God act like one, show me some bloody compassion.' I sense his hesitation and urge him again, 'Please, Father, I need you.'

Silently I move towards him. His arms are trembling as he lifts them from his sides. A moment later I feel their warmth on my back and instantly feel better. We stay like that for a long time, neither speaking nor moving, just holding each other very tight. I can see Brendan, not as he'd looked latterly, but how he was when I'd first met him. His wicked laughter is ringing in my head and his voice above it implores me, 'Take life by the horns hold on tight, Kate, and don't let go. You blink and it's over.'

'I need you, Declan, tonight more than any other.'

'Your need is about your loss, Kate. Go home and grieve for your husband.'

'Kiss me,' I beg.

'No, Kate, if I kiss you I might not be able to stop.'

I begin to shake and he rubs my back and shoulders. 'I'm going to take you home.'

'I don't have a home. Brendan was my home. He was my family. I can't bear to think how much I'll miss him. Tonight I need to be with you.'

Grabbing his hand, I press it hard on my breast. 'Feel my heart, Father, it's like a bloody battering ram. Do you know why?'

'You're distraught.'

'I need to be loved.' Not letting go of his hand I direct it up inside my skirt, pressing his palm on the inside of my left thigh. With a helpless moan, his fingers fumble with the crotch of my panties. I'm impatient and help to guide him inside. Once there I thrust my hips forward, parting my legs in submission. 'I'm ready for you, Declan, I've been ready for many years.'

Without a word and without shifting his eyes from my face he removes his hand and like a madman begins to tear at my clothes. I help him undo the tiny buttons on my blouse and with equal frenzy begin to rip the fastenings on his pyjamas. My anticipation mounts with each article of clothing I take off and pull from him. I long to see him naked. I want him to be big, and hard and strong as he'd always appeared in my fantasies. Naked, the muscled lines of his body are taut, youthful, and covered in hundreds of freckles pale gold in the flattering lamplight.

In a tremulous voice I murmur, 'You're beautiful.'

Falling to his knees he loops his thumbs in the sides of my panties and in one tug pulls them down to my ankles. Still kneeling, he gazes in awe at my golden mound of pubic hair, then very gently he touches it.

'You are the most beautiful thing I've ever seen.'

Parting my legs I urge, 'Look at me, Declan, I'm yours to do with as you will. I've always been yours.'

I can feel his gaze burning into me like a blast of hot air. An intense surge of power grips me once again, tempered now with an overwhelming desire. This, I know, is how it should be, how it should feel. At last I have the man I want, the one I've always wanted, and I know for certain that Brendan would have rejoiced.

Wordlessly he leads me by the hand upstairs and into his bed.

Countless times I'd imagined this moment, but my imaginings were nothing compared to the reality. His face filled with longing; me offering myself without embarrassment or awkwardness. The newness, the discovery; it was like being the first two people in the world to make love. The joy of yielding to desire, and the triumphant empowerment of possession. Minutes after our lovemaking, still hot and wet and entwined, Declan whispers, 'How do you feel? Tell me honestly, was it good? Or was it about assuaging your grief?'

I'm amazed he can't see the answer written all over my face. 'You made me very happy, and what's more I feel no guilt. Above all, Brendan wanted my happiness, as I did his.' My next words are twinged with regret. 'Now I can move on.'

Resting on his elbow his head in his hand, he looks down into my face. 'Are you sure it was all right?'

I kiss his parted lips. 'It felt completely right.'

I didn't go back to Elgin Crescent that night. I couldn't. The thought of leaving Declan made me feel physically sick. At ten past six the following morning, rain clattering on the window pane wakes me. Quiet as a mouse, I slip out of his arms and bed, recalling all the times I'd done the same thing in the orphanage after lights out. The door, slightly ajar, makes no noise, but every other stair creaks and I expect to see him appear on the landing at any moment.

I locate the telephone in the hall; shivering, I punch out my home number. Mrs Keating answers the phone; she sounds drowsy.

'Thank God you've called. I've had the constabulary out scouring the city for you.'

'I was distraught. I just wandered around then spent the night with a friend.'

'I've called Mr Fitzgerald's family and a few of his close friends. Will you be back soon?'

'I'm on my way.'

Chapter Fourteen

The day of the funeral is very hot, the hottest day of the year so far. The weather forecast threatens thunder and torrential rain. I pray it holds off until after the burial. Friends and family determined to pay their last respects had descended on Elgin Crescent. A distant cousin called Fanny had even travelled from New Zealand with her two noisy precocious brats in tow. It said a lot about the man.

Madeleine, Brendan's much despised sister, had insisted on organizing the entire event. Madeleine is a bully and, like all bullies, used to having her own way. I'd protested vehemently, knowing Brendan wouldn't have wanted a pretentious wake. Ignoring me in her inimitable manic fashion she'd managed in the space of a few days to mount the sort of wake befitting a head of state. The day after his death a marquee was tacked on to the back of the house, and a stream of florists, caterers and event organizers prowled the house and grounds as if they'd lived there all their lives. On the afternoon before the funeral, in the midst of the mayhem, I'd waylaid Madeleine on her way towards the garden, a clipboard and pencil in her hand.

'Brendan would have hated this vulgar display, Madeleine, you know that.'

Openly hostile, she'd shrugged. 'You've been his wife for a few months, what do you know compared to me? I'm his sister. I adored my brother all his life.'

The pretence was laughable. 'Come on, Madeleine, you

and Brendan were never close, admit it. You didn't get on, even as kids he said you hated his guts.'

Madeleine scowls. 'That's just not true.'

Countless times I've bitten my tongue in the past but now Brendan is dead I no longer have to contain my contempt.

'You and I know the truth, Madeleine. I loved your brother, very much. I can say that with all honesty, my hand on my heart. You didn't even like him. You despised his sexuality, resented him for being everything you were not: intellectual, witty, charming and popular. But most of all you hated your brother because he had what you wanted more than anything else. The love of your father. So why pretend? Does it assuage your guilt, make you feel Christian? Or is it simply about putting on a show, playing to the fucking gallery? You're a fraud, Madeleine, and when this is all over I don't want you to come near this house, do you understand?'

It takes a lot to ruffle Madeleine, but I'd succeeded. I experienced a perverse frisson of pleasure as I looked at her mouth, downturned and contorted in anger. 'I never liked you, nor did Mother. We both thought you were a bad influence on Brendan.'

'I'll let you into a big secret, Madeleine: the feeling was entirely mutual.'

She'd had enough and without so much as a word or a glance in my direction she stormed out of the room.

After our confrontation I'd deliberately managed to avoid her until today when we are forced to share the family hearse.

The morning sky over the church is a clear blue without so much as a wisp of cloud. I'd insisted on choosing the hymns and readings for the service: two pieces, one by Oscar Wilde, and the other by Brendan's favourite writer, James Joyce. Liam Hennessy, Brendan's long-term occasional partner, read a poem by Yeats and another friend of Brendan's sang, much to my distaste, 'Londonderry Air'. I'd tried to dissuade him, arguing that Brendan had hated the song, but to no avail; he'd been told he sang it well and had to have his few minutes of fame. Pathetic. The choir sang 'The Lord is My Shepherd' and the Reverend John Macguire gave a moving sermon.

I sat through the entire service dry-eyed while all around me sobbed. I'd done my crying, selfish tears, all about me and my loss, bleating, whingeing, self-pitying grief. The night Brendan told me he was going to die he'd made me promise not to grieve for him and to wear something bright at his funeral. Recalling his words, I touch the tip of my wide-brimmed hat. It's banana yellow with a black band. Bright enough, I ask him. He chuckles, a warm sound I remember so well, like water rippling over stones.

He's talking to me. 'It's perfect. As usual you look beautiful, Kate.' He winks. 'Don't grieve for me, Kate, life's too damn short, over in the wink of an eye. Get on with it, don't waste a bloody minute.'

The reverend interrupts. 'Let us pray.' I lower my head. Brendan is gone.

Dropping to my knees, I mumble the Lord's Prayer and, on rising, catch a glimpse of Liam Hennessy, tight-lipped and dead-eyed. I'd never liked him, and had warned Brendan about his insincerity. Brendan, a mischievous twinkle in one eye, had winked with the other, saying, 'He's very GIB.'

Perplexed, I'd raised my eyebrows. 'GIB?'

'Good in bed, my darling girl!'

Michael O'Leary, a life-long friend of Brendan's, is seated next to Liam, unshaven, his face white and crumpled. A couple of feet from him sits Roland Fizgerald, Brendan's uncle, who had emigrated to America as a young man. I scan the church. It's full to capacity – a bloody good turn-out! Brendan would have said. There are a lot of unfamiliar faces, people I've never met. Some are from his distant past, students, school friends, pensioned staff and casual acquaintances. I'm certain they are all in church because in some way Brendan had touched their lives. He'd packed a lot into his fifty-four years, despite his fears about having achieved nothing. This thought gives me strength and a surge of optimism, making his death more acceptable.

As we leave church I'm aware of a strong breeze picking up the hem of the Reverend's gown. Tightly I hold on to my hat, and glancing to a field on my right I recall the first time Brendan had taken me to his country house in Tipperary. It had been a day like today, sunny with a strong westerly wind. He'd pointed to a field similar to this one, saying, 'See the wind on the grass? It looks like a vast lake.' I'd agreed and spent the remainder of the afternoon sketching the field. The subsequent watercolour, 'Field of Water', had sold a couple of years ago for a quarter of a million dollars.

The dull patter of dirt hitting the lid of the coffin breaks the silence. 'Ashes to ashes, dust to dust,' the Reverend intones.

Only words, meaningless words. They offer no comfort. Everyone said time, the great healer, was the only thing that actually worked. I'm not sure about that either. I feel like a colossal chunk of my heart has been torn out of my body. Sure, the open wound can be padded with all manner of dressings: work, friends, sex, anything to stanch the bleeding, and in time it will close, scar, and feel better, but it will never be the same again.

Brendan had helped me to grow, and, like a concerned father, had watched me every tentative step of the way. I was going to miss him. He'd given me so much, taught me things I'd never have known without him, things about myself. He'd said I didn't trust much or many, and had blamed my childhood. 'Don't live in the past, Kate,' he'd once said.

'The past lives in me,' I'd replied and had gone on to say: 'I don't blame the nuns for my character. Our fundamental make-up, I believe, is inherent, genetic, no more no less. We make our own luck.'

A diamond pinkie ring on the finger of a stranger glints in the sunlight; the wind drops to a low murmur. Madeleine sniffs loudly, making a big show of dabbing her cheeks with a delicate lace handkerchief. I'm positive Mrs Keating's noisy sobs will be heard in the next county, and Liam Hennessy looks like he might pass out at any moment. Pain, I'm surrounded by pain – not least my own.

I long to roar and scream, to screech blue murder at God. I want to rant in a voice as hard as rock, as hard as his heart, for deserting me, not once but time and time again. A great many things have caused me to lose my faith, not least losing Brendan before I was able to repay the enormous love he gave me. I gaze upwards to where a black cloud is charging across the sky and vow never to set foot in church again.

I love trains. For me it's the only way to travel. The repetitive metallic clatter of train on track; the rolling motion; and the sense of freedom and adventure all contrive to stimulate me like no other form of transport. I would have dearly loved to have lived in the age of steam. What romance: the wonderful huffing and puffing sound, the gleam of highly polished brass glimpsed through great white gusts of steam.

When I was much younger, every time I boarded a train I used to play a scenario in my head. I'd sit opposite a man. He was always handsome and always Italian, although once, after seeing *Dr Zhivago*, he'd been Russian. We'd share a few words and lots of long meaningful looks, his dark and brooding, mine coy and teasing. He'd always be someone very important, a diplomat or aristocrat on a secret assignment. Depending on the length of the journey he'd either declare love at first sight and insist that I accompany him to some exotic location, or he'd arrange to meet me the following week for dinner in his suite at the Ritz in Paris.

Today, travelling to Leinster House, Brendan's country estate in Tipperary (now mine, I remind myself), a totally different scene is playing in my head. The lead roles are played by me and a tortured priest torn between two loves.

I understand Declan's dilemma and sympathize, yet stubbornly refuse to give him up to God, who, after all, has taken so much from me and given little in return except perhaps my painting. A gift from God, Mother Peter had said. Why should he have Declan, I ask myself, he's got plenty of followers, hundreds of ordained servants, why couldn't he give me one? No big deal, no great loss. But God isn't like that, he doesn't always plays fair, and it always had to be his way or not at all. Well, fuck the Almighty; this time I get what I want. I'm warning you, I'll fight you and whoever else tries to take him from me, do you hear?

In the past couple of weeks I've sensed Declan retreating from me. It scares me and I'm starting to feel like a runaway train careering out of control. Brendan had provided for me very well. In his will, much to Madeleine's fury, he'd left me the house in Elgin Crescent, his country estate and the contents, a generous allowance and one million pounds in trust. On the condition that I continue to paint.

Resting my head on the back of the seat, I listen to the sound of train on track; concentrating on that I gradually empty my head. My eyelids droop, I can feel my head getting heavier and heavier, until eventually I fall asleep.

A voice, distant yet insistent, wakes me. 'It's the end of the line, miss.'

I blink rapidly, trying to focus on the owner of the voice. 'What?'

'The end of the line: Limerick.'

I jump up. 'Damn, I've missed my stop.'

Peering over the top of his bifocals the conductor asks, 'Where you headed?'

I stand up, pulling my tote from the overhead rack. 'To Templemore in Tipperary. I should have got off in Roselea.'

Looking down at his wristwatch, he shakes his head and seems to delight in saying, 'Not another train for nigh on two hours from Limerick back to Roselea, if me memory serves me well, and that without looking at the timetable.'

I wasn't listening. 'I'll take a taxi. It's not that far. How far do you reckon to Templemore from here?'

The deep crease between his eyebrows deepens. 'I'd say fifty-some miles. Taxi will cost you a fair bit.'

I'm walking down the carriage and he's following me, obviously enjoying the drama. It's probably the most exciting thing to happen to him in years. Alighting, I turn to the conductor, who is still on the train. 'Where will I get a taxi?'

He points over my head. 'Across the road. Paddy O'Sullivan's place.'

I'm smiling. 'I can't forget that, it's my name.'

O'Sulliva axis the sign above the shop doorway reads. It could be selling anything from kebabs to building supplies.

A sullen girl with peroxide hair, an inch of black roots, and the kind of snotty nose that takes me back to my childhood, is sitting behind a glass partition reading a magazine. Reluctantly she tells me that Paddy O'Sullivan is out on a job, and won't be back for at least half an hour. In Ireland that equates to more than an hour. After further intensive questioning that makes me feel like an inquisitor, I discover Paddy is a one-man band who, she doubted, would want to drive all the way to Templemore at this time of the day.

'It's not exactly late,' I snap.

'Too late for Paddy. He likes to be at the pub no later than seven. Often jokes about his first pint. If it's not hitting his whistle by a quarter past seven he'll have no crack for the rest of the night. It's gone five now, he wouldn't be back before eight-thirty or nine, that's if he was to leave this minute.'

Exasperated, I try to quell my rising impatience. 'Do you think fifty pounds might persuade him?'

For a split second a spark flares in her vacant eyes, then it's gone.

'Francis Barry has a taxi. He could do with the money right now.'

My eyes light up. 'Can you call him?'

Slowly she begins to dial the number, then stops abruptly. 'I forgot – sure, I'd forget me head if it wasn't screwed on. His wife went into labour this morning. Sure as eggs is eggs he'll be at the hospital.'

'He might not be. She may have had it by now. Try calling him.'

She sniffs, and a mucous bubble bursts through the crust on the end of her right nostril. The sight turns my stomach; I can't look at her any longer and turn to face the window fronting the street.

'Don't like to disturb him, it's their first baby.'

Spinning round, I push my face close to the glass. 'Give me the number, I'll call him and see if he wants to make fifty pounds.'

'Fifty pounds for what?'

I turn to face the owner of the voice. 'To take me to Templemore as soon as possible. Are you Paddy O'Sullivan?'

A lopsided grin splits the man's handsome, mobile face.

'It's myself. Fifty pounds, is it? Your carriage awaits, miss.'

Five minutes later we are heading out of town on the N7 towards Nenagh. Suddenly I remember Sylvester Ryan, the odd-job man at Leinster Manor. Odd is the accurate title. Yesterday I'd called Mrs Hickey, the house-keeper, with the train times.

'Old Sylvester will pick you up, Mrs Fitz – that is, if I can find him. Always shirking, that one. Never could understand why Mr Fitz kept him on so long.'

I'd asked Brendan the same question the second time I'd gone to Leinster Manor. I recall Brendan's reply: 'When I was a small boy, Sylvester Ryan used to take me fishing – a young man at the time, he'd be twenty-eight, maybe twenty-nine. We used to talk a lot – well, I did most of the chattering, as you can well imagine, Sylvester the listening. One day, against Sylvester's wishes, I'd insisted on wading into the river, way past my depth. I was about eight, and a good swimmer. I'd assured him I'd not get out of my depth. There was a strong current that day, I slipped, hit my head on a rock, and was very quickly swept away. Sylvester wasn't a strong swimmer but he risked his life to save mine. On the journey back to the house I made him promise not to tell my parents. He kept his promise and I kept a secret one I made in my head that night. I could always trust Sylvester Ryan and he would always have a job with me.'

Visualizing the old man patiently waiting at the station, I ask Paddy to stop at the next telephone box. It's broken, and we have to travel another fourteen miles to find one that works. Mrs Hickey answers the telephone. Sylvester hadn't rung, and was now no doubt on his way back to the house, or holed up in the pub; she suspected the latter.

Back in the car, Paddy is smoking. Hastily he flicks the smouldering butt out of the open window, drawing a sparking arc of orange light in the darkness. Putting the car into gear, he moves slowly away from the kerb. 'You from these parts?'

'No, I'm from Dublin.'

'You don't sound like you've got a Dublin accent.'

Foreigners, particularly Americans, frequently comment to me on Irish friendliness, hospitality and joviality. They don't understand. The Irish are just plain nosy. Like Mr Molloy always said, 'We have to know the far end of a fart.' Taxi drivers and small village shopkeepers are the worst offenders. Many times I've been tempted to tell them to look out for their own bloody business. The trouble is they don't have enough of their own business and have to live vicariously through other people.

'I used to live in Cork.'

'Got a good deal of family in Cork. Where was it you lived?'

My irritation evident, I reply curtly, 'In Friday Wells, a little village. I don't suppose you've heard of it.'

'I have indeed. Well, well, it's a small world. My sister lives in Friday Wells; she's a nun at the Sisters of Mercy orphanage.'

My heart begins to gallop. 'What's her name?'

'Her given name is Marion O'Sullivan. The name she took after she was professed is Mother Peter.'

The galloping slows to a trot, and I take a deep breath. 'I know your sister, very well.'

He laughs. 'Sure, what did I tell you? It's a bloody small world, it is that.'

'I grew up in the Sisters of Mercy orphanage.'

I can see him in the rear-view mirror, his face a study in bemusement. 'Well I never. Fancy that! Wait till I tell my missus.'

'Your sister is a good woman. She showed me a lot of kindness. The next time you see or speak to her, will you tell her you met me? If she's ever in Dublin I'd love to see her. I'll give you my name, address and number.'

'I haven't seen our Marion for a good few years. She writes sometimes, and sends stuff for the kids, books on Christianity and the like. They never read them, more interested in sitting in front of the telly. Marion, I'm sure, thinks I should spend more time in church and less in the pub. She's never said so, but I get the feeling she doesn't approve of me. She had her calling when she was very young – about twelve, I think. I'm six years younger and can't remember exactly when she decided to give herself to God. My mother encouraged her, but even if she hadn't, our da always said that wild horses wouldn't have stopped our Marion becoming a nun. God bless her. Aye, sure, it's a small world.'

We both fall silent. Fifteen minutes later the towering entrance gates of Leinster Manor are illuminated in the white beam of the car headlights. I get out, speak to Mrs Hickey on the intercom, watch the entrance gates slide open then jump back into the car. We travel down a long beech-tunnelled drive, at the end turning sharp right to the front of the house. The night sky over Brendan's childhood home is velvety black. Some windows glow with light, others are as black as the sky above. As Paddy stops the car in front of the mellow stone-porticoed entrance to the seventeenth-century manse he lets out a long low whistle. 'Nice place.'

When I get out of the taxi once more, Mrs Hickey appears, her stocky frame filling the bottom half of the open doorway, light from the hall shining through the narrow gap in her stockinged legs.

I hand Paddy three twenty-pound notes.

He hands me one back. 'Sure, forty will suit me fine.'

'I said fifty and fifty it is.'

'Ah, to be sure that's very generous, miss.' He fumbles in his pocket for the change while I take a business card out of my case. We swap. He reads it and, scratching his head, says, 'Kate O'Sullivan . . . sure, I know that name.'

'I'm an artist. Maybe you've heard of me, or my work.'

With narrowed eyes he begins to shake his head. 'No, nothing to do with art. All as I know about painting is how to emulsion a wall. This is to do with our Marion, Mother Peter to you.'

I'm confused. 'Has she talked about me?'

'No . . .' He's still scratching his head, looking perplexed. 'I'm trying to remember where I've heard the name before – it's a good few years.' He frowns in concentration. 'I've got it.' He points to the card. 'Kate O'Sullivan, sure – now I remember. I'd just bought my first taxi – now, let me think . . . that was a few months after my twenty-third birthday, so it must have been in '62.'

'The year I was born,' I mumble.

Seeming not to hear and bubbling with excitement he rambles on, 'We was living in Dublin at the time. Hadn't been married long. Ellen – that's the wife – was pregnant.' He scratches his head again. 'Or had she had Finlay? I can't remember. I'd been away on a job, see, and when I got back it was late. Ellen was in bed but she'd put a note on the kitchen table saying my sister Marion left a message to ask if – well, not ask exactly, *demand* I pick someone up the following morning from the airport. It's very urgent, she says, can't trust anyone else to do the job. I've to take them from Dublin to Cork, it's a fair old drive and I'm rubbing me hands thinking of the fare. The flight time and details are all written down in Ellen's neat hand. So, feeling very important, I sets off the following day in plenty of time, arriving at the airport twenty minutes early . . .'

I'm tired and cold and dying for a cup of strong tea and a rasher. The housekeeper moves forward out of the light towards the car. 'Everything all right, Mrs Fitz?'

I turn my head slightly. 'Fine, Mrs Hickey. I'll be with you in one minute. Get on with it, man,' I say, not unkindly, but if I know anything about Irish shaggy-dog stories they can go on all night without a particularly amusing or interesting punchline. 'Is this going to take much longer?'

Seemingly oblivious, Paddy continues as if he hadn't been interrupted. 'As soon as I walk into the arrivals hall in Dublin airport who do you think I should bump into?'

Suppressing a yawn I say, 'I've no idea.'

'Our Marion, hurrying across the concourse carrying a parcel of what at first looked liked a bundle of rags. I call her name, she spots me and a minute later she's by my side. You can imagine my shock when I see the bundle in her arms move and realize what she's carrying.'

I'm alert now.

'A baby, a bloody baby! Can't be more than a few weeks old, all wrapped up in a brightly coloured blanket. Like a Mexican poncho.'

With a jolt I recall the conversation I'd overheard between Paddy Fitzpatrick, the fruit and vegetable man, and Mother Peter. He'd mentioned Father Devlin carrying a baby wrapped in a blanket that had, he thought, looked Indian or Mexican.

All ears, I hang on Paddy's every word. 'You know how nuns are usually all serene like and calm? Our Marion is the calmest of the lot, nothing would ruffle her feathers, even as a child she never got a bit upset over anything. So you can imagine my surprise first to see her, then to see her so jumpy, like she's nervous, real worried over something. She's pale, as white as a bloody ghost. With barely a Hello, how are you, Paddy, she pushes me out of the airport. Once in the car she seems to relax a bit; kept reasonably calm even when the baby began to cry. I drove her to Friday Wells, to the house of a priest. I think his name was Father Delany or Devlin – can't be certain on that one, though; it could have been Dillon. It was a bloody long time ago. On the journey to Friday Wells we didn't talk a lot. Marion seemed preoccupied with the baby, didn't listen to my news, didn't even show much interest in my new Ford Escort. Before getting out the car I ask her where the baby had come from and she tells me it's none of my business. OK, I say, a bit huffy. Well, at least tell me the baby's name. To be honest, I don't know why I asked, I wasn't much interested. I suppose it was just something to say.

'I'll never forget our Marion's face. She can't tell a lie, you see. Never could. I knew she was having a problem with her conscience. "I can't tell you, it's a big secret, but I'll tell you the name I've given her." '

I know exactly what's coming and feel the blood in my veins turn cold. I hold my breath then feel my heart begin to race when he says,

' "Kate O'Sullivan." '

Later that night in the silent hours when most of the country is asleep, I lie completely still and wide awake. Since I'd lost Brendan more and more often I've thought of my past and my parents. When I'd received twenty thousand punts on my twenty-first birthday, Brendan had suggested we start some serious enquiries. He had a friend, a journalist, who he felt sure could help. After almost a year of investigative research we'd come up with nothing. At that point I'd been so bound up in my rising star as an painter I'd decided to put finding out who I was on hold. 'Let sleeping dogs lie,' I'd told Brendan, who'd shrugged and said: 'It's only worth opening up old wounds if they haven't healed properly.'

I'd thought long and hard about what he'd said and decided my scars weren't visible unless you dug very deep. Life at that time was good.

When we were young, Bridget had, with a hint of envy, frequently suggested I wasn't Irish. Sometimes the notion would hurt, at others give rise to fantasies of glamorous origins. I'd imagine my parents to be film stars, or aristocrats who had been the victims of a terrible hospital blunder. Once when I was about thirteen I'd read a story of two baby girls being muddled at birth and given to the wrong parents. It was possible the same thing had happened to me, and my real parents had unknowingly raised the wrong daughter. In my imaginings this appalling mistake was rectified, and I was returned to my real parents. They loved their adopted daughter and we became close like twin sisters.

What Paddy O'Sullivan had told me tonight was absolute proof that I'd been born overseas and brought to Ireland in secrecy. The trust, the bracelet: both signposts – but to where? America, it had to be America. I cling to the thought, wrapping myself up in it like a warm blanket on a freezing night. Now more than ever I'm convinced my mother had got rid of me because she'd had no choice. I was the love child of someone important; he was married, she was threatened. 'I can't tell you, Paddy. It's a big secret,' Mother Peter had said to her brother.

Drawing up my knees, I hug them with both arms, letting my head fall into the soft downy pillows. Paddy's words, 'it's a big secret,' keep returning. I've got to speak to Mother Peter, even if it means going back to Friday Wells and the Sisters of Mercy.

'I took a vow of silence, Kate. I'm sorry.'

Exasperated, I try again. 'I understand, Mother Peter, but it means so much to me.'

The telephone line echoes as if someone has picked up a party line.

'I'm thrilled at your success, Kate. I always said you were special.'

'Why did you say that? Was it because my parents were special? Important, clever?'

'Like I've just said, I'm pleased to see how well you've got on. I do hope you still say your Catechism every night and thank God for all your achievements.'

'God didn't do it, why should I thank him?'

'He was there to guide you, Kate. In your heart you know he's always by your side.'

I want to scream a repeat of what I'd said earlier: *Why did you tell your brother my name was a secret?* Instead I ask, 'Where is Father Devlin?'

I hear her sharp intake of breath. 'He's dead.'

'Mother, if you can find it in your heart to give me just one clue, I promise I'll never bother you again . . .' I pause. '*Please* . . . it's very important to me . . . Mother Peter, are you there?' I'm talking to myself. Mother Peter has hung up. I redial, to be told by a Mother Superior whom I don't know that Mother Peter is busy.

The message is repeated verbatim several times during the next hour until eventually I'm told in no uncertain terms that Mother Peter does not want to speak to me.

'Hardly Christian spirit,' I grumble after the sixth call to Mother Superior, who is clearly losing patience.

'Mother Peter does not wish to be harassed in this way. I must warn you if you continue to do so I'll have to call the police.'

'OK, you've made your point. I promise not to call again, if you'll promise to give her a message.'

'I will not be bullied or blackmailed into anything, Mrs Fitzgerald. By all means, give me a message and if I see fit I'll pass it on.'

I visualize the Mother Superior. I don't know what she looks like but can easily imagine her sitting behind the highly polished walnut desk, the toes of her black-shoed feet peeking out of her habit in the square of space beneath the desk, a slice of dusty sunlight picking out the silver inkwell next to the telephone. I recall the first time I'd seen the inkwell. Funny the way some things stick, I was about six and the inkwell was the most beautiful object I'd ever seen in my life. So engrossed with fingering the intricate silver leaves engraved on the base, I hadn't seen the ruler until it was rapping my knuckles repeatedly, accompanied by Mother Superior yelling, 'You're supposed to look, not touch.'

On my way back to my room I'd licked my stinging fingers and planned a daring escape. I'd steal the inkwell, sell it to one of the market traders, and use the money to run away.

'If she changes her mind and wants to talk she can call me any time at home on Dublin 603 0645.'

As I replace the telephone I experience a surge of anger tightening my chest. My hands are shaking and my mouth feels dry. I want a drink. It's eleven in the morning, too early to drink. Conversely, I think, why not? I walk from the hall to the drawing room, cross to the far corner and stop at a drinks trolley. I pour a small measure of gin and fill the glass to the brim with tonic. Sipping the drink, I walk back in the same direction across the hall into what used to be Brendan's study. This, as far as I'm concerned, is the best room in the house. One entire wall is glass, long, elegant shuttered windows opening out on to a stretch of lawn sloping down to the lake. The view of the lake from this room, although partially obscured by a vast willow, is by far the best. Brendan used to argue that the view was better from his bedroom directly above, whence one could see the entire sweep of the lake and the spare land beyond below the craggy hills, snow-capped in winter, alive now with great gashes of yellow grass, but I disagreed. The room faces south-east and enjoys the morning sun. Today it's very bright, throwing a portrait of Brendan hanging on the opposite wall into inky shadow. I'd painted it for his birthday three years ago. Not my best, I must say. Yes, I'd captured his patrician features, the glint of mischief in his eyes, but I'd failed to recreate their warmth. But he loved it, and that was all that mattered. The painting refreshes a memory of the first time Brendan had brought me here, and dulls some of my earlier anger. We'd taken a tiny boat out on the lake and had laughed so much we'd almost capsized.

There is a sour taste in my mouth. I drink; it feels worse. I abandon the stale gin and tonic with a grunt.

My thoughts return to Mother Peter and her brother's revelations. I feel angry, frustration tugging at my breast. In that moment I hate Mother Peter, and if I could get my hands on her I'd shake the truth out of the stubborn old bitch. I have a right to know where I came from – Australia, America, the fucking moon, or Mexico, as the blanket I was wrapped in suggested. Even my name is a lie. Limboland, that's where I live. Am I, I howl inwardly, destined to live there for the rest of my life?

Lost in thought, I'm not aware of another presence in the room, and I jump like a startled cat when Mrs Hickey says, 'Telephone call for you, Mrs Fitz.'

'Who is it?'

She has an infuriating habit of wringing her hands in a Uriah Heep fashion. She's doing it now. 'Gentleman. Didn't give a name.'

Leaning against the desk, I pick up the telephone as Mrs Hickey, still wringing her hands, backs out.

'Kate, is that you?'

With a start I recognize his voice. 'Where are you?'

'I'm in Dublin. Mrs Keating gave me the number.'

'When did you get back?'

'This morning.'

'I thought you were coming back on Saturday.'

'I was, but I couldn't stop thinking of you. I need to see you, Kate. When are you coming back to Dublin?'

'I'd planned to stay for a few days until you came back from Lourdes.'

'I need to see you, Kate,' he repeated. 'Something has happened. Can you get back sooner? Tomorrow?' I detect the urgency in his tone.

'Is it that urgent? Can't it wait a couple of days?'

Declan says dramatically, 'This won't wait.'

'If I catch the direct train at ten twenty-five in the morning, I should be there early afternoon. I'll come to the church.'

'No. Meet me at my house at four.'

'Is there anything wrong, Declan?'

He couldn't lie. 'Yes, Kate, there's something I have to tell you.'

Frantic, I say, 'Then tell me now. I can't endure hours of waiting and wondering.'

'We need to talk, Kate. I've been offered a post in New York. A very important diocese that could lead to great things. Several before me have gone on to become bishops.'

My insides are numb. Fuck being a bishop. I can't begin to think about him leaving me, choosing his vocation over love. I don't even want to consider it. 'I'll come with you.'

'That won't be possible. You of all people must understand.'

'I'm sick of understanding. I don't want you to go. I'm warning you, I'll follow you to London, New York, Australia, wherever you go. There isn't a corner of the earth you'll be able to hide from me. I won't let you go, Declan, do you hear me?'

'You're overreacting.'

'You ain't seen nothing yet,' I growl. 'Just try leaving me.'

He sounds resigned. 'We'll talk tomorrow, Kate.'

The line goes dead. If I was angry before, it's nothing compared to how I feel now. As I storm out of the room I see the retreating figure of Mrs Hickey who, I suspect, has been listening at the door. Slowly I mount the stairs towards my bedroom, a warning bell clanging in the back of my brain. Mrs Hickey has never liked me. Once I'd suggested to Brendan that she was in love with him. This had elicited a peal of derisive laughter. 'Jean Hickey, in love with me? Are you mad?

I hadn't argued, but nor could I deny my female intuition. Brendan was blind to the insidious ruses the housekeeper employed at every opportunity to gain his attention, or to demean me.

I flick a switch at the bedside and the room is tinged in yellow light. I take a pillow from under the counterpane; it smells of starch and lavender linen spray. Lying down, I rest my head, asking myself furious questions: How could Declan think of leaving me? Why can't I go with him? I close my eyes, listening to the movement of the house, the beams creaking; Mrs Hickey calling to Sylvester; the opening and shutting of doors. Clenching and unclenching my fists, I fight the impulse to jump in the car and drive non-stop to Dublin to confront Declan.

I glance at my wristwatch. It's ten to twelve. With a bit of luck I could be in Dublin by late afternoon. Grabbing my sweater and handbag from the back of the chair I bound downstairs calling Mrs Hickey. When I reach the hall the housekeeper appears. 'Something up, Mrs Fitz?'

'I'm going back to Dublin.'

She frowns. 'When?'

'Now.'

Her eyes narrow suspiciously. 'But you only just arrived.'

'Sorry, Mrs H, but what I've got to do won't wait.'

Chapter Fifteen

From where I'm standing on the doorstep Declan is clearly visible through the corner of the bay window. He's slumped over a book asleep. When I ring the bell he jumps, instantly alert, and strides from the room. There is an expectancy about his manner when he opens the door, grim resignation in his voice when he says, 'I thought it might be you.'

'Can I come in?'

Without speaking he steps back. I follow him into the darkened hall and wait for him to close the door before continuing into the drawing room.

Before I have a chance to speak he says, 'I want to end our affair, Kate.'

Shaken, 'Just like that?' I manage to say.

I detect a hint of exasperation in his tone. 'You have to understand, Kate.'

'The problem is I do. It was fun while it lasted, too bad it lasted longer than it was fun.'

He chooses to ignore my sarcasm. 'I've got an opportunity to do God's work in New York, something I've always wanted. A chance to move on to greater things.'

Relieved, I say, 'I can live and work in New York. Nothing need change.'

'It has to change, Kate, don't you see? I can't go on like this, it's driving me insane. Conflicting hungers eating me alive. I can't sleep, I can't concentrate properly, worst of all I feel so guilty – I'm riddled with it. Everywhere I go I see your face, but it's distorted in the shape of the

269

devil. I tell you I'm going mad!' His anguish is almost tangible. It weighs heavy on his shoulders, I know, yet I feel little sympathy. I'm angry.

'Running away again, are we, Father? Taking the easy option?'

'I'm not running away, I'm trying to explain.' I hear him sigh. 'When I'm inside you, every emotion I've ever experienced, going back as far as I can remember, surfaces. It's as if I've been storing them all up for that one defining moment. Like I'm exploding . . . and when I lie with you in my arms afterwards I'm awed by the magnitude of what has happened.'

Satisfied, I say, 'It's the same for me.'

'During the last few months it's been hard to live in peace with thoughts of you. What's happened between us threatens the very foundation of my life, and I don't just mean the lovemaking. I enjoy your company, I look forward to seeing you, I count the hours. You are music and dance. You've introduced me to another world. I even enjoy watching films, if only to discuss them with you afterwards. I've never shared my life with a woman before.' He pauses. 'With anyone, apart from God.'

'So, why deny yourself?' Before he can reply, I add, 'Do you want me, Declan?'

'I think you know the answer to that.'

I do but I want to hear it from his lips. 'Tell me.'

'Yes. Constantly.'

A great surge of power sweeps over me once, then again, and again, each charge more powerful than the last. I realize that nothing he can say or do will stop the inevitable. Even if he walks away we'll meet again – next month, next year, sometime in the future. We have unfinished business.

'Then nothing can stop what we have to do. We've been denying it for too long. You and I are victims of a force stronger than both of us. Running away won't solve anything.'

'I keep telling you, Kate, I'm not running away. I'm merely trying to repair a disaster that threatens to destroy us both.'

'I think, as usual, you're overreacting, Declan. I've told you what to do – more than once.'

'Give up my faith, deny my calling, turn my back on the Church?' He takes a step nearer to me. 'Would that make you happy?' Without waiting for a reply he continues, 'You profess your undying love for me, so answer me this: Would it make you happy to see me desperately unhappy?'

I say nothing.

'Answer me, Kate! How would you feel, knowing you'd forced me to give up the church for you, knowing deep in your heart it goes against everything I've ever believed in? Don't assume I haven't thought about it. I've thought of little else since the day in church when I joined you and Brendan in marriage. Don't you see, Kate, I'd be a different man, not the Father Steele you idolized as a young girl, nor the Declan you love as a woman. I'd be a lesser person.'

'Not in my eyes.'

'In *mine*, Kate.'

His desperation silences me. I can think of nothing but the pain of being parted from him. We both remain silent, preoccupied with our fears. After a few moments' hesitation, I say, 'When I'm not with you I feel like I'm living behind a glass wall looking out at the world from the other side. When I'm with you I feel the opposite, totally at one with the world.'

Miserably he adds, 'I love you, Kate, but I love God more.'

'Can't you do God's work in some other way? Teaching, perhaps, or charity work?'

Rounding on me, his eyes blazing, he screeches, 'You don't give up, do you? All these years you've waited for me when you could have had any man you wanted. Why?'

'Simple. I've never wanted anyone else but you since the moment I saw you. I want to marry you. Do I have to spell it out? Is it not written all over my face, tattooed on every piece of my flesh? I wear my heart on every part of my body like some bloody lovesick snot-nosed kid. I can't imagine my life without you. When you're not with me I feel like I've lost a limb. We can't deny what's happened between us, any more than we can deny our love for each other.'

'I'm confused, Kate. I can't come to terms with the magnitude of my betrayal.'

'So it was OK to fuck me a couple of times a week? I suppose God accepted that, did he? Have you confessed, Declan? Talked to him in depth? Sorry, just one of those things Mr Almighty, you know: lust, temptation, happens to the best of us. I'm sure I'll get over it eventually, return to the fold.'

'For God's sake, Kate!'

'Don't talk to me about God, Declan. Right now I don't want to invite him into this conversation.'

He lifts his face and concentrates on the ceiling. 'Why do I always feel guilty? Why do I carry all the blame? The first night you came here, the first time we made love after Brendan's death, I begged you to leave – yet still you stayed.'

'You wanted me to stay, Declan, admit it. As much as I wanted to.'

He's not listening. 'You were determined to have me, I know that now. Was it a power trip, Kate? With all your beauty, talent, resources, was I the one thing you couldn't have? Because I belonged to another? Is this your way of avenging the Sisters of Mercy, the nuns who abused you, and a God you felt had deserted you? Was it about love, Kate, or revenge?'

His words crawl under my skin, roping themselves

around my heart. He doesn't flinch as I lash out, slapping his face hard, my hand stinging when I scream, 'Is that what you think? I don't know how you can even suggest such a thing, Declan. All my life I've wanted, longed for, craved to feel the way I feel when I'm with you. You make me whole. Nobody has ever done that for me. Brendan made me feel secure, but he never made me feel complete.'

Completely still, a white handprint clearly defined on his left cheek, Declan begins to speak. I barely recognize his subdued voice, yet feel certain he's telling the truth. 'I'm sorry. I'm distraught, confused, but I do know deep in my heart I don't want to leave the church. I've been thinking about it for weeks and I can't imagine my life outside. I've talked to God, I intend to talk to the Bishop. I've got an appointment with him next week.'

'Will you tell him about me . . . us?'

'Yes. I intend to tell him everything.'

'You're not a good liar, Declan, I can see it in your eyes. You have no intention of telling him everything. He might excommunicate you.'

'I have no choice but to tell him. I can't carry on swallowing the lie to the Church, to God. If he allows me to continue, I'll make a vow never to see you again. I intend to keep it.'

I feel like a huge weight is crushing my body, so much so I can't breathe. I'm helpless. I try to speak but the words won't come. I try again, opening and shutting my mouth like a goldfish in a tank.

In one long stride he's next to me. I can taste his breath as he enfolds me in his arms murmuring, 'Kate, my beautiful Kate, you must understand I love you. I've never loved anyone like I love you, but I love God more. I can't carry on with this madness. I feel like . . .' he struggles to find the right metaphor '. . . I'm being driven by a powerful locomotive forced to travel at breakneck speed to forbidden destinations. Once there, I abandon myself to the illicit pleasures yet am full of bitter remorse on the journey back.'

With both hands he cups my chin. I'm a little girl again begging Mr Molloy for a square of chocolate. In a small, childlike whimper I say, 'How will I survive without you?'

'You will move on. I know you have the strength, the resources to turn the corner into the next street.'

I begin to cry.

Declan is clearly moved. Tenderly, he wipes my tears with the sleeve of his soutane. I stroke his face, letting my fingertips trail to the nape of his neck. Tilting my head I find his mouth. It's dry: I wet it with my tongue, slowly forcing his lips apart with mine. The taste of his breath increases the ache in my groin, in my heart, in my entire being. I'm whimpering, 'You have such power to hurt me, Father, but my need is greater than God's. Without you I'm nothing.'

Now he's crying, his chest heaving with loud, tormented sobs. 'Kate, my love, my beautiful Kate, I have to leave you, don't you see? I can't carry on like this.'

I'm not listening. 'Take me, Declan,' I urge. 'For the last time. It will be the last, I promise.'

Gently he holds me at arm's length. 'No, I can't, it won't be the last time, you know as well as I do, it will be the last time until the next time. I have to stop, we have to stop.'

Knotting my fingers in his, I squeeze tight, my voice deliberately controlled: 'I understand how you feel, Declan. I want you to be happy. I swear by almighty God that this will be the last time we make love. I'll walk away, Declan, for ever. No forwarding address, nothing. I want you inside my body for the last time.'

As I speak, I'm leaning into him, pressing my body hard against his. I lean forward, he fills his mouth with my hair. He's taut and erect; a beat of triumph throbs in my chest. He desires me, and that, for the moment, is all that matters.

My hands fumble with the fastenings on his soutane, his begin to claw at my clothes. He forces me down to the floor, eagerly I submit, and as he enters me I'm startled by a feeling of total invincibility. I knead his buttocks, urging him over and over again to take me, use me in any way he wants, for the last time. Afterwards, knotted in each other's arms, my eyes fixed on his face, I begin to plot. Let Declan think our affair is over, it'll lull him into a state of complacency. Little does he know I will never give him up, not as long as I live.

'You can get dressed now, Kate.'

I sit up, swing my legs over the examination bed and let them dangle. 'Everything OK, Doctor?'

Dr Clancy is smiling. 'Couldn't be better. When you're ready I'll see you in my office. We'll have a chat.'

I'm on my feet reaching for my clothes as the doctor leaves the examination room. A few minutes later I'm seated opposite him at his handsome mahogany desk. He's humming, his head bent, methodically jotting notes with a smart black and silver pen. Nonchalantly I glance around the dowdy familiarity of the room. A thick wedge of primrose paint had faded on the wall opposite the bay window, the heavy Victorian reproduction furniture is covered in its habitual film of dust, the doctor's desk is a clutter of thumbed papers, manila files and books. David Clancy had been Brendan's GP, as Brendan always put it, 'for more years than I care to remember'. I've never found out exactly how many. I first met him four months after I'd moved in with Brendan. Hearing me coughing one night, Brendan had sent me to consult Doc Clancy, silencing my protests with a firm: 'That's a nasty bark you've got. David will sort you out, young lady.' Just as well

Brendan had insisted. It turned out I'm asthmatic: any infection left untreated would very quickly deteriorate into bronchitis. Up to that point I'd thought the chronic cough I'd had several times as a child was flu. The sisters had never called for the doctor. I'd been treated with a Vick rub on my chest, two dabs, only two, on my vest, and a vile-tasting mixture Mother Superior swore by. Once I'd been so ill Mother Peter had insisted on calling the doctor, who'd given me antibiotics. After two days I'd felt much better, but once out of bed I'd been told Mother Thomas had lost the remainder of the course. I'd suspected, but had been too afraid to say, that she'd lost them on purpose.

'When was your last period, Kate?'

I know exactly: two weeks before Brendan's death. 'May the twentieth.'

'You're sure about that?'

'Absolutely.'

More scribbling before Dr Clancy looks up, fixing me with his penetrating icy blue gaze. 'You're approximately twelve weeks pregnant, Kate. It's impossible for it to be Brendan's child.' A long sigh, then, 'Pity.'

'I know the baby isn't Brendan's.'

'Do you know who the father is?'

'Yes, but I can't disclose his name.'

There is a long silence, punctuated by the rustle of paper and the doctor clearing his throat. 'I know it's none of my business, Kate, but I'm speaking to you now as a friend. Do you have any plans to marry the father?'

'No.'

'How do you feel about bearing and raising an illegitimate child?'

'Not great, but I have very little choice.'

'How about putting pressure on the father to acknowledge his responsibility?'

'He can't.'

'Is he married?'

I lie. 'Yes.'

Dropping his pen the doctor leans back in his chair; with his right hand he rubs the side of his face. 'Before his death, Brendan told me of his desire for a child. I did all the tests for him, sperm count, the lot. He loved you, Kate; not in the conventional sense, I know, but I really believe if he'd lived he would have been happy to adopt this child as his own. If you want my advice . . .' I nod. 'Pass this child off as Brendan's. It will carry the Fitzgerald name, be the heir he so desperately craved. Your reputation is maintained, the father can relinquish his responsibility and keep his marriage intact, if that's what he wants. As long as you can make your peace with God, all will be fine. Can you do that?'

Rising to my feet I say, 'I've no problem passing the child off as Brendan's. In fact, I'd already considered it. I'm sure the father will be more than pleased to relinquish his responsibility. As for God, I walked away from him the day of Brendan's funeral. I'd left him before that, but Brendan's death was the final straw.'

'I don't think you really mean that, Kate.'

Placing the flat of my hands on the desk top, I look directly into the doctor's eyes. 'I've never been so certain about anything in my entire life.'

The sky over the church is inky black, pricked with stars. My eyes are glued to the door of the sacristy. When it opens and he steps outside I can see him clearly in the light above the door. He's talking to someone inside whom I can't see. As his mouth moves I concentrate on his profile. A soft breeze shifts a tuft of hair on his brow; my fingers itch to pat it back into place. Hidden in shadows like a mugger, I wait for my prey, silently ticking the seconds off in my head as he finishes his conversation. The closing door makes a dull thud closely followed by his soft footfalls on the path. He's walking in my direction. When he is almost upon me I step out of the shadows to block his path. Startled, he jumps like a rabbit caught in the glare of car headlights.

'I've come to say goodbye, Declan.'

'I thought we did that already.'

'We did, but I heard you were leaving Ireland next week. I wanted to give you a parting gift.'

I sense his nervousness.

'I'm expecting your baby.'

Dazed, he reaches out for support. Finding none, he staggers a little before regaining his balance. Momentarily speechless, he stares at me as if I'm some kind of alien monster who has just landed in his path.

'Say something,' I demand after at least four minutes of silence.

'I thought you'd put on weight.'

'Is that it?'

'What did you expect? Jubilation? Are you certain?'

For a second I hate him. I'm shaken by the violence of my fleeting emotion and want to tear into him, scratch at his eyes, tug his hair, draw blood. 'I saw the doctor this morning. He confirmed I'm twelve weeks pregnant.' Trying hard to remain calm, I add, 'How do you feel, Declan?'

He drops his head in his hands. When a moment later he lifts his head, I see his eyes have grown sadder, as if he's realized he's failed me. 'Do you want the truth?'

I can't contain my sarcasm. 'Sure, Father, you always tell the truth.'

Shaking his head, he says, 'I feel physically sick. My entire world has splintered into hundreds of tiny fragments. I feel unreal, like I'm living a book, a story. It's going to come to an end soon, I know it must.'

'Do you enjoy being unhappy, Declan?'

'What sort of question is that?'

278

'An honest one, because it seems to me that you do. You're an impostor. You pretend, hide behind your own back, play games, lie to yourself. What you see is not what you get with Father Steele, folks!' When he doesn't respond, I appeal: 'We could be a family, Declan. Imagine that, *our* family.'

'I've got a family. I don't want a wife and child. Can't you see what this means? God will never forgive me now. I'm living a perpetual lie.'

I loathe the conciliatory tone that has crept into my voice. 'Do you really think God gives a shit about your little world? Anyway, having a baby doesn't change anything, Declan. I can pass it off as Brendan's child. Or I can go to London, have an abortion.'

'No, Kate, never! I can't, I won't let you. Would you, could you kill our child?'

I take a step closer to him; he backs away. Miserably I mutter, 'It was just a threat. I wanted to see how you would react.'

Without hesitation, he says, 'Did I pass the test, Kate?' Then, before I can reply, 'I understand now. It's about manipulation, isn't it? It's all a deliberate game to get me to give up the Church to marry you.'

'Absolutely not.'

'Be honest, Kate. I've always known when you lie. Why can't you understand I refuse to give up the Church? Why is that so difficult for you to accept? Do you want to know what I think?'

Mutely I nod.

'I think you're sick.'

Outraged, I shout, 'What do you mean, sick?'

He points to his temple. 'Sick in here, Kate. I don't mean insane, just a little unbalanced. All your life you've been searching for someone to love. In your adolescence you saw me as the perfect role model, a mixture of brother, father, friend. Now you have cast me as your lover, husband, father to your baby. I'm just a vehicle to fuel your obsessive need.'

Calm now, I respond, 'You're wrong, Declan, totally wrong. I found my father in Brendan, and happily I've filled lots of other gaps with my work. What I feel for you is not remotely like anything else. I can't bear to lose you, the thought makes me feel so desolate it's pathetic. I hate myself for this dependency. If that's obsession, then so be it. But there is something I have to know, I want the truth.' I pause then ask, 'Do you love me?'

After a moment's hesitation, he replies with an emphatic, 'Yes.'

'That's why I'll never accept it. I'm sorry, Declan, but you do see that I can't let you go, ever.'

The moon has risen high in the overhead sky; it streaks the path and lawns silver. The top of his head looks coppery in the moonlight, like the colour of the floor in Mother Superior's office after I'd polished it for five hours. I'm trapped inside the glass box again, my face pressed hard against the window, reality moving slowly past on the outside. The sense of isolation and despair is like nothing I've ever felt before. With profound regret and sadness, I watch him turn and begin to walk away. I call his name, but he doesn't stop. Instead he increases his pace.

The painting is the biggest and most ambitious I've ever attempted. A life-size portrait painted from memory. For five days and nights I've worked almost non-stop, the fatigue and emotional input taking me back to the early days with Brendan.

I'm with Brendan in the studio in Elgin Crescent. His spirit inhabits this room as if he'd never left. I'm playing his favourite Vivaldi at full volume, and with every violent brushstroke I hear his voice.

'Kate, my beautiful genius, Kate. I wonder who gave

you those magic hands? Was it your mother or father, grandfather perhaps? Or were they sent from God? Let me worship at their shrine.' Without restraint I'd laugh, oh how I'd laugh as he fell to his feet to kiss one or both of my hands.

I miss the laughter, Brendan's as much as my own. I haven't laughed like he made me laugh since his death. Until I lived with Brendan I had no idea how to do it freely. In the orphanage, laughter – when there was anything to laugh about – was subdued, hidden behind hands, sinful, wicked. The Sisters of Mercy don't know a lot about having fun, and, as Bridget had said, 'Only a feckin eejit would dare laugh with, at, or within earshot of Mother Thomas.'

'Fucked up.' That was how Brendan described the Catholic Church. How can the human spirit evolve constrained by the shackles of a doctrine that is opposed to all human joy? I recall the first few months of living with Brendan, how he'd gradually taught me not only how to enjoy life, but how to develop an eye, an appreciation of the aesthetic: fine antiques, classic architecture, the cut of a handmade suit, the clink of pure crystal, the lines of a thoroughbred mare. I grew to adore the sensuality of linen sheets; I learnt to savour food instead of bolting it like my last supper; I was introduced to the pleasures of aged claret and port, and vintage champagne that caught in the back of my throat, and the best vodka martini (according to Brendan) outside of Manhattan. But, more importantly, it was Brendan who made me address my fundamental character. 'You're a free spirit, Kate. The nuns tried but were unable to quell that spirit. Now you've no restraints. Let it loose, it's a special gift. Promise me you'll never change, nor forget that if you love yourself it's easier to love and be loved.' Now in my head I hear his laughter, loud as if he's standing right next to me.

Suddenly I feel a white hot blast of anger. I throw the

brush I'm holding across the room; a blue blob marks the spot where it hits the wall before landing on the wooden floor. I can feel the tears like sharp needles pricking at my eyelids.

'You selfish bastard,' I howl at the painting of Declan. Then, addressing the blank wall to my left, I scream, 'I need you, Brendan. Why the fuck did you leave me? Am I not worthy of love? You can't answer that, can you? I'm having a baby, Brendan, the child of a Catholic priest. How do you feel about that? Tell me, for Chrissake, give me a sign. Do you really want this child, this Catholic child, to carry your name? Before you make a decision, let me warn you, the father is as fucked up as the rest of the God squad. Totally repressed, a good God-fearing man, Father Declan Steele. His passion, he's decided, after much oral and full penetrative sex, is reserved for God. He's the type you love to hate. Doesn't laugh a lot – dour, you'd say, or worse, boring. The sort of man you always claimed said three hundred Hail Marys after fantasizing about a blow job or a good fuck. But I'm in love with him, Brendan, have been since I was a kid of fifteen. He's the one. Like you always said, the Big L is as unpredictable as it's indiscriminate, totally irrational. That's what makes it so fascinating. I can't let him go. The mere thought terrifies me – I'm afraid of what I might do. Help me, Brendan, if ever I needed your advice, it's now.'

I fall silent, wondering if I'm going mad – all this ranting aloud at a dead man, as if he were standing next to me. I let a tear fall, then, using the back of my hand, I swat it like I would a fly. The sense of isolation is crowding in on me again. Gripping the base of the easel, I take a deep breath. My chest tightens; I'm back in the dark days of Mother Thomas. I'm shaking, whimpering, 'Please don't hurt me, I promise to be a good girl, please don't . . .' The nun's mouth is folded in at the corners, her lips are dry and crusted. I hope she's in hell. The probability cheers me. I pick up another paintbrush. Dipping it in the oil, I begin to paint Declan's mouth. Easy, I know it as well as my own. With each stroke of the brush I feel his lips forcing mine apart, his tongue traversing my body, finding my most intimate parts while I submit with absolute abandon. The recollection makes me wonder if I'll always feel this way. I see myself in years to come: a withered old bird, dry as a prune, still hankering after a long-dead priest. I touch my belly. At least I'll have his child. I'll never feel lonely again. Every day I'll see my child's face, knowing Declan and I had made him in love. At least my son (it must be a boy) would have the love of a mother. A lot more than I'd had. I'd already decided I'd compensate for the lack of a father. My child would never know a day without love.

Standing back a couple of feet I study my work. It's good. I've succeeded in capturing his dual personality: Declan the man, and the pious priest. The sombre black soutane, heavy baroque cross, bible clutched firmly in one hand, are in direct contrast to the dishevelled hair and wild passionate gaze. Conflicting hungers, he'd said. I hadn't seen him look like that often. It was what I saw immediately after he entered my body, and in the few exquisite moments before his climax.

This canvas shows a bold, charismatic figure, proud and strong: every woman's hero. There's a little romantic idealism on my part – in fact Father Declan Steele is made of much weaker stuff. It doesn't make me love him less; on the contrary, I love him more. I'll be damned if I'll give him up. As I touch up the corners of his mouth with a small brush, an idea pops into my head.

It wouldn't be difficult to find out where Declan would be living in New York. My exhibition was due to open in two months and I'd agreed to attend the first night. I'd make some discreet enquiries as to the whereabouts of Father Declan Steele and at the same time take up Susie

Simon's repeated offer to find a Manhattan apartment for me.

I'd have the baby, quietly, in Ireland, well away from prying eyes. When the child was old enough to travel, we'd join his daddy.

Invigorated by the plan I hum to the strains of Vivaldi, dabbing Declan's usually pale cheeks with colour. I'm so engrossed I don't hear the telephone ringing or Mrs Keating's footsteps until she taps me on the shoulder.

Startled, I spin around fast, daubing Mrs Keating with splurges of paint. Carefully she wipes her cheek. I'm aware of the ugly way her flesh puckers on her chin. Fighting to be heard above the music, she shouts, 'Mrs Fitz, I think there is something you should know.'

Strolling to the stereo I cut the music. As I walk back across the room I notice Mrs Keating staring at the portrait. She is very white and, concerned, I ask, 'Are you OK?'

Wringing her hands, her bottom lip trembling, she says, 'Terrible news.' She points at Declan's portrait. 'Him – the priest, he's dead, a news flash just now. I can't believe it. Two nights ago I was confessing how I'd lost faith in God after Mr Fitz's death, and now this, the good Father dead.'

I feel light-headed but am able to mumble, 'I don't understand.'

Holding the flat of her hand to her mouth she sobs, 'It's Father Steele from St Patrick's . . .' Again she points to the painting. 'The priest you've painted, the one who married you and Mr Fitz – he's dead. For the love of God, why would a handsome young priest like him take his own life? Jesus Mary and Joseph, what's the world coming to?'

Her voices drops to a whisper and dies. Unable to grasp what I've just heard, I'm speechless. I can do nothing but stand very still, shaking my head. I'm hot, there's a strange tingling in my hands and Mrs Keating's face is blurred. I try to tell her I'd like a glass of water but I can't speak. As I slump forward I'm only vaguely aware of hitting my head on the corner of the easel. Then merciful blackness.

Part Three

THE GODS

I wonder if the dead I have loved will live on inside my head for the rest of my life, or if time and age will deaden the voices, fade the images. To be betrayed is one thing, but to be abandoned, not once but twice, is contemptible. I thought about joining them. It would be easy: an end to pain. Brendan stopped me; he convinced me it was too soon.

I listened to him, I always did, I always will. I wasn't angry with him for deserting me, not any more. My anger is reserved for Declan. Had he, in the darkness and silence of his own selfish despair, spared a thought for our child? What would become of him?

I recall something Brendan said to me a long time ago: 'There are good men in bad places, and bad places in good men.' I know deep in my heart I'll never forgive Father Steele.

Chapter Sixteen

'SUICIDE PRIEST HAD SECRET ARTIST LOVER.'

My agent had sent me the *New York Times*; it arrived this morning with a brief note: 'Now I know why you were never interested in any of the men I put in front of your nose.' I read the headline for the third time before fixing on the photograph of Declan. In the image taken several years ago he looks no more than a boy. I'm pictured in a column below, a paparazzo shot taken in London less than a year ago. Groaning inwardly, I let the newspaper fall from my grip to the floor.

Lighting a cigarette, I inhale deeply. I'd started to smoke the day after Declan's death. It helped; a bit, not a lot – the vodka helped more. The shrill ringing of the telephone invades the part of my brain still functioning and I move with the automated jerkiness of a robot to the telephone located on a table close to the window.

'Is that you, Kate?'

Instantly I recognize the voice and feel my heart swell like a balloon in my chest. Bubbling over with indescribable joy I can barely get my words out. 'Bridget? Is it really you?' Then again, 'Bridget, I can't tell you how good it is to hear your voice.'

'It's myself, Kate. I read about you in the newspaper. How are you?'

'I've felt better.'

'How are you holding up?'

'Not good, Bridget. The media are hounding me. In Dublin I felt like a prisoner. The press had set up camp outside the door. I had to leave Elgin Crescent by the back way, like a bloody fugitive, under the cover of darkness. That was two days ago. Since then I haven't set foot outside Leinster Manor's grounds. But it's only a matter of time before they track me down. One British tabloid got to Mother Paul; she described me as an evil whore who seduced the good priest when I was sixteen. I'd always been a bad influence, she said, and had laid the responsibility for Mother Thomas's death firmly at my door. I quote, "Bridget was under that wicked girl's influence. She did everything Kate O'Sullivan said."'

'Have you given an interview? Your side of the story?'

'No, and I don't intend to. The entire country has cast me in the role of temptress from the wrong side of the tracks. Do you really think, given Catholic determination to ignore what they don't want to know, my tiny voice will be heard above the furore? I've caused the death of a priest. I'm to blame. If Brendan had been alive he would have protected me from all this.'

'Are you sure about that?'

For a couple of minutes I consider Bridget's question before saying, 'He knew me very well – better than I know myself. I believe he would have understood what drove me into the arms of Declan Steele.'

'What?' Bridget asks.

'I was in love with him. Hopelessly, passionately, unconditionally. I wanted him to abandon the Church and marry me.'

'I'm sorry, Kate.' A pause, then: 'I need to sort out a few things here, but if you hang on a couple of days I'll get back to Ireland.'

My eyes streaming, I mutter, 'I've missed you, Bridget.'

'I'll be there on Friday morning. Where will you be?'

'I'd planned to stay here in Tipperary, away from the press, but I could meet you somewhere discreet in town.'

'Nah! I'll drive to you. The country air will do my

lungs the power of good after the pollution in Chicago.'

'I don't need to tell you that it's not often I'm stuck for words, but I can't start to tell you what this means to me.'

'It's the bloody least I can do.'

'Thanks, Bridget.'

'See you Friday. And, Kate . . .'

'Yes?'

'Don't ever forget what you always said to me when we were kids: "As long as we're together we can lick 'em all, the long and the short and the tall." '

As I replace the telephone it rings again and I hear a male voice, American. 'Mrs Fitzgerald?'

Pulling on the cigarette, I ask, 'Who wants to know?'

'I don't know whether you remember me – I'm the clumsy guy who doused you with champagne at your exhibition in New York.'

I remember the journalist I'd liked on sight. 'Tom Gregson. Did your wife like her painting?'

'My soon-to-be-ex wife didn't seem to appreciate it very much at the time, yet it's the only thing we've fought over in the divorce settlement.'

'I'm sorry.'

'Don't be. Under the circumstances your sympathy should be kept exclusively for yourself. The press have given you a hard time.'

I laugh hollowly. 'Well, naturally the Irish press have cast me as the villain, with the devout Father Steele the victim.'

'How about telling your side of the story?'

'I doubt it will make a difference.'

'That's where you're wrong. There are always two sides and it's important your side is heard. People can then make a choice based on the truth. The other option is to hide away until you feel it's safe to venture out, but you'll always be wondering if your colleagues, friends, acquaintances, or the man in the street is pointing the finger of guilt at you. Do you really want to live the rest of your life like that?'

In my head I've formed a very clear image of Tom Gregson: the impish suavity, the boyish grin, the gap between his front teeth. 'People have short memories, they move on to the next thing very quickly. It would only take the Bank of Ireland to cut or increase interest rates and I'd be forgotten.'

'Don't be too sure, Mrs Fitzgerald. I agree, people have short memories, but you know as well as I do the Catholic Church looks after its own. They won't let you forget.'

I sigh, accepting the logic of his words. 'You're very encouraging.'

I imagine him grinning. 'No, just realistic and honest. I won't deny I'd love to write your story, tell it how it is, let the world and Ireland in particular know how it felt and feels for you. Were you in love with Father Steele?'

The rebuke, None of your fucking business, jumps into my head but I hold back.

'Yes, very much.'

'All the more reason to tell your side of the story. It takes two to tango. We can't make out alone. If I were you, I'd be very angry. My lover priest absconds by committing suicide and gets an automatic acquittal before the jury have heard all the evidence.'

'You're very convincing, Mr Gregson, and right about me being angry.'

'Call me Tom.'

'Suicide is so bloody cowardly, it makes me feel physically sick to think Declan could have left me this way.'

'Will you consider granting me an interview?'

I ask, 'Which publication?'

'New York Times.'

'It's a deal.'

I hear a note of triumph when he asks, 'Where and when?'

'Here in Leinster Manor, Tipperary, tomorrow afternoon. Any time after lunch. Can you make it?'

'I'll catch the six-thirty flight out of here to Dublin.'

'Where are you now?'

'Upstate New York.'

I give him the address and directions and, before I put the telephone down, add, 'No photographers.'

He sighs before agreeing, 'OK.'

Lighting another cigarette I leave the study, cross the hall and mount the stairs to my bedroom. As soon as I enter I feel better. It's the one room in the house where I feel secure. I lock the door and lie on the bed, inhaling the last of the cigarette deep in my lungs. I grind the cigarette out on a saucer next to the bed, then, my legs curled up to my stomach in a foetal ball, I shut my eyes tight. It's how I used to sleep in the orphanage after the nuns had inspected the dormitories to check all the girls were sleeping with their arms outside the covers, crossed over their chests.

The thought of Bridget coming warms me like a thick blanket on a bitterly cold night and for the first time since I'd heard of Declan's death I feel alive.

Is this to be my fate? I ask myself. Are the men I love destined to die? Without a thought for how I would survive without them? Single-minded and downright selfish. I quake with anger when I think of Declan; I despise him for his weakness. I rub my belly. How would I explain to our son that his father had killed himself? What a despicable legacy.

How could you do this, Declan? Did you not for one moment think of what would become of me? How I would bear the impossible baggage you've dumped on me? I recall our last meeting when I'd told him I was pregnant; I see again a veil of sadness covering his eyes, then the outrage and the evident despair. I begin to rock, singing softly, 'Hush little baby, don't say a word, Daddy's gonna buy me a mocking bird. An' if that mocking bird don' sing, Daddy's gonna buy me a diamond ring. An' if that diamond ring don' shine, surely will break this heart of mine . . .'

That night I drink a bottle of vodka. At three-thirty I fall asleep and at ten-thirty awake to Mrs Hickey's insistent knocking.

'Mrs Fitz, there's a telephone call for you.'

Forcing my eyes open, I shout, 'I thought I'd unplugged all the bloody phones.' Shambling out of bed, a throbbing at the back of my head, I open the door. The housekeeper, in her matter-of-fact tone, says, 'You forgot the kitchen.'

Holding my head, I mumble, 'Who is it?'

She frowns. 'Some fella from the *Irish Times*. Said he had some information you might be interested in.'

'How did he get this number?'

'Search me.' I notice the contempt in Mrs Hickey's face as she shrugs. 'Reporters have ways and means. How did that fella who rang yesterday get the number?'

'I know Tom Gregson.' Then, 'Did you ring the *Times*, Mrs Hickey?'

Shifting her eyes from my face to the empty vodka bottle lying on the floor next to the bed, she says, 'Sure I did no such thing.'

I wouldn't put it past her to do it – for money or out of sheer spite. Mrs Hickey has never forgiven me for marrying her Mr Fitz.

Adeptly changing the subject, she comments, 'Mr Fitz would have hated you getting drunk like this. Always hated women who got drunk.'

I grimace. 'Mr Fitz is dead. No lectures please, Mrs Hickey, I've got a sore head and I feel very sick.'

'You'll get no sympathy out of me. Self-inflicted pain.'

'I don't want sympathy. I want something to ease my

head.' Holding my throbbing forehead I add, 'Please.' Then stumbling back to the bed I lie down.

'What shall I tell the reporter fella?'

'Tell him to bugger off,' I mutter. I shut my eyes, not opening them again until Mrs Hickey returns a couple of minutes later with a glass of water and two white tablets. 'Here, take these. They'll make you feel better.'

Struggling to sit up, I take the tablets from the palm of her hand and, popping them on to my tongue, ask, 'What are they?'

'Strong stuff I had from the doctor when I had my gallstone operation last year. I always keep them in my bag just in case. In no time at all you'll be feeling right as rain.'

She's right and when the telephone rings forty-five minutes later I'm ready to take the call.

Without preamble, I confront the journalist with, 'How did you know where to find me?'

'I'm a journalist, what can I say? I'd like to introduce myself properly. I work for the *Irish Times*, the name is –'

'I'm not interested in your CV. Just get on with it, man.'

Quickly he says, 'I believe you were born in America to American parents.'

A gob of mucus catches in the back of my throat. I clear it and demand, 'Where did you get this information?'

'If you give me an exclusive interview, I'll tell you. Fair exchange?'

After a moment's hesitation, I say, 'I can't, I've granted one to the *New York Times*.'

The line goes silent. 'You still there?' I ask.

'Call them and tell them it's off.'

'I can't. But what I will do is ask if the stories can run simultaneously. If not, then you get to print the next day. You have my word I won't speak to anyone else.'

'OK, you got it. A few days ago a woman called my office. Said she had some information concerning Mrs Fitzgerald née O'Sullivan to sell.'

'Who was this woman?'

'She refused to give her name but agreed to pass on conclusive information concerning your birth and subsequent adoption. I've got the info sitting on my desk in front of me.'

My heart instead of my head is pounding now. 'Tell me about it.'

'No can do. Not until you keep your side of the bargain, but I'll give you a taster. You were born in America, to American parents and came to Ireland in 1962; June the fifth, to be precise, on a BOAC flight.'

'Is that it? I could have told you that.'

This seems to throw him. I hear the hesitation when he hurriedly continues, 'I've got more. When can we meet?'

'On Friday at one in the Crooked Man pub in Templemore, County Tipperary. I think you know what I look like.'

That night I drift in and out of sleep, returning time after time to the affirmation of what I'd always suspected. I wasn't Irish. American parents, the reporter had said. At least it explained why I look so different from all the other girls I know. I wake at dawn to a thick slice of sun filling a gap in the half-drawn curtains.

I wrap up warm in a long coat and, with my feet slipping in Brendan's size ten Wellingtons, I trudge out of the garden, up the lane past Cassidy's farm, and take the track out across spare land between flocks of lazy sheep knee deep in yellow grass.

An hour later on returning to the house I bathe for the first time in three days and dress in the most garish dress I own: a vivid print in varying shades of reds and blues. I put on black patent leather shoes with pointed toes, high heels and a narrow ankle strap. Brendan always called them my 'come and fuck me shoes'. The recollection makes me smile and for the first time since Declan's death two weeks ago I do my hair and apply some make-up.

Tom Gregson arrives early at fifteen minutes to three. Mrs Hickey lets him in; in her overly effusive manner I hear her bombarding him with offers of all manner of fare, from sandwiches to biscuits, apple pie, beer, whiskey, tea, coffee – the poor man is spoilt for choice. Fundamentally she's a good woman, but that doesn't mean I have to like her or her constant prattle.

Her jowls appear before her when she comes to announce the journalist, and I'm struck by her ugliness all over again. Last in the queue that one; 'Mrs Hickey has overdosed on ugly tablets,' was Brendan's wicked description. His banter and my own laughter ring in my ears. I'm going mad, I tell myself, then, with a reassuring shrug, think it can't be any worse than the way I've felt in the last weeks. It might even be preferable.

When Tom Gregson enters the room I'm struck by his presence. I don't remember him being so tall – six three or maybe four, with wide American-footballer type shoulders – but I do recall his riot of inky curls reaching almost to his shirt collar and his suave easy charm.

For once deserted by my confidence I quietly mumble, 'I just want to say, it's good to see you again.'

He's smiling tentatively, showing the gap between his two front teeth and a deep dimple in the centre of a prominent chin. Both are very attractive. He has blue eyes, bright and inquisitive like an over-zealous child, in distinct contrast to his worn face, which is deeply furrowed on brow and cheeks.

'I heard Mrs Hickey overwhelming you with hospitality. I'm afraid she doesn't have her adored Mr Fitz, my late husband, to spoil any more.'

'How long has he been dead?'

'I'm surprised you don't know. Come on, Tom, I'm sure you know more about me than I know of myself.'

Again the boyish grin. I like the way his eyes curl at the corners and dance inside. Laughing eyes, always the best. Brendan's eyes had danced a jig most of the time except when he was angry.

'I seem to recall you telling me once you had Irish blood?'

'Yes, on my father's side. Way back, County Wicklow.'

I light a cigarette, offering the open pack to him. Vigorously he shakes his head, which makes his hair stick up on end. 'Don't tempt me. I gave up a few years ago but still get the urge. Regularly.'

Hunched over my lighter, from the corner of my mouth I say, 'I just started.'

Looking up I see the door open. It's Mrs Hickey bearing a tray containing a teapot, two cups, milk and sugar and a plate of neatly cut sandwiches. With extreme care and unwarranted fuss she places it on a small butler's tray. 'I've prepared a bite. I'm sure you must be half-starved, coming in from New York and all. They serve naught but rubbish on them flights. Mr Fitz always said our cat gets better grub.'

Hands neatly clasped in front of the starched white pinny, Mrs Hickey backs out of the room, her I-know-best look directed at me. It never fails to irritate me and no amount of trying on my behalf to forge some sort of friendship with the woman has made a scrap of difference to her attitude. A few weeks before my marriage to Brendan I'd overheard a conversation between the housekeeper and Sylvester. I recall having felt stung when she'd said, 'If the young mistress thinks I'm going to change to her ways she'll do well to think again. Sure as eggs is eggs, I'll be the same Mrs Hickey the master has been happy with for a good some years. Meself, I'll be having none of it. She's a bloody upstart, that one. Stuck-up –

Tuppence-halfpenny looking down on tuppence – you'd think she came from something grand instead of a back-of-beyond orphanage. "Always the worst," my mother used to say, and she worked for all types in her time. Called them *nouveaux riches*. "Toffee-nosed lot," she'd say to me when I was first starting out in service. "Watch out for the ones that have come from the wrong side of the tracks. Think they know it all."'

Sylvester had grunted something I couldn't catch in reply.

In passing I'd mentioned it to Brendan, who'd supported Mrs Hickey, adding that all staff were, if you allowed them to affect you, a pain in the neck.

'Tea?' I ask, dragging my mind back to the present. I begin to pour before he nods. 'Do you like tea? I thought most Americans preferred coffee.'

'I'm not a great fan of either. My mother was into health food and alternative therapy long before it became fashionable. She brought us up on fruit and vegetable juices. No caffeine ever darkened our door. After college, when I became a journalist, it felt great and kinda illicit to drink gallons of strong black coffee and smoke untipped Gitanes cigarettes while hammering out a story through the night.'

'Where were you brought up?'

'In the South, near Charleston. My mother was a Southerner, a beautiful belle in her time. Yes, ma'am, a real beauty; still is. My father was the demon Yankee who stole her heart and took her North. I was born in Boston but we moved back South when my maternal grandfather died leaving most of his estate to his only child, my mom. My father, God rest his soul, was a writer. He produced racy crime novelettes that sold millions and beautifully crafted short stories and poetry that didn't get published. Something I intend to get round to soon. Novel-writing, I mean.'

I sip my tea, studying him from under half-closed lids. Clearly uncomfortable under my scrutiny, he shuffles from foot to foot trying to concentrate on anything but my gaze.

Taking a tape recorder out of his jacket pocket, he places it on the table between us.

I glance at the tape recorder. 'Do you have to?'

'It's difficult for me to work without it.'

I sit down. 'Tough.'

With a sigh he sits on the opposing sofa and fishes a notebook and pencil from the breast pocket of his shirt. He flicks open the pad, saying, 'Let's do it the old-fashioned way.'

I point to the cup sitting next to the tape recorder. 'Your tea's getting cold.'

Lifting the cup, he takes a small sip, then sets it down again. 'When and where did you first meet Father Declan Steele?'

Letting my head fall back I shut my eyes tight. I see myself crouching in St Winifred's church in Friday Wells, cold and wet, suppressing a sneeze, waiting, watching, listening for his footsteps.

'In 1978, in church, in Friday Wells, Cork – the village where I grew up. I was taken there as a baby, barely new born, and lived there for sixteen years. I was a young girl, I'd never been held, or kissed, only abused and chased by boys – and the nuns with their canes and leather straps. The Sisters of Mercy, they called themselves. We called them by other names,' I spit.

'Other than the warmth we girls gave each other, we had nothing – just the cold, the brutality of the regime in the orphanage, and our dreams.'

'How old were you?'

'Fifteen.'

'How old was the priest?'

'Twenty-nine. He was the curate. I just want to say it

was love at first sight – for me, that is. I don't think the curate thought about me in that way. Well, not then.'

'When?'

My eyelids flutter open but I can't look at Tom. Instead I focus on a Hopper drawing Brendan bought for me several years ago. I can't remember exactly when but I do recall my utter delight. With a beat of regret I think of how different my life might have been if Brendan had been straight.

'Declan's – that is, Father Steele's interest in me began when I started to work for him.'

'Where?'

'In his cottage in Friday Wells. I was becoming a woman damn fast. Approaching my sixteenth birthday, it was time for me to leave the orphanage. I'd planned to go to Dublin but put them on hold when a job as housekeeper to the curate became available. I jumped at it. I would have worked all hours that God sent to be near him. It was just me and Father Steele. I was totally besotted. You might describe it as an adolescent crush, and, given my circumstances, that's understandable. But I knew it was more than that, much more. With every ounce of my being I wanted this man, and the longing never went away. Even after I left to go to Dublin and he left Ireland.'

'Where did he go?'

'Missionary work in South America.'

'And you, what became of you at that point?'

'I left Friday Wells for Dublin, believing I'd forget him in time. I applied to art college and worked as a life model for art students. That was how I met Brendan Fitzgerald. He changed my life. Brendan was the dearest, sweetest, warmest human being. A big man in physique, personality and heart. I adored him, as he did me, but ours was a platonic relationship. He was a guru to me, taught me almost everything I know.'

'Brendan Fitzgerald was a lot older than you?'

I'm smiling as I say, 'Will you answer a question for me, Mr Gregson?'

'I'll try.'

'Why is it journalists waste time asking questions they know the answers to?'

'A good reporter, if he's done his homework, will know a lot of the subject's background. Invariably what he doesn't know is the human emotion and motivation hidden beneath the detail. A good interview should reveal something of the subject's character, provide insight, inspiration, and a knowledge of the fundamental human forces that drive us to do the things we do.'

I like the sound of his voice, the soft Southern drawl is soothing. I feel some of my pent-up tension relaxing.

'Without that vital element the interview is dead in the water. Might as well be scrapped. Today it's difficult to achieve – just getting past the pack of publicists and hangers-on surrounding most celebrities is a mammoth task. Once you get to them, for the most part they are so guarded it's infuriating. It makes me so angry. We, the press, make these people, they use us when they want something and abuse us when it isn't exactly word for word how they anticipated. You in comparison were relatively easy to access.'

'You make me sound like a computer file.'

He grins. 'Sorry. Occupational habit. I spend a large part of my life accessing information.'

'Forgiven, and to answer your earlier question Brendan *was* much older. But that made no difference to our relationship. When we met he was forty-seven, I was sixteen and greener than that grass –' I point to the lawn beyond the window. 'I was eager to learn and I could paint. He encouraged both. I just want to say, ours was an unusual relationship but it worked.'

Not looking up from writing, Tom asks, 'You lived with him for many years before you married, is that right?'

'Yes. Three weeks after I met him he insisted I move in to his house. That was, I must admit, after he'd seen my work.'

'Did you submit some paintings?'

'No, I was modelling for a class he tutored. Brendan, as you no doubt know, was a very wealthy man. His family go way back. For most of his adult life he'd had a love affair with the arts. He painted a bit himself, not great, but good enough to hang. Once after class I criticized a life study of myself by one of his pupils. Brendan challenged me to do better.' Secretly I smile, thinking of Brendan dramatically stripping off his clothes to pose naked for me.

'And did you?'

'Yes, a lot better, so much so Brendan seemed convinced he'd discovered genius.'

I pause and am only vaguely aware of Tom pulling a press cutting from a brown manila file he'd earlier placed on the table. He wafts it in front of my face. 'According to this review in 1984 after your debut American exhibition your husband was right. I quote: "... emotional depth and innocent clarity that sears the soul with the flame of youth and genius ..."'

Modestly, I say, 'Very flattering, but merely one critic's opinion, not enough to warrant genius. I've got a long way to go to catch up with the masters.'

'But many of the masters weren't recognized until after their death. You're enjoying some notoriety in your lifetime, and at –' he looks down at his notes – 'twenty-four, I believe you're a millionaire?'

'What has money got to do with anything?'

'A naïve question, Mrs Fitzgerald, if you don't mind me saying. Money, and the acquiring, keeping, stealing, hiding, increasing of it, are all fundamental driving forces. People commit terrible crimes because of it, some of us crave it so much we lie, cheat, deceive and betray our loved ones and friends and family to acquire it. Avarice is one of the deadly sins, Mrs Fitzgerald, like its associate, lust; not to be taken lightly. Which brings me to my next question . . .'

Anticipating it, I turn to face the window, reminding myself that I'm not under oath, not forced to answer.

'When did your love affair with Father Steele begin?'

'Pass.'

A deep sigh escapes his lips. I hear his pencil drop and from the corner of my eye see his big frame hunch over the glass table. A curtain of silence falls between us. I wait for him to speak, acutely aware of his concentrated patience. Eventually, after a long few minutes, Tom asks, 'Is it painful?'

I utter, 'Very,' feeling my stomach bunch up in a tight fist. 'I just want to say that all my life I've worked hard at not feeling sorry for myself. When you grow up in an Irish-Catholic orphanage it's easy to become either a martyr – and I've met enough of them to know I never wanted it to happen to me – or a fucked-up mess, constantly blaming your background for all your inadequacies. The regime at the orphanage was grim. Some of the nuns were very cruel. Punished for almost everything, we lived in constant fear. Thank God, I had talent, something to cling to; my painting was my escape, or God forbid what might have happened to me.'

'I doubt it. I sense that you've got what Americans call guts, chutzpah. You're the kind of woman who survives against all odds. You came through the beatings. Am I right?'

I shrug, then pull myself out of the chair and light a cigarette. Blowing out smoke I cross the room to the window. Looking out towards the lake I see the stooped figure of Sylvester moving slowly on the far side. Ducks flap and fly in an arc in front of him. As I watch, the scene freezes in vivid grass green with great splurges of yellow and crimson like a surreal painting. I inhale and turn to face the journalist. 'Would you mind if we adjourned until tomorrow?'

He removes his hands from behind his head and rises. 'You're not on trial, Mrs Fitzgerald. I'm sorry if it feels that way.'

My attention is back at the window. I see the painting has changed; now all is grey: steely light, sombre water, and dappled grey lawns. Sylvester has gone. I prefer this mood, dismal and foreboding.

'I think it's going to thunder.' Then, 'I'm afraid of thunder. The devil clapping, the nuns used to say.' I pause. 'Brendan once said the richer you are, the less you pay for.' I smile enigmatically. 'But I've got a feeling we all pay in the end.' In two steps I've reached his side. 'I'll see you out.'

I'm aware of his confusion but don't care. I've done enough talking for one day. I'm tired. Now I want to be alone with my memories.

Chapter Seventeen

From the hall window I watch Tom open the car door and unfold his long legs. He leaps a couple of the deep puddles littering the drive before he reaches the door. I feel a flicker of exhilaration as he spots me and waves. I return the wave, then walk briskly to the front door to let him in.

'Good morning.'

I'm smiling. Not my best smile, but close. 'A better morning, after last night's storm. At least it's not raining for a change.'

'Hope the thunder didn't scare you too much.'

I grimace, thinking back to my terror. I'd spent the entire night curled up in a ball on the floor of Brendan's study, convinced that since it had the smallest window in the house I'd be safe. 'A little,' I admit.

I'm barefoot, and as we cross the hall my feet make no sound on the polished wood floor. A moment later I notice Mrs Hickey appear in the rectangle of space at the end of the inner hall leading to the kitchen and utility rooms. Like a bloody genie out of the lamp, I think. Would I ever get used to servants? At first it had been impossible. I'd made my own bed and had insisted on folding all my clothes in neat piles. As for being served at table, the urge to jump up and help or clear the plates had been irresistible and, if Brendan had not insisted otherwise, I would have ended up washing, ironing, and polishing floors.

It had been the same with Mrs Keating. 'Servants make cowards of us all, if we let them,' Brendan had said. At the time I hadn't been sure what he meant; now I knew.

Since Brendan's death I'd reverted back to doing for myself and had insisted that neither Mrs Keating nor Mrs Hickey interfere. They both resented my independence and stayed with me, I'm sure, purely out of loyalty to Brendan. If I wasn't careful I'd lose them both and be very sorry.

Smiling brightly, the housekeeper says, 'What can I be getting you? Sure, if you've travelled some distance perhaps you'd enjoy a bite?'

'If it's no trouble, I'd love something to eat,' Tom replies.

'It's no trouble at all. Now, just you be saying what it is you'd like. Perhaps you could be tempting Mrs Fitz to eat something? Rashers and eggs perhaps?'

The mere thought of a plate of bacon and eggs makes me feel sick, but to please Mrs Hickey and to join Tom I say, 'I'll have some of your home-made sour dough bread, toasted, with a thick slathering of golden marmalade.'

Her face splits into a wide grin. 'And fer the gentleman?'

'I could sure use the rashers and eggs – sunny-side up?'

Mrs Hickey looks confused. 'Sunny-side up?'

'Sorry, it's an Americanism. The yolk on top, not overcooked.'

'Sunny-side up it is, with tea, coffee, toast and freshly squeezed grapefruit juice.' Briskly she turns on her heel, calling over her shoulder to no one in particular, 'I'll set up in the morning room.'

The morning room is located on the corner wing of the house facing south-west. A circular table covered in a white linen cloth sits in front of the deep bay window affording uninterrupted views of untamed woodland and rolling hills beyond. This morning they are shrouded in mist.

I take a seat with my back to the window, gesticulating to Tom to sit opposite. 'You have the view.'

He sits and is about to speak as Mrs Hickey bursts into the room carrying a tray. Making fussy little mewing sounds in the back of her throat she begins to set the table with crockery, cutlery and the finest linen napery. Feeling edgy, I light my fifth cigarette of the day, deliberately blowing smoke close to the housekeeper who I know loathes smoking. 'Filthy habit,' she's fond of saying. 'When my Dan was alive I never let him smoke, not once. Mother of God, he would have sooner taken his own life as light up within ten miles of our house.'

Poor Dan, I'd often thought, not allowed to smoke in his own home. What else, I wonder, did she ban? Probably never got his dick within ten miles of her either. Old Dan had died of consumption when he was fifty. 'The Lord takes the best first,' Mrs Hickey had commented at the time. Then I hadn't agreed with her; I do now.

When at last Mrs Hickey leaves the room I grind my cigarette out in a saucer and look quizzically at Tom when he says, 'You look different today.'

Self-consciously I smooth my hair. 'I'm not wearing make-up.'

'It suits you.'

I'm accustomed to admiration so I'm surprised by the frisson of pleasure his compliment causes. I blush and lower my eyes. 'Thanks.'

'You look younger and even more beautiful.'

Now I know I'm as red as a turkey's neck. Feeling ridiculous, for once I'm grateful to see Mrs Hickey reappear. With a flourish the housekeeper places a plate in front of Tom. Looking at it and grinning, he says, 'Wow, this looks great.'

Mrs Hickey beams and puffs out her chest. 'A good Irish breakfast. That'll put hairs on yer chest.'

He winks in her direction. 'Who says I need any more?'

To my amazement, Mrs Hickey winks coquettishly back. 'I like a man with a hairy chest.' Without so much as a glance in my direction she places a basket of toast and pastries in the centre of the table next to a pot of freshly brewed coffee and a pot of tea. When we are alone, I exhale loudly.

'I can't believe what I've just seen. Mrs Hickey flirting with you.'

He blushes. 'Am I that bad?'

Not intending any offence, I recover quickly. 'In all the years I've known her, she's never acted remotely like that. Her husband died quite recently, he was only fifty; since then I think she's only ever looked at one other man: my husband, but she was very careful how and when.'

Slicing into an egg he says, 'I thought the old boy lurking in the woodshed was her husband.'

'No, that's Sylvester, an old retainer. He came to Leinster Manor when he was a boy. Worked for Brendan's father.'

Helping himself to toast, Tom ladles it with bacon and cuts into the open sandwich with gusto as I pour coffee and nibble the edge of a slice of toasted soda bread. I pour myself tea and continue to watch Tom attacking his breakfast with the fervent zeal of a starving man.

I sit in silence until he's eaten every morsel and wiped the plate clean with the last piece of toast.

'Do you want more?'

He shakes his head. 'That was great.'

'When did you last eat?' I ask, watching him screw his napkin into a tight ball.

'Last night at the hotel, but I left most of it. I skipped breakfast in favour of a jog and three espressos.'

'Which hotel?'

'The Falls.'

'No wonder, it's a dreadful place, not exactly known for its gourmet cuisine.'

'I've stayed in worse,' he comments, pouring a fresh cup of coffee as I light up another cigarette. 'Can we return to where we left off last night?' Noticing the grim set of my jaw, he says, 'Look, I know it's a delicate subject, but I promise to treat the piece with extreme sensitivity.'

'How do I know I can trust you?'

'You don't. All I can offer you, as a man of integrity, is my word.'

My hand is shaking as I extend it across the table to rest on the back of his. I turn his palm up and he grips tight. In a faltering voice I say, 'I'm clean out of trust and I'm scared and filled with an indescribable rage. It hurts like hell, I don't think I can take much more.'

His grip tightens. 'You *do* have my word.' Silently I nod, reluctantly sliding my hand back to rest on my lap. Quickly I glance out of the window. 'Look, the sun has come out. That's a good sign. I want to feel the sun. Would you like to take a walk, Mr Gregson?'

He jumps to his feet. 'I'd love to.'

We descend the stone steps into the garden, our feet lit by a tame autumnal sun. A flock of wood pigeon takes flight, stirring the sullen lake. Silently we traverse the perimeter of the water. At intervals the toes of my Wellingtons kick at a tangle of storm debris.

Looking out across the lake, his hand shading his eyes, Tom says, 'This reminds me of my mother's home. I used to fish the lake as a boy with my maternal granpop. By all accounts the old man was a tyrant but I never saw any evidence of it. To me he was just like a big old teddy bear, kind of worn but lovable. One of those men who could find wonder in the ordinary.'

'How old were you when he died?'

'Ten. That's when my parents moved to Charleston. My grandmother never got over his death and deteriorated rapidly. Carried on till almost ninety, minus her faculties.' He pauses, then: 'If you keep distracting me, we'll never finish the interview.'

I grin. 'So ask away.'

Extracting a pen and notepad he makes notes as we walk, stopping from time to time to scribble frantically. He opens with the question we'd left hanging yesterday: 'When did your love affair with Father Steele begin?'

'Nine months after he married me.'

'He married you?'

'My marriage should have been conducted by Father Francis Malone. The night before my wedding Father Malone was rushed into hospital for emergency surgery. Father Declan Steele, new to the diocese and due to take over from the retiring Father Malone, had to take over. You can imagine my shock when I saw him for the first time since I'd left Friday Wells. I want to tell you, I almost passed out. Here I was, being married to a man whom I loved but not in the passionate sense, by a man whom I'd adored from afar since I was fifteen, a man who came to me every night in my dreams. Declan handled it adeptly but admitted later he'd been shaken to the core. I was away for a month on honeymoon; after that I pursued him. I went to services and confession countless times, until eventually I got lucky. He was taking confession. I confessed the way I felt about him; naturally, it had a profound effect. There was nothing either of us could do to stop it. It was inevitable, it consumed us both. Declan tried to fight it, but deep down we both knew we'd make love. But we didn't sleep together until after my husband died.'

I stop walking and, standing very still, my ears pricked, I listen for a bird call. It's a gull. I fish deep in my coat pocket, pulling out a pack of cigarettes and lighter. Tilting my head forward towards the flame, I light up yet again, inhaling deeply and ignoring the dry cotton woolly taste in my mouth.

Tom is watching me intently. 'How long did the affair last?'

'A couple of months. Declan broke it off just before his death.'

Tom stops walking. 'Did he ever mention taking his own life? Was he given to black moods, depression?'

I shake my head. 'Not to my knowledge.'

'His suicide note said he couldn't come to terms with his betrayal. In your opinion, did he mean betraying you or God?'

I can feel the rage welling up in my throat. I'm brimful and overflowing. 'There were always three of us in the relationship. In the end, the Almighty won, he always does. I told him, warned him I would follow him wherever he went. I said I'd never let him go, kept repeating that I worshipped him to the point of being pathetic. I'd invent things, anything to make him laugh – which, believe me, was difficult. Declan had little sense of humour. I'd beg him to tell me over and over he loved me, refusing to sleep until I was firmly wrapped up in his arms.' Flicking the cigarette into the lake, I hug myself. 'Have you ever been worshipped, Tom? They say the only reason to be a man is to have the love of a good woman.'

He thinks carefully before answering. 'As you know, I was married. But Jenni didn't love me, she needed me. That's different. But I live in hope.'

A chill breeze sweeps across the lawn, displacing Tom's curls and sending ripples across the surface of the water. I shiver. 'Children?'

'No, thank God. She didn't want kids. Well, not with me. She's now pregnant.'

I sense rather than see his sadness. 'Do you think happiness has to be worked at, Tom?'

'Yes, absolutely. I believe some people have a greater capacity for happiness and some, I'm certain, enjoy being unhappy.' Tom's eyes narrow as he asks, 'Did your husband know about the priest?'

Still hugging myself tight, I say, 'No. He died the same day as I made love to Declan for the first time. I was with Brendan when he died and less than ten hours later I was making love to another man. I had no control over it. Do you think that's shocking?'

His expression turned for an instant to surprise. I'm not sure whether he's surprised by my actions or my questioning. I suspect he's choosing his words carefully. 'I think we are all in control of our own lives, but you'd suffered a gamut of conflicting emotions after the death of a loved one. Clearly you were very vulnerable.'

'I'm not sure any of us have complete control over our own lives. Brendan was terminally ill when he proposed. He had bone cancer, but all the experts had given him at least eighteen months. The reason for marrying was to have a child. Brendan wanted an heir before he died.'

'Why did you guys not marry sooner?'

'My husband was a homosexual.'

Tom looks visibly shocked. He stops walking. 'That didn't come out in my research.'

'Brendan never came out officially, but neither did he keep it a closely guarded secret. His friends and family knew. I would appreciate it if you didn't print it.'

'Now I understand, it all makes perfect sense. You were a young vulnerable orphan who needed to be loved. You fixated on the priest, who became an obsession, and found a surrogate father in Brendan Fitzgerald. The priest's rejection in favour of God incensed you so much you decided –'

I interrupt. 'I think you've got it –'

Raising his hand, he says, 'Let me finish.'

Angered by his arrogance, I growl, 'No, I won't let you finish. I resent your presumptuous summing up of my life in a few clichés. If you don't mind me saying, I think you're full of shit.'

Tom looks suitably subdued and I feel my anger quickly dissolve.

'You're right, I'm sorry. Who am I to start pontificating on your life? I've got a big mouth.'

'Exactly. How would you feel if I did it to you?'

'I'd tell you to mind your own fucking business.'

'My sentiments entirely.' My bottom lip quivers.

He looks concerned. 'You cold?'

'A bit, let's walk back.'

We fall into step side by side. It's unseasonably cold and will, I suspect, get much colder.

At the foot of the garden where the steps leading to the terrace run the length of the house, Tom stops. He's smiling, it reaches his eyes. 'I think you're a very courageous young woman.'

'I just want to say, I'm strong-willed and single-minded. Neither have anything to do with courage.'

I deprive Mrs Hickey of fussing over lunch and insist we go to the local pub. We have to blink to adjust our eyes to the murky darkness of the windowless snug. I'm thankful for the dim lighting and the lack of customers, yet still I keep my head down when I order a pint of Guinness and lemonade. Tom has a pint of draught bitter. We order a ploughman's lunch with crusty bread and Irish cheddar, and for the first time in days I've got an appetite.

As we leave the pub I feel Tom's strong arm push me back inside. 'Get out the back. The front is crawling with photographers.'

I run through the bar to the back door. It leads to a yard enclosed by a stone wall. A path leads to a padlocked door. I scale the wall like I had as a kid to steal pears from the nuns' domain and scramble down the other side in time to see Tom running towards me followed by a photographer. Using his body to shield me, he hisses, 'Don't move.'

I hear a man's voice behind Tom, 'Come on, mate, give us a break, I've come all the way from London. Just one snap.' The paparazzo lets his camera drop and flashes a wily, lopsided grin.

To my astonishment, Tom says, 'OK.' Still protecting

me with his body, he steps forward, catches the photographer off guard and wrestles the camera from the man's hands, shouting at me to run.

I set off at a sprint, taking the bridle path across Mullen's Wood and not stopping until I'm a few hundred yards from the gate leading to Leinster's six-acre paddock. I skirt the field and enter the house by the back door. Taking off my muddy shoes, I'm still panting when I hear Mrs Hickey talking to Sylvester in the kitchen. 'Jesus, Mary and Joseph, if it wasn't for me needing the money so bad and jobs being short I'd be gone. Everyone is talking about it in the village, asking me how I can stay under the same roof as Mrs Fitz. I tell them to mind their business unless they want to feel the lash of my tongue. It's unforgivable, what the missus has done. How could she do it with a priest? And him, Mr Fitz, such a good man. He adored her, that was clear from the start. It was him who got her all them fancy exhibitions. If it hadn't been for Mr Fitz, she'd be nowhere.'

Sylvester interrupts, 'I think she's a grand painter, no doubt about that.'

'Aye, with a lot of help from Mr Fitz. He taught her everything she knows. First time he brought her down here it was plain as the nose on my face what she –' Mrs Hickey is cut short by the loud pealing of the doorbell. I hear her footsteps on the flagged floor and when they reach the door I slip unseen into the study, appearing a minute later in the hall. Tom is standing in front of the closed door, his hair dishevelled and a red swelling on his left temple. Mrs Hickey is next to him, her arms folded across her ample chest.

I run towards him. 'What happened?'

'A little scuffle, nothing much.' He touches the side of his head. 'They'll be camping out in the grounds soon. If I were you, I'd make arrangements to go away somewhere safe. How about New York?'

Jutting my chin out defiantly, I say, 'I'll not be driven from my home. Let them camp out; let them hound me. They'll get tired eventually and crawl home with their tails between their legs.'

'I'm not so sure about that. According to local gossip, the press are here from all arts and parts.'

I round on the housekeeper. 'You gossip far too much, Mrs Hickey. Can you make yourself useful and get an ice-pack for Mr Gregson's forehead?'

Mrs Hickey stands her ground. 'And what exactly do you mean when you say I gossip, Mrs Fitz?'

'Exactly what I said. You gossip too much. Please, let's not argue, just get something for Mr Gregson's head – it's swelling up like a balloon.'

To the housekeeper he says, 'It's nothing. Don't worry about it.' And to me: 'I've got to get back to my hotel. I need to file copy before close of play today. Thanks for the interview. I'll discuss the piece with you before it goes to print. I might, if it's OK with you, have to ask a few more questions.'

'You could give me copy approval?'

'Impossible.'

Adopting a persuasive tone I say, 'Why not? It wouldn't hurt just this once.'

His eyes darken. 'How would you react if I told you how to paint my portrait?'

I concede defeat. 'Fair comment.' Then, holding his gaze: 'I just want to say, it was good to meet you again, Tom. Thanks for saving my life back there. If you'll for-give the old line, if you're ever in Ireland again there'll be a welcome on the mat.'

He's grinning. 'And I just want to say . . .' he winks '. . . the same applies to New York, New York.'

I laugh. 'Shit, sorry about the "just want to say". I say it all the bloody time, terrible habit.'

'Jeez, no, it's not, it's amusing. Our foibles, idiosyncrasies make us original, interesting – in some cases, fascinating. The most important thing is not to take yourself too seriously.' He fishes a card out of the breast pocket of his shirt. 'Look me up. Sometimes I can run to real fancy dinners, but if I knew you were coming into town I'd take out an overdraft.'

'Where I come from fish and chips wrapped in a newspaper was a luxury.' I read his card adding, 'I'm in New York for an exhibition in about six weeks' time. I'll look you up then – if I like the piece you write.'

'Is that a promise, Kate?'

'I don't make rash promises I might not be able to keep.'

Resting his hand on the door, he looks at me intently. He'd done it a few times since we met, an opaque expression as if unable to make sense of what he's seeing. 'By the way, if you used peroxide on your hair and cut it short you'd look exactly like a young Marilyn Monroe. Has anyone ever told you how much you resemble her?'

'Once, a long time ago, a friend's mother.'

'I noticed the resemblance as soon as I met you. I've been meaning to mention it ever since.'

'When I was a kid I used to dream my mother was famous, a film star or celebrity who had been forced to have me adopted. As soon as she got her life sorted out she'd come for me. I fantasized about it so much I actually started to believe it and it wasn't until I was ten Mother Thomas shattered my dream. She told me I was the daughter of a prostitute, and all girls born of prostitutes became prostitutes themselves. They all die young of terrible diseases, she said, and when the devil got them he and his disciples stuck their things into them for all eternity. You can imagine how terrified I was, and how ashamed.'

Shaking his head in utter bewilderment, Tom says, 'What sort of woman tells a child stuff like that?'

'A Catholic nun, believe it or not. Mother Thomas. An evil woman who was killed by my best friend – an accident,' I add quickly. 'I wouldn't have blamed her if she'd stuck a knife into the wicked old bag and twisted it a hundred times.'

Mrs Hickey crosses herself, and, as if in the presence of the devil himself, she hurriedly crosses the room mumbling, 'Oh my Lord,' under her breath as she stumbles out of the hall.

'Have you ever thought about searching for your parents?'

'Yes, umpteen times, but each time something else got in the way.'

Eagerly Tom says, 'How about I help you?'

After a few minutes' consideration, I suggest, 'Write the interview first, then I'll decide.' Tom seems reluctant to leave. Again he says, as if prolonging his time with me, 'Thanks for the interview. Take care, Kate. Just in case I don't see you again, I want you to know I think you're an exceptional woman.'

Somehow I think he really means it. I feel lighter than I have for weeks. 'If you need to reach me I'll be staying here for another week, then I've got to go back to Dublin. The Bishop is making a lot of noise about meeting me. He needs to reconcile the role of the Church in all of this hype. I expect he's going to try and persuade me to keep my mouth shut.'

'A bit late for that,' Tom comments as I scribble my Dublin number on the back of his newspaper. Standing by the open door, I watch him walk to his car, get in and shut the door. Tom's crown touches the roof; his hair, flying out from his ears, is splayed across the top of the window. As his car starts to move he waves. Standing completely still I fix my eyes on the rear headlights until they are out of sight.

Chapter Eighteen

At five past four in the afternoon I hear the sound of car wheels crunch on the gravel drive. From where I'm standing at the window located at the top of the stairs I have a clear view of anyone approaching the front of the house. The car, a dark blue Ford something or other, looks like a hundred other similar small hatchbacks. I assume it's a hire car. When Bridget steps out I feel a flicker of apprehension, but as I make my way downstairs it's quickly replaced by a great wave of joy. When I reach the door I hear the sound of Mrs Hickey's brisk footsteps in the corridor connecting the kitchen to the hall. Throwing the door open to a startled Bridget, her finger poised about to press the bell, Mrs Hickey's shout reaches us: 'If that's John Moran with the laundry, tell him to go to the back door.'

Ignoring her I open my arms wide; I'm not sure whether to laugh or cry as Bridget steps into them. We hug, gripping each other very tight, both reluctant to pull away, like we used to do in the orphanage when one or the other of us was in trouble. We don't need words, we never did. I'd started the hugging thing one night in the dormitory after listening to Bridget, her knickers on her head, crying herself to sleep. We were about six or seven at the time. It was a Thursday. I know that because we had to show our knickers to Mother Thomas on Thursdays. We'd form a line in the dormitory and she'd inspect every pair. If we'd soiled them in any way we were made to wear them on our heads for the remainder of the day. After lights out I'd crept into bed beside Bridget and with my usual reckless spirit had taken her knickers off her head, ignoring her protests, and stuffed them under her pillow out of sight. She'd been terrified Mother Thomas would return and beat her. I'd assuaged her fears, reassuring her that Mother Thomas slept very deeply, and rarely if ever came into the dormitory after ten. I'd taken her in my arms and hugged her very tight. She'd sobbed, saying in between sobs she'd never been hugged before. I didn't admit, not then, that it was the first time for me too. 'If we hug really tight,' I'd whispered, 'my love will pass into your body and make you feel better.' It worked and she'd slept.

After at least five minutes we part. Holding her at arm's length, I say, 'It's so good to see you, Bridget.'

'Ditto.'

We are both smiling as Mrs Hickey appears on the doorstep. 'Are you two going to come in or catch your deaths out there?'

'We're coming in right now and I think we'll both have a cup of tea – unless Bridget has changed her drinking habits since moving to America. Bridget?'

'God forbid I stop wanting a cup of tea, or for that matter a good Irish breakfast. Sure, I miss that more than anything.'

Mrs Hickey looks delighted. 'A girl after me own heart! You look like you need feeding up, and perhaps you could persuade Mrs Fitz here to get rid of those rank-smelling cigarettes and eat some decent grub. She's fading away.'

Bridget looks amused. I'm not. I grind my teeth in irritation, glaring at the housekeeper. It's lost on the thick-skinned Mrs Hickey who begins to trot across the hall.

'I've got the kettle brewing right now, tea coming up and' – she beams – 'I've made fresh scones and fruit cake.'

Bridget licks her lips. 'Sounds grand.'

I wait until the housekeeper is out of earshot before

hissing in a stage whisper, 'She's a tyrant. Sometimes I feel like I'm back with the Sisters of no Mercy. No sooner are you over the threshold, and even before your coat is off your back, she pounces. Demanding you eat something or other she's cooked.'

Unbuttoning her coat, Bridget raises her eyebrows. I notice they've been plucked to a fine black arch. 'I wouldn't compare that sort of hospitality to the orphanage. It's obvious she simply wants to please. To feel needed.'

I sigh grudgingly, acknowledging, 'You're probably right, but I can't help it if she irritates me.' I pause to help Bridget out of her overcoat, an ankle-length camel wool. Unknotting a scarf underneath she stuffs it down the arm of the coat, reminding me that old habits die hard; it was something we always did as kids.

'It was blazing sunshine in Chicago yesterday. I can't believe it's so cold. I almost didn't bring a coat at all until I remembered how unpredictable the weather is here.'

Under the coat she's dressed in a pair of casual classic-cut navy trousers and a roll-neck cashmere sweater in a lighter shade of blue.

'You've lost weight,' I comment approvingly. 'You look great.'

Looking down at her body, Bridget pats her ample bottom. 'Everywhere but here.'

We wander into the drawing room and sit side by side on the sofa. I'm hungry for her news. 'First and foremost I want to hear all about the baby, Patrick, your work, Chicago, everything.'

As Bridget begins to talk I take in every detail of her face. I haven't seen her for more than two years and in that time she's changed. She hasn't perceptibly aged, it's more that she's acquired an aura of self-esteem, a confidence that I suspect has something to do with motherhood.

'Chicago sucks. I hate it. Myself, I'd relocate to New

York tomorrow, but Patrick is happy in the Mid-West and doing well. His uncle got him started, got him a green card. He's worked bloody hard and it's just starting to pay off. We've recently moved into a new apartment, new to us that is. It's bigger, more space for Eugene. I named him after Pat's father.'

Instinctively I touch my stomach. 'How old is Eugene?'

'He's eight months and a big boy – fat, actually, or as Mrs Molloy would say, a bonny baby.'

'Have you got any photographs?'

'Dozens, but I'll show you later, there's something I want to say first . . .'

We both look up as the door opens to admit Mrs Hickey bearing a tray full of the usual goodies. She places it on the table in front of the sofa. 'Get stuck into those scones with fresh cream from Cassidy's farm and me own home-made strawberry jam. I don't want to see a crumb left, else it'll go to the birds again. Must have the fattest birds in the county,' she mutters crossing the room towards the door. 'They sure as hell shit a lot, according to Sylvester.'

We both stifle giggles until she is out of the room then burst out laughing. Springing to my feet as light as a girl I pour the tea and, handing Bridget a cup, ask, 'Scone or cake?'

'Both! I can afford to put on a few pounds. I lost a stone and a half after Eugene was born and haven't put it back on yet. Pat says I'm scrawny. Like most men he ogles top models but at home prefers a bit of meat on the bone.'

I help myself to a thick slice of fruit cake and settle down next to Bridget, balancing the plate on my lap. My friend is piling a thick wedge of cream topped with strawberry jam on to a scone.

Between mouthfuls I mumble, 'It's like being back at Mrs Molloy's. Remember her tea cakes slathered with real butter and that lemon curd she used to make? I used to dream about Sunday afternoon tea at Lizzy's house.'

Wiping a gob of cream from the corner of her mouth, Bridget says, 'That's the only reason you befriended Lizzy.'

'Not true! I liked her.'

'Come on, Kate, admit it.'

I swallow a lump of cake. 'Mrs Molloy's cooking, I suppose, played a certain part in our friendship. But Lizzy did all right. Without me she would never have got into college. She could barely spell her name before she sat next to me in class seven.'

Picking a few crumbs from the plate into her mouth, Bridget smacks her lips. 'That was grand. Thank God I don't live with this woman – I'd be as fat as I was as a kid.'

'You were plump, not fat.'

'I was fat, Kate, and you know it. Sure, I've no idea how I got so fat on what they fed us in the home.' Bridget holds her cup on her lap and concentrates on stirring the tea with a delicate silver spoon. 'I'm sorry we lost touch, Kate.'

I open my mouth, poised to say it was her to blame, then swallow the rebuke. What use is recrimination? She was here, she'd come to me, that was enough.

'I could say many things, Kate, make excuses – I've thought of lots, but they all sound lame and insincere. I never stopped thinking about you, I just wanted to get on with my new life with Patrick. America was a fresh start. I suppose the truth is I wanted to get rid of the past. Cut it out like a malignant tumour. You, Ireland, were part of that past. But we have a duty to the past, it lives on inside. I now know I can't deny it. What I'm trying to say, not very well, is I'm sorry. I missed you, Kate, very much, and when I read about you in the newspaper my heart went out to you. We shared such a lot, and you were there for me when I really needed you. Particularly

323

after reform school when I thought I might not make it. Sure, wild horses wouldn't have stopped me being there for you now, Kate.'

'You've made me very happy, Bridget, happier than I know how to articulate. Sometimes words aren't enough. I missed you, but seeing you today has made me realize just how much. It's about the past for me as well. We went through the same shit, and came out the other end smelling of *feckin'* roses. It takes some doing.' I pause, waiting for Bridget to finish her tea. 'There's so much I want to say to you, I don't know where to start.'

Placing her cup on the tray she kicks off her shoes and, curling her feet under her, she smiles. 'I've got all the time in the world so why not start at the beginning?'

Where is the beginning, I ask myself. Do I go back to working for Declan in his cottage in Friday Wells? Tell Bridget about the time he'd kissed me, and later destroyed the portrait I'd painted of him? Or do I start with our subsequent meeting at my wedding to Brendan? I decide to begin with Brendan's bizarre proposal. Bridget, knowing Brendan as she did, would appreciate the story. As I begin to speak I can feel the warmth of my friend's love. It's almost tangible and suddenly it's as if a great load has been lifted. I feel as light as air.

We talk – in truth, I talk until the light fades, the sky turns velvety black with a rash of stars. At the point when Declan and I make love for the first time Bridget interrupts. 'I'm dying to know: how was it?'

'How was what?'

Her cheeks colour. 'You know, making out with a priest. Did it feel different?'

My eyes mist over. 'The man I loved was inside me. It felt completely right.'

I suspect it wasn't the answer Bridget sought, but I'm reluctant to elaborate. I continue, holding nothing back except my pregnancy. It's gone midnight when, no longer able to keep her eyes open, Bridget yawns then says, 'I'll have to get to my bed before I fall asleep on the sofa. It's been a long day.'

We mount the stairs together hand in hand like a couple of kids. Before leaving Bridget at her bedroom door I kiss her on both cheeks, then say, 'I'm having a baby, Bridget.'

Bridget grabs both of my hands. 'Who is the father?'

Surprised she hasn't guessed, I say with a hint of indignation, 'Declan, of course. Who else?'

Lowering her lids (something she always did when she didn't wanted to confront or address an issue) she asks, 'Are you going to have the child?'

'I don't believe in abortion, I think you know that. I want this baby more than I've ever wanted anything – apart from the father himself. It's his parting gift. That's the way I think of this child. How could I even think of killing it?'

'A priest's illegitimate child, Kate. Think about it carefully. You're only twenty-four, you've got the rest of your life to have babies, with a good man, a husband, someone who will be there to support you. Think on it, please.'

'I've thought of nothing else. Declan betrayed me by committing suicide. I'm still angry with him. I've been cast as the villain, the slut, the whore who seduced a priest. I'll never forgive him leaving this way, without a thought for me or our child. I'm so bitter it gnaws at my belly constantly. The only relief I have from the pain is thinking about my child.'

Backing into her room, Bridget says, 'Sure, you always had enough spirit for yourself and another half a dozen girls, and strong will. You were the only girl who dared stand up to Mother Thomas. I don't suppose anything I say will make you change your mind.'

I resist the urge to remind Bridget that she had pushed Mother Thomas to her death and say instead, 'Sleep tight, don't let the nun bite; if she does, squeeze her tight, then she won't come back another night.'

A flicker of sadness creases Bridget's face. 'I used to say the verse over and over again, convinced she wouldn't come back. But she did.'

Throwing my arms across her shoulders, I place my lips on her brow. 'Not any more, Bridget, not any more.'

That night I dreamt of the orphanage, only it wasn't the same. This surreal place was serene and beautiful, filled with golden light and exquisite furnishings. The nuns wore white like angels and seemed to float. Bridget and I were dressed like identical twins, and hand in hand we glided through perfumed gardens towards a high wall where the dream ended.

I oversleep and when I come downstairs for breakfast Bridget is sitting in the morning room surrounded by the newspapers. She looks fresh, her dark hair shining like an oil slick on the high collar of her cherry-red sweater. Looking up from the *Irish Times*, she smiles. 'Good afternoon, Mrs Fitz.'

I grin. 'Sorry, I overslept.'

'No problem. Mrs Hickey has had the time of her life regaling me with the local gossip. I now know everybody's business – including yours.'

I grimace, then glance at an envelope on top of the pile of mail. It's handwritten in an untidy childish scrawl. I pick it up, noticing the Limerick postmark. Tearing it open, I glance at the foot of the page. It's from Patrick O'Sullivan. My heart begins to prance as I read:

Dear Kate,
I'm not sure if the fella from the Times *in Dublin has spoken to you yet. but it's been preying on my mind, so it has, for some days past. About the airline ticket. In truth I forgot all about it till I got back the night after I took you home. I'd had a few jars in*

the local then gone straight home. I was tired after the long drive and wanted naught better than to fall into bed next to the missus. But she wants to know where I'd been, the in and outs, the long and the short of it, all the bloody details. Somebody had seen you in the office and, I don't have to tell you how gossip flies around small villages. So I tells her the story and, lo and behold, a few minutes later she hands me a wallet. Shiny leather with gold writing on the front, like you get from travel companies. She explains that she'd found it in the back of the car a couple of days after I'd picked you and our Marion up from Dublin airport. Myself I would have tossed it in the bin, but not our Ellen, no, she keeps most everything. Never know when things might come in handy, she's fond of saying. She'd kept her bus pass and store coupons in the wallet.

Must be honest, I was shocked to read about the priest, and thought long and hard about getting in touch with you. But it was our Ellen that called the newspaper. She said big newspapers paid all sorts of money for information, any kind of information. She said it took a lot for her to pick up the phone, and if it hadn't been for our John John (the youngest who needs an operation on his foot) I don't think she would have had the bloody nerve. He's been on the waiting list nigh on two years and limping worse every day.

The fella at the *Irish Times* has got the wallet with the boarding card and flight details, but I took a copy so if you want to know what stork brought you to Ireland give me a call.

With my best regards,

Paddy O'Sullivan

PS I haven't told Ellen I was writing to you, so if you do call I'd be grateful if you didn't breathe a word.

327

Bridget is looking at me with characteristic concern. 'You OK?'

Nodding, I pass the letter to Bridget. As she reads I pour myself a cup of tea. It's cold. I discard it and pour a cup of coffee instead. I sit down next to Bridget and wait in silence until she's finished.

'I don't understand, Kate. What does it mean?'

'It means I was probably born in America and sent over to Ireland as a baby. My mother, father – or someone – desperately wanted to keep my birth a secret. He, she, they, I don't know, made elaborate plans to ensure I was never found. A journalist from the *Irish Times* called me the other day. Now, thank God, I don't have to do the interview he wanted in exchange for the information. I can get it from Paddy.'

Bridget frowns, 'Who is this Paddy?'

'He's Mother Peter's brother. I met him purely by chance. He's got a cab company in Limerick. He drove me here from the station one night. We got chatting, and it turns out in 1962 he'd picked Mother Peter up from Dublin airport. She arrived on a transatlantic flight with a baby. I believe that baby was me.'

Bridget lets out a long low whistle. 'Your mother or father or both could have been high profile and your birth might have caused some sort of scandal.'

'Exactly.'

'Perhaps your father was married, your mother penniless, afraid – or threatened even.'

'When I first heard about my trust fund I was desperate to find out who had set it up. I tried with Brendan's help, but after a few leads had come to nothing I shelved it to concentrate on my work. Since Brendan's death I've thought more and more about tracing my parents. He, as you rightly suggested, was my surrogate father, but more than that he was my entire family. With him I never felt alone, nor did I feel the compulsion I felt as a kid. But since

328

his death the compulsion has returned with a vengeance.'

'The compulsion to do what?'

'Find out who I really am.'

'When I had Eugene I stopped craving that knowledge. I'm sure the same will happen to you when you have your child.'

'That's where you're wrong. Having a child will make it worse. What do I tell my son of his ancestors? How do I reply when he asks me about his grandparents? I don't even know their names.'

'You tell him the truth. He'll have a mother. That's a lot more than you or I had.'

Walking to the window I look out on to manicured lawns. The sky is like flint. The newspaper rustles, reminding me of mornings similar to this one spent in this very room with Brendan heatedly debating the news. Sometimes, intimidated by his intellect and articulation, I had hesitated to express an opinion but he'd always encouraged me to speak up. 'Confront the issue, Kate, you're no shrinking violet. Say what you think. Even if they don't agree, people will admire you for your courage.'

With a purposeful stride I cross the room. At the door I turn to face Bridget. 'I'm going to call Paddy.' Five minutes later I return, my voice tinged with frustration. 'No bloody reply.' Then: 'How long before you've got to go back, Bridget?'

'Eugene is with my sister-in-law. She's got three kids of her own but has offered to have him until next Wednesday. I made a reservation on the Tuesday morning flight.'

'That gives us three days.'

'To do what?'

Turning from the window, I look at Bridget. 'Will you go back with me?'

'Back where?'

'To the orphanage.'

Her look of horror dashes my determination.

'Jesus, that's a tall order, even for you, Kate. And why, for the love of God, would you want to go back to that hell-hole?'

'To speak to Mother Peter, née Marion O'Sullivan.'

'And what makes you think she'll talk to you? Even if you strap her to the nearest tree and horsewhip her till the blood spurts, she'd die willingly before breaking her vow of silence. I think you might be wasting your time.'

Bridget has a point. 'Possibly, but it's worth a try, don't you think?'

Throwing the paper down, she sighs. 'I've just told you what I think.' Leaning back, she folds her hands across her chest. Familiar protective body language, it makes me want to hug her again. 'Don't lay this one on me, Kate. I vowed I would never go back, so did you.'

'But these are exceptional circumstances.'

We both fall silent, occupied with our own thoughts and fears.

'I just want to say it holds bad memories for me too, Bridget, but it might also hold the key to my past and my future. Mother Peter knows more than she told her brother. I have to give it a shot.'

On her feet now, Bridget is frowning. I can see she's grappling with her conscience. 'Determination was always your strong point, Kate O'Sullivan. My God, when you want something neither hell nor high water can hold you back.' Unfolding her arms she lets them drop by her side. 'If I don't come, you'll go alone, won't you?'

'Yes.'

'Well, that settles it. I can't let you go back there on your own. When do you want to leave?'

'No time like the present.'

'I was afraid you might say that.'

Chapter Nineteen

The day grew overcast. When we reached the outskirts of Friday Wells it began to rain. Huge drops as big as raisins spatter the ground. In my head, I hear Mrs Molloy's voice: 'Sure, it's raining cats and dogs' – the first time I'd heard this odd expression I ran to the window expecting to see real animals pouring out of the sky. As I turn my car into Potters Lane I hear Bridget's sharp intake of breath. A quick glance at her ashen profile tells me she's not well. Concerned, I ask, 'You OK?'

'No! Can you stop the car for a minute? I feel sick.'

I pull over at the side of the road. I stretch my arm across the seat and take her hand from her lap; I squeeze it gently. She's shaking.

'Would you rather I dropped you in the village? You can have a cup of tea and wait. I won't be long. Mother Peter will probably refuse to see me anyway. Even if she doesn't, our meeting won't take all day.'

Staring straight ahead, Bridget bites her bottom lip. 'I feel such a bloody coward.'

'You're not a coward. If anyone understands that I do. Come on, I'm taking you to the village.'

She doesn't object, so I begin to turn the car. As I do so I spot the figure of a man rounding the corner. He's very tall and wearing a long black overcoat, his face partially obscured by the black canvas of a vast umbrella. As he gets closer I bend my head to see under the umbrella and recognize the face of Father O'Neill. Silently the electric window glides down. I poke my head out a couple of inches, feeling a blast of cold air on my cheeks as I shout, 'Father O'Neill, is that you?'

The priest takes a step closer. Bending slightly from his knees, he leans his colossal bulk into the car frowning. Father O'Neill has aged; his face is red-veined and lumpy. I count three, wait, four chins and one side of his face has dropped as if he's had a stroke. He's wheezing badly, not remotely like the intimidating giant of my memory. 'Do I know you?'

'Yes. I'm Kate O'Sullivan.'

His face darkens. He backs away from the car as if afraid. 'I think you should turn this fancy car around and drive straight back to where you came from. You're not welcome here, Kate O'Sullivan.'

'Don't judge me too harshly, Father, before you know all the facts.'

He lets his umbrella fall back to show his face, angry red, and overblown. 'I know enough. You're an evil woman who led a good priest astray.'

Angry myself now, I say, 'Father Steele had nothing to do with it, of course. A lamb to the slaughter, is that how you see it?'

'Away with you, woman. Don't taint this village with evil.'

It was useless to argue. 'I'm looking for Mother Peter. Is she still at the orphanage?'

He begins to cough, spittle flying from his open mouth. Shaking his head, he stares at me as if I'm the devil incarnate.

'I asked you a question, Father.'

Ignoring me, he begins to stride purposefully down the lane. I watch his black hulk as it retreats. Seething with frustration, I close the window, sigh deeply and hit the steering wheel with my clenched fist. 'Bloody narrow-minded, bigoted, ignorant . . .'

'What did you expect, Kate? A welcome party?'

'You're right. In fact, I'm taking my life in my hands. I might get lynched.'

'Lets go back. Coming here won't do any good. You'll get the same reception at the orphanage – if they let you in.'

In silence I turn the ignition, pull away from the kerb and drive slowly towards the village. 'I've come this far, Bridget, I've got to go through with it. If Mother Peter won't see me, fine. At least I'll come away knowing I did everything I could.'

'I think you're wasting your time.'

In my innermost heart I know she's right but I can't ignore the determined little voice in my head that keeps urging me on.

The village High Street looks almost the same as it had when I'd left, except Mrs O'Shea's is now a trendy hairdresser's and the post office has moved to bigger premises.

Pulling her coat from the back seat, Bridget says, 'I could do with something stronger than tea. Drop me on the corner of Fonthill and Furze Lane outside Mac-Sweeny's Pub.'

I do as she asks, pulling the car to a stop outside the pub. A couple of people point openly at my Mercedes sports car. When Bridget alights, a boy runs up to the open door, a good-looking kid with dark eyes and a bruise on his left temple. 'How much does a car like this cost, missus?'

Bridget shoos him away with, 'Money and fair words.' Then, turning to me, she says, 'I'll stay here all day if necessary, though I doubt you'll be that long. Good luck.' She slams the door and I wait until she's inside the pub before driving back the way I'd come.

On the journey down Potters Lane I anticipate the inevitable flood of terrible memories. A few hundred yards before the entrance to the orphanage my heart begins to race. I take a very long deep breath, resisting a strong urge to stop the car, turn around and go back to the pub for Bridget. You can do this, I tell myself. What can they do to you now? The nuns can't hurt you, the worst they can do is turn you away.

The stone wall enclosing the yard is partially covered in tiny pink flowers, blossoming from cracks. It looks strangely less imposing, as do the entrance gates, now painted gloss white. As a child they had seemed huge and impenetrable. I let out a long sigh of relief when I see the gates ajar. I drive past the wrought-iron sign above my head: *In Jesus We Trust*.

The house is smaller than I remember, and worn out. Of another era, I think, another time. I feel strong when I get out of the car. I'd anticipated an unwelcome return of my worst demons, yet surprisingly there is nothing, as if none of it had actually happened and I'd dreamt the first sixteen years of my life. With forceful steps I stride to the covered porch leading to the front door. The four glass panes have been replaced; the woodwork, a bright lemon, looks fresh, as if recently painted. I tug at the bell and hear it peal throughout the house. The sound is the same. Straining my ears, I hear the faint patter of feet, recalling my own and Bridget's clatter. At the ring of the doorbell we'd always race to the nearest window, rest our elbows on the sill and crane our necks to see who was at the door.

The feet belong to a novice who opens the door a chink. 'Can I help you?'

Only part of her face is visible, but the bit I can see has the glow of youth.

'I've come to see Mother Peter.'

'Is she expecting you?'

'Yes.'

The door opens a few inches wider and the girl, who is no more than seventeen, looks me up and down, furtively

334

glancing over my shoulder towards my car. 'I'm sorry, but Mother Peter isn't here.'

'Where is she?'

'Hospital. She's very poorly. To be honest, I'm not entirely sure what's up with the good sister. Night and day we pray for her recovery. Mother Paul is here, perhaps she can help . . . ?' Her lips part; her teeth gleam in the dark hall.

I manage what I hope is a reassuring smile. 'Has Mother Paul been here long?'

'She left here a good few years ago, and came back just before Christmas last year, a few weeks after I started.'

There seems to be little sign of life. 'Is this still an orphanage?' I ask.

'No, not since 1982 when it became a school for novices.'

I'm about to ask where I can find Mother Peter when a black-clad figure appears next to the girl. The woman is bespectacled, tall and reed thin, thinner than I recall. She's wearing bifocals instead of the thick horn-rimmed specs she used to wear. It's clear she doesn't recognize me because she's smiling warmly, a crooked, yellow and black smile. I don't ever recall having seen Mother Paul smile – well, not in my direction. I feel a great surge of hurt and rage pour out of me, and the urge to get very close and whisper, 'I'll wipe that smile off your face,' is overwhelming.

Still smiling, her voice like saccharine, she asks, 'Can I help?'

'I came to see Mother Peter, but I'm told she's in hospital. Do you know which one?' Behind the glasses I detect a flicker of recognition.

Slyly she answers my question with another: 'Who shall I say called?'

'It's very urgent I see her today. I've an important message for her. If you won't tell me where she is, I'll find out for myself. It won't take long to ring around the hospitals.'

Thank God for the impetuous spontaneity of the young, I think, as the girl pipes up with, 'She's in Blackrock Clinic in Kilmallock –'

'Shut up, Theresa, and go to your room at once. I'll speak to you later.'

With downcast eyes the girl retreats; my sympathies go with her. Mother Paul's intense focus is beginning to unnerve me. I can feel the first stirring of fear and with it the urge to run away. Without a word I turn and walk towards my car. She follows, tapping me on the shoulder before I reach the car door. I turn. We are approximately the same height, our eyes are level.

Behind the thick glass she studies my face. 'Don't I know you?'

'Yes. My name is Kate O'Sullivan.'

I see recognition fill her watery gaze and decide to act quickly before she has a chance to speak. Bunching my fist I put all my anger and rage behind it and hit her hard below her rosary beads, dead in the centre of her belly. Not waiting for her reaction I jump into the car and lock the doors. Her face is way past red, almost purple, and she's stooped, gripping her stomach with both hands.

I let the window down and shout, 'It hurts like hell, doesn't it, Mother Paul?' before putting my foot down and speeding out of the drive.

Bridget is aghast. 'You did what?'

'I punched her as hard as I could in the stomach. My God, it felt good. I can't remember the last time I felt so good.'

Bridget is laughing. 'I wish I'd been there.'

'Her glasses were hanging off the end of her nose. She looked so bloody shocked, I thought she was going to have a heart attack. I can't tell you the sense of satisfaction it gave me. When I think of all the times she thumped me for no particular reason.'

'And me.' Bridget's expression darkens.

'Funny. I was dreading going back, thought I'd be filled with terrible memories, but I wasn't. In fact it all seemed to have diminished. Smaller and meaner than I remembered, and less menacing. Oddly enough, it felt as if I'd never lived there. Like I'd dreamt it. I'm pleased I went back. It's a chapter in my life I can now close.'

Bridget repeats, 'I wish I'd been with you.'

'Forget it, Bridget, you didn't think you could handle it so you did the right thing. Why subject yourself to more pain? You said last night that since having Eugene you've been able to exorcize the past, so why let the demons back in if you don't have to? Just because I felt OK doesn't mean you would.'

'You're bloody brave, Kate. You always were.'

I give her the same answer as I gave Tom Gregson: 'I'm not. I'm single-minded and instinctive; that's not courageous. If I had courage I'd have accepted Declan's decision to serve God and not hounded him into what he eventually did. It takes courage to walk away, to make a sacrifice for someone else. Instead I was selfish, determined to have my own way as usual. Now I have to live with the consequences. Obsession is like that, it's corrupt, and is never satiated. It knows no reason and invariably ends in disaster.'

Bridget twists her mouth, pinching the corners in. 'If Father Steele chose to take his own life that's not your fault. Where was his courage?'

'However much I intellectualize it, Bridget, I'll always bear some of the guilt for Declan's death. I could have put a stop to the affair any time. I should never have started it in the first place. The world is full of eligible men, why did I have to fixate on a priest?'

Bridget relaxes, softening her mouth and the furrows on her brow. 'You fell in love with him. Is that so bad?'

'I should have walked away,' I say emphatically. We

both fall silent. After a few minutes I ask, 'So tell me about Patrick. You've hardly mentioned him since you arrived.'

Teasing, she chides, 'Sure, I haven't had a chance.'

I grin. 'That's true. Sorry, I've been talking too much as usual.'

'That's what I came here for, to listen. This trip was about you. I'll let you into a big secret, it feels good to be there for you for a change. For the first time in years I've felt you really needed me. When we were kids it was a mutual need. Then the hearing and the trial and when I was in the reform school you were there for me. I'll never forget your support. It helped save my life. I dread to think where I might have ended up without you. When you became successful ... don't get me wrong, I was happy for you – very happy – but I felt left out, and when Patrick came along he filled that void. He needs me. You may not think so, but beneath all his bluster and arrogance he's a mass of insecurity and low self-esteem.'

I'm very tempted to say, You could have fooled me, but I bite my tongue. The last thing Bridget needs is to hear me criticizing her husband. 'Does he makes you happy, Bridget?'

'Yes, very, and he's a wonderful father. I think he's surprised himself. We want to have at least three.'

'I'm happy for you, Bridget, you came through against all odds.'

'I couldn't have done it without you.'

'Nonsense. You've got the crack, the intelligence, and you kissed the Blarney Stone more than once. You'd have made it with or without me around to bully you.'

From the corner of my eye I see her wry expression. 'You and I both know that's not true.'

Simultaneously we see the sign: *Kilmallock 10 miles.* It's stopped raining but the roads are like wet glass. I regret not having the foresight to drive the Range Rover instead of a grand tourer designed for a German autobahn on a glorious day.

On entering the centre of the small town I see a hospital sign which turns out to be St Luke's General. At the entrance Bridget opens her window to ask a passing nurse for directions. 'Do you know where Blackrock Clinic is?'

The nurse bends forward. 'Sure, I used to work there. It's not far from here, a couple of miles. If you take the road out of town towards Limerick you can't miss it. It's just before you get to the village of Adare on the right-hand side of the road.'

Less than twenty minutes later we drive past the gates of Blackrock. When I stop the car, Bridget points to the sign above the entrance: *Blackrock Hospice. Care for the terminally ill.*

The receptionist, a woman well past her prime and clearly trying to hang on to it with the aid of peroxide and make-up, is jabbering on the telephone. It's impossible to detect from the conversation if it's important or not. My impatience rising, I'm about to rap on the desk when she replaces the phone and looks with barely concealed boredom in our direction.

'Yes?'

'We've come to see a patient, a nun, Mother Peter.'

Glancing down at her register, the woman frowns. Without looking up, she asks, 'Could she be registered in another name?'

I try, 'Marion O'Sullivan?'

'That's it. Ward 3a. Do you know your way?'

We both shake our heads.

With a pencil she points to a set of glass doors directly in front. 'Go through the doors, take the lift to the third floor, turn left when you get out, then carry on to the end of the corridor. You can't miss it.'

Walking side by side, Bridget and I push the double doors, stopping outside the lift. After a couple of minutes the doors open; side by side we step in. As the lift begins to ascend, I whisper, 'She's dying.'

Silently Bridget nods.

On leaving the lift we pass an unmanned desk, a nurse helping a woman to the toilet, and a male nurse lifting a patient into a wheelchair. Our rubber-soled feet squeak on the highly polished floor sounding ridiculously loud in my ears. On entering the ward I instantly spot Mother Peter. She's sitting on the edge of her bed, an open bible on her lap. There are two other women in the ward. One is sleeping, the other furiously knitting what looks like a pair of pink baby booties.

I nod in her direction. Bridget looks straight ahead.

As I move closer to Mother Peter a big lump enters my throat. She's thinner, much, but to my relief doesn't look as ill as I'd expected.

'Mother Peter?' I say softly.

After a moment she lifts her head and I'm given the most radiant smile I think I've ever seen. The bible she'd been reading is firmly shut and she has eyes only for me.

'Kate O'Sullivan, I've been thinking about you a lot.' Patting the edge of the bed, she says, 'Sit, I want to look at you.'

When I'm settled a couple of feet from her I say, 'You look well.'

'As well as can be expected since I'm dying. Don't look so sad, Kate, I'm not. I'm going to a better place. I know it's hard for the young to accept death. They're not in touch with their mortality and that's as it should be.'

Turning her neat head towards a nearby window she asks, 'Is it still raining?'

'No, but it's cold, and I think it's going to get foggy later.'

Her gaze returns to me and I notice the whites of her

340

eyes are mushy and discoloured like sour cream. 'Have you come far?'

'From Templemore in Tipperary.'

'Thanks for coming. I don't get many visitors.'

'We brought you some flowers.' I call to Bridget who is standing next to the window on the far side of the ward. She crosses the room, holding the flowers in front of her face. When she lowers the bouquet Mother Peter frowns and begins to claw at the bedclothes in agitation. 'I don't want flowers.'

I signal for Bridget to back off. She gets the message and drops the flowers on the end of the bed before leaving the room.

'Why is Bridget here?'

Containing my irritation I say with deliberate calm, 'Bridget is a good woman. She's done penance. She's married now with a baby boy. She's a good Catholic, a God-fearing woman who never misses church.' I'm telling the truth. 'Don't judge her so harshly. What was it our Father preached about judging others?'

The nun shuts her eyes and, placing her hand on the bible, quotes, "Do not judge or you will be judged. For in the same way as you judge others, you will be judged, and with the measure you use it will be measured to you." Matthew chapter seven, verses one to two.'

Patiently I wait for her to open her eyes, tenderly stroking the back of her hand. It's cool, a tangle of veins is clearly visible through the wafer-thin skin.

Afraid that she might drop off to sleep, I say, 'Mother Peter, I want to ask you a question. I think you know what it's about, but before you answer I want you to consider how profoundly important this is to me. All my life I've been searching for an identity, something, anything to cling to. To call my own. Have you any idea what that feels like? Not knowing is scary. The possibility of never knowing is even more so. I need to know who I am.'

Her eyelids flutter open. 'You may not like what you find, Kate.'

'Don't you see, that doesn't matter? At least I'll know. If you care about me at all, Mother Peter, please, I beg you, tell me all you know.'

Lowering her head, she concentrates on the back of my hand, then turning it over, she circles the palm with her fingertip. 'You were an exceptional baby, beautiful inside and out. If I hadn't been in the service of Our Lord I would have gladly adopted you myself. It was Father Sean Devlin who organized your adoption. I was chosen to be the courier. I was given instructions as to where and when to collect you. We flew into Dublin airport, you and me, on June the fifth, 1962, at two-thirty in the afternoon. I arranged for my brother Patrick to pick us up and take us to Friday Wells.'

I don't see the point of telling her I know all of this and pretend to listen intently.

'It was me who called you Kate O'Sullivan, after my grandmother.'

'Where did I come from, Mother Peter?'

'The flight was from New York to Dublin via London.'

'Is that it? Where in America did you pick me up? From whom? Tell me, Mother Peter, I have to know.'

'I nursed you, Kate, you were such a good baby. I was loath to let you go.' Her lips are trembling.

I squeeze her hand affectionately. 'I would have been proud to have you as my mother.' Judging by her beatific smile, this pleases Mother Peter. Pressing her further, I urge, 'Have you any idea why I was sent to Ireland in such a bizarre manner?'

Her eyes cloud. 'Dutifully, I did as I was told. Father Sean Devlin knew the details.'

Unable to quell my rising irritation I implore, 'But someone must have met you in America. I couldn't have simply appeared out of nowhere.'

342

She repeats, 'Like I said earlier, Father Devlin made the arrangements.'

'Where can I find him?'

'In St Patrick's churchyard, Donegal. He died six years ago.'

Bitterly disappointed, I mumble, 'You were telling the truth when I called.'

'Of course, Kate, I wouldn't lie to you or anyone. I'd taken a vow of silence. You must understand.'

'So why tell me anything at all?'

'I'm dying, Kate. It won't be long before the cancer has colonized my vital organs. I don't want to leave any regrets.' Her eyelids are beginning to close.

It's obvious she's not going to reveal any more. I lean forward to plant a kiss on her brow, undeterred by a whiff of rancid breath. As my lips leave her, she grabs my hand. 'Have you still got the book I gave you when you left the orphanage?'

'Yes.'

'Have you read it?'

Shame-faced I have to admit, 'Not all. I'm sorry, I know I should have, but I've been too busy working, living . . . you know how it . . .' My voice trails off as with a start I realize I've no idea when I last saw the book or for that matter where it is.

'Read chapter six. It's very interesting.'

Her lids droop and close, flying open a second later. She looks agitated. 'I never liked him.'

'Who?' I ask.

'Father Steele. He had a dark side. I knew that from the very first moment I met him. A dangerous combination of corruption and charm.' She finds my hand. 'Don't blame yourself for his death, Kate. He isn't worth it. You have a good heart, it will help you to move on.'

I want to take her in my arms and hug her tight, breathe new life into the frail body. Leaning forward, I touch her cheek. 'Thank you, Mother Peter. I can't start to tell you how much that meant to me.'

'I'm tired. I want to sleep.' Her eyes close, her mouth slackens and her breathing becomes very shallow.

For a long time I stand completely still next to the bed, looking at her for what I know will be the last time.

Chapter Twenty

On the long drive back to Leinster Manor and during a restless night I rack my brain trying to remember where I'd put the book Mother Peter had given me as a leaving present. At one point I think, incorrectly, that I'd left it at Father Steele's cottage. Then I recall having seen it in the bottom of my case when I'd moved into Magenta House.

The following morning after breakfast I'm climbing the stairs when the sight of Mrs Hickey opening the top drawer of a tall-boy chest jogs my memory. Now I know exactly where I'd put the book. Racing back downstairs, I rejoin Bridget in the morning room. 'I know where the book is.'

Not looking up from the political section of the paper she says, with, I detect, a lack of interest, 'Where?'

'In a chest of drawers in my bedroom in Elgin Crescent. Unless that busybody Mrs Keating has moved it.'

'You don't like housekeepers, do you?'

'No, but that's irrelevant. I'm certain Mother Peter was sending me a message last night. There's a clue to my birth in that book, in chapter six. Come on, Bridget, we've got to get back to Dublin.'

With a deep sigh Bridget drops the newspaper. 'I was looking forward to a long walk, some good crack and Mrs Hickey's plum crumble.'

'What's more important, Bridget, plum crumble or my life?' Her face begins to split. Before she can reply I say, 'Don't answer that, just get packed. I can't bear the thought of the train and pointing fingers. I'll drive.'

Folding the paper and tucking it under her arm Bridget rises. 'Can we take the Range Rover? I'm not sure I could stand a journey like last night. You drive so fast. Sure, before I went to sleep I thanked Our Father a hundred times for getting me back safe.'

'The Range Rover it is. Now hurry.'

Side by side we march towards the front hall, passing Mrs Hickey arranging freshly cut flowers in a vase on a circular table in the centre of the hall.

'As soon as we've packed, Bridget and I are going back to Dublin.'

Angrily she stabs a petunia into the vase. Water splashes over the brim, wetting her hands. As we mount the stairs she begins mumbling under her breath. I can't catch what she's saying and on the fourth step I stop, urging Bridget to carry on upstairs.

'Are you speaking to me, Mrs Hickey?'

Scowling, she strides to the foot of the stairs, gripping the handrail with one hand, her other clutching a dripping flower. 'What about your lunch, and dinner for that matter? I've prepared both. What am I supposed to do with all this wasted food?'

'Don't waste it, give it to Sylvester. He looks like he needs feeding up.'

Blowing out her cheeks she opens her mouth, no doubt to give me a stream of complaints, but for once I'm determined not to be intimidated. 'I'm sorry, but I've got to get back to Dublin urgently. This might be very difficult for you to understand, Mrs Hickey, but what I've got to do is more important than eating your plum crumble.'

Red-faced, she is clearly struggling to contain her anger as she splutters, 'Don't know why I put up with your odd ways. Never understood why Mr Fitz did. I knew what you were the moment I first laid eyes on you –'

I cut in. 'What was that, Mrs Hickey?'

Wild-eyed she blurts, 'A scheming little madam who was after Mr Fitz for his money.'

My outrage must show on my face as I see Mrs Hickey's cheeks pale. 'How dare you suggest such a thing! I loved Brendan Fitzgerald with all my heart. I was devastated by his death.'

'I suppose the priest helped you get over your grief?'

I grip the balustrade very tight, my knuckles shining white. I suppress with huge effort the urge to run downstairs to wipe the smug smile off Mrs Hickey's face. 'I'm going to pack now. When I come down I want you to be gone. I'll forward your money on to you.'

I carry on climbing and am at the top of the stairs when I hear her shout, 'Mr Fitz said I had a job for life.'

Without turning I shout back, 'Mr Fitz is dead.'

'You're a bloody slut, Kate O'Sullivan,' she screams, venting all her pent-up anger, stuff I'm certain she's stored for years. 'Worse than a feckin' whore. At least they're honest.'

I'm shaking as I lean over the balustrade. 'If you don't get out of my house now, I'll come down there – and if I do, I'm warning you I won't be responsible for my actions.'

Mrs Hickey stands her ground. 'You don't scare me – you never did. That was the trouble, wasn't it? I was all for Mr Fitz.'

'The problems, Mrs Hickey, are all yours. You were jealous, and still are. You were in love with Mr Fitz. I told him once – he thought I'd gone mad. Do you know what he said?' Not waiting for her to reply I rush on: ' "Mrs Hickey makes my eyes sore. Poor woman has taken an overdose of ugly tablets. Thank God she can cook." '

Her expression turns for an instant to profound sadness, reverting a moment later back to resentment. 'I don't believe you. If you can do it with a priest, your good husband still warm in his grave, you're capable of doing

347

or saying anything. You're an evil bitch, a bad lot, you'll end up with the devil downstairs, in hell and –'

I finish for her: 'Damnation. Now get out.' I point to the door. When she doesn't move I screech, 'Get out!'

I wait until I see her storm out of the hall before breaking into a trot towards my bedroom. I'm still shaking with anger as I change my slippers for comfortable driving brogues and pull a sheepskin jacket and scarf out of the wardrobe. I grab my handbag from the seat of a chair, checking I've got my wallet and keys. When I descend the stairs, Bridget is in the hall standing near the door next to her case. A brown leather handbag is slung over one shoulder and she's gripping her camel coat with both hands.

'Just got to get the keys to the Range Rover,' I say, racing past her towards the kitchen. I spot them hanging on the key rack, next to the back door. There is no sign of Mrs Hickey. A blast of cool air greets us as I open the door. I spot Sylvester walking towards the garage. 'Sylvester!'

He turns, touching the side of his peaked cap. 'Missus.'

We walk towards him. 'Have you seen Mrs Hickey?'

'Yes, a few minutes ago. Went striding out of the drive, a million miles an hour, set me thinking that there was something wrong. Her granddaughter is having a baby, so I'm thinking perhaps she's started labour.'

I shake my head. 'She's left and she won't be returning.'

Bridget looks surprised, but wisely keeps her mouth shut. Sylvester nods, a small smile playing at the corner of his mouth. 'Sure, I'll miss her grub, but I won't miss her crack.' He tips his cap. 'Always was grumpy, but then so are most old women.' He winks. 'That's why I've stayed single.'

Bridget chuckles as I help Sylvester open the garage doors to reveal a gleaming Range Rover sitting between a tractor and my dirty Mercedes. 'I think she could do with a rub down, Sylvester,' I comment, pointing to the Mercedes.

'I'll have her looking as good as new, don't you worry 'bout that, Mrs Fitz.'

Climbing into the car, a thump of regret jumps in my chest. Brendan had bought the four-wheel drive three months before his death. He'd only used his new toy twice. I turn the ignition, the engine roars into life and we sweep past Sylvester doffing his cap and using it to wave.

The gates of Leinster are only a few hundred yards behind when I put my foot down intent on getting to Dublin as soon as possible.

Do not suddenly break the branch, or
Hope to find
The white hart behind the white well.
Glance aside, not for lance, do not spell
Old enchantments. Let them sleep.
'Gently dip, but not too deep',
Lift your eyes
Where the roads dip and where the roads rise
Seek only there
Where the grey light meets the green air
The hermit's chapel, the pilgrim's prayer.

At first glance the poem by T. S. Eliot seems to hold no clue to my birth. After the fifth rendition, Bridget makes a suggestion: 'Has it occurred to you that Mother Peter was trying to tell you to let sleeping dogs lie?'

Frustrated, my patience wearing thin, I growl, 'No. I think she was trying, without breaking her vow of silence, to give me a clue.'

'Don't get irritated with me. I'm only trying to help.'

I toss the book to one side and it lands on the bed between Bridget and me. I jump up, knot my fingers and stretch my arms out to full length in front of my chest.

Idly, Bridget begins thumbing through the book as I pace between the bed and the window overlooking the back of the house. 'Has Mother Peter ever been to Mexico?'

I shrug. 'I haven't got a clue. Why?'

'Just something here on the inside cover. A stamp, I think. It's faded and most of it's missing, but it looks like it says Mexico City.' She points at the book. 'Can you read that?'

Holding it up to the light, I read the word 'Mexico', the letters followed by the numbers 9 and 2. You're right, it looks like a stamp of some sort.'

I'm still trying to figure it out when Bridget says, 'I've got a hunch. What if Mother Peter collected you not from New York but from Mexico?'

For a few minutes I consider Bridget's suggestion. 'Possible, but why?'

'Money,' Bridget says. 'The priest and she were paid.'

'I can't imagine Mother Peter doing something for money alone.'

'Nor can I, but how can you explain the book from South America?'

'There could be a hundred feasible explanations. Someone could have sent it to her, a friend on missionary work or holiday.'

'That's true. Try her brother Patrick. He might know if she's ever been to Mexico.'

Without a word I'm trotting out of the bedroom and taking the stairs down two at a time. In my study I locate Patrick's card in my briefcase. There's no reply from his office. I punch out the numbers to his home; a woman replies.

'Is Patrick O'Sullivan there?'

Cautiously the woman asks, 'Who wants him?'

'We haven't met but I assume you are his wife, Ellen?'

'It's myself, and you are . . . ?'

'Kate O'Sullivan. Your husband may have mentioned me.' I'm about to ask where I can contact him when the phone goes dead.

I try again but it rings repeatedly. After five more attempts the woman answers. 'Before you put the phone down again I want to offer you a deal.'

Silence, but I know she's still on the line by the sound of her shallow breathing. 'What sort of deal?'

'Money for information.'

'I'm listening.'

'Do you know his sister Marion well?'

'I'm not answering a bloody thing till I know how much.'

'A hundred pounds if you can supply the answers to a couple of questions.'

Less hostile now. 'Ask away.'

'How well do you know Marion?'

'Well enough.'

'Enough to confide in you?'

'No, but I knew what she was up to when she brought you to Ireland in 1962.'

'What do you mean, Ellen?'

'It was her who fetched you from overseas. Even Paddy doesn't know that, he's a gobshite. Gabs to all and sundry down the pub.'

Suspicious, I ask, 'How do you know?'

'By chance. When I got the message from Marion about our Paddy picking someone up from Dublin airport I called the orphanage. She wasn't there and one of the lay helpers told me to get in touch with Father Sean Devlin. It was him who let it slip. I wasn't prying, you understand. I had naught to be suspicious about. I just wanted to check the flight times so as to make sure our Paddy got there in good time. I was young, nineteen, and aeroplanes and airports were a mystery to me. Still are, only been abroad once in me life. A boat trip to Calais.' I hear hollow laughter. 'We're broke, stony, bottom-of-the-barrel broke. The kids all need new shoes, and clothes, we'll have the bailiffs banging on the door soon, and him still pouring his bloody earnings down the back of his throat.

'Father Devlin said that Marion had a long journey from Mexico and would be grateful to see a familiar face at the airport. He urged me warn Paddy the connecting flight from London to Dublin was often delayed because of fog over the Irish Sea. I got the impression from the priest he and Marion were acting for some important people. It was all very hush hush, cloak and dagger like.'

Unable to contain my curiosity for a moment longer I ask, 'Did the letter say where the flight originated?'

'What?'

'Which town or city?'

'A hundred pounds, you said?'

Impatient I snap, 'Yes.'

'I've got a letter Father Devlin sent me with the flight details. Kept it all these years. I'm a hoarder, see, never know when things will come in useful. Hold on, I'll get it.'

The waiting time seems endless. Eventually I hear the rustling of paper and a mumbling, 'Flight departs New York –'

I interrupt. 'Her journey must have started before New York.'

I hold my breath, hearing the rustle of paper again.

'Yes, here it is. Mexico City. Do you know it?'

'No, but it looks like it's the place I was born, or where my parents took me for some reason or other.'

'When do I get my money?'

'When you send me the letter, I'll send you a cheque by return.'

'No cheques, I want cash. I haven't got a bank account. A money order will do.'

'A money order it is. Thanks, Ellen.'

'Don't thank me, thank Marion. If it wasn't for her who knows where you might have been today.'

I replace the telephone. On my return to the bedroom I stand in front of Bridget. 'Fancy a trip to Mexico?'

Bridget looks glum. 'Sorry, Kate, no can do. I have to get back. This one you have do alone.'

I fully intended to go it alone, and would have if Tom Gregson hadn't called on Monday night at ten-thirty. I was in bed. Bridget and I had decided on an early night since she had a seven-thirty flight to London the following morning to connect to Chicago. I'd promised to drive her to the airport.

Sleepily I answer the telephone. 'Hello?'

'Hi, Tom Gregson here. Is that Kate Fitzgerald?'

I mumble, 'Yes.'

'Sorry, did I wake you? What time is it over there?'

'It's ten-thirty, and no, you didn't wake me. Ten minutes later and you might have.' Shuffling into a sitting position I rest my head on the headboard and move the telephone to my other ear. 'How are you?'

'Great. I've done the piece. It's good, my editor wants to run it this weekend. I need a recent photograph of you and a couple more questions.'

Wide awake now I say, 'Fire away.'

'Do you know if Father Steele ever had any other affairs?'

His words trigger a memory of standing outside the living-room door in his cottage, hearing Father Steele talking to a woman. 'It's possible. I once overheard him talking heatedly to a woman called Siân.'

'Did he ever make any sexual overtures to you when you worked for him in Friday Wells?'

'What are you driving at, Tom?'

'Come on, Kate, no need to get touchy, just say yes or no. You can trust me.'

'How can I be certain of that?'

An exasperated sigh follows. 'My word. It's all I've got.'

I decide to let him have it all. 'I think the man and the priest were in constant conflict. He so desperately wanted to be a good priest he tried hard to deny the man. He failed. He even went abroad to put distance between us, get out of the way of temptation. We didn't see each other for over six years and our next meeting, as you know, was a twist of fate, mere chance, not planned or premeditated. After that meeting Declan made no attempt to find me, or get in touch, although it would have been very easy. I sought him out, I had to see him to confess the way I felt about him. I loved Brendan, but I was in love with Declan. I wanted him to know that. But our affair didn't begin until after Brendan's death.'

The line is hushed. 'Are you still there, Tom?'

'Yes, I'm scribbling.' Then: 'Are you sure you want me to print this stuff?'

'Absolutely certain.'

'Fine, but don't go all defensive on me when you see it in print. Now, I need a recent shot of you, looking suitably glamorous.'

'Difficult for tomorrow. You could try Susie Simons, Simons & Lake on 76th and York. I think she's still got some trannies of me taken last year at my summer exhibition.'

'Great, I'll call her now. By the way, I did a little research on the stuff we talked about.'

I sit bolt upright. 'Turn up anything interesting?'

'Yes, but I don't want to talk about it over the phone. How about I come over to Dublin next week and take you out for supper?'

'That won't be necessary. I'm coming to New York on Friday.'

'Like this Friday, the end of the week?' He sounds surprised.

'Yep, I'm in town for two nights.'

'Can you spare a few hours for an old hack?'

'I'm meeting Susie on Friday evening. She's throwing a small supper party for me at her apartment, but I'm free on Saturday.'

'How about lunch?'

'Great, where?'

'Leave that to me. I know a great little place that you might get a real buzz out of.'

'I'll look forward to it. Probably my last decent meal for a while. I'm flying to Mexico the next day, and I hate Mexican food.'

'Why Mexico?'

'I've been doing a bit of research, and have discovered that Mother Peter brought me to Ireland as a baby, from Mexico City.'

'Who told you that?'

'Paddy Fitzgerald, Mother Peter's brother. He picked her up from the airport, and has subsequently sent me a copy of the airline ticket.'

'What was the date on the ticket?'

'June the fifth, 1962. The journey originated in Mexico City.' I pause 'Why do you want to know?'

'I might make a few enquires of my own, see what I can come up with by Friday.'

Someone once told me journalists can't resist a challenge. 'I can't imagine you'll find out much in three days.'

I'm grinning when he comes back with, 'Just watch me.'

When I arrive at the Carlyle Hotel, there are two messages waiting for me. One from Tom: 'The feature is in tomorrow morning's edition. I hope we've still got a lunch date after you've read it.' The other from Susie, apologizing that she's had to cancel dinner, but was sure I'd understand a million-dollar deal in San Francisco was more important.

Bullshit, Susie, I think. No doubt in my mind that she'd got a hot invitation from the San Francisco-based banker she's been fucking for the last six months. On the way up to my room I feel very relieved; I hadn't been looking forward to confronting Susie's smart dinner guests.

Exhausted from a combination of jet lag and sleepless nights, I fall asleep as soon as my head hits the pillow, waking at my normal time of seven-thirty GMT, two-thirty a.m. New York time. I drink two small bottles of Evian from the mini bar and lie in the dark, gazing out of the window at the glazier gleam that is the Manhattan skyline. I try to imagine Declan in New York, wondering if he'd have been happy. I romanticize, imagining him in church not in Ireland but here in Manhattan; not in some swanky uptown diocese but in a poor neighbourhood, recounting tales of Ireland to a group of impoverished kids.

I begin muttering under my breath: I'm sorry it turned out the way it did. It could so easily have been different. A strangled sob rattles in my throat as an image of myself replaces that of Declan. I'm very old with long hair flowing down to my waist; it's grey – not the grey of slate but whiter, with a single golden thread. My skin is papery and very wrinkled like a prune. But my eyes are bright and I'm fit and healthy and painting prolifically. My painting will be with me until I draw my last breath. No one can take that away from me.

Declan no longer comes to me at night in my bed. It wouldn't make any difference, I'm numb from my waist down. My image begins to fade but not before I see another figure. It's a child, he or she, I'm not sure, is running towards me. Yellow hair flies back from a heart-shaped face, piercing blue eyes are framed with brows and lashes black as the night. I want to reach out, touch, feel, speak to our child. I know it's our child, mine and Declan's. I stroke my stomach in circular movements round and round, whispering, 'I've got you. I don't need anyone else. The rest of the world can go fuck themselves.'

Breakfast arrives at seven-thirty along with the *New York Times*. With a cup of coffee in one hand, and the newspaper in the other, I begin to read Tom's interview with me:

HOLDING BACK THE TEARS

After the death of her surrogate father and the suicide of her lover, artist Kate O'Sullivan talks of forbidden love.

'It was love at first sight, I couldn't help myself. You have to remember I was just 15, I'd grown up in an orphanage in a tiny village. I'd seen nothing of life. Then suddenly here's this amazing Adonis, handsome, compassionate, caring – I wanted him to sweep me up and take me away and love me forever.'

Kate O'Sullivan's eyes are sparkling even though she's barely rubbed the sleep out of them and it's mid-afternoon. She's been up most of the night and slurps black tea greedily as she talks.

'We were just young girls, we'd never been held, or kissed or chased by boys – only the nuns with their canes and leather straps. Other than the warmth we gave each other, we had nothing – just the cold, the brutality of the regime in the orphanage and our dreams.'

The young internationally acclaimed artist is trying to explain why a 15-year-old orphan girl would tempt the wrath of a God beaten daily into her hide by trying to seduce a priest.

O'Sullivan is tall with long sleek legs, a pinched waist and a voluptuous bosom. To call her figure scandalous would be an understatement. Her fine-boned face and long, elegant fingers add to the allure which is topped by a fine cloud of platinum blonde curls. She could be Marilyn Monroe's taller, classier twin sister.

Already a millionaire, with her work on an international tour that arrives in New York next month before moving on to Chicago and San Francisco, O'Sullivan commands $250,000 a portrait. Inspired by the old masters, her genius is the depth of character she achieves by light and shade alone, but O'Sullivan is unimpressed by her success.

I'm intrigued by the critics' conviction that the horrors of a repressive orphanage and a childhood lived in monotone are what guides her brush and I ask her about the nuns.

'Sisters of Mercy, they called them. We called them by other names,' spits Kate. 'I was taken to Friday Wells as a baby, barely new born, and lived there 16 years.'

I watch her face, looking for the tears of a painful memory dredged, but Kate's eyes are cold and stark.

'The regime was grim,' is all she'll say, without a hint of self-pity.

She could have added other adjectives. The Friday Wells orphanage regime has already been well-documented in a government inquiry – punishment beatings for bed-wetting, institutionalized violence, children sleeping in soiled sheets for days on end, inedible food and sexual assaults.

I try to draw Kate on the subject but she doesn't budge. 'I'm not sure all that is relevant to my life now or my work –'

I suspect she's being coy, or just plain obstructive, but move on. I ask her about the death of a nun and she dries up completely, feigning ignorance. Kate's best friend in the orphanage pushed a particularly brutal nun down stairs. She was convicted of manslaughter. The sentence might have been life if Kate hadn't made an impassioned plea of justification on behalf of her friend to the court, detailing the systematic sexual and psychological abuse inflicted on her friend by the nun.

'I suppose if you push me on my childhood I'd have to admit that painting was my means of escape from it all. Then suddenly there was Declan, Father Steele.

'I was besotted, love at first sight. After all those dirty, grimy, dark, cold, wet, hungry days and nights, Declan was a miracle: tall, strong, handsome, passionate – all the things we girls had no idea existed outside Friday Wells.'

She talks freely now, drawing on a cigarette, the black tea going cold on the table in the morning room of the country house she shared with her husband. She talks of Declan now not with love or adoration but sadness; she is reflective rather than regretful.

'I don't think he thought of me in the same way at first. I was a novelty, a child to him, but I was also becoming a woman damned fast. Approaching my 16th birthday it was time for me to leave the orphanage. I'd planned to go to Dublin, but Father Steele asked me to become his housekeeper. It was just me and him in his cottage, alone most nights. I gave him painting lessons, and in return he taught me about life.'

It's clear the tension between the two, the adolescent, adoring girl, the innocent young celibate priest, reached boiling point.

I hesitate to ask if the young Kate deliberately encouraged the priest, and she's already moving on.

'Anyway – let's just say it got impossible. Declan fled. I went to Dublin and met Brendan. He taught me that art was not an escape from life but a means of embracing it. He was the dearest, sweetest, warmest human being . . .'

Now I notice her eyes are misting. Brendan Fitzgerald died of cancer recently. More than 30 years her senior, he was Kate O'Sullivan's mentor, guru and guide. When last year he was diagnosed with bone cancer and given months to live, he proposed to Kate.

'Brendan desperately wanted to leave something behind – a child, our child. That's why he proposed. Ours had been a beautiful platonic relationship, like father and daughter, but I loved him unconditionally and said Yes – not to make him happy on his death bed, but because I truly loved him.

'You can imagine the shock I got when I walked down the aisle and there was Father Declan Steele officiating at *my* wedding. My heart beat almost as loud and as fast as Declan's,' explained Kate.

In the ensuing days Kate, now a woman, and Declan Steele rekindled the passion they'd stirred in the cottage in Friday Wells five years earlier. Inexorably they slid into the Catholic taboo of broken vows and illicit sex within the Church.

'There was nothing either of us could do to stop it. It was inevitable, it just consumed us both. Declan fought it for weeks but we both knew deep down we'd make love. We could see the compulsion in each other's eyes.

'The man and priest conflict tore him apart. For certain, he tried to deny his desire for me, but eventually it got the better of him, and I don't think he ever came to terms with it. There were always three of us in the relationship. Me, Declan and the Almighty, and as usual He won.'

Now O'Sullivan acknowledges that she encouraged the priest. She's angry and feels partly responsible for his death.

I suggest that we are all in control of our own lives and if we choose to end it there is no one else to blame.

She doesn't agree and says, 'I'm not sure any of us really have complete control over our lives.' Then with a winsome smile adds, 'I wish.'

Undoubtedly she has unaffected charm, but people who underestimate or misjudge her untutored naturalness should watch out. There's definitely a controlling side to Kate O'Sullivan. 'Steel and determination,' her US agent Susie Simons told me. 'Couple that with beguiling beauty and incomparable talent, and you have Kate O'Sullivan.'

She smiles a lot, it makes her look younger, and her voice is deep and throaty with the resonance of Irish pub singing.

O'Sullivan looks out of the window across the garden. 'I think it's going to thunder – devil's clapping, the nuns used to say.' She pauses, then in a breathy voice says, 'Brendan once said, "The richer you are the less you have to pay for."'

She faces me with an enigmatic smile, 'It's true, so true, but I've got a feeling we all pay in the end, one way or another.'

Tom is at the restaurant when I arrive, seated at a corner table. He's drinking what looks like a whiskey and water.

He stands up and, visibly nervous, grins. 'Punctual – unusual for a woman.'

I sit down opposite. 'No ordinary woman.'

He sits very still, grinning Cheshire-cat like. 'That's for sure.'

He hands me a menu, then, before I can look at it, says, 'Well?'

I know what he means but can't resist teasing, 'Well, what?'

'What did you think of the piece? I can't eat until I know.'

'Oh shit!' I cover my mouth with the flat of my hand. 'I forgot the interview was today.'

He lets out a long sigh. 'How the hell could you forget?'

I begin to laugh, and I see him relax. 'It was great. As interviews go, I thought it was candid, to the point, and in parts very flattering. Thanks, Tom.'

He blushes, acknowledging my thanks with a wide beam. 'Have you ever thought about an autobiography, Kate?'

'No, never. Why do you ask?'

'This morning I had a call from an editor I know at Random House. She asked me how to get in touch with you. She's very interested in your autobiography.'

I'm struggling with chopsticks and trying to look and act enthusiastic about the Japanese food, which I hate. Swallowing a whole piece of some sort of raw fish I gag and quickly wash it down with a gulp of still water. 'Who would write it?'

'Me, if you agreed.'

Right now I don't want to think about an autobiography but in the short time I've spent with Tom Gregson it's become clear he's very persistent and since I'm in no mood to be badgered I concede: 'I'll think about it.'

'Promise?'

'I promise,' I say, popping a prawn in my mouth. As I chew I watch Tom digging into the food with relish. Earlier when he'd called I hadn't the heart to tell him I loathe Japanese food. I'd even fixed a delighted smile on my face when he'd led me through the red lacquered door whispering that the Konikiti was the best-kept secret in New York.

Still hungry but finished with the Japanese rubbish, I place my red chopsticks decoratively on the black plate and wipe my mouth with a taupe napkin. Pushing the serving plate in front of my face he presses me to eat more.

'I'm full up to here –' I indicate an imaginary space above my head.

With a mouthful of food he manages to mumble, 'Was it good?'

I lie with practised ease. 'Great.'

He looks dubious. 'You didn't eat much.'

'Breakfast was lunch to me. I was famished. I'd been awake half the night. I pigged out on bacon and eggs.'

I'd demanded during the meal that Tom tell me what he knew about my birth in Mexico. He'd resisted my persistent questioning, insisting that I wait until after lunch. 'Now, will you give me all the news on Mexico. I've been patient long enough.'

Tom runs his tongue across his top lip before saying, 'I think you were born in the Celestine private clinic, located in a place called Puerto Vallarta on the Pacific coast of Mexico sometime in the early part of 1962.'

I'm impressed but don't show it. 'How did you find out?'

'After I left Ireland on the plane back to New York, I couldn't stop thinking about you. The circumstances of your birth, the way you look – like I said, a young Marilyn Monroe. I was and am intrigued. I'm an investigative journalist – what can I say? It's in my blood. Anyway, after you told me about the airline ticket I started a few discreet enquires. I began with an old buddy, a fellow journalist, Mike Moran. He worked in Mexico for six years as a foreign correspondent. He's very well connected. I gave him the information, suggesting that your birth was probably a secret. He made some enquiries about private clinics operating at the time, and came up with a list of female babies born in February 1962 to unmarried mothers in and around Mexico City. At the time, the very expensive and exclusive Celestine Clinic in Puerto Vallarta was run by a consultant gynaecologist called Dr Juan Perez. He performed illegal abortions, at a price, and delivered and organized adoptions for many high-profile families. Usually the illegitimate offspring of rich kids and mistresses of high-powered men. We think your mother may have been delivered by him. There's no record of the mother, but a record of a baby shows a premature female born on February 28th, 1962. Incubated and taken from the clinic a few months later on June the fifth. It fits. A few years later the doctor disappeared. Probably unconnected, but we might get lucky with the nursing staff. I've told Mike to keep digging.'

I feel a surge of optimism. 'That's great news, it's my first concrete lead. If I can find this Dr Perez, or one of his staff, I might be able to persuade –'

Tom interrupts. 'Perez might be dead. The clinic no longer exists. Trying to trace the staff will not be easy. You're going to need help. Do you speak Spanish?'

I shake my head. 'Do you?'

He rotates his hand. 'A little, but Mike Moran is fluent. He lived there, and understands the indigenous culture. How about I accompany you, we meet Mike, and do it together?'

Unused to having my space invaded, I say, 'I want to do this alone.'

'I understand the emotional logic of that, but I can't let you go down there on your own. Not to Mexico.'

'I've been all over the world alone.'

'Maybe so, but always, I'm sure, in protected situations. London, Sydney or New York for an exhibition. You're met at the airport in a limo and escorted to your hotel suite in a five-star hotel. The back streets of Mexico City are no place for a lone woman. You want to find out who your parents were?'

'Stupid question – you know I do.'

'Then don't fight me. I know a bit more about this sort of thing than you do, and believe me it's dangerous. I'd hate to read about you as a missing person or, worse, dead. I'm serious, Kate: there are people down there who'd stick a knife in their own mother if they could sell her body parts.'

He lets the wisdom of his words sink in, waiting patiently for me to speak.

'I give in, but I want to do my own thing. I need space

364

and I don't want you bullying me, telling me what I can and can't do all the time. Deal?'

Extending his hand across the narrow table, Tom says, 'You're a tough nut, Kate Fitzgerald, but I've got a sneaking suspicion there's a soft centre.'

Ignoring this, I grab his hand and repeat, 'Deal?'

He grins; light sparks from his pupils. 'Deal.'

Chapter Twenty-One

Mike Moran, Tom's friend and colleague, meets us at Mexico City airport. I'd travelled first class, Tom in tourist. After sitting next to a heavy-drinking crew member I'd longed for Tom's urbane company.

Mike is a burly, genial man with a robust personality, ruddy complexion and warm brown eyes. He looks to me more like a Kerry dairy farmer than a top investigative journalist. As we troop out of the arrivals hall I notice Mike is limping. Tom in hushed whispers tells me he'd been a foreign correspondent in 'Nam, injured in action in Saigon. Later that evening in the Hotel Eden bar, Mike informs me he'd been born with one leg slightly shorter than the other. Confused and unsure who to believe, I'm about to ask Mike when Tom winks and begins to laugh. Instantly cottoning on, Mike asks, 'What line did he spin about my limp? Was it the Vietcong, Beirut, or maybe a croc in Mozambique?'

'Saigon, injured in action.' I grin.

'That's an old one, Tom, try and come up with something a bit more original. The next round is on you, I'll have a double Scotch and a big fat Cohiba. It's the only way to ease the trauma of my terrible wartime injury.'

Puffing on a cigar, Mike relates his findings. Maria Días had been the mistress of Dr Juan Perez from 1959 to 1964. Now the Condesa Maria Sanchez Márquez, respectably married to an aristocrat, she has refused to talk to Mike or anyone else, and has threatened legal action if he harasses her in any way.

I decide to call her myself, insisting she might talk to me. She takes the call, speaking in heavily accented English. 'Yes, I'm Condesa Márquez.'

'We haven't met. My name is Kate O'Sullivan, I'm a painter. I recently had an exhibition in Buenos Aires, you may have read about it or heard of my work?'

There is a few moments' silence, then, '*Sí*, I read of you in the newspaper. For long time I am admiring your work. A good friend of me, the wife of the Mexican ambassador, has painting from you her husband was getting in New York last year. I ask my husband to buy a painting from you but always he say too expensive.'

I feel a wave of elation. I had something to trade. 'I wonder, Condesa, if I could come to see you, or if we could meet? I have a proposition to put to you.'

'I not understand.'

Very slowly I repeat, 'A proposition – something for you to consider.'

She repeats, 'No understand.'

I speak slowly, pausing after each word. 'I'll give you one of my paintings if you'll help me.'

She falls silent. 'How to help?'

'It's difficult to discuss over the telephone. Can we meet?' I sense her hesitation. 'It won't take long. Half an hour.'

'*Sí*. You come here, my house, tomorrow afternoon by four.'

'I'll be there. Can you give me the address?' I scribble the address on the hotel notepaper, then say, 'See you at four.'

After replacing the telephone I spin around to face the two men with a look of triumph. 'Well, say something.'

In unison they shout, 'Bravo!'

The taxi drops me outside a large apartment building in the centre of the Avenida Insurgentes. I ask the driver to wait; he seems unsure but brightens up when I force

367

several notes into his hand. The door is answered by a uniformed maid who shows me into a grand salon. The walls and ceiling are decorated in elaborate Rococo plasterwork depicting wood nymphs and musical instruments. On one wall three sets of tall casement windows overlook the street; two are shuttered against the afternoon sun, the third in the centre is open a fraction to let in a whiff of polluted air. Light from a cut-glass chandelier casts a yellow glow on the gleaming floors and there's a distinct smell of stale tobacco and polish. The room has the heavily laden, hushed air of a museum. After about five minutes a butler, also uniformed, arrives, carrying a small circular silver tray. Two glasses and a decanter sit on top of an inlaid coat of arms. With a curt incline of his sleek head he offers me sherry. When I accept, he begins to pour sherry into a fine cut glass. We both look towards the door as it opens.

A statuesque figure appears, dramatically dressed from chin to mid-calf in silver-grey silk, a diamond and pearl choker glimmering at her throat. She has an abundance of shoulder-length chestnut brown hair – a wig, I suspect. With a few curt words she directs the butler to hand me the glass of sherry, then, waving her manicured hand, she dismisses him, directing her attention and the same hand to me.

'Maria Sanchez Márquez. Pleased to meet you.'

'Kate Fitzgerald, née O'Sullivan.'

A short uncomfortable silence follows before she indicates a set of chairs placed in an orderly half-circle in front of a vast fireplace. The grate, I notice on sitting down, is filled with an arrangement of dusty dried flowers. We both sit upright on high-backed chairs side by side. I feel gauche, like I'm having an audience with the queen.

Maria, on the other hand, is detached and cool. She crosses her long elegant legs before speaking. 'You are more beautiful than in the photograph.'

'What photograph?'

'In the *New York Times*.'

'Thank you.' I take a sip of sherry; it's very sweet and extremely smooth. I raise the glass a fraction. 'This is very good.'

'I don't drink. No good to the skin. You are young.'

I say honestly, 'Your skin is flawless.'

The compliment produces her first smile. 'You are kind to old woman.'

There are some people I know who soak up flattery, sincere or insincere, like a sponge. You can't give them enough. This woman is, I suspect, one of those. 'You don't look old.'

Again she says, 'You are kind,' elongating her long neck in preening-swan fashion. 'I lucky. I have the skin of my grandmother. On her death bed all who saw her said she had the skin of a woman –' she slices the air with her hand – 'half her age.'

'If I look like you when I'm –' careful here – 'older I'll be over the moon.'

'Over what?'

'Sorry. Delighted, pleased, thrilled,' I say quickly.

Unnecessarily patting an imaginary strand of hair into place, she asks, 'What age am I?'

I err on the good side: 'Forty-eight?'

She laughs. 'Sixty-three,' she says triumphantly.

Now I'm genuinely stunned. I had in truth put her age at early fifties. 'You're an inspiration! What is your secret?'

'No secret. To 'ave the love and desire of a good man.'

I use this as a cue. 'Which brings me to the reason I'm here . . .'

She leans slightly towards me. 'My ears are yours.'

'Did you know a man called Dr Juan Perez?'

Perceptibly she stiffens. 'You are the second person to enquire of this man. Why?'

'I believe he delivered me.' She looks puzzled. 'Brought me into the world. My mother, whoever she was, is, had me adopted when I was a baby. Are your parents still alive, Condesa?'

Her brown eyes harden like polished stones. 'My father died when I was twelve, my mother two years gone. I am missing of her every day. She was . . . how do you say in English? Formi . . .'

'Formidable.' I finish the word.

'*Sí*, for-mid-able.' She enunciates the syllables.

I decide to appeal to her feminine side. My instinct tells me a real woman exists beneath the brittle manufactured perfection.

'Can you imagine not knowing who your parents were, what they did for a living, how they looked, how they felt?' She shakes her head as I continue: 'I need to understand what motivated my mother to give me up. If it was simply because she didn't want me, then I'll have to accept that and move on. But I have to know, I can't start to tell you how important this is to me. Have you any children, Condesa?'

'One son. A lawyer. And' – spreading her fingers on her left hand – 'five grandchildren.'

'You're a very lucky woman. Let me put it to you this way: your son is adopted at birth, given a different name and brought up by strangers. All his life he craves an identity, to know who he is. He's now a grown man, married with five beautiful children, but they will never see or know of their grandmother. It's hard to forge a future without a past. I was lucky, compensated by a gift – I can paint. It's been my salvation.'

'Your mother, she dead.'

At first I think she is asking me a question, then realize it's a statement. 'How do you know?'

Her eyes darken to almost black. 'She die after you were born.'

Anticipation burning in my chest, I ask, 'Did you know her?'

'No, but she was loving you. She very much wanted you, much difficult at the time.'

'What was her name?'

The Condesa directs her hard gaze to the middle distance. 'Ask Juan Perez.'

'Where is he?'

Still staring into space, she says, 'Sometime he write to a friend, Antonio Cortez.'

'Where can I find Señor Cortez?'

Rising, she crosses the room. She stops next to the fireplace, and with a scarlet talon presses a bell to the right of the mantelpiece. 'Jorge will give you the address and telephone number. I sorry to say goodbye, but I rushing to dress for a state banquet.'

Clearly the meeting is over. I'll get nothing more out of the Condesa. I stand up. 'The painting – have you any preference?'

For a moment I think she's going to refuse it, but I'm wrong.

'The fruit. I like very much the fruit.'

'A still life it is,' I comment, following her across the room. Before we reach the door it opens and the butler reappears. Maria speaks to him in rapid Spanish. I understand a couple of words: *sí* and *bueno*.

As he backs out, I turn to the Condesa. 'Thank you for your help.' She studies me intently, her head set at a haughty angle, a ghost of a smile playing at the corners of her mouth. 'I'm pleased for helping.'

I'm about to respond when the butler hands me a slip of paper. The address of a Dr Antonio Cortez is at the top right-hand corner; below there's another.

The Condesa extends her hand. I take it; we shake. 'You will be sending the package to that address.' She points to the address beneath that of Dr Cortez.

Reading the address of a bank in Panama, I smile. 'It will be there very soon, I promise.'

'I will telephone to my friend Dr Cortez and explain with him. Good luck for you.'

I fold the paper and slip it into the inside pocket of my shoulder bag. We exchange knowing looks. 'Goodbye, Condesa.'

'*Adiós*, Miss O'Sullivan.'

I step through the open door; she remains inside, her hand resting on the door knob. 'You have the look like your mother,' she says before shutting the door firmly in my face.

It takes me a few moments to adjust my eyes to the brilliant sunshine after the gloom of the Márquez apartment. The taxi driver is dozing, his open mouth pressed against the window. When I get into the back of the car he jumps awake, bumping his head on the roof. I hand him Antonio Cortez's address. It is, he indicates with his thumb and forefinger, a little way from here.

I point to my wristwatch, urging him to drive fast. After five minutes of the most hair-raising driving I've ever encountered, I'm praying for him to slow down. Several times I try to stop him careering at breakneck speed through a series of back streets, but to no avail. He merely laughs maniacally, shouting, 'Me Ayrton Senna!'

I feel physically sick, certain at any moment I'm going to throw up. My hands are aching from gripping the back of the seat as we screech to a halt in front of a multi-storey glass box. Turning to face me, the driver beams. 'Many, many cars, me quick. *¿Bueno, sí?*'

Pleased to be alive I fish in my purse and hand him his fare and a few dollars' tip. I don't ask him to wait as I get out. I check the address before mounting the wide marble steps to a revolving glass door. A board located on the wall behind the reception desk tells me Dr Cortez is a consultant plastic surgeon and is located on the sixth floor. I've never consulted a cosmetic surgeon and have no preconceived idea of how the surgery will look. The receptionist, to my surprise, is plump and elderly with sun-charred skin and several chins. She clearly has resisted the knife.

In perfect English, she asks, 'Can I help you?'

'My name is Kate O'Sullivan. I've come to see Dr Antonio Cortez.'

'Have you got an appointment?'

'No, but I believe he's expecting me. I'm a friend of Condesa Maria Márquez.'

The name seems to impress her. 'Take a seat in the waiting room. I'll tell him you are here.'

The waiting room has one other occupant, a beautiful young woman with a perfect retroussé nose. I assume she's a post-operative patient.

I flick through American *Vogue*, idly glancing at the glossy images. After a few moments the girl is called. I wait for a further half an hour before hearing a deep voice speaking in Spanish. I look towards the sound coming from a man dressed in a blue shirt and white surgical coat. A moment later the man is introducing himself to me. 'I'm Dr Antonio Cortez.' I stand up, towering above the diminutive doctor.

'I'm Kate Fitzgerald.' A look of confusion flashes into his narrowed eyes. 'My married name. O'Sullivan is my maiden name.'

With a brisk nod he says, 'Come through.'

I follow him through a labyrinth of passages punctuated by doors. Eventually he opens one, leading me into a large office. His desk sits in front of a wall of glass covered with white vertical blinds. The floor is blond wood, the walls and ceiling surgical white; two large contemporary paintings offer the only relief. One I recognize immediately as Miró, the other I think I should know but don't.

I'm studying the painting when he supplies, 'Dali, very early work,' then, 'Please sit.'

I sit on the opposite side of his desk.

'Maria called me, said to expect you. I know what you want but I don't think I can help.'

He speaks very fast, not pausing between sentences. I can't resist saying, 'You speak very good English.'

'I was educated in America and spent my post-graduate years in Florida. I married an American and for many years lived between the two countries until I divorced. But getting back to you. The only person who could have helped you is Dr Juan Perez.'

'Why past tense?'

I feel my heart sinking as he replies, 'He's dead.'

'The Condesa didn't know he'd died?'

'I didn't know myself until a few weeks ago. I've been travelling. I intended to tell her on my return, but you know how it is. Life is so hectic. I forgot.'

Confronted with what may be the truth, my disappointment manifests itself in disbelief. 'I don't believe you. He can't be dead. It's just too convenient for him to be dead, too tidy. Send me back to no man's land to live the rest of my life not knowing. But then, so what, who cares? Certainly not you. I suppose you've got parents, grandparents; ascendants, heritage, mementoes, photographs, memories. I've got fuck all.'

I'm trembling like an old woman and have to grip the lip of his desk to stand. I lean towards him. 'You have to tell me the truth, Doctor. If this man is still alive my search won't be futile. It's a lifeline, something to hang on to.'

Spinning his chair round to face the window, the doctor sits in silence, rotating a pencil in his left hand. I wait patiently, praying inwardly that if Dr Perez is still alive I've pricked his friend's conscience.

To his back I say, 'I implore you, please find it in your heart to help me, I'm desperate to know who I am.'

His expression when he spins back into view has changed. A flicker of hope springs into my eyes as I spot a hint of compassion in his.

'The last time I spoke to Juan Perez he was living in relative luxury in Miami, Florida.'

'When was that?'

'Two months ago.'

He hands me a photograph. It shows a man who looks in his late forties; he's wearing a Panama, a cigarette dangles from the corner of his mouth, he is staring at the camera out of insolent eyes. As he scribbles on a notepad, Dr Cortez says, 'That was taken in 1978, but the last time I saw him, about three years ago, he hadn't changed much.' He hands me a slip of paper. 'This is his last known address. I doubt he'll talk to you, but then again he might. Juan could never resist a beautiful woman, particularly a vulnerable one. I'd appreciate it if you were discreet about how you found him. We've been friends a long time. I want to keep it that way.'

'You have my word.' I put the notepaper in my pocket. 'Did you meet my mother?'

He shakes his head. 'I wish.'

'Before I go, will you answer one further question?'

With a curt nod he replies, 'I might.'

'Will you tell me her name?'

He stands up, his gaze hard as rock. 'No.'

'Why? Is it because she was famous?'

'You said one question.'

I plead, 'Please, Señor Cortez, please.'

With a quick glance at his wristwatch he walks round his desk. 'I have a patient waiting.'

'Just answer yes or no, and I promise I'll leave.'

With a deep sigh, he says, 'Yes.' Then he pauses, clearly deliberating his next words.

I wait, my heart battering against my chest.

'And so was your father.'

Chapter Twenty-Two

'I think I've got him. I saw him go into the surgery on Biscayne, about half an hour ago. Fits the description, looks like the photograph, his age is right, about fifty-six.'

I hear the animation in Tom's voice when he asks, 'Did you notice if he had a small scar below his left earlobe?'

'He was too far away. But I definitely think it's our man. I'm going to wait for him to leave the surgery. I'll follow him – hopefully to his home. See you back at the hotel later.'

I sense the concern in Tom's voice when he warns, 'I don't think he's dangerous, but it pays to be careful, Kate. A hint of trouble and you get out of there fast, understood?'

'Yep,' I say, my sights fixed on the surgery entrance. 'I'm a bit scared. I've never done anything like this before.'

'All the best operatives are scared, it gets the adrenaline pumping. Go get him, Kate.'

I leave the telephone box, and with my head bent to my chest I run back to my parked car. At ten minutes past twelve Dr Perez emerges, blinking rapidly against the strong sunlight. He pulls a pair of sunglasses out of his breast pocket, puts them on, then, leaning heavily on a walking stick, stumbles across the car park to an old silver Mercedes coupé. As he gets in his car, I turn the key in the ignition and follow the Mercedes down South Bayshore Drive. Thankfully, he's driving very slow and I can keep on his tail easily. After a couple of miles he indicates left. I follow him into the car park of the Easy

Over Diner. I wait for him to park, then I park close enough to see him, but not close enough to be seen. I watch him struggle out of his car and hobble towards the entrance to the restaurant.

I reapply a coat of lip gloss, push a few stray strands of hair into the baseball cap I'm wearing and fix a pair of dark glasses to my face. Inhaling deeply, I step out of the car, cross the lot and enter the diner. Instantly I spot the doctor sitting in the window facing the street. He's got a mass of steel-grey hair and is smoking a cheroot and reading the front page of the *Miami Herald*.

'Waitress service only, miss,' a young girl pouring coffee informs me. 'Take a seat and someone will be right with you.'

'Is anyone sitting here?'

The doctor's eyes move from the newspaper to me. His smile is inviting. He's eyes are as cold as the bloody Irish Sea. 'Be my guest.'

I sit down opposite him, glance briefly at the menu for a couple of minutes then ask, 'Are you familiar with the food in here?'

'I take lunch here every day – is that familiar enough? The girls joke that I don't have a home to go to. It's become a ritual – you know, like brushing my teeth, and besides, I enjoy familiarity.'

'What would you recommend?'

'It's all good. If you like omelettes, the mushroom is –' he kisses his bunched fingers – '*magnífico!*'

'Are you American?'

'Latin American, like the other three-quarters of the population of Miami. And you? Are you British?'

'No, I'm Swedish, but my accent sounds strange because for most of my life I lived in the North of England.'

'Where in Sweden were you born?'

'Stockholm, but my family moved to England when I was eight.'

377

This seems to satisfy him. 'How long do you intend to stay in Miami?'

'I arrived three days ago. I'm staying for two weeks. Do you live here?'

'I live not far from here, ten minutes walk.' He takes a sip of water. 'Are you on vacation alone?'

I nod as the waitress approaches the table. He orders for me.

'The young lady, on my recommendation, is going to try one of your glorious omelettes, Barbara. I will have my usual. Why spoil a habit of a lifetime?'

'Omelette comes with hash browns, country fries or bacon.'

'Hash browns, please.'

'Wholewheat, rye, pumpernickel, English muffin?'

'Wholewheat.'

'Tea, coffee, juice, beer? We got grapefruit, orange, pineapple, tropical fruit –'

The doctor cuts in: 'Try the orange juice, it's great.'

'Orange juice it is, and tea with milk.'

Barbara sticks her pencil through a coil of hair fastened to her crown. She smiles cheerfully in the doctor's direction. 'You want beer or wine with your usual, Doc?'

'A glass of chilled Chardonnay would be very civilized.' He grins, making no pretence at discretion as his eyes follow Barbara's buttocks bouncing down the centre of the restaurant.

'Wow, I'm exhausted before I start.'

'American fast food. It's an experience I wouldn't miss for the world, and this, in my opinion, is the best place to eat it authentically. I adore the great American brunch. I eat it here most Sundays when I'm in town, which, I have to add, is most Sundays. A lot of restaurants have spoilt it with European inventions. Eggs Benedict, smoked salmon and scrambled egg with brioche. Whoever heard of Americans liking brioche and croissants? The majority of Americans have never been out of their own state, let alone to France. Do you know, only six per cent of the population of this country own passports?'

I didn't know. 'Really. That's extraordinary. But then, Europeans travel a lot, we're very different.'

'I know, to my sorrow.' Like a conspirator he leans close to me. 'I was married to an Italian. A mistake. My mother warned me, but I was, to put it mildly, besotted. She was the most beautiful woman I'd ever seen, and it wasn't only her looks. She had fire in her soul. God, that woman was wonderful. Full-blooded.'

'What happened?'

He frowns, lost in thought. In repose his mouth is cruel. He begins to wave his hands wildly as if wafting irritant flies away. 'She left me. The bitch ran off with another man.'

Our food arrives, my plate groaning with golden hash browns and a perfectly formed omelette, his with a minute steak and thinly sliced French fries. I'm hungry and cut into the food with genuine relish.

As if talking to himself he murmurs, 'It's rare for me to talk to strangers. Occasionally I may pass a courteous good morning, maybe a comment on the weather, but never a conversation. I'm not – how do you say in English – a dirty old man, if that's what you are thinking.'

I swallow a piece of omelette. 'I wasn't jumping to any conclusions. It's pleasant to chat. What harm is there in that?'

'None, but try telling that to any beautiful young girl in this town. If you so much as glance in their direction they respond with a stream of abuse. Can you tell me why they wear such revealing clothes if they don't want to be gawked at?' He takes a sip of wine, then continues, 'Age. That's the problem. Getting old. Sometimes I forget I'm an old man. It's very easy to forget. The trouble is, I don't feel old in here –' he points to his head. 'Or here –' he thumps his chest. 'How old are you?'

379

Biting into a bread roll, I say, 'Twenty-four. And you?'

He sighs and looks deeply troubled. 'Old enough to be your grandfather.' Tearing a chunk from his bread roll he mops his empty plate, and pushes it to one side. He finishes his wine in one gulp and coughs, as if to clear his throat. 'Now I have to go. Time, never enough of it, not in this country. Everyone is always racing – and in pursuit of what?' I watch him reach for his walking stick hooked over the back of the chair. He stands, and with his back poker-straight he takes hold of his stick, leaning on it heavily. 'It was nice meeting you. I've got an appointment with my physiotherapist. Doesn't do much good though.' He taps his right leg with the rolled-up newspaper. 'Gout got me years ago. Enjoy the rest of your stay here in Miami.'

I smile. 'Nice meeting you. I enjoyed our chat. I'm staying in a hotel close by. You never know, we might bump into each other again.'

'Like I said, I'm in here every day same time, same place. Always been a man of rigorous discipline. Not sure it got me anywhere, but can't get out of the habit. Too old to change. Have a good day.'

I turn and watch him leave the restaurant with a brave attempt at a dignified walk.

Tom is wearing shorts, docksiders and a polo-style T-shirt when I join him in the lobby of the Turnberry Isle Resort. I whistle. 'Mr Tourist.'

Taking my arm he steers me in the direction of the restaurant.

'I made a reservation for lunch.'

With a smug smile, I say, 'I've had lunch with Dr Perez.'

His brows arch as he whistles. 'You don't waste time.' Then, 'How did you manage that?'

'I followed him from the surgery to the Easy Over

Diner, on Bayshore Drive. Apparently he eats there every day, so we know where to find him.'

'How was he? Did you guys hit it off?'

I grin. 'Big time. He's interesting. I'm sure he was very handsome, and still has a lot of charm. Clearly a ladies' man.'

Tom pushes open the glass door to the restaurant. 'I'm starving. Wanna drink while I eat?'

I nod and follow him to where a hostess is waiting to seat us. When we are comfortably seated at a circular table next to a window overlooking the swimming pool, Tom says, 'Don't be fooled by the doctor's charm. Beneath that sophisticated veneer, he's as tough as they come. Charm and corruption, a lethal combination.'

'You could say that about a lot of people. I'm not intimidated.'

After Tom has eaten we walk along the shoreline, to all intents and purposes the archetypal tourists, a couple dating or on vacation together.

'Do you think the old man will talk to me?' I ask.

'He lives in a fancy apartment, so I doubt he can be bought. Yet, who knows? Tax-free money deposited in a Panamanian account is not to be sniffed at, but in my experience you can never tell. Sometimes the people you think will take a bribe don't. Nobility, integrity. Not that I've come across it a lot in my time.'

The light is strengthening. I look across to a boat hoisting its mainsail and with a pinch of envy say, 'Brendan used to take me sailing off Kerry Head.'

'Do you like sailing?' Tom asks enthusiastically.

'I love it.'

'OK. Let's do it.'

Tom had spent a large part of his childhood sailing with his father in the Carolinas. His handling of the forty-two-foot ketch we charter for the afternoon is impressive, but I'm more impressed by his modesty. There is, for me,

381

something very romantic about being on the water. I'm always gripped by a sense of freedom mixed with adventure. Some of the most profound conversations I'd ever had with Brendan had been at sea.

We couldn't have chosen a more perfect day to sail. The wind was a westerly force three past the harbour, reaching a steady force four. While Tom had chartered the boat I'd bought bread, cheese, cold meats, fruit and beers: a veritable feast, Tom had declared, helping me aboard.

We drop anchor for supper; tearing the bread and cheese with our hands and folding the ham and pastrami into bite-size pieces, we eat on our laps.

'How long were you married, Tom?'

'Eight years.'

'What happened?'

'We were childhood sweethearts. It was the usual story: married too young. I travelled a lot. I was working on the *Washington Post* as an investigative reporter. I worked on crime. It took me away from home. I didn't think anything was wrong, and it hit me like a ten-ton truck when she announced out of the blue that she wanted a divorce.'

'You didn't have kids, did you?'

'No, thank God, that's a blessing. Lots of my friends have separated in recent years and, boy, have I seen big changes in the behavioural patterns of their kids. But I want kids, desperately. I've been seeing a woman recently who has a four-year-old son. We've bonded big time. If I can feel that way about someone else's kid I can't start to imagine how it must feel to have your own. How about you, Kate, do you want kids?'

I consider telling him I'm pregnant, but something holds me back. 'Not until I'm absolutely certain I can give them the sort of balance and security I never had. I want my kids to have it all.'

He pulls the ring on a Bud. 'That's not always possible.'

'I can try. Anyway, what are we without dreams, ideals, romantic imaginings? When I was a little girl I dreamt up an entire family history for myself. My parents had been tragically killed in a car accident in America. My mother was from Ireland originally but had moved to America when she became a famous actress. When my parents died her sister brought me back to Ireland but couldn't afford to keep me, so I was put into the orphanage. The sister died not long after and I was forgotten. I'd dream about my father's brother finding a letter from the sister saying where I was, and him arriving to take me back to America. Everyone in the village would be talking about the big limousine and the tall handsome American who'd come to take Kate O'Sullivan to live in New York. They were childish dreams but they helped me through the hell of the orphanage. Kept my spirits up, fuelled my aspirations and my self-esteem. I just want to say I was convinced, still am, that I'm not Irish.'

He winks and, mimicking my Irish lilt, repeats, 'And I just want to say, I don't think you look Irish.'

'Do I say, "I just want to say," a lot?'

He's laughing. 'All the time. You preface almost every sentence with it.'

'I just . . .' I stop myself in time and, laughing, yell, 'You tease me remorselessly.'

'I just want to say . . .' he begins, then, 'Like I said before, you look like a young Marilyn Monroe. You have a natural sexual grace, like she had.'

Holding my windswept hair back from my face I take a swig of beer. 'Perhaps I'm Marilyn's daughter. Now that –' I point at him with the can –'*would* be a sensational story.'

'The story of the decade, the fucking century.' He grins impishly, a man–boy. Finishing his beer and crushing the can, he says, 'She was desperate to have a child, lost and aborted several. Poor old fucked-up Marilyn, adored but never loved, one of life's victims.' Holding on to the rudder he gazes out to sea, his mood sombre. I understand this retreat into the sanctuary of his own reflections and don't press him to converse.

At dusk the weather changes. Tom sets course for home, the strong wind out of the north-west helping the boat make fast time back to the harbour. Once safely in we tie up, grab our shoes and walk hand in hand down the slip next to the water, flat now and still, reflecting the fading yellow light.

Back in the lobby of the hotel, Tom regains his usual ebullience and suggests a nightcap.

I yawn. 'I'm exhausted. Early to bed, early to rise to stalk Doc Perez again. I think I might make an appointment at his surgery.'

'You're not going alone.'

'Why not? What do you think he's going to do to me in his surgery?'

'Who knows? I think the diner is the best bet. Tomorrow lunch, and we take him on together.'

Too tired to argue, I feign a yawn. 'Anything you say, Mr Gregson.'

'Don't be facetious. I'm serious, you could be in danger.'

'Oh, come on, Tom, all I want from him is information, and I'm prepared to pay. I think he'll welcome me with open arms.'

'Surely that depends on a lot of things. Not least of which is who your parents were . . . are.'

He's right and I concede. 'Point taken. Now I want to go chill out.'

'Sure I can't tempt you with a vodka martini, and my amusing conversation?'

'The vodka martini sounds inviting, but I'm not sure about the other . . .' I deliberately let my voice trail off.

He pulls a long face. 'That's what they all say, the

women that is. Never sure about the other bit. The part after the vodka martinis. Story of my life.'

I'm certain a man as attractive and erudite as Tom Gregson has had a lot of success with women; this makes his self-deprecating humour all the more appealing. I wink. 'I don't believe that for one moment.'

He grins, the man–boy again. 'Would I lie to you?'

'Probably, if you had to – but then, don't we all?'

'Sometimes it's necessary. Sensitive people understand that.' He groans. 'Now I'm faced with yet another rejection. How will I cope?'

I pinch his arm. 'You'll cope. I'm off to soak in a hot tub, drink gallons of mineral water, watch a bit of TV and sleep. Goodnight, Tom.'

In a quiet voice he says, 'Sweet dreams.'

He recognizes me immediately, his expression instantly alert, his body language taut and guarded. 'What do you want?'

'Answers.'

I see his hand move towards a drawer on his desk. 'Who are you?'

'I'm not sure, that's where you come in.'

A flicker of comprehension crosses his face, and I see Dr Perez visibly relax.

'You are Juan Perez, are you not?'

'That depends.'

'Before we go on, I want you to know that I'm not alone. I've got back-up in your waiting room, and outside in the car park. Just in case you decide to do anything hasty.' I feel like an actor in a bad B movie, and any moment expect the director to shout, Cut!

Dr Perez repeats, 'Who are you?'

'My name is irrelevant. It was given to me on my adoption. I have reason to believe you delivered me in the Celestine Clinic in Puerto Vallarta in early 1962. I

385

was taken from the clinic by an Irish nun, and brought up in a Catholic orphanage in Ireland. Does it ring any bells, Dr Perez?'

Now infinitely more relaxed, the doctor leans back in his chair, an enigmatic haze in his eyes. 'I assume since you got this far, you've done your research, so it seems a little futile to lie. I owned and was the senior consultant at the Magdalen and Celestine clinics from 1954 to 1965. The best days of my life. The Celestine was a wonderful building, perched on a hill overlooking the Pacific. It had been a monastery; a fragrant, idyllic place.'

'Do you remember a baby being collected by a nun?'

'Several babies were taken from the clinic by nuns. Mexico is a Catholic country; some of the girls were young, they gave their children up for adoption to Catholic families, to convents. One nun looks like the next.'

'I believe I was born in February 1962. You must have kept records . . .'

'Of course, but they were all destroyed. The Celestine burnt down in 1965.'

With both hands on the lip of his desk he supports himself as he begins to stand. 'Now you'll have to excuse me. I've got an important meeting to attend.'

I stand, facing him. 'You performed illegal abortions – is that why you destroyed the records and left Mexico?'

He laughs. 'What nonsense is this? I think you've been watching too many American movies.' Grabbing his stick he rests his weight on it, his eyes narrowed.

'Just tell me if you can remember a baby being picked up by an Irish nun. Surely all the nuns weren't bloody Irish?'

'I tell you, I can't remember. I may have been operating at the time – who knows? It's a long time ago.'

'Will two hundred thousand dollars jog your memory?'

Contempt pours from his icy gaze. 'Corruption joins us once again. He's never far away, been my close friend, and enemy, for the majority of my life, and I'm tired of the relationship.'

Angry tears cloud my vision. 'All I want to know is who I am. Who my mother was. Tell me, Dr Perez, I beg you. I know you know.'

Using one hand to steady himself, he walks evenly around his desk, stopping next to me. His breath smells of nicotine, and I notice a mole on the side of his left cheek, close to his ear. 'You're right, I do know.'

'Jesus, Mary and Joseph, man – tell me!'

'Why should I?'

'Why not? Is two hundred thousand not enough? Will half a million loosen your tongue?'

I can hear the scorn in his voice when he growls, 'This is not about money. I have enough. But I can see you're determined, you're not going to go away without a fight. Give me a good reason, a better one than bribery, and I might consider confiding in you.'

'Compassion for a fellow human being?'

'Don't talk to me about compassion!' He spits out the words as if emptying his mouth of something foul.

I decide to appeal to him, yet feel in my heart it's hopeless. 'I was brought up in a grim orphanage, in a place God forgot. I was different, I looked different, felt different, and I could paint. I'm now an internationally renowned artist, and when I sign my paintings it's always with a deep sense of regret. K. O'Sullivan – O'Sullivan was the nun's maiden name. I want to know what my real name is. For the love of God, I need to know.' I begin to cry, real tears. 'Is there anything, or has there been anything, that you wanted so bad you'd be willing to do almost anything to get it?'

For a few moments he doesn't speak, then fumbling in his pocket he pulls out a handkerchief. He hands it to me, saying, 'Stop crying, I can't bear to see a woman cry. Particularly a beautiful one. I understand need, and longing, and the bitter taste of regret and failure. I've wanted something for a very long time, and now at last I have my dream. I'm leaving here soon, in a few short weeks, to spend, I hope, the last years of my life free.' Looking at me intently he continues, 'The loins you sprung from, and the womb that conceived and carried you, belonged to extraordinary people. Are you prepared for that knowledge?' Before I can reply, he adds, 'I think not. I'm not sure you are. I see it in your eyes, an innocent. But I like you, you've got that fire in your soul. Believe me, I don't encounter it often. My wife had it. I've wished a million times I had. Chutzpah, the Americans call it, I think it's courage. I'll think about you, K. O'Sullivan, and what you've said, and if you come to the Easy Diner the day after tomorrow, we'll talk. I'm not making any promises, and I don't want your money.'

Tom meets me outside the doctor's surgery. I take a deep breath and smile tremulously.

'How was it?'

Ignoring his question I say, 'Will you take me out of town, Tom?'

We walk towards the car. I feel shaky and my legs are leaden.

'Where?' he asks, surprised.

'Anywhere. I need some space.'

As we drive west on Alligator Alley, through the Everglades, I recount my conversation with Dr Perez. Tom listens intently – not commenting until we reach Naples. Once there he says, 'Don't expect to see Doc Perez again. In my experience men like Perez don't talk, they walk.' With a dismissive shrug I suggest that we check into a small hotel on the beach. I want to take a shower, so does Tom, and we arrange to meet in the lobby in an hour.

Fifteen minutes later someone is hammering on my door. Wrapped in the hotel bathrobe, I open the door.

Tom's face is white. 'Can I come in?'

Concerned, I ask, 'What is it? You don't look so good.'

Once inside, Tom says, 'I'm fine, but old Doc Halliday isn't.'

I shut the door with my back. 'What do you mean?'

'He's dead, just seen it on a news flash in the bar. Shot outside his apartment building. Apparently, the good doctor was involved in a huge narcotics operation the FDA and the police have been trying to crack for a couple of years.'

A great wave of rage sweeps over me. I want to lash out, hit the wall, scream abuse, smash something. Angry tears spring to my eyes as I yell, 'I don't believe it, I can't fucking believe it! To get this close – I'm positive he was going to tell me. You know, like I said earlier, in the car, I felt it in here –' I touch my stomach. 'Instinct, call it what you like, but I really felt he was going to tell me who my parents were, are. He wasn't afraid, just tired, you know, like he'd had enough, and why not do someone a good turn? He said he'd found his dream, and was leaving.

'Now I know why he didn't want my money. I don't believe it! Shit, we were so close. I thought, I hoped, at last, at long bloody last, I'm going to know.' My eyes feel gritty as I fight the urge to cry. Tom is next to me now. I can feel the heat of his breath on my face. It feels natural to wrap my arms around his neck. I'm only vaguely aware of him kissing my neck and his hand in my hair. Sucking in my cheeks, I gasp for air, muttering, 'It's over.'

'No, it's not, it will never be over until we find the truth. There are avenues we haven't explored yet. The doctor must have had friends. He liked women. He'll have a girlfriend somewhere, she might know. You can't give up, Kate. I'll help you to find out who you are if it's the last thing I do. You can't give up.'

My mouth connects with his. It's warm and solid and safe. I press my body hard against his, sucking and holding his breath in my mouth like I'm drowning. Taking his hand, I feed it inside my bathrobe, drawing in breath as he exposes my left breast. I fumble with the belt, then abandon it to Tom's one easy tug.

It falls open. I lift it off my shoulders and let it drop.

'You're very beautiful, Kate. I'm almost afraid to touch you.'

With my fingertips I trace the line of his mouth. He sucks my finger, biting the tip.

'You have a beautiful mouth. Deep-lipped.'

Images of Declan begin to swim in front of my vision. I close my eyes, stumbling forward as if drunk to hang on to Tom for balance. 'Make love to me, Tom, make me forget. I need you tonight. I need you very much.'

When he doesn't reply, I open my eyes to see him backing off, holding me at arm's length. He's whispering. I strain to hear him.

'I want you to need me, Kate. But not like this.' Purposefully he picks up my bathrobe. Gently resting it on my shoulders, he says, 'You're not ready yet.'

Chapter Twenty-Three

The morning sun sparks off the wings of the plane as it dips, dissecting the clouds. The inky Irish Sea, white-capped and choppy, comes into view. I feel a great surge of happiness. I'm home.

When I emerge from immigration, Joe McNamara, the driver, is waiting for me in the arrivals hall. He's wearing his grey uniform and cap, the one I know is two sizes too big and stuffed with newspaper.

The familiarity and certainty of home are reassuring. We talk little on the journey into Dublin. It's always the same: I make a few polite enquiries about his family, he asks me about the weather in America, or wherever it is I've been; then we settle into a comfortable silence. It's how we both like it; it's grand, it is that.

When I arrive at Elgin Crescent Mrs Keating is waiting, stiff backed, starched and predictable. I refuse breakfast, opting instead for a pot of tea and bed. After soaking in a hot bath for over half an hour I slip between linen sheets, shutting down my thoughts. I awake with a start at three in the afternoon. I've slept for more than seven hours. Sitting up in bed, I let my head loll and, dozing, I replay the last few weeks in sequence. Scene by scene it returns to the final denouement when I'd announced to Tom I was giving up the search and returning to Ireland.

Tom had wanted to carry on, wanted me to stay, more I suspect out of his growing attraction for me than any-thing else. I'd watched the colour bleed from his cheeks; every feature on his mobile face had frozen for what had seemed like a long time but in reality was a few minutes.

'I can't go on, Tom. We've, you've tried everything, no one could have done more. I'm tired . . . I want to go home.'

'The nurse from the clinic promised to call Mike tomorrow. She might have good news. I know I've been saying that for weeks, but I've got a hunch we're right on the brink of the truth. I'm certain we are almost there. I feel it in the old bones.'

Ignoring the note of hope in his voice, I'd said, 'I've heard it all before, and I'm tired. I want a break. You understand, don't you?'

'No, I don't understand how someone as passionate and determined as you could give up so easily. That confuses me. In truth, I'm baffled.'

'It's not about giving up, it's about putting on hold. I'm exhausted and I need a rest, that's all. A couple of weeks to reflect. Come on, Tom, give me a break.'

'Give you a break – how about me? I've worked my ass off on this, because I believed in it, in you. And now you want to give up, run back to Ireland to reflect. Bullshit, Kate, and you know it! You're running away. I'm warning you, if you go now, you'll never know the truth. You'll go to your grave not knowing who the fuck you are. Is that what you want?'

Angrily I'd retorted, 'Fuck you, Tom Gregson. You know that's not what I want. But I'm sick of the disappointment, the leads that lead nowhere, the hopelessness of the whole fucking thing.'

'It's not hopeless, not while there's still a chance of finding out more.'

Resigned, I'd said, 'It feels hopeless . . . dead, and nothing you can say or do will change the way I feel.'

For a long time Tom was silent. When at last he spoke I'd been shocked by the disappointment in his voice. 'I really thought you were special, made of different stuff to the majority of the pack. But it seems I was wrong, I misjudged you.'

'You judge me too harshly, Tom. I'm a lone woman, who is tired and wants to go home. Is that so bad?'

'Not bad, Kate, just defeatist. Like I said, I thought you were made of different stuff.' With that he'd turned and left without saying goodbye.

The following morning Tom was at the airport check-in desk when I arrived. He looked weary. 'I couldn't let you leave without saying goodbye.'

I'd laughed out of sheer joy. 'I can't start to tell you how happy I am to see you. Last night, after you left, I felt like I was walking through turd. I haven't slept, and want you to know I'm not giving up. Give me a couple of weeks to sort myself out, and I'll be back.'

I'd sensed an air of defeat about him that hadn't been there the previous night. 'I'm sorry about last night. I was angry, and hurt. You leaving feels like a rejection. I mean a personal rejection.'

'It's not. I want a break, that's all.'

'From me?' he'd asked.

I'd thought carefully before answering truthfully. 'Partly, but only because you are bound up in the search, and it's the negative aspect of that I want to escape, for a while.'

He took a step closer to me, then, as if he'd changed his mind, backed off. 'I'll keep in touch if I have any news.'

We didn't embrace, because he insisted it wasn't goodbye. I waved from the departure gate, then watched him melt into the crowd. I knew I'd miss him. I already was.

Downstairs Mrs Keating is moving around. I hear her footsteps on the stairs and a few moments later a discreet knock on the door.

'Come in.'

Her head appears before her body. 'I wondered if you'd

be wanting any supper. Just in case, I've prepared a light quiche and salad.'

'Sounds grand.' I stretch. 'Right now I could use a pot of tea and my mail.'

'Both coming up.'

I'm in the same position ten minutes later when Mrs Keating returns with a tray of tea, fruit cake and a bundle of mail tied with an elastic band. She pours the tea while I undo the mail.

Most are bills. There's a letter from Bridget enclosing a photograph of a chuckling Eugene. He's chubby, and looks like Bridget. Susie Simons wants me to call her urgently to confirm whether or not I'm coming over for the exhibition. I'd completely forgotten about it. My London agent Caroline Lamb is getting married and has sent an invitation to her wedding next spring. A letter slips off the bed; Mrs Keating stoops to pick it up. As she hands me the envelope I recognize Paddy O'Sullivan's childish scrawl. The letter is brief and to the point.

Dear Kate,
   I thought you'd be wanting to know our Marion died on Sunday.

I glance at the postmark: October 13, three days ago.

   She's being buried on Friday at St Patrick's in Limerick at ten-thirty.
   She told our Ellen that you'd been to see her in the hospice. That was kind of you. Anyways, you'll be as welcome as the flowers in May to pay your last respects. I'll understand, and so would our Marion, if you can't make it due to other commitments. I know you'll be there in spirit.
   Yours,
   Patrick O'Sullivan

It begins to rain when I drive out of the churchyard gates. The sky above the church is metallic; fog further reduces the light. The journey back fills me with dread. I'd deliberately sat at the back of church and slipped out before the mourners. I'd covered the broken ground leading to the grave and, lurking behind a stout oak trunk, I'd watched from a distance. Waiting, listening, hiding. Black thoughts of demons and death consume me in this depot to heaven – or hell?

I see Declan floating above the grave, bone white. He's pointing a finger at me, a bitter reproach on his lips.

I hear my last words to him: *I'm sorry, Declan, but you do see that I can't let you go, ever.* Was it, I wonder, that sentence which tipped him over the edge?

Paddy's directions are very accurate. I find Sunnyside Terrace easily. The street faces due north, it's not sunny at all. Patrick O'Sullivan's house is the last but one, number 24. The front door is painted in candy pink, the sort of colour indigenous to the Caribbean, a bold splash in a squalid landscape.

Through the rear-view mirror I see the leading hearse turn into the terrace. I wait until it stops outside number 24 before climbing out of my car. Ellen alights first. She's totally different to how I imagined from our telephone call: a fat woman, with clear milky skin, a plump pretty face and sparkling green eyes. Seeing me crossing the road, Ellen smiles warmly. She waits for me to join her before following her husband into the hall. The house is similar in size and design to the Molloys', built at the end of Queen Victoria's reign.

'Boxes,' Brendan used to say. 'Can't swing a cat in most of them, let alone a family of six or eight. A couple of spare rooms with not a flower or a blade of grass to brighten the eye and lift the spirit on a spring morning. Soulless boxes for the men and women who are the bloody backbone of this country. Make them slave all hours that the good Lord sends, pay them a pittance for it, and lock them up at night in identical boxes to rob them of their identity. No wonder half the male population are drunks.'

Ellen is what the Sisters of Mercy would have referred to as nipping clean and not just top show. Every square inch of the house is spotless and, like the door, decorated in bright pastel colours.

The small gathering includes close family (Paddy's two sisters and their offspring); a couple of neighbours, one who'd earlier informed me he lived at number 26; an old school friend; and Mother Superior from the Sisters of Mercy Convent. We'd never met; I make no attempt to alter the situation, nor does she. I was thankful not to have to deal with Mother Paul. Paddy had told me earlier that she was very ill. Cancer of the colon.

Forced into a corner by a man who introduces himself as John McHugh, Paddy's brother-in-law, I try, not very hard, to look interested without listening to a word of his small talk. Through a gap created by his shoulder and the close proximity of a mop of peroxided back-combed hair belonging to Paddy's sister, I observe Ellen O'Sullivan holding two plates: one contains curling slices of ham, the other anaemic sausage rolls. She's a bovine hulk of a woman yet feminine and extremely beautiful, one of the rare women who suits being big. She'd be a wonderful subject to sculpt, something I've been longing to do for some time. I'd begged Declan to sit for me nude. He'd conceded after much persuasion, but we'd made love after less than ten minutes. The memory, though painful, makes me smile. Paddy is circulating with tumblers of Irish whiskey. I hate the stuff but take one and pretend to sip.

Soon I can no longer bear the press of closely packed bodies, the loud voices rising above the smoke. Excusing myself from John McHugh, I squeeze past a couple of people to reach Ellen. 'I must go. I've got a friend coming for supper tonight and it's a long drive back.' It's a lame excuse and I wish I hadn't used it. The truth is simpler. I've done what I came to do – pay my last respects. I'm tired, jet-lagged and I hate wakes.

'You can't go yet, we've just got started. Half the village are coming over later. Roddy Flynn has promised to sing, and Dan Doyle from the pub has got some good crack.' She repeats, 'You can't go yet. Paddy wants to show you off. He's always talking about you down the pub – a bloody film star, Kate O'Sullivan, he says. They're all dying to meet you.'

Emphatically I say, 'I'm really sorry, Ellen, I've got to go. Where is Paddy? I want to say goodbye.'

A petulant scowl turns down the corners of her mouth, making her look less pretty. 'I want you to stay.'

Feeling mildly irritated, I repeat, 'I'd love to, Ellen, but I can't.' Before she tries to persuade me further I leave her side in search of her husband. I find him in the kitchen pouring Guinness into a tall glass. 'I'm off now, Paddy. Thanks for everything.'

Concentrating on the fine head he's getting on the beer he says, 'Going so soon? The lads from the pub will be disappointed.'

Not wanting to get into a similar conversation to the one I'd just left, I say, 'Ellen and I have been through all that. I've got to get back to Dublin.'

Paddy holds the glass up to the thin light from the kitchen window. 'A fine head, if I say so meself.'

'It is that, Paddy, it is that.'

Fastening his lips around the glass he polishes off half the Guinness in one swallow. 'I needed that,' he says, wiping his white frothy moustache with the back of his hand. 'I'm pleased you could get here anyways, Kate. I know she was fond of you, and being as she brought you over here from America. Had any luck in that department?'

For a moment a pang of desperate disappointment grips me, then I recollect the promise I'd made to myself on the overnight flight from Miami to London. No good living in the past. I'd been doing that for too long. The future I'd promised myself was the only destination I would consider from now on.

'I'm trying to forget recent events. I think it's time to move on.'

Paddy swigs the last of his beer. 'Sure, you've had a hard time lately, lass. More than most. Losing your husband and all that nonsense with the priest.' He leans towards me, lowering his voice. 'Hypocrites most of them – those men of God, I mean. Either pleasuring themselves with young lads or thinking about getting inside a woman. Men will always be men, love, no amount of bible-thumping and Hail Marys can alter that. So think hard on what I've said and don't go blaming yersel' for things that you have no control over. Our Marion always said, "Don't have any regrets, Patrick, just keep turning corners and marching on. As long as you have faith in the Almighty, you'll have your place in the life ever after." Always preaching, our Marion, God rest her soul, but not in a pious sort of way.'

His eyes shine with tears. 'She really cared, you know, about me and the kids and Ellen. Always said Ellen was a good woman, too good for me.'

'Your sister did care, Paddy, genuinely. She gave me and lots of other girls in the orphanage their first taste of humanity. I hope she rests in peace.' I pause as I see a tear escape the corner of Paddy's right eye. He swipes it impatiently with the flat of his hand. 'I'd best be off. It's a long journey back.'

Paddy walks me down the narrow hall towards the front door. As we pass the open door to the front room, Ellen waves. I wave and mouth, 'Thank you.' At the door Paddy extends his hand. I use it to pull him towards me and plant a light kiss on his cheek. He blushes crimson, a wide grin spitting his face like a melon.

'I'll not wash me face for a week, a month, a year maybe.'

I chuckle. 'That's the nicest thing anyone has said to me in ages.'

Paddy is still grinning when a moment later Ellen joins us. 'I almost forgot, Marion left this for you.' Ellen is holding a small parcel wrapped in brown paper. 'She gave it to me the last time I saw her, a couple of days before her death.' Handing me the package, Ellen says, 'Marion said to tell you she loved you.'

Tom is reading by a single light in the darkened room. He throws the newspaper aside when I appear at the door. Rising to his feet, he peers through the shadows. 'Kate?'

'Yes, it's me. When did you get here?'

'Ten minutes ago. Mrs Keating let me in. Said you'd be back soon.'

I cross the room, tilting my face to the light. Tom looks exhausted, there are dark pouches under his eyes and his skin is tinged with grey. 'You look like shit,' I say, not unkindly, then: 'You OK?'

'I haven't slept for a couple of nights, but apart from that I'm fine.'

'So why are you here, Tom, good news?'

'There's no easy way to tell you this, Kate.'

My impatience is mounting. 'Say it the hard way, then.'

'The day after you left, Mike got a call from the nurse who had worked at the Celestine during the time you were born. She now lives in Guadalajara. Mike and I drove down and met her there. She claims she assisted Dr Perez in your delivery, and that you're the daughter of Marilyn Monroe.'

A beat of silence when I can hear my pulse hammering

in my own ears. I'm unable to make sense of what I've just heard. I manage to utter, 'What?'

'Marilyn Monroe was your mother.'

Shaken to my core, I stumble, lamely reaching out for support; once again it comes in the shape of Tom. Wrapping my arms round him, I lower my head into his chest, my mouth stretched in a silent scream. I feel my insides loosen and my head throb as if being rained with blows.

'I had to tell you myself, face to face. Remember, it may not be true. It's the word of an impoverished woman living off a state pension and meagre savings, who might say anything for a thousand dollars.'

My voice is tiny, barely a whisper. 'Tell me what she told you. Exactly, word for word. Don't miss anything out.'

As he begins to speak I can feel his breath hot on my brow. 'In 1962 Renee Tabora was training in midwifery. She worked for Doctor Perez. At the time he had two private clinics, the Magdalen in Mexico City and the Celestine in Puerto Vallarta. On the afternoon of February 28th she was on duty at the Celestine when an emergency case was brought into surgery, a woman in her thirties in labour. The patient was gowned up for a Caesarean section; at first she didn't recognize her as Marilyn Monroe. It wasn't until later, in recovery, that she realized it was the film star who had just given birth to a premature child. The baby, born at twenty-eight weeks and weighing less than three pounds, was not expected to live. But she survived and thrived in the intensive care unit of the clinic until June 5th when a nun came to collect her. During the first week or so after the birth, Marilyn came to the intensive care unit every day, staying for as long as she was allowed. The nurse recalls her sitting next to the incubator silently staring through the glass. She spoke no Spanish, the nurses little English, so apart from a few odd words they didn't converse. After the second week Renee didn't see the mother again, and like the rest of the world was shocked when Marilyn was found dead in August of the same year. I asked her why she didn't go to the newspapers with her story. She said it was because she'd been afraid, as had her friend, a nursing sister at the time, who is now dead. Dr Perez had warned them both that if they ever breathed a word to anyone their own lives would be in danger. Less than a year after the incident, Perez paid off the nurses and shut the Magdalen clinic. He continued at the Celestine until a fire burnt it to the ground. Time passed, she married, brought up four children and forgot all about Marilyn's daughter.'

'Do you believe her, Tom?'

'It's a bizarre story, but it explains everything. Marilyn was going through a traumatic period of her life. As you know, she'd had an affair with JFK and, if all accounts are correct, was in love with his brother. Marilyn Monroe was in Mexico in February 1962 – she returned to LA on March 2nd.'

'Did the nurse mention the father?'

'I asked. She said she had no idea who he was. Of course she'd speculated at the time about the Kennedys, but had never mentioned or discussed it with anyone.'

We both fall silent. At length I pull away. 'I want to be alone.'

'I don't want to leave you like this.'

'Please, Tom.'

I see a flicker of protest enter his eyes before he reluctantly strides from the room without another word.

The magnitude of what I've just heard will, I know, take a long time to sink in, if at all. I'm light-headed and breathless, drowning in a great wave of bewilderment. Questions: so many form a queue in my head. How could she have left me for weeks on end in intensive care? Why didn't she take me with her when she left Mexico? What was she doing there in the first place? If she'd wanted to keep my birth a secret, surely she could have taken me to a close friend or relative? Last, but by no means least, who was my father?

After about an hour I guess – I've lost track of time – I sense Tom entering the room. His feet make no noise on the carpet. It's the gentle exhalation of his breath that alerts me to his presence.

'There's nothing more we can do tonight, Kate. Why don't you try and get some sleep?'

'Will you sleep with me, Tom? I don't want to spend tonight alone.' I wait for his response. When there is none, I say, 'I need you.'

Reaching out, he takes me in his arms, his mouth full of my hair.

'You're vulnerable, Kate, it would be so easy for me to take advantage of that.' He steps back, holding me by the shoulders.

In a little-girl voice I say, 'I want you to hold me, that's all.'

I feel the soft love from his eyes when he says, 'I'll spend the tonight with you, and as many nights as you need me.'

Deliberately I dress in a baggy pair of men's pyjamas and a big T-shirt. All the better to hide my rounded stomach and swollen breasts. I say the Lord's Prayer, a leftover habit from childhood, before climbing into bed next to Tom, who is wearing a pair of boxer shorts.

Wriggling my bottom into his lap we spoon, his arms wrapped round my chest. We lie in silence. I've no need of words, I prefer the sanctuary of my own thoughts. Eventually I fall asleep wrapped in Tom's furry limbs.

The package was where I'd left it on the hall table along-side my bag, forgotten after Tom's amazing revelation. Picking them up I cross the hall into the morning room. I'd left Tom in bed sleeping like a baby.

Sunlight streams into the room from the window facing the garden. I sit on the arm of a chair in the direct path of the sun, reading a card from Mother Peter. It's short and to the point.

Dear Kate,

After your mother's death, this arrived at the orphanage addressed to you, care of Father Devlin. Before he died, he passed it on to me for safe keeping. It was sent from Dr Greenman, in America, who was treating your mother at the time of your birth and her death. His enclosed note had simply said he thought you should have her diary. I'm not sure how he came to have it, he didn't say. Sorry you had to wait for me to die to find out who you are. I do hope it doesn't cause you pain. God be with you.

Yours,
Mother Peter

The brown paper package contains a box that had, I think, once held something else – a book, perhaps. Inside the box is a diary bound in maroon leather. I open it, my pulse thumping against my temples as I read the first entry:

October 20th 1961
Missed my period again. That's two. Must see the doc.

November 12th
Confirmed pregnant. Twelve and a half weeks.

I leaf through mundane entries for the following weeks, fixing on an entry for December 18:

He wants me to have an abortion. Told me today. This time I'm going to put my foot down. He can go to hell.

I don't want to get rid of this baby. I want it so bad, I'll do just about anything to keep it.

January 24th 1962
Spoke to J this morning. He insists I do it, even after I'd promised not to tell another living soul who the father is. He won't listen, he doesn't trust me. Men are all the same. They want to fuck without responsibility. The ones I've met anyhow.

February 20th/Miami, Florida
Got very drunk last night at the Club Gigi. Isadore was shocked to hear that Arthur was getting married again. Isadore Miller is one of the good guys. He's very sweet. He looked after me reel good. I showed my appreciation. I always do.

March 8th
Looking forward to going to Palm Springs with J. I'll get him in a good mood – I know exactly how to do that, then tell him about the baby. I hope Sam Giancana won't be there. He scares me.

Aware of a shuffling on the other side of the door I stop reading. I'm holding the card in one hand and the diary in the other when Tom enters the room.

'Morning, Kate. You must have crept out of the room as quiet as a mouse. I didn't hear a thing.'

Ignoring this, I wait for him to sit next to me then push the diary under his nose.

'What is it?'

Without a word I hand him the card from Mother Peter. As he reads I notice the dark pouches have gone from under his eyes and a little colour has returned to his cheeks.

He's excited. 'Dare I say it? Marilyn's?'

Slowly I nod. 'It makes fascinating reading.'

'May I?' he asks, extending his hand towards the diary.

I withdraw, holding it close to my chest. 'To your heart's content – after me.'

Tom, using his eyes to register his understanding, rises. 'You're right. I'll leave you to it,' he says before leaving the room.

Eagerly I return to the diary, reading an entry for:

February 22nd/Mexico City, Hilton Hotel
I can't sleep – so what's new? Afraid to take anything in case I hurt the baby. A shot of vodka can't hurt, can it? Someone once told me vodka relaxed the womb, was good for pregnant women. Told him Jose Bolaños had invited me to Taxco. Jose's cute. I think I'll go. They got armed guards in the fucking corridors here. I feel like I'm under siege! Press everywhere. It's a fucking circus!

February 23rd, Mexico City
I'm bored. I hate it here, it smells and the people are reel dirty. I want to go down to the coast to Puerto Vallarta or Taxco. I want to drink piña coladas and dance under the stars. I'll ask Jose to take me today, or maybe tomorrow. I know exactly how and when to ask him.

February 25th
The hotel on the hill in Taxco is just beautiful. Stone floors and huge beds with carved posts and mosquito nets. Jose and I swim naked in the swimming pool set on the edge of the cliff. Jo really knows how to mix a mean margarita and last night he serenaded me with no less than six mariachi bands. Wow – I was blown away.

February 26th
I'm fat, too fat for all my clothes, my tits have grown huge. Jose offers to take me shopping. I don't want to go. I want to sit naked by the pool and get smashed.

February 27th
Don't feel good, got a hangover, I'm bored and I want to go back to LA. I'm scared, having the bad feelings again. I can't sleep, afraid to take the pills in case I hurt the baby. I call B, we talk for a long time, he's reel sweet and tells me he misses me. Eunice wants me to go back to LA, so does Fred Fields – what do they know? I wanna stay here with Joe.

I pause, stunned by the magnitude of what I'm reading. Then with a hammering in my chest I continue.

February 27th
Blood on the bed just like the other times, and pain bad pain. I need sedation I need sleep. Got to have drugs. Jose taking me to a private clinic. I call J he's not in office. I call B he doesn't return my call.

February 28th
She's the most beautiful thing I've seen in my whole life. I sit by her side all day, and every few minutes I press my face close to the glass to get a closer look. I've called her Anne after Nana Anne Karger, my surrogate mother who I love with all my heart. The doctor says she might not live. I know for certain she will.

Anne is thriving against all odds according to Dr Perez. I told her I love her a million times today. I'm sure she can hear me. Dr Perez hangs around me a lot. I've met men like him before, they only like women when their legs are open and skirts are above their heads. I've spoken to J he thinks I've had an abortion. He sounded relieved.

March 1st
I've lost a lot of weight and can't sleep. Today I called Ralph Greenson. I told him about the baby. I didn't tell

him who the father is but I will very soon. I've got to tell someone. Thank God for Dr Perez who has given me some Nembutal. Strong stuff. Tonight I'll conk out.

March 2nd
Spoke to my agent this morning. Wants me back in LA. Damn costume fittings for *Something's Got to Give*. Don't want to leave Anne, but can't take her with me. Not yet.

Told Anne I'd be back soon. She's gained almost a pound. Dr Perez thinks she'll be fit enough to travel in a few weeks. I promise to ring him every day. Before I go he tells me I can touch her. It's the first time. I'm so excited I can't stop shaking. Gowned up I wait, my heart beating hard, for the nurse to open the incubator lid. Slowly I lower my hand, gently touching the soft downy cleft in the centre of her crown. Her hands, bunched in tiny fists, lie by her side. Tenderly I undo her left fist, feeling my chest tighten and a great surge of happiness when she grabs my finger, holding on very tight. Holding my breath, I keep my finger in her fist until the nurse says I've got to remove it. When the incubator lid shuts I kiss my fingers and place the flat of my hand on the glass. I'm crying, my eyes streaming, through my tears I tell her I love her and she's the best thing that's ever happened to me.

Blurred by my own tears I let the diary drop to my lap. A great sadness engulfs me, not for myself but for Marilyn. My tears dry on my cheeks. I lift the diary and continue to read:

March 18th
Back in LA, can't think straight. Lost a lot of weight, costume fittings for the movie not going well, too much weight loss. I speak to Doctor Perez every day. Anne is

doing great. I've told my shrink who Anne's father is, he's warned me to stick to my story about abortion and not to tell another living soul the truth. I want to go back to Mexico. I want my baby.

March 24th
Got very drunk and spoke to Rose. Thought she should know what her son has done, make him face up to his responsibilities. Got cold feet when she told me I was a drunk and not to call her again.

March 25th
I'm confused things are very jumbled had to leave the set early they said I was slurring my lines. I've had a bottle of vodka. I call J he refuses to take my call. I call B he's out of town. I call Rose again this time I tell her the truth.

March 28th
Spoke to Dr Perez this morning he says Anne has put on enough weight to leave the clinic. I call Jose Bolaños who offers to send his private plane for me next week, five days time. I know he'll expect something in return, a blow job for my baby, no contest.

March 30th
Rose Kennedy calls me. I'm in shock it's like getting a call from the Queen of England. Says she's been thinking hard about the baby. In a tone of voice I don't like she suggests the baby should be adopted. She'd find good God-fearing folk to raise her. Discreet people who wouldn't gossip, and I'd be able to see her whenever I chose. She'd be cared for emotionally and financially. Rose said she'd set up a trust fund for Anne. A 'just in case' anything happened to me. When I get angry and tell her I want my baby more than anything else in the world and refuse to give her up Rose turns nasty. She tells me I'm a drunken slut who isn't capable of looking

after herself, let alone a child. I tell her to fuck off and slam down the phone.

April 2nd
Dr Perez called this morning. Bubbling with excitement I tell him I'm coming for Anne tomorrow. I hear his words but can't make sense of what he's saying. Anne is dead ... not sure how it happened ... he'll let me know the results of the autopsy. Very sorry, it happens sometimes with premature babies, not to worry about the burial arrangements he'll see to all of that. So sad, she fought hard, sorry, very sorry.

At this point the writing becomes almost illegible, and I have to hold the page under the light to read:

I've had some bad times in my life, very bad. Times when I've wanted to end it all. But all those other times are nothing compared to how I feel right now.

I should never have left her alone. If I'd been there she would have lived I feel it in my bones.

I'm aching all over, every bit of me aches, even my earlobes. The pills aren't working fucking stupid doc has given me 5mg instead of 10. Ralph and Jose both want to see me but I don't want to see anyone. I want to stay here in bed quiet and safe until the pain goes away.

The final entry is May 19, 1962:

Tonight I'm going to sing for him at Madison Square Garden. Jean Louis did a great job on my dress, I'm wearing nothing underneath, make his eyes pop out when I get in that spotlight. Told Weinstein I've got a heavy period to get out of shooting, he's pissed but what the hell, it's the President's birthday.

Fifteen thousand Democratic delegates are going to

be there to cheer on their leader. But they don't know what I know. Nobody knows the real man. Stuck-up wifey hasn't got a clue. His brother adores him, worships him with canine devotion. In B's eyes his brother can do no wrong. I still love him but it's tainted with hate. I wanted our baby more than anything else in the world. He let me down. There will come a time very soon when I'm going to have to spill the beans. Keeping secrets is hard especially when they're screaming to get out.

I snap the diary shut. Clasping it between my palms I try to absorb the enormity of what I've discovered. My heart feels unbearably heavy, swollen to bursting point with sadness. A picture of Marilyn poured into a nude sequinned dress singing 'Happy Birthday, Mr President' in her breathy voice makes me feel sick. All my life I've craved a father, a daddy to love and admire, now I have to live with the legacy of his philandering, corruption and deceit. He was bad. He'd never loved my mother, I'm certain of that; he'd used her. The word misogynist could have been invented for him.

The weight of anti-climax bears down on me. I'd anticipated an ecstatic sense of freedom, at long last released from the yarns of bitterness and anger that have bound me to the past. I have the knowledge I've craved yet am consumed with regret.

Do daughters become their mothers or their fathers, I muse. I don't want to be either.

Later, when Tom returns, I hand him the diary. I can't find any words to express the way I feel. I leave him reading and slip noiselessly out of the room. I drift up to my bedroom and lie sprawled across the bed face-down.

Inwardly I groan when, ten minutes later, Tom, bubbling with barely contained excitement, bursts into the room.

'It's fantastic, the story to beat all stories. Fucking amazing! I can see it now on the bestseller lists for months.'

Lifting my head I crank it in his direction. 'Story?'

'Your autobiography, remember?'

Turning over, I shuffle to the edge of the bed. 'I seem to recall saying I'd think about it. I've thought. I don't want to do it.'

The hands gripping the diary shake; he looks at me in utter amazement, like I'm some sort of alien.

'You can't be serious, Kate. The world deserves to know about this. It might be the reason Marilyn committed suicide, if, as many believe, she did take her own life. You can't contain a story like this, it's criminal! I can't forget what I've just read. It's the fucking story of the century. It has to be told.'

Leaping from the bed, I say, 'Only if I want it told.'

'How could you want otherwise? It's obvious Rose Kennedy organized the adoption, as far from prying eyes as possible. As a child you were abused, mentally and physically, by a pack of psychopaths masquerading as nuns. You were dragged up by the skin of your teeth in deprivation and forced to work for a priest who clearly wanted to seduce you when you were sixteen.'

'He loved me,' I scream.

'Stop kidding yourself, Kate, and for fuck's sake grow up. I'm sure you had a mirror in the cottage. If you were half as beautiful then as you are now, how could any man living in close proximity not be stirred? Priest or otherwise.'

I try to speak but he stops me with a harsh: 'For once let me finish. You admit you carried a torch for this man since you were fifteen. I believe it was Father Steele who fed your obsession with family, love and guilt. You were never in love with him, not the sort of love I know and understand. Obsession is not about love, Kate, it's about power and inadequacy. Your inadequacy stemmed from not knowing where you were from, who you were. Now you know, you can begin to live. I mean *really* live. Let me write this story, your biography: together we can do it. Don't you see, if you don't do this now you might be bound up with regrets for the remainder of your life.'

'Knowing I wasn't abandoned, that my mother loved and wanted me, is enough. Don't *you* see, Tom, it's all I've ever wanted? I don't suppose you've got any idea how good that feels. How could you? Cushioned by wealth, a close family and comfortable home, what would you know of these things? My mother was a victim, a victim of her own weakness and circumstances. At last I can turn the corner, unashamed and unafraid of what I might find lurking in the shadows. This discovery, Marilyn confirming what I always suspected, is my passport to moving on. It's all I need. I don't have to tell you the furore the story will cause. If you tell the world, I'll be thrown to the wolves. They'll never leave me alone. First the book, then the movie, then the TV documentary. Endless exposure, and for what? I don't need the money or the fame. Why would I want my innards served up to a pack of cynical wolves? My mother had unprecedented fame and it gave her nothing but utter misery. And what happens when eventually they tire of the "Marilyn's daughter" story, what will remain of me?'

A long silence. I watch his eyes dull over, his expression turn from persuasive to determined. He shrugs his powerful shoulders. 'I'm going to write this story with or without your authorization, Kate.' Tom's voice is weighted with intent. Before I can reply he slams out of the room without a backward glance.

Chapter Twenty-Four

The first cry from my baby's lips is the sweetest sound I believe I've ever heard. She's long, angry red, very crumpled and extremely beautiful.

Now I'm pushing again, mustering my final reserves of strength to expel the afterbirth. It slips easily from my body.

Within minutes I've forgotten the pain and can think of nothing but the child now lying in my arms. I'm in love. Deep creases cover the baby's face and neck, a fine skein of golden fluff plastered in half curls to her head looks like the crown of a Roman emperor. I lower my head, place my cheek close to hers. She smells of dried blood and antiseptic. Tentatively I stroke her crown, careful not to dip into the shallow hollow in the centre. I long for her to open her eyes. In my head I speak to her father: I was convinced I was having a boy, certain he would look exactly like you, and I'd feast my eyes on him when your face begins to fade. But I'm not disappointed, she's the most beautiful thing I've ever seen. I forgive you, Declan. Then out loud I whisper, 'And she's all mine.'

My decision to leave Ireland had come late in the night, a waking dream, six weeks after Ria was born. By daylight it had grown stronger, and a month later I'd found the house of my dreams in a small village called Slapton in Devon, between Stoke Fleming and Tor Cross.

Middle Earth was a witchy place, haunted, so the agent said. I fell in love at first sight, seduced by its creeper-clad,

413

stone-flagged, mullioned-windowed presence. The air, cooled by a south-westerly breeze, gusted off the sea. I walked with the agent through the grounds, beneath sun-dappled trees; we followed broken paths leading to woods and endless untrodden meadows, with always the evocative sound of the sea behind us. It was a place of dreams, a timeless place of beguiling solitude. I had to make it mine.

The previous owner, I discovered, had been called Betsy Campbell, a widow of considerable means who'd fallen in love and been deserted by a man half her age. She'd been born in Middle Earth and had died there, so the agent said, of a broken heart. After I moved in I'd found an old steamer trunk in the basement. In it Betsy had left a treasury of letters and photographs. Betsy, a considerable beauty, had had three husbands and numerous lovers, but none, according to the letters, could match Spencer, her last and greatest passion. Using a photograph taken in Africa between the wars I paint Betsy as I'm sure she'd have liked to look: a romantic heroine, beautiful and bold. I hang her above the charred stone fireplace. It feels right to have her back in Middle Earth.

Once, after I'd lived in Middle Earth for about six weeks, I took Ria to Grayshott. I told her about Brendan and how he'd wanted her to have his name. We took tea then retraced the walk to the beach Brendan and I had taken daily on our last holiday together. It wasn't the same. Nothing ever is.

From my bedroom and studio I can see and hear the sea, intoxicating, unpredictable, on the edge. And I can hear the gulls. Brendan had been right when he'd said it was no ordinary sound.

Rarely do I feel alone. I've got my painting and Ria. But sometimes I feel lonely. Usually I know when it's coming, and I've devised distractions to outwit the demons. Often I think of Tom, dwelling briefly on what might have been if he'd tried to understand why I can't authorize my biography. I've discussed it with my daughter; I tell her everything.

'What do you think, Ria? About your grandparents and Tom's book? It's a can of worms that if opened threatens to rock our world.'

I haven't spoken to Tom since I left Ireland. I miss him.

My agent and staff have strict instructions not to give anyone my forwarding address. Tom's dogged determination to write my unauthorized biography angered me; his betrayal as a man had hurt a lot more.

I'd misjudged him. I'd thought him a maverick, married equally to loyalty and mischief, romance and integrity. A shoulder to lean on and someone to dance with. He'd made me laugh, but not in the same way as Brendan. I'd laughed at and with Brendan. Tom had taught me to laugh at myself. I'd believed that I'd be able to persuade him to give up the story, I'd supposed that he'd do it for me. I was mistaken.

Pushing thoughts of Tom away, I think of Ria and our future. For the time being at least we're safe in Devon. Far from Ireland, prying eyes, nosy buggers, and the God squad.

It isn't Mr Summers with my delivery of oil paints. I gawk at the man on the doorstep. He's standing as still as a figure in a painting.

'I thought it was the postman. I'm expecting a delivery.'

'I've been searching for you for months.'

'How did you find me?'

A wry smile. 'I'm an investigative reporter, remember? Even so, it wasn't easy. I won't bore you with the details.'

A gull dips low overhead. My heart leaps into my throat. I cough, then say, 'I suppose you'd better come in.'

He stiffens, his shoulders squared. 'I'm not intruding, I hope.'

Shaking my head, I lead the way to my studio. On

entering, Tom scans the room, saying, 'Wow, great view,' as he walks to the window.

The tide is high. The white-capped waves crash on to a deep arc of shingle beach at the foot of my ragged lawn.

Tom locks his eyes on a painting in progress of Ria. 'Beautiful baby.'

I make no comment, waiting patiently for him to speak further. I don't have long to wait. After a couple of seconds he says, 'How long have you been here?'

'Almost five months.'

'Why here?'

'I came to Devon with Brendan a few weeks before he died. I loved it. I wanted to move on, to leave the memories in Ireland. I had no reason to stay – after all, I'm not even Irish. It was the best move I ever made. As soon as I saw the house I knew I had to have it. It was talking to me, saying, buy me, live in me, I'm yours. It just felt absolutely right. Since I've been here, Ireland and my early life has faded, like an old photograph left out in the sun. Sometimes I think I dreamt it all. Even Mother Thomas no longer comes to me in dreams, or waking thoughts. I think that's because I've forgiven her. Once, after Mother Thomas died, Father Steele had urged me to forgive her. I wasn't able to then, and at the time I thought I would never find it in my heart to understand or forgive what she'd done to me and Bridget.'

'Something happened to me recently, something deeply cathartic that has opened doors in my pysche that I thought were closed forever.' I pause and stare out of the window. 'My garden is waiting for flowers,' I comment. Then, redirecting my gaze back to Tom, I continue: 'My brief to the estate agent was to find an isolated house, preferably period, on the sea, remote, idyllic. So here I am, Middle Earth. If you stand on tiptoe, you can see the lighthouse beacon in the distance. I can paint, be at peace. No prying eyes, no gossip. I don't think half of the people round here even read the newspapers. and I've thanked God countless times for the English reserve.'

I'm studying his face. Two deep creases have appeared at the corners of his eyes since I last saw him. He looks tired. As usual he's wearing his very own suit of armour, I'm positive he polishes it relentlessly every day of his life. Suddenly I realize how gladdened I am by his presence, and how much I've missed him.

'So what incredible event made you forgive that bitch nun?'

With an enigmatic smile I say, 'Would you believe I found God?'

'No.' Then: 'Are you happy, Kate?'

I answer honestly: 'I'm content.'

'Is it enough?'

'For the moment, yes. How about you?'

Digressing, he says, 'I've written the biography.'

'If you've come to try and persuade me to authorize it, Tom, I could have saved you a wasted journey.'

With a resigned sigh, he says, 'I thought you might say that, but I figured it was worth a final shot. I'm supposed to submit it next Monday for publication in spring. Two terrestrial networks are interested, and there's talk of a major movie and, of course, every newspaper across the globe will be hot-footing it to Devon trying to snatch a photograph of you, or a few words. You should probably keep moving, 'cause, take my word for it, they'll hound you. If I had your authorization I could protect you from all of that shit. Vet all interviews, restrict them to a few choice exclusives, guide and protect you throughout the entire circus – because that's exactly what it will be. A fucking circus in relentless pursuit of a slice of you.'

The sound of crying interrupts him. Agitated, I try to ignore it but it gets louder. I mumble something about babysitting before fleeing the room. After ten minutes I hear Tom's footsteps on the stairs, then his voice asking for the toilet.

A moment later his head appears around the nursery door. He's rooted to the spot, visibly shocked by the scene in front of his eyes. I'm feeding. It's my favourite time with Ria. Late at night when I'm about to snuggle down to sleep, or early morning when I'm barely stirring, my ears are always attuned to her faint cry. In a second I'm out of bed and leaning over her cot. Gathering her into my arms I support her wobbly neck as I unbutton my nightdress, inhaling her smell deep in my nostrils. I love it when she finds my nipple, clamping it between her lips, the mewing sounds of satisfaction, and the way her tiny hand rests on the underside of my breast. I talk to her while she suckles; she listens intently.

Nonchalantly I declare, 'Declan's baby. I called her Ria Norma Jean Fitzgerald. Ria was her paternal grand-mother's name, and Brendan, if he'd lived, would have wanted her to have his name. Beautiful, isn't she?'

Tom manages to mumble, 'Beautiful . . . Your profound experience, I assume?' before leaving the room.

Twenty minutes later when I descend the stairs he's waiting in the hall. 'Why didn't you tell me about the baby?'

I shrug. 'Sometimes we need secrets.'

'You stopped taking my calls, didn't reply to any of my letters – surely, I deserved a reply.'

'I was angry and hurt. I couldn't – still can't understand why you are so hell-bent on publishing my story when you know it's not what I want. I've been through so much, the thought of more publicity is unbearable, yet all you can think of is yourself, your story, the story of the fucking century. It's all that matters.'

'I was frustrated and as stubborn as hell. All I could see were the bright lights, the big picture. It's the story every journalist dreams of, the one to kill for, the story of a lifetime. I just wanted you to authorize the book, and couldn't understand why you wouldn't. Now I know.'

'It's not only about Ria, Tom, it's about me. Sure, it would be hell for her, kids at school poking fun, calling her names. It would impact on our relationship as mother and daughter too. There wouldn't be a place left on earth we could hide.' My mouth curls in contempt. 'Can you imagine the quality of life we'd have?'

His eyes grow sad. 'None.' Then suddenly brightening, he says, 'Wait right there. Don't move.'

Confused, I watch him stride out of the house. He returns a few minutes later carrying a manuscript. It's bound in a cellophane folder, tied with printer's tape. He thrusts it into my hands. 'It's yours, Kate.'

There's a considerable silence while I read the title page: *Marilyn's Child* by Tom Gregson. I blink slowly, one, two, three times, like the clicking of a camera. Without looking up, I say, 'My copy?'

'It's your story. I can't do it without your approval.' He pauses, sighs, then says, 'When I was about fourteen a classmate, Paul Spencer, invited me to spend the summer vacation at his father's estate at Cape Cod. The house was a Gatsby-esque spread. Miles of beach, sailing, tennis, swimming pools; his beautiful sisters and their equally beautiful friends; late-night parties; copious amounts of food and drink; in fact, everything a boy of fourteen fantasizes about. The problem was I'd already invited Josh Denver, a lifelong friend, to stay with me. Josh had no folks, no place else to go. I'll never forget my pa's words when I asked his advice: "Do the right thing, son."

'I have to admit it took some doing. I remember longing for Cape Cod and resenting Josh for the first week of our vacation together. Two days before we were due to go back to school, we heard that Paul and the friend he'd invited in my place had had a fatal boating accident. It took three days to find their bodies. I've never forgotten that I could have been dead if I hadn't done the right thing.'

I move closer to him. I feel his breath warm on my face. A flash of sunlight from the window above dapples his crown, yellow and ruddy brown. 'Have you ever danced the tango under the stars?'

Perplexed, he says, 'Strange question.'

I'm smiling. 'Have you?'

'I've danced under the stars, but not the tango.'

'What about swimming naked in a tropical sea lit by moonlight?'

Now he grins too. 'What is this?'

'Have you?'

'Yes, on honeymoon in Maui.'

'White-water rafting?'

'No, but I'd like to.'

'Gotcha. Eaten fish and chips from newspaper?'

'Hell, no – sounds gross. Can I join in the quiz?'

Just one more: 'Have you made love under canvas in Malawi?'

'Under canvas but not in Africa. Wanna try it?'

My cheeks colour. 'In Malawi?'

'I was a mean boy scout, I can pitch a tent in the back yard if you like. But if it has to be Malawi, I'm sure I can arrange it.'

I wink. 'The back yard sounds like it could be fun. So many places I want to see, things I want to do.' I hug the manuscript tight to my breast. 'Now I won't waste precious time with fears of the future. Thank you, Tom, I appreciate it very much.'

'I owe you that much, Kate. And who knows? There may come a time when *you* want to tell the world your story.'

Leaning forward provocatively, I lower my eyelids and, parodying Marilyn's breathy voice say, 'Anything's possible, almost . . .'

Lynne Pemberton

Eclipse

'Rising star in the blockbuster firmament' *Observer*

Lucinda Frazer-West: daughter of Lord Nicholas and Lady Serena, a young actress with a glittering future beckoning.

Luna Fergusson: daughter of West Indian businessman Royole, reluctantly accepted by his wife Caron, and developing a high-flying business career.

Two successful young women, unaware of the bond that links them. They are twins, the product of a one-in-a-million biological chance, following a liaison between Serena and Royole: twin sisters, one white, one black.

Now, twenty-seven years later, events are destined to bring them together, and to unmask the secret of their birth.

0 00 649005 0

Win a trip to New York

with

Sȍvereign

Sovereign, the premium tour operator is offering a prize of a three-night stay in the city that never sleeps, New York, for one lucky *Marilyn's Child* reader and their guest. Visit the most famous statue in the world, shop until you drop and enjoy late night Jazz in Greenwich Village! New York is just one of the 65 destinations offered by Sovereign Cities and Short Breaks and the prize includes return flights and room-only accommodation, subject to availability and must be taken before the end of November 2000.

Also included in the prize are tickets to a Broadway Show, a champagne dinner for two in the famous Carlisle hotel and brunch with the stars at the Palm Court in the Plaza Hotel. Everything you could wish for for the ultimate Big Apple experience!

All you need to do for your chance to win is answer the following question: Which famous pair are linked to Kate in *Marilyn's Child*?:

A - Marilyn Monroe and JFK
B - Audrey Hepburn and Cary Grant
C - Marilyn Monroe and Richard Nixon

Then, in not more than 15 words, complete the following tie-breaker:
'If I could be related to someone famous it would be...'

Send your entry on a postcard, together with your name, address and phone number to the following competition address by 30 June 2000:

Dept: LMC, HarperCollinsPublishers,
77-85 Fulham Palace Road, London W6 8JB

For a copy of the Sovereign Cities and Short Breaks brochure and reservations call Sovereign on 08705 768373.

No cash alternative is offered. Only one entrance per household. The competition is not open to employees of HarperCollins, Sovereign holidays or either of these companies' agents. If the winner is under 18, their travelling partner must be aged 18 or over. Draw will take place on 1 September 2000. The winner will be notified by post. Result may be discovered by sending an SAE to the address above.